A WOMAN WITH A PAST

"Have you found your compatriots welcoming even though your relatives have returned to France?"

Her mouth twisted. "The grand émigrés in Soho will have nothing to do with a woman who was a whore in Turkey."

He winced. "Surely no one said such an appalling thing!"

"The aristocratic ladies did. Their husbands tried to corner me in empty rooms," she said tartly. "I decided I would be safer among my more humble countrymen here in St. Pancras."

He bit off a curse. "You deserve so much better than this, Suzanne!"

She sighed. "If there is one thing I have learned, it's that no one 'deserves' anything more than the right to struggle for survival. I'd rather be here altering gowns in a cold room than living in luxury in a Turkish harem and wondering which night might be my last, so I think I am doing well." She raised her teacup in a mock toast. "Will you drink to my survival, Simon?"

"I can do more than that," he said, his gaze intense. "Marry me, Suzanne."

Books by Mary Jo Putney

The Lost Lords series
Loving a Lost Lord
Never Less Than a Lady
Nowhere Near Respectable
No Longer a Gentleman
Sometimes a Rogue
Not Quite a Wife
Not Always a Saint

The Rogues Redeemed series
Once a Soldier
Once a Rebel
Once a Scoundrel
Once a Spy

Other Titles
Dearly Beloved
The Bargain
The Rake
Mischief and Mistletoe
The Last Chance Christmas Ball

MARY JO PUTNEY

ONCE A SPY

ZEBRA BOOKS
KENSINGTON PUBLISHING CORP.
www.kensingtonbooks.com

ZEBRA BOOKS are published by

Kensington Publishing Corp.
119 West 40th Street
New York, NY 10018

All Kensington titles, imprints, and distributed lines are available at special quantity discounts for bulk purchases for sales promotion, premiums, fund-raising, educational, or institutional use.

Special book excerpts or customized printings can also be created to fit specific needs. For details, write or phone the office of the Kensington Sales Manager: Attn.: Sales Department. Kensington Publishing Corp., 119 West 40th Street, New York, NY 10018. Phone: 1-800-221-2647.

Zebra and the Z logo Reg. U.S. Pat. & TM Off.

First Kensington Books Hardcover Printing: August 2019
First Zebra Books Mass-Market Paperback Printing: October 2019
ISBN-13: 978-1-4201-4810-7
ISBN-10: 1-4201-4810-9

ISBN-13: 978-1-4201-4813-8 (eBook)
ISBN-10: 1-4201-4813-3 (eBook)

10 9 8 7 6 5 4 3 2 1

Printed in the United States of America

Chapter 1

London, February 1815

Even though Suzanne was working under the small window in her room to get the best light, it was now too dark to continue sewing. England was much farther north than where she'd been living, and in midwinter the days were short and often rainy or overcast. She might have to buy candles to finish these alterations by the end of the week.

She set aside the gown and stood to stretch. Perhaps she should go for a short walk. The day was raw and her old cloak barely adequate, but she loved having the freedom to go outside whenever she wished.

Solid steps sounded on the stairs outside her room and she recognized the dignified approach of her landlord, Mr. Potter. He knocked on the door and announced, "Madame Duval, there's a fellow here who says he's your cousin, Colonel Duval. He's down in the sitting room. Do you have a cousin who is a colonel?"

Suzanne opened her door, surprised. After the last tumultuous years, she had no idea what relatives might still be alive, or what they had been doing. "I might, but I'll have to see him to be sure. I assume he looks respectable or you wouldn't have allowed him in."

"He has the look of a soldier, not that being one would make him a saint," her landlord said dourly. "I'll go down with you in case you want me to send him away."

She nodded her thanks. Mr. Potter was very protective of the female tenants in his boardinghouse. It was one of the reasons she'd chosen to live here.

She peeled off the fingerless gloves she wore to keep her hands warm while sewing, brushed a casual hand over her dark hair, and straightened her knit shawl over her shoulders, glad that her appearance was no longer a matter of life and death. Then she followed her landlord down the narrow stairs.

When she opened the door to the small sitting room, the dim light revealed a man gazing out the window, his hands clasped behind his back as he studied the shabby neighborhood. Lean and powerful, he did indeed have the bearing of a soldier. His wavy dark hair was in need of cutting and he had a familiar grace as he turned at her entrance. His searching gaze met hers and he became very still.

She froze, paralyzed with shock. *Jean-Louis!*

But her husband was dead—she'd seen him murdered with her own eyes. Also, Jean-Louis had been twice her age when they married. This man was younger.

When she saw his cool, light gray eyes, she remembered a young second cousin of her husband. Simon Duval had been a boy, only a couple of years older than she'd been as a very young bride, but he'd shared a strong family resemblance to her husband. The years had emphasized subtle differences in his features and she guessed that he was a shade taller and more broad-shouldered than Jean-Louis had been.

Realizing she wasn't breathing, she inhaled slowly. "Well met, Simon. Or should I call you Monsieur le Comte?"

"So it really is you, my cousin Suzanne," her visitor said with soft amazement. "The name is not uncommon and Hawkins didn't say you were the Comtesse de Chambron. But though you are a countess, I am no count. Merely a distant cousin by marriage who is very glad to see that you are alive."

He spoke English with no hint of French accent and she remembered that his mother had been English. "Though I no longer think myself a countess, you might be the Comte de Chambron if enough members of my husband's family have died." Which was true, but even more true was that the world where French courtly titles mattered seemed very far away. She extended her hand. "Mr. Potter announced you as a colonel. Which army? British, French royalist, or French imperial?"

"So many possibilities! The British army, though I'm going to sell out now that the emperor has abdicated." He smiled a little as he took her hand and bent over it, a gesture wholly French. "I'm glad to see you well and more beautiful than ever. I'd heard you were dead."

His hand was warm and strong and competent. She released it with reluctance. "You flatter like a Frenchman, Simon," she replied, returning his smile. "I am no longer a dewy young bride and I was very nearly dead several times over. But yes, I have survived."

Her landlord cleared his throat and she realized that he'd been monitoring this meeting from the doorway. "Madame Duval, I imagine you and the colonel have much to discuss, so I'll bring you some tea."

"That would be lovely, Mr. Potter." After he left, she knelt on the hearth and added a small scoop of coals to the embers of the fire. "Indeed, we have much to catch up on, cousin. It's been a dozen years or more."

Simon had been one of many guests at her wedding to the Comte de Chambron. She'd been only fifteen, dazzled by suave Jean-Louis and thrilled to be making such a grand marriage. Since Simon had been near her age, they'd developed a teasing friendship in the days before the wedding, but that had been a lifetime ago.

She settled in the chair to the right of the fireplace. "How did you find me?"

"Captain Gabriel Hawkins." Simon took the seat opposite her. "He and I shared an alarming adventure in Portugal some years back. By chance we ran into each other and, as we exchanged news, I learned that he'd just returned from a voyage to Constantinople and you were a passenger."

She stiffened. "Did he tell you my circumstances?"

Voice gentle, Simon said, "He said you were in the harem of a powerful and deeply corrupt Turkish official, and that your aid was invaluable in rescuing two English women, including the young lady who is now his wife."

Those were the bare facts. She hoped that Hawkins had said no more than that. "And in return, he rescued me and brought me here."

"Hawkins said he offered to take you to France, but that you chose to join émigré relatives who were in the French community in Soho." His perceptive gaze was evaluating her and the clean but worn sitting room. She could guess his thoughts. In London, Soho was the French quarter where the wealthy émigrés lived. The poor ones struggled to make a living in this rundown neighborhood in the St. Pancras parish.

Answering his unasked question, she said, "After Napoleon abdicated, those cousins returned to France to reclaim their property. I was not surprised to find them gone. But no matter. I prefer to make my own way in England rather than return to France. There is nothing for me there."

His gaze flicked around the worn sitting room again. "Forgive me for asking, but how are you managing?"

"I sew well and I've been doing piecework. Soon I should be able to find a permanent position." She smiled wryly. "But I do wish I'd been able to bring the jewels I had when I was a favorite in the harem! I'd have been able to buy my own shop."

"Money makes everything easier," he agreed, his brow furrowed. "I'm fortunate that my mother came from a successful English merchant family and her fortune remained on this side of the Channel."

"Very prudent of your mother and her family." She cocked her head to one side. "Are you here only to look up a distant family connection? Perhaps you are bored now that you've sold out of the army?"

"Not bored, though I am rather at loose ends," he admitted. "But as soon as Hawkins mentioned you, I wanted to see if you were the right Suzanne Duval, and if so, to learn how you are faring."

Mr. Potter returned, a tea tray in hand. The tray was dented pewter and there was a chip in the spout of the teapot, but her landlord presented the refreshments with the air of a duke's butler. There was also a dish of shortbread.

"Thank you, Mr. Potter!" Suzanne said warmly. "You and your wife have outdone yourselves."

"The pleasure is ours, my lady." He inclined his head and withdrew from the room.

"My lady?" Simon asked as she poured tea for them. "He knows that you're an aristocrat?"

"He was just being polite, though you might have changed that." She sipped her tea, then offered him the shortbread. "Have a piece. Mrs. Potter is a wonderful baker."

He followed her advice and murmured appreciatively after he bit into it. "She is, and she doesn't stint on the butter." He finished his tea in a long swallow and set the cup down with a clink. "I wonder if I might find old friends or relations in the émigré community. Have you found your compatriots welcoming even though your relatives have returned to France?"

Her mouth twisted. "The grand émigrés in Soho will have nothing to do with a woman who was a whore in Turkey."

He winced. "Surely no one said such an appalling thing!"

"The aristocratic ladies did. Their husbands tried to corner me in empty rooms," she said tartly. "I decided I would be safer among my more humble countrymen here in St. Pancras."

He bit off a curse. "You deserve so much better than this, Suzanne!"

She sighed. "If there is one thing I have learned, it's that no one 'deserves' anything more than the right to struggle for survival. I'd rather be here altering gowns in a cold room than living in luxury in a Turkish harem and wondering which night might be my last, so I think I am doing well." She raised her teacup in a mock toast. "Will you drink to my survival, Simon?"

"I can do more than that," he said, his gaze intense. "Marry me, Suzanne."

Chapter 2

Suzanne set down her teacup so quickly that the tea sloshed out. "Good heavens, Simon! You look so sane, but clearly I misjudged."

He smiled, enjoying the musical lilt of her French accent, the grace of her petite, perfectly proportioned figure, the shine of her rich, tobacco brown hair. "I am as astonished by my proposal as you are. Yet it feels right."

"Why?" She tilted her head, her startling green eyes curious and amused. "Why ask, and why does it feel right?"

This was a question he needed to answer for himself as well as her. "I have spent years of my life working for the demise of Napoleon," he said slowly. "He and his regime cost me much of my family and the girl I loved. Now he is gone, for good, I hope. What does a soldier do when the wars are over?"

"What do any of us who survived do?" she asked softly.

It was the question that had haunted him for months,

and gradually he was finding answers. "Cultivate the ways of peace. I'll open my long-neglected house. Put away my uniform. Plant a garden. Take a wife." He studied Suzanne's lovely face. In many ways she was a stranger, but on some deep level, familiar. "You have survived great losses and tumult in your life, so perhaps you want the same things?"

She set her teacup down and rose to drift across the room. Ending at the window, she gazed absently at the street outside. "You and I met a dozen years ago during the Peace of Amiens. The naive and optimistic girl that I was then thought the wars were over and we could look forward to bright futures. Then the world dissolved once more into violence and chaos. Perhaps your proposal stems from a desire to recapture those days of peace and optimism? But they are gone forever."

"That time has passed," he admitted, "but weren't we friends even though we didn't know each other for long? I enjoyed your intelligence and warmth and envied my cousin his choice of bride. You seemed to enjoy my company as well. Isn't that worth building on?"

"That is a frail, distant connection," she said as she turned from the window to look at him. "We are strangers to each other now."

"Are we?" He caught her gaze. "Much has happened to us both, but do you feel as if you are a different person from that young bride? I may be battered and weary, but I feel that at heart, I'm the same man I was when we met."

"I suppose I am also the same deep down." Her expression tightened and he saw pain in her eyes. "But I don't know if I'll ever be suited to marriage again."

When she fell silent, he asked tentatively, "Are you willing to say why?"

At first he thought she'd refuse, but then she sighed. "Years in a harem where my survival depended on being a whore and pretending to enjoy it have damaged me, perhaps beyond repair. I'm not sure if I'll ever know desire again. The way I feel now, the answer is probably no."

He winced internally as he recognized how much pain lay under her flat, honest words. Yet he felt a surprising kinship with her. "My circumstances were nothing like yours, but I do understand the death of desire." For a brief, piercing moment he remembered the intoxicating mutual madness he'd known with his fiancée, Alette. "For me, desire is not much more than a memory, buried with all the other bright memories. Yet I can imagine a satisfactory marriage without physical intimacy. Can you?"

She looked startled, then thoughtful. "For myself, yes, I can imagine it. But you're a man in the prime of life, and in my experience, men are more physically passionate. What if desire returns for you and not for me? I should be a great inconvenience to you then."

It was an important question. He thought before replying, "You would still be my wife and my friend. I would do nothing to humiliate you. What if the reverse is true and you recover desire and I don't?"

"Like you, I would be discreet and do nothing to bring shame on your name." She laughed suddenly, her face alive with amusement. "This is a very French conversation!"

He laughed with her. "So it is. Perhaps we would be very sophisticated and both quietly keep lovers on the side. But this is mere speculation. All we can know is this moment, how we feel now. And what I feel is that I would be profoundly grateful if you agreed to share my life."

"But why?" she asked a little helplessly.

If there was to be any chance she would accept his proposal, he must be honest and vulnerable. "I have felt lonely for many years, Suzanne," he said quietly. "When I walked into this room, my first emotion was great happiness to see that you are alive. And in the next moment, I realized I didn't feel lonely anymore."

Her gaze was searching. "I also feel less alone, but what if we don't suit?"

"We courteously go our separate ways within the marriage and treat each other with respect and kindness. That shouldn't be too difficult. It's great passion that creates anger. If we are both beyond passion, surely we can be friends."

"The idea sounds simple, but human beings are seldom simple," she said skeptically.

Just talking to Suzanne made him feel more alive even when they disagreed. "You're right, of course. But let us not overlook the shockingly practical side of my proposal," Simon said. "As my wife you could live quite comfortably. Not with the luxury of a countess, but you will not have to work long hours in order to eat."

"I can't deny that has appeal," Suzanne said. "But marriage is a great leap of faith at the best of times, and I scarcely know you. The same difficult years that are something of a bond between us might also have produced deep scars that could prove hard to live with."

"Those are all good points, but we need not decide today. Let us spend some time together. Become reacquainted."

"That is *essential*! At the moment, sir, you are a pig in a poke."

He laughed outright. "I have been called many unflattering things, but never that." He gestured at the lightening sky outside. "The sun is attempting to shine. After calling here, I planned to visit my London house. I've been staying in a hotel since returning to the city, but it's time to move into my own home."

She glanced out the window at the brightening day. "I should finish my sewing commission while there is light."

After a moment's thought, he said, "If you join me for this small excursion, I will supply candles so you can work into the night."

"You are courting me with candles?" she asked with interest.

"If you find that appealing, they can be courtship candles. Or you can think of them as merely helpful."

She studied him thoughtfully, then nodded. "Candles will indeed be helpful, and I should like some fresh air. Let me get my cloak."

He watched her depart, and wondered if he was mad to offer marriage. But he felt no inclination to withdraw his offer.

Suzanne felt a little reckless as Simon handed her into his curricle, then swung up beside her and took the reins from his groom. Reaching under the seat, he pulled out a dark blue carriage robe. "You might find this useful. There's a hint of spring in the air, but warmth is still some distance off."

"But this is very pleasant after days of rain." She adjusted the robe around her. It was woven from some marvelously soft wool and she enjoyed the touch of luxury. Even more she enjoyed his consideration.

As Simon deftly turned the carriage in the narrow street and headed west, she studied his profile. Now that the initial shock of his resemblance to her late husband had passed, she was seeing the differences. Jean-Louis had had the air of a jaded sophisticate while Simon was contained and . . . enigmatic? She thought of still waters running deep. He surely had interesting tales to tell. As did she.

She enjoyed studying the streets and buildings and energetic inhabitants they passed. "It's pleasant to finally see something of London."

"You're not familiar with the city?"

She shook her head. "I'd never been here before I arrived from Constantinople."

"You were willing to risk your future in an unknown place?"

She shrugged. "It's easier to become a new woman here. By the time I sailed the length of the Mediterranean on an English ship, I was reasonably fluent in the language and I knew I could manage."

He nodded, understanding the desire to start a new life.

"You've seen more of Europe's great cities. Which is your favorite?" she asked. "Paris? So many people love Paris."

"But you are not one of them," he said in what wasn't a question. "All the great cities have their own souls, their beauties and blemishes. Paris, Rome, Vienna, Lisbon. I'm particularly fond of Lisbon, a lovely city of light and wide vistas. But my favorite is London because this is most my home."

"Did you live here when you were a child?"

"Yes, my mother's father gave her this Mayfair House when she married to make it easy for her to visit her family, so when we fled the Reign of Terror, the house was waiting to receive us. I've spent more time in England than in France."

The neighborhoods became grander until Simon drew up in front of a substantial town house in a square with a small green park in the center. Turning the curricle over to the young groom who'd ridden on the back of the vehicle, he helped Suzanne from the carriage and up the few steps to a dark green painted door. The door knocker was a polished brass lion that glinted confidently in the afternoon light.

Simon hesitated for a long moment, visibly steeling himself as he produced a heavy key from his pocket. "The old knocker was an eagle that looked too much like Napoleon's imperial eagle standard, which French troops carried into battle. I had it changed to a British lion."

"Symbols matter." After a long silence, she asked quietly, "Are you reluctant to return because the house holds too many bad memories?"

"Too many good ones. This is part of the golden past that is forever gone." Face set, he unlocked the door and ushered her into the small vestibule.

A gilt-framed mirror hung above a polished mahogany table opposite the door. Suzanne and Simon were reflected there and she felt a jolt of surprise, as if he was a stranger. When he'd first greeted her, for a stunned moment she'd thought he was her late husband. Then she remembered him as Simon, a charming young man she'd liked very much in the golden days before her marriage.

But the image in the mirror reflected the man he was now. Austerely handsome. Quietly masterful. A man at case in any situation, as dangerous as he needed to be—and carrying a bone-deep weariness that was eating away at his soul.

She drew a shaky breath as she absorbed this fuller understanding of the man who wanted her for his wife. Oddly, in that mirror they seemed well matched: She looked attractive and had the cool elegance of the countess she'd once been even though she wore an altered, secondhand gown.

But the strongest resemblance was that she shared his weariness. Was soul deep fatigue a foundation strong enough to support a marriage, or reason for her to run in the opposite direction?

Her thoughts were interrupted when Simon opened a door on the right and revealed a drawing room. The draperies were drawn so the light was dim, but she could see the elegant lines of the furniture and appreciate the softness of the Turkish carpet beneath her feet.

As she entered, she brushed her fingertips across the gleaming surface of a satinwood table. "It's a handsome house. Has it been empty for years?"

"No, a French couple who served my father's family for many years live here." Simon moved to a window and drew the draperies back, allowing the pale winter sunshine into the room. "When war erupted after the Peace of Amiens, I helped the Merciers out of France. They needed a new home and the house needed caretakers. A fortnight ago I sent a message that I'd be returning soon, and asked that they take the Holland covers off the furniture and prepare the house for me to take up residence."

He crossed the room and pulled the bell rope by the fireplace. A distant ringing sounded on the floor below in the servants' quarters. "I haven't been here in years. It's rather eerie to see how nothing has changed."

Well-proportioned tables, chairs, and sofas were clustered into conversational groupings, the upholstery only a little faded with time. Her gaze was drawn to the portrait that hung above the fireplace. A dark-haired woman with a warm smile sat in a chair in this very room, an older man standing behind her with his hand on her shoulder.

"Your parents," she said. "I met them briefly before my wedding, but I met so many of Jean-Louis's relatives then that I did no more than exchange a few words." There was a strong resemblance between Simon and his father, a resemblance shared by her husband. The Duval family blood ran strong.

Simon joined her, his gaze on the portrait. "This was painted at a happy time. My father was French to the bone, but he was philosophical and made the best of his exile to England. The world would be changing, he said, so he made sure I was equally fluent in French and English. The plan was that I would attend school here and university in Paris if the wars were over by then, but that wasn't possible."

"What school?" She searched her memory for the names of the most famous British schools and came up with only one. "Eton?"

"Harrow. Like Eton, it's close to London." He smiled a little. "As an old Harrovian, I am honor bound to say that my school was superior to Eton, but in truth they are much the same."

Her brow furrowed as new memories surfaced. "Do you have a brother? I remember you talking warmly about a Lucas."

"He was my cousin, but yes, as close as a brother. Our mothers were sisters. He was orphaned young and came to live with my family." He gestured to a smaller portrait that hung over a sofa. It showed two young boys, perhaps ten years old. One was clearly Simon, and the other a boy with fair coloring and mischief in his eyes. "We attended Harrow together and looked out for each other."

"Is he . . . gone?" she asked softly. "Another victim of the wars?"

"Yes," Simon said bleakly. "Lucas was in the Royal Navy. His ship was sunk with no known survivors, though I've never quite given up hope that he might be a prisoner of war somewhere in France."

She frowned. "Weren't all prisoners released after the emperor abdicated?"

"Yes. But hope is a difficult habit to give up."

Their conversation was interrupted by the arrival of a middle-aged couple who were clearly the French caretakers. The broad, capable-looking man bowed deeply. "Milord, how good to see you home and well!"

Madame Mercier, round and sharp-eyed, bobbed a curtsy. "All is in readiness, milord. Will you be moving in today?" Her curious gaze slid to Suzanne.

"Perhaps tomorrow," Simon replied. "I've brought my cousin, the Comtesse de Chambron, to see the house. I'd thought her dead, so it was a great pleasure to find her alive and recently arrived in London."

Suzanne smiled at the Merciers and said in French, "The house is lovely and you've kept it well."

Looking pleased, Madame Mercier replied in the same language, "Thank you, Madame la Comtesse." After a moment's hesitation, she added, "Would monsieur and madam like to have a light luncheon here? There isn't time to prepare a proper meal, but I can offer simple bistro fare, a beef bourguignon stew and good French bread."

The thought made Suzanne's mouth water. She had too little money to eat well. "I should like that above all things! It's been years since I've had decent French cooking."

The couple gave approving smiles. Mercier suggested, "Would monsieur and madam like a glass of wine while the meal is prepared?"

Good French wine, Suzanne hoped, but she said, "I'd like to see the rest of the house, Simon, if that's not too impolite of me."

"I'd like to show it to you. I'll ring when we're done, Mercier. We'll eat in the breakfast room."

The Merciers inclined their heads and withdrew, probably to speculate on the meaning of Suzanne's presence at their master's side. She wished them luck with their speculations since she, herself, had no idea what the future held.

Simon offered his arm. "Shall we explore, milady?"

She took his arm with a smile. Even if she decided marriage would be unwise, at the least she'd get a good French meal out of this expedition.

Chapter 3

~

Wishing he could read Suzanne's mind, Simon kept a close eye on her as he showed her through the public rooms, then led her upstairs to the next floor. Her gaze was calm and unreadable as she studied her surroundings. Though he'd always loved this house, it was modest compared to the palatial homes Suzanne had lived in. But it was certainly better than the boardinghouse where she lived now.

Their first stop on the bedroom floor was his parents' rooms at the back of the house. "This bedroom on the left was my mother's." He opened the door for Suzanne so she could enter. "My father's room is the mirror image on the other side of the house and there's a small sitting room between. My mother liked the quiet in the back of the house, and there's a good view of the garden."

Suzanne moved to the window and gazed down. "Even in February, the garden looks pleasant. In summer it must be beautiful."

"My mother loved gardening, though this one has been

neglected for years. The planting season is coming so I need to find a good gardener."

She turned from the window. "Where is your room? Or would you rather not visit that?"

She was perceptive in picking up his uneasiness, which made him doubly glad to have her company on this painful return to his home. "My bedroom was at the front of the house next to Lucas's room. The better for us to commit mischief together."

She smiled. "Then by all means I'd like to see it."

He escorted her the length of the house to his room, bracing himself as he opened the door. As Suzanne moved by him, she asked softly, "Too many good memories here?"

Suppressing a sigh, he replied, "I didn't know how happy my life had been until I lost all the people I cared about."

She nodded with sad understanding, then drifted around the canopy bed, her fingertips brushing the coverlet, her gaze scanning the overflowing bookcase. She paused by the open shelves that held his childhood collection of interesting rocks and crystals and small wooden carvings of animals. She lifted one to study it more closely. "A British lion, I see. Did you carve these? They're very well done."

"Lucas made them."

She must have heard something in his voice because she carefully set the lion back in its place and moved to the window that looked out on the quiet street below and the iron-fenced park in the middle of the square. With her elegance and perfect proportions, even her back was lovely to observe.

Beauty. It had been so long since he'd felt the beauty of the world. Women were one of God's most beautiful creations, yet he had stopped recognizing that a long time ago. He tried to remember back to the time before desire had been burned out of him by war and violence. The young man he'd been then would have wanted to move behind Suzanne and wrap his arms around her waist and murmur sweet words in hopes of invoking a matching response in her.

He could barely remember that young man, but he could at least recognize that Suzanne had the beauty of grace, experience, and wisdom. It was a deeper beauty than she'd had as a radiant young girl, and more interesting. The weary man he was now wasn't interested in seduction, but he liked being with her.

He crossed the room to stand beside her, careful not to touch. But he couldn't prevent himself from asking, "Can you imagine yourself living in this house?"

"This has been a happy house," she said slowly. "I can feel that, and how it yearns to come alive again. And yet . . ." She turned to face him, her expression troubled. "I have spent almost all my life caged by men. As a child, as a very young wife, and as a harem slave. I enjoy the freedom I have now."

"But not the poverty, I assume."

"Definitely not the poverty," she agreed. "Yet if I have a roof over my head and enough to eat, it's preferable to some of my other living situations."

That adaptability was probably why she'd survived so much. "Though I've never been actually poor, in my army years, I sometimes lived like a beggar." He smiled ruefully. "I most certainly did not enjoy the hunger, cold, and general miseries, but the experience has deepened my appreciation of life's comforts."

"Do you miss the camaraderie of being in the army?" she asked. "Leading your men into battle, sharing triumph and loss as well as the miseries? Is the lack of that camaraderie why you yearn for companionship now?"

"Most of the time I wasn't a field officer," he replied. "Because I know several languages and could draw maps, I became an exploring officer, doing reconnaissance behind enemy lines. For that kind of work, I wore my uniform for the most part so if I was captured, which I was a time or two, I'd be treated as a prisoner of war rather than a spy."

Noting his caveat, she asked, "Did you also act as a spy on occasion, wearing civilian clothing and risking a spy's death?"

He nodded. "When that seemed necessary, yes. Once in Portugal I was captured with several Englishmen. We were all condemned as spies and sentenced to be shot at dawn. One of the other men was your friend Hawkins. Working together, we all managed to escape."

"And I'm glad of it! If not for Hawkins, I'd still be a slave, or dead." She shrugged. "More likely the latter. My owner, Gürkan, was growing tired of me. When that happened with one of his slaves, it never ended well."

He winced at her calm words. He had also learned that detachment was essential for survival. "Often I worked alone, and you're probably right—that's a strong reason why I yearn for companionship now. Traditionally, husbands and wives see a great deal of each other. I find the idea appealing."

"That's only true if they get along well," she pointed out. "I fear giving up my freedom. What if we don't like each other well enough to be companions?"

"That could happen," he admitted. "But I'm willing to chance it. Are you?"

Her brow furrowed. "I risk more if this marriage of . . . of friendship fails."

She was right. He asked, "What would it take to make you more comfortable with the idea of a marriage of friendship?"

She considered. "As we discussed earlier, we need to know each other better. We need to talk and spend time together."

"Those are very reasonable suggestions." He smiled

and offered his arm. "And we can begin by sharing a meal. Our luncheon should be ready by now."

Her eyes lit up as she took his arm. "Lead on, sir! Is your wine cellar as French as your food?"

"I'll be surprised if it isn't." As they headed downstairs, he felt cautiously hopeful that he and Suzanne might have a future together.

There was little conversation over the meal. Suzanne was grateful that Simon didn't distract her while she was enjoying the best meal she'd had in years. The beef bourguignon was marvelously flavorful and so tender that the chunks of meat almost dissolved in her mouth. There hadn't been time to make fresh bread, so a baguette had been split and spread with butter and garlic and finely chopped chives, then grilled till it was crisp and fragrant.

It was simple peasant food—and sublime. She emptied her bowl twice and considered asking for a third serving, but regretfully concluded that she didn't have room to eat any more.

Simon smiled as he leaned forward to top off her glass with a red Burgundy wine perfectly suited to the food. "I like to see someone enjoy a good meal."

"It's the best food I've had in many years. Meals in the harem were lavish and sometimes very fine, but they were not French." She chuckled. "It would almost be worth marrying you for Madame Mercier's cooking."

"She is definitely an asset to the house. I believe a lemon tart and coffee will appear eventually. Will that be enough to tip the balance?" he asked with mock hopefulness.

"No, but I shall enjoy them." She turned her glass, admiring the deep crimson of the wine as light reflected through it. "In our discussions, we must be honest with each other, no matter how appalling the truth is. Will you swear to that?"

His gaze was steady. "I have spent too many years keeping secrets. I pledge always to be honest with you unless the truth belongs to someone else."

"That is fair." She studied his face. "What did you think when we first met all those years ago? Surely you didn't fall in love with me at first sight."

"No, I knew you were not for me, and even at that age, I saw no reason to pine for the impossible," he replied. "But I thought you were enchanting and was honored to become your friend. I vaguely hoped that someday, when I was ready to marry, I'd find a girl like you." After a silence, he added in a quiet voice, "When I heard you were dead, I lit candles for you."

She was touched by his words. "Strange how the world works," she mused. "Here we are discussing the possibility of marriage, though I'm only a faded echo of the enchanting girl I was then. Look hard before you commit to a future with me, milord."

"You no longer have the dewy perfection of fifteen," he agreed. "But you are so much more interesting now."

"I'm glad you think so." Her mouth curved. It hardly seemed fair that men tended to improve with age. Simon had been an attractive young fellow, and he'd matured into a strong, handsome man who would draw glances from any normal female. She was no longer normal, but she did find him pleasing to face across a dining room table.

He asked, "What did you think of me when we met? Not 'enchanting,' I'm sure!"

"No, but charming. Intelligent, a good companion." She tried to recall that first meeting. "I thought that Jean-Louis must have been like you when he was your age. Though in that, I was wrong."

"In what way? I didn't know him well."

She hesitated, wondering how to describe her late husband without saying more than she felt like discussing. "I think you are more interested in your surroundings and the people around you than Jean-Louis was. He was very much a French aristocrat while you have become a man of the world."

His expression was curious, but he didn't pursue the topic, for which she was grateful. Perhaps someday it would seem right to discuss her marriage, but not today.

When Madame Mercier entered the room to serve the lemon tart and coffee, conversation languished. The tart was as good as the rest of the meal, a deliciously bittersweet taste on her tongue, and the strong, hot coffee was the perfect complement.

After Simon had finished off his tart, he said, "Now that you are mellowed by good French food, I'll ask what it would take to coax you into risking marriage. What if I settle a lump sum of money on you that will permit you to be comfortable and independent even if we separate?"

"You want this so much?" she exclaimed, startled. "Surely there are other women who would be charming, accommodating wives!"

He smiled a little. "I don't know any such women, but I know you."

"A convenient female for a marriage of convenience? I suppose that makes sense."

"There's more to it than that," he said seriously. "I've always felt easy with you even when we were both very young and you were on the way to the altar with another. I feel easy with you now despite the strangeness of this conversation. Do you feel that way, or is it just me?"

"I've felt much the same," she said slowly. "As if we were natural friends. In the years since, we've both lived complicated lives. There is ease in not having to pretend to be normal."

He grimaced. "I often feel like that, that I'm pretending to be normal. But there are a good number of other former soldiers around, so I'm not that unusual. There are few if any European women who have escaped harems as you have."

"It's a distinction I would prefer to have avoided," she said dryly. She studied his face, wondering if she was mad to consider this proposal. "If I am to accept your offer of a settlement, we'll have to trust each other. You must trust that I won't take the money and run away, and I must trust that you won't push me down the stairs to free you from an unsatisfactory marriage."

"I like your directness," he said, amused. "I swear not to push you down any stairs, and I trust that you won't take the money and leave without making a good faith effort to create a companionable marriage."

"If I accept your proposal, I swear I will try my best," she said seriously.

"One can ask no more." He glanced out the window. "Night falls so early at this season. I need to return you to your home."

Suzanne nodded agreement, then asked, "Now that we've broken bread together, what next, milord?"

"First I'll take you home so you can finish your alterations. Tomorrow, shall we meet some of each other's friends?"

She liked that he respected her work even though alterations must seem trivial to him. But the rest of his comment was irrelevant. "I have no friends in London except for Mr. and Mrs. Potter and the other women in the boardinghouse."

Simon smiled. "Aren't you friends with a certain Lady Aurora Lawrence, informally known as 'Roaring Rory'?"

"Rory is still in London?" Suzanne exclaimed. "I'd love to see her! Surely her captain is not far from his bride."

"Glued to her side by all appearances, with a wide, happy smile on his face," Simon said with affectionate amusement. "Tomorrow evening, several veterans of the Portuguese cellar and their wives will be dining at the home of Lord and Lady Kirkland, so you can meet Rory and some other amiable ladies."

Suzanne glanced down at her gown, appalled. Correctly interpreting her expression, Simon said, "You have the Frenchwoman's gift of elegance, Suzanne. You will look very well, and from what I hear, the other ladies who will be present are not the sort who claw other females for sport."

The idea was still rather intimidating, but it would be wonderful to see the exuberant Rory and perhaps her quiet, lovely cousin Constance. Suzanne was also curious to meet the friends Simon had made when under sentence of death. "I shall be pleased to accompany you. Who are the Kirklands? Was he in that cellar?"

"No, but he has been a friend to all of us. Kirkland has extensive shipping interests and many useful connections. When Lady Aurora's mother was desperate to find a reliable agent to negotiate her daughter's freedom in Algiers, Kirkland produced Hawkins for her. He's very good at such things."

Suzanne smiled. "Surely the captain exceeded his orders by not only rescuing the lady but marrying her."

"Perhaps, but there are no complaints from any direction. I think the lady's parents are relieved to see her safely married off."

"Safe" wasn't the word Suzanne would have used to describe Lady Aurora, but she and Hawkins clearly suited each other well. Rising from her chair, she said, "It will be an interesting evening."

With impeccable timing, Madame Mercier entered the breakfast room and offered a basket to Suzanne. "Your candles, milady."

Suzanne looked into the basket and saw a wrapped bundle of what she suspected were the best beeswax candles, alongside a wrapped parcel of bread and a small crock that smelled deliciously of beef bourguignon. "Thank you, madam! You are very generous."

Madame Mercier murmured in French that it was her pleasure, but her conspiratorial glance at Simon said that she was hopeful this long neglected house would soon have a new mistress. The idea was beginning to seem . . . possible.

Chapter 4

In a tribute to her skill with alterations, the shimmering green gown Suzanne wore for dinner with Simon's friends produced a bow of admiration when he collected her at her boardinghouse. "You look splendid, milady. The green of your gown makes your eyes seem impossibly emerald."

She made a face as she took his arm, and they left the house together. The evening was damp and bitingly cold, but the battered cloak she'd found at a rag shop was mercifully warm. When she had time, she'd refurbish the cloak with braid and brass buttons, but for now, she preferred comfort to style. "Those emerald eyes probably saved my life. My master, Gürkan, liked exotic looks in his harem slaves. He'd not seen eyes like mine before and they intrigued him enough to spare my life."

Simon flinched as he helped her into the carriage. "It is hard for me to imagine the uncertainty and danger of harem life."

"I was told that many harems were pleasant places that gave beautiful young girls the chance for a better life."

She settled on her seat and pulled her cloak tight against the chill. "But Gürkan was mad. Evil. He had fits that put him into a killing rage. No one ever left his harem for a better life, until the night of our escape."

Simon took the reins and set the carriage in motion. "You speak of these things so calmly. Was that how you kept your sanity?"

She shrugged. "Collapsing in a weeping heap would do me no good. Detachment and acceptance of the fact that I might be killed at any time were necessary."

"You would have made a magnificent soldier," he said pensively.

"I expect I would have enjoyed that a good deal more than being a harem slave." She studied his silhouette as they passed through a splash of light from a house. She liked his firm, handsome profile. "But women have few choices."

"Which is why you are reluctant to put yourself into a man's control again," he said as he turned the carriage into a wider street. "I do understand, though I hope to change your mind."

He was making some progress, but she preferred not to tell him that. "Enough about the past. Tell me about that mad night in Portugal, the men you shared it with, and whom we will dine with tonight."

"That mad night was in 1809, when the French were invading northern Portugal," he said. "They had reached Porto, so the retreating Portuguese army destroyed the bridge over the Douro River that separated Porto from Gaia on the opposite side. They wanted to slow the French advance, but in the process they also destroyed the escape route for Portuguese civilians fleeing the French army."

She frowned as she thought back. "There was a disaster, wasn't there?"

He nodded in the darkness. "A bridge was improvised by lashing small boats together so they reached from shore to shore. Desperate people were surging across even though it was unsteady and dangerous. Then the bridge broke and the refugees were pitched into the water screaming." He drew a rough breath. "The current was swift. I was one of many who tried to rescue the victims from the water. It was chaos."

She shivered at the image of a river full of desperate, screaming people. "I once fell into a stream and was dragged down by my saturated skirts. I would have drowned if a servant hadn't pulled me out."

"Many of the refugees were women and children," Simon said grimly. "The five of us who were captured and sentenced to death were rescuing a group of nuns and schoolgirls. Some English was spoken, and that alerted a French colonel who arrested us, declared we were all English spies, and locked us in the damp cellar of a house where he'd set up his headquarters. The other four men were British. I became very French but the colonel decided I was a royalist spy and I was locked up with the others."

"Why were you there?"

"I was observing the invasion, as a reconnaissance officer does, but I wasn't wearing my uniform, so I was fair game."

"What a difference a uniform makes! Why were the other Britons in such a dangerous place?"

"None of us discussed that, though I later found that our group included another British army officer." His voice turned wry. "We were a proper scruffy set of rogues. As we waited for dawn and the firing squad, we drank bad brandy provided by a couple of the French guards who thought we shouldn't go to our deaths sober."

"How very French!" Suzanne exclaimed. "Though a pity the brandy wasn't better. What does one speak of on such a night?"

"A major topic was what we'd do to redeem our wicked lives if we escaped."

She laughed a little. "One may have very saintly aspirations when death is inevitable. Were you really such rogues?"

"I can't swear to the sins of any of the others, but what man doesn't have regrets?"

"What man or woman?" she said softly.

"Very true." After a long silence, he said, "I'll be curious to learn what the other Rogues Redeemed have done with their survival."

"Who will be there tonight?"

"Hawkins and his lady, of course. Masterson, who was the other army officer. A fellow who called himself Gordon and who could be called a soldier of fortune. Kirkland said they were bringing wives, so perhaps they're settling down to quieter lives."

"You would be the fourth man in the cellar. Who was the fifth? Has he survived the wars?"

"I don't know. He called himself Chantry, but there was an assumption we weren't necessarily using our real names. We arranged to send letters to Hatchards bookstore to update each other on our situations, but I haven't yet had time to call at the store and check for messages."

"It sounds as if a deep connection formed among you in mere hours," Suzanne said thoughtfully. "This reunion will be interesting."

"We have nothing in common other than that one night of shared danger. We worked together to escape and the bond is real, but it won't necessarily make us friends." Amusement sounded in his voice. "As you say, it should be interesting."

"Have you seen any of the men other than Hawkins?"

"I met Masterson in Spain after the emperor's abdication. I sent him on a mission that very nearly got him killed."

Simon's amusement deepened. "He wrote me a thank-you note later."

Suzanne blinked. "Why?"

"Apparently he thought the benefits outweighed the dangers." Simon turned the carriage into an area of parkland and grand houses. "This is Berkeley Square. Kirkland House is directly across from Gunter's confectionery shop, which is famous for its ices. I'd like to take you there when the weather is warmer."

She tugged her shabby cloak closer. "That won't be anytime soon."

"Spring will come eventually. The weather is no worse than Paris."

"And no better!" But she would take rain and cold over the scorching sunshine of Constantinople any day.

Suzanne schooled her expression to polite amiability as they entered Kirkland House. With Hawkins and Rory attending, at least not everyone would be a stranger.

The butler accepted her worn cloak with no visible sneer. "The guests are gathering in the drawing room," he said as he ushered the new arrivals into a spacious room on the left.

Their hosts approached to welcome them. Lord Kirkland was dark and handsome and fashionably detached, though his greeting was friendly. His lovely blond wife was warmer, with a smile that made Suzanne feel immediately at ease.

Lady Kirkland was performing introductions to the guests who had already arrived when a newcomer cried out, "Suzanne!"

Suzanne turned and was engulfed in a swift, rose-scented hug. "I'm so glad to see you!" Lady Aurora Lawrence exclaimed. As golden and vivacious as always, Rory stepped back, radiant with pleasure. "When the *Zephyr* arrived in London, I was so excited about seeing my family that I didn't say a proper farewell to you, and later I realized I didn't even have an address."

"We owe this reunion to our gentlemen of the Portuguese cellar," Suzanne said, delighted by Rory's exuberance. "Are your cousin and her husband still in England?"

"No, Constance and Jason sailed for Maryland almost immediately to avoid the worst of the winter storms. Just yesterday I received a letter, though. Constance loves America, and Jason's family loves her. She sounds thoroughly happy."

"I am so glad to hear that," Suzanne said sincerely. "Though you must miss each other dreadfully."

"Very, but we both have compensations." She glanced mischievously up at Hawkins, who was at her side. He returned a swift, intimate smile that made Suzanne feel a pang of envy.

Tanned and solid and reliable as the earth, Hawkins looked more relaxed than Suzanne had ever seen him. "I'm glad Duval has found you, Suzanne," he said, returning her greeting. "I gather you're cousins by marriage?"

"We are." Simon laid a light hand on her lower back as he replied. "I am also courting the lady, but the outcome is uncertain."

Suzanne felt herself flush, sure that she was red from her hairline to her décolletage. A tall woman said with amusement, "Colonel Duval, full frontal assault may work well in battle but it's not the best of courtship techniques."

She offered her hand to Suzanne. Though not beautiful, she was striking and had an air of natural authority. "I'm Athena Masterson and it's my pleasure to meet you. Since dinner is half an hour or so away, shall we ladies take a bottle or two of claret into a corner and become acquainted while the men trade their war stories?"

"What a fine idea," a dazzling woman with red-gold hair agreed. "You can tell us whether you want to say yes, no, or maybe to the colonel. We shall support you in whatever decision you make." She offered her hand. "I'm Callie and that handsome blond fellow with the shifty expression is my husband."

The handsome blond fellow was grinning, uninsulted, and Suzanne decided this evening would be more entertaining than she'd expected. "Lead me to the claret, ladies, and let us become friends!"

Smiling, Lady Kirkland ushered them to comfortable chairs set around the fireplace. The butler, a quick thinker, followed with claret and glasses.

Suzanne settled in her chair, saying, "It's early in the evening for the men and women to separate, but I'm sure the Irredeemable Rogues need time together. I hope Lord Kirkland doesn't feel too left out."

Lady Kirkland chuckled at the reference to the Irredeemable Rogues. "Kirkland went to school with two of these rogues and he is eternally curious about people, so he'll manage very well." Her thoughtful gaze settled on Suzanne. "Have you and Colonel Duval known each other long?"

"We met when very young. I was on the verge of marriage and Simon was a second cousin of my fiancé. We struck up a friendship, but I haven't seen him from then until yesterday. So we've known each other long, but not well," she said candidly.

"If you're uncertain what sort of man Colonel Duval is now, I can give him an unqualified endorsement," Athena said seriously. "I met him in San Gabriel, a small country in the mountains between Portugal and Spain. San Gabriel had been ravished by the French, and Duval was instrumental in getting the country back on its feet."

"Simon said he sent Masterson on a mission that almost

got him killed, and Masterson wrote him a thank-you note?" Suzanne said with a questioning tone in her voice.

Athena laughed. "I didn't know about the thank-you note, but it's true that Will came far too close to being killed. Luckily he survived and was made a knight of the Order of Saint Deolinda, patron saint of San Gabriel. He got a grand shining medallion that is large enough to block bullets. Colonel Duval has one, too."

"What did Simon do to win such honors?" Suzanne asked.

"The details are lengthy. Best ask him to explain," Athena replied. "But I assure you that he acted with intelligence, compassion, and honor throughout."

Suzanne would have guessed as much, but it was good to hear Simon's better qualities confirmed. Her gaze moved around the other four women. "I suspect that none of you had what is considered a normal courtship. I know your story, Rory, having seen some of it firsthand, but what about the rest of you? I'd love to hear how you met and mated with your rogues."

Callie grinned. "You may be sorry you asked, but I'm happy to tell you in as much or as little detail as you like."

"This may take more claret," Lady Kirkland said with a mischievous smile. "A good thing Kirkland's wine cellar is extensive!"

Chapter 5

As the ladies moved off en masse, Kirkland's formality fell away and he said with amusement, "Do any of you actually prefer sherry? If not, we can collect decanters of brandy and whiskey and move to a separate corner."

"A fine idea," Hawkins said, his interested gaze moving to Simon's face. "You and Suzanne? During the voyage from Constantinople to London, I enjoyed getting to know her. A lovely woman with nerves of steel."

"She'll need them if she accepts me," Simon said dryly. The other men laughed as they settled into leather upholstered sofas at the opposite end of the room from the ladies. The alert butler followed them with a tray of decanters and tumblers.

As Simon accepted a brandy, he studied the group, surprised how much at ease he felt even though they'd known each other only for a matter of hours, and Kirkland he'd known only by reputation.

But though at first glance they could be any group of well-off English gentlemen at their club, a deeper study revealed more. All of these men had lived beyond the borders of fashionable society. All had navigated danger and survived, and all of them seemed to have reached places of stability and happiness. Exactly what Simon would like to find for himself.

The feeling of ease was similar to his reaction when he'd met Suzanne. Apparently he was no longer as relaxed with people who had lived normal, uncomplicated lives. Aloud he said, "We look so respectable now that I'm not sure I'd have recognized anyone."

"It would be difficult to look worse than when we met after floundering about in the Douro River," Hawkins said dryly. "That night we didn't speak of our pasts, but I'd like to know more about everyone. Where do you come from, what have you been doing, what brought you to that cellar?"

"My background isn't particularly interesting," Simon said. "Though I presented myself as French in Portugal, I'm Anglo-French. My mother was English and I've spent more time here than in France. When the Peace of Amiens collapsed, I decided to join the British army and eventually became a colonel of military intelligence." He smiled a little. "Usually I did reconnaissance in uniform. I ended up in the cellar with you because of a foray out of uniform."

"Dangerous, that," Masterson said with understanding. "I did the same, which is why I ended up in the cellar next to you. But in general my life has been straightforward. I was born in Oxfordshire and went to school with Kirkland." He hesitated an instant as if wondering how much to say. "I'd always wanted to join the army, so I bought a commission and marched off to fight for king and country. I spent most of the next years on the Peninsula and I sold out of the army at the first reasonable moment."

"And you found yourself a magnificent Amazon on your way home," Simon pointed out.

Masterson laughed. "That was the best part."

"I'm disappointed. Remember how just before we went our separate ways in Portugal, it was acknowledged that we might be using names that weren't entirely accurate? Yet here you two are, Duval and Masterson, as originally labeled." The blond man grinned. "Technically I'm Kingston now, but I prefer to be called Gordon as I was in the cellar. It's one of my names, so more or less legitimate."

"What was your path before and after that night?" Hawkins asked.

"I left school when an attack of nobility got me transported to New South Wales," Gordon said succinctly. "After I escaped from the penal colony, I wandered widely and rather randomly, doing different things in different places. After Portugal, I decided I should start working toward the redemption we discussed, so I returned to London and became something of a problem solver."

"And a very good one," Kirkland said. "From a professional point of view, I regret that you've retired to respectability."

"Your fault for sending me on that last mission." Gordon gestured toward Hawkins. "I needed transport across the Atlantic and Hawkins was willing to take the risks of sailing into a war zone. We deepened our acquaintance over brandy on the journey over."

"Speaking of changing names, I'm another who was using a variation of my own name," Hawkins said. "Though my family name is Vance, I started using my middle name, Hawkins, when I was cashiered from the Royal Navy. After that I became a merchant seaman and eventually acquired a ship of my own through rather dubious means." He grinned. "A very fast ship, very good for blockade running."

His words jolted through Simon. He leaned forward, his body tense. "Are you the Lieutenant Vance who was forced out of the navy because you carried a wounded midshipman belowdecks during an engagement? Because all your superior officers were killed or wounded, you were charged with abandoning your post during battle."

Hawkins stiffened. "That's what happened. How did you know?"

"Because the young man you rescued was my cousin, Lucas Mandeville." Simon swallowed hard. "More like a brother, really."

Hawkins also leaned forward, his gaze intent. "Did he recover from his wounds? Lucas was so gravely injured that the surgeon didn't hold out much hope and I never learned his fate."

"He recovered, though it took some time," Simon replied. "He returned to active duty when he was well enough. He said that was his obligation since the navy lost a future admiral when you were cashiered for saving him."

Hawkins shrugged. "Perhaps, but I like the way my life has turned out. In the same circumstances, I'd do exactly the same thing again. I'm glad to hear that Lucas recovered. What has happened to him since? I'd like to see him again if that's possible."

"His ship was sunk by the French and he was listed as missing in action. There's a slim chance that he was captured and interned in France, but he sent no letters and his bank says he never wrote asking for money to make captivity more comfortable." Simon's mouth tightened. "It's been almost a year since the emperor abdicated and there's been no word, so I must accept that he's gone."

"Searching for a missing friend, I became something of an expert on the various places France interned British officers," Kirkland said slowly. "Have you had a chance to investigate your cousin's disappearance more thoroughly?"

"No, I've been busy on the Peninsula until quite recently." Trying not to hope, Simon asked, "Did you find your missing friend?"

"Yes, in a rather unexpected place. If you're interested, we can discuss the material I collected while searching for Wyndham."

Be damned to reason; it was impossible not to feel a small flare of hope. "I'd like that very much."

"We'll talk later," Kirkland promised.

Simon nodded his thanks, then asked, "Four out of five of us are here and looking reasonably fit and happy. Has there been any news of Chantry?"

"I met him in Constantinople," Hawkins said. "He was a sort of special projects aide to the British ambassador, meaning he spoke Turkish like a native and had many interesting local connections. He was invaluable in our rescue of Rory, her cousin, and Suzanne. At his request, I deposited a letter confirming his whereabouts at Hatchards. Gordon, you'll be pleased to learn that his real name is Ramsay."

"Good! At least one of us was suitably sneaky," Gordon said with a grin.

Across the room, a footman entered and murmured something to Lady Kirkland. She nodded and rose, saying in a soft but clear voice that reached everyone in the room, "Dinner is ready, so I suggest we continue these interesting conversations in the dining room." She smiled. "Seating will be informal, so you may sit beside your favorite person."

Better and better. Simon stood and made his way to Suzanne. She looked younger and happier, like the girl he'd met all those years ago.

She rose and took his arm, her green eyes sparkling as she gazed up at him. He smiled back, thinking how much he liked her. "You enjoyed your gathering?"

"Indeed I did! They're a very diverse group of women and much friendlier than the aristocratic émigrés who scorned me."

That was enough to make Simon like the other women, even the ones he hadn't properly met. "I look forward to conversing with them. The only one I know is Athena Masterson, whom I met in San Gabriel shortly after the emperor abdicated."

"I'd never heard of that country till tonight," Suzanne said. "There is so much news of Europe that I missed while I was in Constantinople! I was intrigued to learn that you were made a member of the Order of Saint Deolinda and you have a great gaudy medallion to prove it. Would it really stop bullets?"

"I wouldn't stake my life on that," Simon chuckled. "But it is impressive. Athena and Will both have the medals as well and deserve them more than I do. She's probably too modest to tell you her story, but I will if you're interested."

"I am very interested." Suzanne's hand tightened on his arm. "None of them flinched when I spoke of my background. It was very refreshing."

"You told them?" he said, a little surprised.

"I thought if we were to be friends, I must be honest." Her mouth twisted. "And if they despised me, no more time would be wasted."

"That's a very pragmatic approach," he said, impressed by her courage.

"Living in a harem will remove one's illusions." She gave Simon a slanting glance. "The whole discussion was very frank. I think it would have sent you gentlemen fleeing if you'd heard. But we found that we had much common ground. For example, Callie, the beauty with the rose-gold hair? She also had to earn her living with her needle. I look forward to talking more with her."

Callie, who looked like the most delicate of aristocrats, had been a seamstress? "She must also have interesting stories."

Suzanne nodded. "How did your gentlemanly discussion go? You said that shared danger didn't mean you would necessarily become friends."

"True, but as it turns out, we get along very well, being rogues working toward redemption." He realized that they'd been talking while the other couples had moved past them to the dining room so both resumed walking.

"Doing dangerous, necessary work doesn't make you a rogue," Suzanne said as they entered the dining room. "Foolhardy, maybe, but not a rogue."

"Perhaps not, but staying alive while one does such work can be very ungentlemanly." He pulled out her chair. Since they were the last to enter the dining room, there were only two seats left and they were opposite Hawkins and Lady Rory. All the couples had chosen to sit together, and he was pleased to see that the table was narrow enough to converse across. He liked the way the Kirklands entertained.

"As an expert in the pragmatic art of survival, I'm in no position to criticize," she said with a touch of dryness.

"I'd say something we all have in common is being survivors," Simon said thoughtfully. "Hawkins, would you agree?"

"Without question," the other man said. "I've had more close calls than I care to count! Rory has had her share as well."

"I'm going to take notes on all these narrow escapes," Rory said, a gleam in her eyes. "They'd make wonderful episodes in outrageous Gothic novels!"

Suzanne chuckled. "As long as the details are changed to protect the guilty!"

Their teasing comments were typical of the dinner conversation. The food was excellent and the discussions even better. Simon couldn't remember a more enjoyable meal.

He and Hawkins discussed the sailing life and memories of Hawkins's friendship with Lucas; Athena and Callie discussed life in the war zones they'd known; and Gordon told hilarious and hopefully exaggerated stories of his traveling days.

Kirkland listened to everything with interest, probably taking mental notes. Simon knew the other man was something of a legend in the intelligence gathering community, and part of his success was due to his genius for collecting information.

As the meal came to an end, Kirkland said, "Before we temporarily separate, I have a question for you since collectively your experience is vast. I'm sure you've all heard rumors and speculation that the emperor will escape from Elba and return to France to reclaim his throne. What do you think will happen?"

The long silence that followed was broken by Athena Masterson. "I think that's very likely," she said slowly. "I recently made the acquaintance of several French soldiers in San Gabriel. Some are tired of war and want only the chance to build a peaceful life, but others know only war and have nothing else to go back to. Napoleon is still worshipped by many of his soldiers. If he returns and raises his banner, many will march again."

"Very true," Simon agreed. "The new Bourbon king has not been endearing himself to his subjects and it's said that Napoleon is growing bored with his miniature kingdom on Elba. If he can escape, he will."

"And sooner or later, he *will* escape because there are so many people willing to support him," Masterson said soberly. "Enough of the French people will welcome him back to trigger new wars."

"Old wars continued." Simon could think of many ways the situation might play out, none of them good. "He should have been exiled to a far more distant place. Botany Bay, perhaps. Elba is much too close to Italy and France."

Kirkland nodded, his expression grave. "That confirms my own fears. In the long run he can't defeat the Allies, but he can devastate the Continent again before he is defeated once and for all."

The new silence was broken when Lady Kirkland rose to her feet. "Now that gloom has been evoked, it's the traditional time for the ladies to withdraw to sip tea and for the gentlemen to gossip over their port. I do hope you'll join us soon, sirs."

"We don't gossip," her husband protested as he stood. "We exchange valuable information and insights."

"As you say, my dear," she said sweetly.

The Kirklands exchanged private smiles before Lord Kirkland said, "Duval and Madame Duval, will you join me for a few minutes?"

"Of course," Simon said, and wondered warily what Kirkland wanted.

Chapter 6

❦

Kirkland led his guests into his comfortable private study, then lit lamps as they settled onto a small sofa opposite the desk. Suzanne studied Kirkland carefully, a habit that had been crucial for survival in the harem. She sensed that he was not a cruel man, but that he could be ruthless in pursuing goals he considered vital. Stopping Napoleon from reclaiming his throne would surely be in that category.

Though she concealed her nervousness, Simon's calm was real, she thought. He and Kirkland came from the same world and understood each other. "What do you want to know, Kirkland?" he asked. "I don't have any special insights into what Napoleon might do."

"No, but you do have entrée into the French émigré community if you choose to use it," Kirkland replied. "After all, it's possible that you are the Comte de Chambron."

Simon's expression was pained when he glanced at Suzanne. "So many of our relatives have died?"

"It's hard to be sure. As the Revolution shattered the old order, French aristocrats fled in all directions. Many moved to Britain and even Canada, while others fled east into Russia. It's hard to get information this far away."

"Then I shall hope I have healthy cousins living in Russia."

"If so, we should find out eventually," Suzanne said quietly. "But I suspect that at the moment, Lord Kirkland is hoping to use your possible rank."

"Exactly so," Kirkland said. "As a possible French count who served with distinction in the British army in the fight against Napoleon, you would be welcomed into the highest London émigré circles."

"I am not French enough to be the Comte de Chambron," Simon said dryly. "Why would I *want* to be welcomed by aristocratic émigrés?"

"The London émigré community may contain highly placed Bonapartist spies or informers who have been passing information to the emperor's supporters in France," Kirkland said succinctly. "That's not as critical now as it was several years ago when the fighting was more intense, but it would be useful to identify any such people. Particularly if they might have some knowledge of Napoleon's plans."

"And you would like me to turn spy again to investigate them," Simon said flatly.

"You wouldn't be a spy, merely a trained observer. If you're willing, the information could be useful." Kirkland's gaze moved to Suzanne. Uncannily perceptive, he said, "I've heard that you were not treated well by your countrymen when you recently arrived in London."

Her face turned hot with shame. "Your information is correct. Does everyone in England know of my ruination?"

Simon touched her hand. "You were not ruined," he

said softly. "You have become strong as tempered Damascus steel."

She gazed into his clear, light eyes and almost wept as she saw his belief in her. She had thought of her captivity as a trial she'd barely survived, not as an experience that had made her stronger and better.

She drew a shaky breath and turned to Kirkland. "Surely you have enough spies that you don't need Simon's help in this."

"I have some informants among the émigrés," Kirkland admitted, "but none are well placed enough to be useful in this matter. Colonel Duval has rank and experience of intelligence gathering. As his wife, you would be accepted also if you accompany him."

"I have no desire to be accepted by those people!" she snapped, going rigid as she remembered the humiliation and pain she'd experienced when she'd expected to be welcomed and comforted by her countrymen.

"That's understandable," he agreed, his expression sympathetic. "But wouldn't there be some satisfaction in returning to those circles as a countess with a heroic husband on your arm?"

Simon said sharply, "Suzanne might not be ready to make this decision, and I will not allow her to be coerced!"

"Nor do I wish to coerce her," Kirkland said seriously. "But you both know as well as I what horrors will be unleashed if Napoleon returns to his throne. There may not be any vital information to be found among the émigrés, but there might be something that would save lives."

"The hell of intelligence work is that one never knows if the information gathered will be useful," Simon said tartly.

"Sometimes it isn't, yet other times it spells the difference between triumph and disaster," Kirkland agreed. "You saved San Gabriel and its people from a bloody invasion. I'd say the work you did there made up for any number of dead ends."

As Simon nodded reluctantly, Kirkland turned to Suzanne. "Madame Duval, marriage is a grave step to take and the business of no one but you and Colonel Duval. Such a decision is not to be rushed, but collecting information is a separate issue. If you're willing to work with the colonel, an actual marriage isn't necessary."

Her brows arched. "A false marriage? No, thank you! I've spent too much of my life living lies."

"Our marriage could be real," Simon said quietly. "But only if you wish it."

She studied his strong, familiar features, drawn to him and the life of ease he was offering her. She wanted the women she'd met tonight to become her friends, and as a practical Frenchwoman, she wanted the security and comfort that Simon could provide.

Was that enough for marriage when the thought of putting herself into a man's power again terrified her? Though her mind said "Accept," the wounded girl deep inside wanted to burrow back into anonymous poverty.

There was only one way to reconcile these impulses. Choosing her words carefully, she said, "It is time we discussed your proposal in greater detail."

Simon's eyes lit up. "Indeed we should. Kirkland, will you mind dreadfully if I ask you to leave?"

The other man chuckled. "Not at all. Take as long as you wish. I hope you'll join us later with good news." He crossed the room and closed the door quietly behind him.

When they were alone, Suzanne said wryly, "Have you noticed that happily married couples encourage everyone to join them in that estate?"

"Yes, while unhappily married persons urge flight. What we must decide is which best suits us," he said.

"Most betrothed couples yearn to share a bed. That

isn't what we'll be doing." Her gaze searched his face, trying to look beneath his calm. "Are you sure this is what you want, Simon? As the melancholy of war fades, you may regret contracting a passionless marriage. You are buying the cow but will receive no milk."

"A cow?" He laughed out loud. "I see myself marrying a lovely, intelligent woman of the world whose company I have always enjoyed. Even in the most passionate marriages, people don't spend all their time in bed. They'd starve if that was the case."

"Friendship is powerful, but I think most of the advantages of our marriage would go to me," she said seriously. "What would you receive in return?"

"Companionship," Simon said immediately. "A woman I can laugh with, or discuss the issues of the day, or take to the theater. Someone I'll enjoy seeing at the breakfast table. A wife who will care whether or not I come home." He hesitated, then continued, "Someone to cherish. To give purpose to my life."

She frowned. "I can be your companion, but I can't promise to be your salvation."

"Companionship is enough. Anything more will be a bonus. You have your doubts, understandably. Is it me, the fact that this is so sudden, or the idea of marriage itself that you object to?"

"It isn't you. We are old friends and I don't think you will turn into a monster. My head says to accept because I won't get such a good offer again. But this is happening so suddenly." She swallowed hard, knowing she must be honest with him if there was to be any chance of their building a lasting relationship. "And I do fear marriage. With anyone."

"I'm grateful that you don't think I'll become a monster," he said with wry humor. "The practical advantages of this marriage are obvious, but emotions run much more deeply. Do you understand the source of your fears?"

When had she known a man who wanted to understand her mind and emotions? Never. "I went from child to wife to harem slave," she said bluntly. "The thought of putting myself in a man's power again terrifies me."

She waited for him to become affronted, but instead he said, "That is entirely understandable. There are times I've been in the power of others and I've hated it, and those situations were surely less threatening than what you've endured." He cocked his head to one side as he thought. "Is there anything that might help allay your fears?"

"Money is protection against many of the world's ills," she said diffidently. "You said you would settle an income on me. How much would that be?"

His brows drew together as he thought. "A thousand pounds a year? You won't be able to live in the grand style you knew in France, but it's enough for comfort."

Her eyes widened. "That's very generous! You would draw up a legal settlement to guarantee it?"

He laughed and raised her hand to brush a light kiss on her knuckles. "My practical Frenchwoman! Yes, there would be a legal settlement to protect you."

She flushed and pulled her hand away. "I don't feel I need protection from you. But life is dangerous and uncertain. If something happened to you, I wouldn't want to find myself in desperate circumstances again."

"Of course you wouldn't. You must have funds that are yours alone." He regarded her thoughtfully, his eyes narrowing. "Is there anything besides money that would help dispel your fears?"

She hadn't thought beyond money, but an answer came swiftly to mind. "I'd like to learn to defend myself! Men don't expect women to resist and they are right. Most of us are used to submitting tamely. We don't know how to fight back. I'd like to learn how to shoot a gun or wield a dagger."

"Not against me, I hope! Unless I deserve it. I can give you shooting lessons. I can show you how to use a knife and how to conceal it when you travel in dangerous places. I can also teach you some defensive moves that can be effective against assailants larger than yourself."

Suzanne's eyes widened in amazement. She hadn't really expected an answer, much less one so specific. "I would love all those things!" She thought of Rory, who had known how to fight back when necessary. "The mere idea of being able to defend myself effectively makes me feel stronger. Safer."

"Then it shall be done." He gave her a slow smile. "The thought of learning how to wreak mayhem makes you glow. What an extraordinary woman you are!"

She thought how Jean-Louis would have reacted to her desire to learn how to shoot and fight. He'd have been appalled. Despite his physical resemblance to her late husband, Simon was a very different man. She thanked heaven for that. She blushed. "For years, I have yearned for freedom, independence, and power over my own life. Is it possible for me to have all those things as your wife?"

She meant her question seriously, and Simon answered with matching seriousness. "Any marriage, even one as unconventional as what we're negotiating, will involve some compromises for both of us. But I swear that I will never try to coerce you into doing something you don't want to do."

It was impossible not to believe him, but still she hesitated. "If ever our marriage should become so unbearable that I leave, will you promise not to try to find me? With your abilities, I'm sure you could hunt me down no matter where I might try to hide."

He winced, but answered. "I pray God that matters between us never become so painful! If you wish to leave, I'll let you go, but I reserve the right to speak with you once to see if the situation might be resolved."

Her imagination produced the image of a murderous Simon cornering her so she had no escape. . . . *No.* That was her fear speaking and had nothing to do with him. If their marriage failed, it would be with a weary sigh, not violence.

"I can't imagine that we would reach such dire straits." She smiled wryly. "You must think I'm a little mad to ask about such absurd possibilities, but the more we talk, the better I know you. You really listen to me. That is rare and valuable."

One corner of his mouth lifted in a half smile. "So I'm passing your test?"

"It's not precisely a test," she said. "But you're doing a good job of allaying my fears. Am I making you have second thoughts about your proposal?"

"No, you're convincing me that you will be a most excellent wife if you accept me," he said promptly. "You're cautious, intelligent, experienced, and wise. I value those qualities greatly. No flighty debutante could match them."

She liked the way he saw her, though she didn't quite believe his words. Turning again to practicalities, she asked, "What kind of life would we live? What will you do now that you're out of the army? I don't imagine that you'll spend all your time drinking and gambling, but what will you do with yourself? Seek a government post, perhaps?"

"Definitely not a life of gentlemanly dissipation, and I've no interest in a government post." He looked almost embarrassed. "I've said that I had a comfortable inheritance. In fact, it's quite substantial. Besides the town house, there's a sizable estate in Berkshire and I'm part owner of several businesses inherited from my mother's merchant family. The properties have all been in the hands of capable managers, but it's time I took on my responsibilities. They'll keep me busy and out of trouble."

She blinked, surprised at the extent of his wealth. "An estate. Would I be able to have a horse again?"

He looked startled. "I hadn't thought of it, but I suppose you couldn't ride during your time in Constantinople."

Her mouth twisted. "If they'd let me near a horse, I'd have been halfway to Greece so quickly they wouldn't have seen me go!"

"I believe that. You were a superb horsewoman even at age fifteen. Yes, you can have a horse. As many as you want."

She smiled a little ruefully. "It's been far too long since I've been on horseback. Remember how we rode through the countryside in the weeks before my marriage? We always outran the grooms."

"Good times," he murmured. "I didn't realize how good until much later."

She had never felt more free than when she was on horseback, galloping with the wind and a good companion at her side, and she'd never had a better companion than Simon. Choosing her words carefully, she said, "I look forward to riding with you over the hills of our estate."

He became very still. "Does this mean you're accepting my proposal?"

She drew a deep breath and stepped off the cliff, praying that she was doing the right thing. "I do believe it does."

Chapter 7

~~~~~~~~~

Simon felt a surge of pure delight that was as startling as it was welcome. Taking Suzanne's fine-boned hand in a warm clasp, he said, "I'm so very glad to hear that! Fear doesn't vanish in an hour, but I presume it's now diminished to a manageable level."

She gave him the sweet, bright smile that had enchanted him when she was a young bride-to-be looking forward to her future. "There is still some fear, but more anticipation. What will our life together look like?"

"What would you like it to be? We have many choices."

She looked thoughtful. "I envision us with friends who are interesting and open-minded, like the people we met tonight. Even more important, I see you and me sharing a library after dinner. We'll sit by a fire and read or write letters with a cat or dog or both to keep us company. Domestic peace with good French cooking."

He contemplated the picture she created and found it good. "That's very appealing. We've both had too much adventuring. You like cats?"

"Yes, in the harem there were several long-haired Turkish cats. They were charming. There was a beautiful silver-haired fellow who graciously allowed me to brush through his long silky hair. I felt very honored."

"Cats do have the ability to make us believe we're privileged to be their slaves," he agreed.

"Omar was certainly of that sort. Captain Hawkins has a very different sort of cat. The Spook was a rangy, odd-looking ship's cat who hunted for vermin and presented his trophies to favored humans." She chuckled. "Most often the ship's cook, who was his special friend, but I was the fortunate recipient of several of his gifts. Hawkins and Rory planned to move him ashore, so he's probably patrolling their kitchen now."

Simon laughed. "A working cat, very different from the decorative sort. I'd like either kind of feline. Both! And I want to get a dog or two now that I'm finally going to be in one place long enough to provide a proper home."

"Dogs are good companions and less expensive and less work than wives," she pointed out. "You wouldn't really need me at all!"

"Dogs have many fine qualities, but they're poor conversationalists. So I need a dog *and* a wife." He loved that she was relaxed enough to tease him. "When shall we marry? It won't take my lawyer long to draw up the legal settlements for you."

She drew a deep breath. "I see no reason to wait. A special license means we could marry soon, doesn't it?"

"Yes, right away and in a time and place of our choosing." Remembering an important question, he asked, "Do you want a Catholic ceremony?"

She shook her head. "I haven't been a true Catholic for many years. Since reaching England, I've sometimes attended services at the local parish church. You may choose as you like."

"I was christened both Catholic and Anglican and never felt there was a great deal of difference," he admitted.

"Nor do I." She hesitated, then asked diffidently, "Could you advance me some money from the income you're settling on me? I'd like to give gifts to the other women in the boardinghouse as well as to the Potters. They have been kind to me."

He knew how much difference even a few pounds could make to people living on the bare edge of poverty. "Of course, and as your friends, they must be invited to the ceremony and the wedding breakfast."

"We must also invite those people we've met tonight," she said warmly.

"Certainly," he agreed. "They are well on their way to becoming our friends."

Suzanne laughed. "The women will probably want to swoop in and organize the wedding. If so, they are welcome to do so!"

More seriously, Simon said, "There is the matter of spying for Kirkland, but as he pointed out, that is separate from our marriage. Like an old warhorse, I must answer the call of duty, but you don't have to join me."

She smiled ruefully. "If we meet the émigrés as a couple, it will be more effective, won't it? I am gaining so much by this marriage that it is only fair I keep you company while you see what you may learn."

He gave an inward sigh of relief. "Thank you, your presence will be valuable. It's also another reason to marry soon since anything might happen with Bonaparte." He rose and offered his arm. "Shall we join the others and announce our news?"

"I'm sure all those romantic couples will be pleased." Suzanne rose gracefully and took his arm, but her fingers felt cold even through the fabric of his coat. She still had her fears, he realized, but he guessed that now she had chosen her course, she would not turn back.

As they made their way to the drawing room, Simon felt a warm sense of—no, not possessiveness. Suzanne had made it clear that she would be no man's possession. More a sense of belonging. Yes, that was it. They belonged together. He'd do his best to see that she came to feel the same way.

When they entered the drawing room, where tea and coffee were being served, there was a hush as all eyes turned toward them. Simon announced, "Suzanne has done me the honor of accepting my proposal. We haven't worked out the details, but the wedding will be in about a week, and you're all invited."

A babble of congratulations filled the room. Callie with the sunset hair exclaimed, "There is scarcely time to make up your bride clothes, Suzanne! We'll need to get busy."

"I don't need anything new. Our wedding will be a small affair." Her voice lowered. "I'm a widow, you know. This is not my first marriage."

"God willing, it will be your last," Callie said seriously. "This will be a special day and you deserve to feel special. I have a length of green silk that will look ravishing on you."

"Perhaps the gown could be trimmed with silver ribbon and lace for a touch of extra richness," Rory said thoughtfully. "Since you're new to London, Suzanne, do you need help organizing the wedding? I'm at your service."

Suzanne realized that she'd need a witness, and Rory was the woman she knew best. "Rory, will you stand up with me?"

"I'd be delighted," her friend said promptly. "After all you did to make my wedding special, I'm happy to return the favor!"

Simon said, "I need a man to stand at my side, also.

Masterson, are you willing? Since you thanked me for almost getting you killed, that seems only fair."

Masterson laughed. "I'm not sure I follow your logic, but I'm honored to accept."

Tears stung Suzanne's eyes as she saw the genuine pleasure everyone felt for her and Simon. Would their marriage live up to these good wishes even though it was made without passion? She hoped so.

As the women's wedding discussion became animated, Kirkland strolled to Simon's side. "You're a lucky man, Colonel."

"I know." Simon's gaze lingered on his bride-to-be. She sparkled with laughter, and the sight made him happy. "I wasn't sure I could coax her to the altar."

"Is she also willing to join your investigation of the émigrés?"

"Yes, and the business will be more enjoyable with her on my arm." Simon sipped at his tea. "I've heard that a good number of émigrés have returned to France in the months since Napoleon's abdication, presumably to reclaim their former lands and wealth."

"Which makes one wonder about the ones who have remained in London," Kirkland observed. "Some have put down roots here, others may be waiting for the situation in France to stabilize, but I'd be surprised if there aren't a few gathering intelligence to support Napoleon if he decides Elba is not a large enough kingdom for a man of his talents."

"Which of the remaining émigrés do you think bear watching?"

Kirkland's brow furrowed. "I consider Roubaix, de Chaurry, and Moncoutant most likely. I don't know that they could be considered spies, but they may know interesting things. I'll also let some influential émigrés know of your arrival so that you can be added to invitation lists."

"I'll see what I can discover." Simon couldn't restrain his smile as he gazed at Suzanne. "But just now, I'm far more interested in the fact that I'm getting married."

By the time Simon collected Suzanne to take her home, she was tired but happy. She'd been scarcely more than a child at her first marriage and she'd had no voice in planning it. Organizing a wedding with a small group of supportive new friends turned out to be much more rewarding.

Because of the damp, bitterly cold weather, Simon had hired a closed carriage and driver for the night. After handing her into the vehicle, he tucked a soft wool blanket around her.

"Are you warm enough?" he asked as he took his seat beside her.

"Between the blanket and the hot bricks for my feet, I'm cozy as a kitten in hay," she assured him.

"What wedding plans have emerged?" he asked.

"Lady Kirkland has offered their home for the wedding breakfast. She said they entertain often so it's easy for her to arrange. Does that suit you?"

"Very generous of them," he said. "Do you wish for the ceremony to take place there as well? With a special license, we can do that."

She considered that, then shook her head. "I want to be married in my parish church. They've been welcoming to poor émigrés like me."

"A church makes a wedding seem more official," he observed. "After the service, I can arrange to have carriages take your friends to Kirkland House for the wedding breakfast, then drive them home again later." He glanced sideways at her. "Do you want to move out of the boardinghouse tomorrow? I'm sure the Kirklands would be happy to have you as a guest until we marry."

She shook her head. "The boardinghouse has been my home and it seems right that I be married from there."

"As you wish. What about your wedding gown? From the bits of conversation I overheard, that was a major topic of the discussion."

Suzanne laughed. "Indeed it was. The consensus was that the green silk Callie suggested would suit me well. She has a modiste who can produce a fine gown in mere days. I'll have to have fittings and buy things like slippers and shifts and a bonnet, though. It will be a busy week!"

"We also need to visit my solicitor for the settlements. Shall I engage a separate lawyer to protect your interests?"

She blinked. "Is that necessary?"

"I'll tell my lawyer to write the document in language clear enough for a normal person to understand, but I can also arrange for you to have your own advocate to ensure that you're treated fairly."

She studied his calm, handsome profile and realized that she couldn't imagine him cheating her on this matter. "As long as the language is clear, I don't need a second lawyer."

He accepted that with a nod. "When would you like to start on your lessons in shooting and self-defense?"

He really was serious about granting her requests. "There won't be much time this week, so better to start after we're married," she decided. "Are we going to have a honeymoon? It's not necessary."

"I thought after a day or two in town to recover from the wedding, we could visit my estate. *Our* estate. White Horse Manor is in Berkshire, not far from London." There was a smile in his voice. "You can try out the horses and learn to become dangerous."

She laughed. "The perfect honeymoon! Yes, please."

"Tomorrow I'd like to take you to the house again so I can introduce you to the Merciers as their new mistress."

"I don't think they'll be surprised at the news. I assume more servants will be hired now that the house will be occupied?"

"Yes, several. A groom, a footman, several house and kitchen maids. A lady's maid for you and I suppose I need a valet." He looked hopeful. "As mistress of the household, hiring staff is surely your job?"

She smiled at his reluctance. "I expect it is. I'll ask the Merciers what they need for the household staff, but I have some thoughts about our personal servants."

She glanced up at him. "Two of the older women at the boardinghouse, Mrs. Brown and Mrs. Parker, are both widows who have been longing to set up a small shop for sweets and baked goods. With the gifts you've agreed to settle on them, I expect they'll do well."

"Isn't there another woman?" he asked.

"Yes, Jenny Dunne. She's younger, about my age. We were both supporting ourselves doing piecework and sometimes we'd sew together. She has a lovely hand with a needle." Suzanne bit her lip. "I wonder if she could work for me. She was a lady's maid, but she was turned off without a reference."

"Did she say why?"

"She was assaulted by the son of the house and her mistress blamed her," Suzanne said, unable to suppress her anger.

"It's a common story," Simon said, his expression grave. "If you want to hire her, by all means do so. If she was exaggerating her experience as a lady's maid, we should be able to find something else for her in the household."

"Thank you, I will. I'm sure she'll do a good job. But there's more."

Simon raised his brows encouragingly, so Suzanne continued, "I'd like to give her some time to visit her family in Dorset. She hasn't seen them for years. She's also desperate to see her sweetheart, who recently returned to his home village. He was in the army, an officer's batman."

Simon grinned. "I think I see where this is going. Are you recommending him to be my valet?"

"Yes, but there's a problem. He was injured in the Battle of Toulouse. Jenny was told by her mother that his face is scarred and his left hand was damaged and isn't as strong as it was. His own mother is very worried because he feels worthless, like a burden on his family because he can't do any kind of heavy work anymore."

"Most valet work isn't heavy. If he's been a batman, he should have a good idea of what's needed. Have her bring him along when she returns to London. Unless he and I hate each other, he can work for me."

"You are being so kind to me!" she exclaimed. "I don't deserve so much."

"Ah, but you do, milady," he said softly. "You see me as an individual, and you're willing to take me on even though I'm a war weary Anglo-French soldier with too much history. You can't know how much I appreciate that."

She hadn't fully realized that before. But she did now.

Chapter 8

❧

After a busy week of rain, meetings, rain, fittings, rain, and gatherings with her new friends, the day of Suzanne's wedding dawned bright and clear. A dusting of snow veiled the city with a brief moment of white purity. Suzanne had hardly been able to sleep from a combination of excitement and alarm. She didn't fear Simon, but the thought of marriage still made her skittish.

Then Rory arrived with the dawn, her bright enthusiasm dispelling doubts. Suzanne heard the knock at the front door and hastened down the steps to find Mr. Potter admitting Rory and her husband to the sitting rooms. Seeing Suzanne, Rory explained, "Since I'm standing up with you, I thought I should arrive early to help you dress, hold your hand, and soothe your nerves."

"Thank you! I need all those things. Captain Hawkins, I see you have been enlisted to carry the wedding gown." She gestured at the long canvas-covered bag that was draped over his arm. "Or are you here to defend your lady from the perils of early morning London?"

He smiled at her. "Some of both, but my main reason is to ask if you'd like someone to walk you down the aisle. Rory made it very clear to me that no man is giving you away—you're giving yourself of your own free will. But would you like having a friend at your side?"

She bit her lip as her eyes teared up. "What a lovely idea! Thank you, Captain. I'd like that very much."

He gave her a warm hug with the arm that wasn't encumbered by the gown. "So would I." Carefully he draped the canvas bag over the back of the sofa. "I've also brought a basket of cakes and biscuits and sausage rolls to provide breakfast for everyone in the house."

"You are a saint!" she said, hugging him back.

The next two hours were spent in laughter and eating in the sitting room. The Potters and the other boarders joined in.

The boardinghouse residents left for the church while Rory was making the final adjustments to Suzanne's appearance. The green and silver gown matched the green and silver ribbon-trimmed bonnet she'd ordered, and Athena Masterson had given her a delicate emerald and pearl necklace set that was the perfect complement.

Suzanne turned to gaze into the mottled mirror in her bedroom. Though it was too small to show her full image, it was clear enough to make her throat tighten. She looked her best. More than that, she looked like her own woman in a way that she never had before.

"You look beautiful," Rory said warmly. "Even more beautiful than usual. But don't you *dare* cry and ruin all my work!"

The comment made Suzanne laugh. "I'll do my best not to."

She lifted her skirts to examine her green and silver slippers. Rory had really done an amazing job in creating this ensemble so quickly. "I'm glad it's not raining. I'd hate to ruin these." Then she left her small, cold room and moved down the steep stairs toward her new life.

Hawkins was waiting there with their warm cloaks. Suzanne's was dark green velvet trimmed with dark fur, a gift from Callie. Such generous friends she'd acquired!

Their carriage waited outside for the short drive to the parish church, but the distance was long enough for Suzanne's nerves to begin to flutter again.

"You're doing the right thing," Rory said with a pat on Suzanne's gloved hand. "Marriage is a very fine institution and Colonel Duval is a very fine man. Hawkins said that he was the one who took the most risks in escaping from the cellar where they awaited execution. Ask him about it."

"I will," Suzanne said a little unsteadily. She'd met Simon half a lifetime ago, and even though they hadn't seen each other in years, she trusted him. And if the marriage didn't work out, she now had the means to leave and live comfortably.

But she wanted rather desperately for it to work. She owed that to Simon. Even more, she was tired of being alone.

They arrived at the church and Hawkins guided them up the steps with a lady on each arm. He was such a kind, reliable man, with the courage of a lion as she had observed firsthand. She sensed that Simon had similar qualities of courage and rock solid reliability, which was good. She had no taste for volatile charmers.

Events began to blur. Music filling the church, bouquets of winter flowers, and then gripping Hawkins's arm while Rory walked gracefully down the aisle carrying a nosegay of golden daffodils that matched her hair.

Suzanne's heart caught as she saw Simon waiting for her at the altar, with Will Masterson at his side. Simon wore his scarlet army uniform and was so dazzlingly handsome her knees felt weak. How had she gotten so lucky as to be this man's chosen bride? There was no answer, but then he smiled warmly at her and that was enough.

It was time for her to walk down the aisle with Hawkins, unsteady but no longer unsure. Looking on were her friends from the boardinghouse, the friends she'd made with Simon, the Merciers, and a scattering of other friends of Simon. So much goodwill.

The gray-haired vicar greeted them all in his sonorous voice and the ceremony began. As Suzanne listened and made her responses, she realized she'd never attended a wedding in the English language. The words from the Book of Common Prayer were lovely, and the vows solemn and a little fearsome.

Though the words "with my body I thee worship" were bitterly inappropriate, the arrangement they made suited them both. She and Simon would learn how to be happy together.

And then they were married and the rest of their life began.

The Kirklands knew how to host a fine wedding celebration and there was an abundance of good food and friends and toasts to the newlyweds' health and happiness. Nonetheless, Simon was happy to finally be home with his new bride, fulfilling her domestic dream of a quiet evening together.

The sitting room between their bedrooms was small and cozy with warmth, and the previous week he'd bought a pair of very comfortable wing chairs to place on each side of the fireplace. They'd both changed into relaxing garments when they'd returned home. He'd packed his uniform away, not sure if he'd ever wear it again since soon he'd be officially out of the army.

Looking forward to this peaceful evening, he'd changed into loose trousers and shirt and a warm navy blue banyan.

Suzanne wore a soft gray wool robe and looked thoroughly enchanting even though there wasn't a square inch of her visible below the neck. She had curled up in her wing chair and was pulling pins from her hair as she gazed idly at the flickering fire.

Knowing that she liked red wine, Simon poured two glasses of a particularly fine claret and set them on the table between their chairs. "All we need now are the cat and the dog, and that lack will be remedied soon."

He settled into his chair and sipped his wine, content to gaze at his bride. From what he'd observed, first marriages burned with hope and passion and eagerness for a shared future. But this would be different even though it was a first marriage for him.

"I remember your first wedding so clearly," he mused. She'd been vividly pretty and eager for life. "You were the loveliest bride imaginable. I'm sorry that your hopes and dreams on that occasion didn't come true."

She combed her fingers through her hair, loosening it to fall over her shoulders in a shining cascade. "I doubt that anyone's bridal dreams come fully true, but being caught in the tides of war certainly fractures the maximum number of dreams."

He hoped she'd say more, but she fell silent. He wondered about the years between her marriage and her escape from the Turkish harem. What had happened to her husband, the handsome, debonair Jean-Louis, Comte de Chambron? How had she been captured and sold into slavery? How had she survived so much disaster?

But if she didn't want to speak of it, no matter. There was much of his own past he didn't like to discuss. Safer to discuss domestic matters. "I suspect your new friends have been working to get you a whole new wardrobe suitable for a lady of means."

Suzanne smiled. "I've already ordered several gowns from the modiste who made my wedding dress. She's very talented and has good assistants so she can work very quickly. After they finished my grand green gown, they started work on a riding habit. She promised it for tomorrow since we were planning on going to your estate for a honeymoon." There was a slight questioning note on the last sentence.

"And you want to be ready to ride," he said with a chuckle. "I'm looking forward to visiting White Horse Manor. I haven't been there in years. The estate belonged to my grandfather and we spent long visits there in the summer. The stables will contain several decent riding hacks, I'm sure."

"All I need is a docile mount with good manners so I can relearn everything I've forgotten," she assured him. "I don't want to ruin my new riding habit by being thrown immediately!"

"It will all come back quickly. You were a natural rider. I was always impressed by the way you could charm a horse into doing your bidding. A horse witch."

"I did then." She shrugged and began to plait her hair into one long braid. She had the haunting beauty of a sorrowing Madonna. "Now, well, we'll see."

"You look a little sad, milady," he said softly.

After a long silence, she said, "A little, perhaps. Life's milestones call to mind other milestones, and the older we get, the more of them we've passed." Her gaze touched his and held. "I'm happy to be married to you, though, so this is a good milestone."

"It's one of the best milestones ever," he said honestly.

Smiling, she tied off her braid with a thin ribbon, then covered a yawn with one hand. "Weddings take energy to prepare and perform. I'm ready to sleep."

"In the morning, we can fulfill one of my marital fantasies, sharing breakfast together." He stood and offered his hand to help her from her chair. "I know you'll look lovely across the table."

"Don't be too sure!" She didn't need his help to stand, but he enjoyed the warm clasp of her fingers. She released his hand to smother another yawn, then moved through the door to her bedchamber. "Sleep well, milord."

Since Simon wasn't yet ready to retire, he poured Suzanne's unfinished wine into his own glass, enjoying the intimacy of finishing his wife's wine. Very domestic, and besides, the wine was too good to waste.

But as he sipped the claret, he felt a little melancholy. He'd emptied the glass before he realized why. Though he was delighted that Suzanne was now his wife, he realized he wanted more closeness. More touching. He would have liked to give her a long hug before she retired. He would like to feel her soft body pressed against him, relaxed and content.

But their relationship was too new and he didn't know how much touching she would permit. She didn't mind taking his arm or similar casual contacts, but he wasn't sure she would accept more than that.

Intuition said that he must go slowly with Suzanne. He wasn't sure a man could truly understand what she'd endured in the harem, but he couldn't forget what she'd said when they'd first met: *"My survival depended on being a whore and pretending to enjoy it."*

He had accepted her stipulations because he desperately wanted her companionship. Their marriage was based on an agreement that her body was her own.

And yet, he wanted more.

He heard her moving around her bedchamber as she prepared to retire. He imagined her removing her robe. It was still winter so she'd be wearing a warm nightgown underneath. There was a faint rattle as she put a scoop of coal on the fire. Then the light went out and there was silence. He pictured her sliding between the sheets and pulling the covers over herself.

He hoped she rested well and woke up without that

sadness. She might be feeling some of the same kind of melancholy he felt. Marriage was the goal of courtship, but it was also the beginning of a journey together, one he hoped would last the rest of their lives. Perhaps tomorrow they could discuss touching and how much she was willing to accept.

He propped his feet on the footstool and let his thoughts wander over his childhood in this house. His loving parents, his beloved foster brother, Lucas, a world of possibilities, now gone.

Then he consciously released that past. He would never forget it, but now he was starting a new phase of life. It was time to look forward, not back.

As an adult, he'd discovered new possibilities he'd never imagined as a boy. He'd done good work in dark and dangerous places, and now he'd married a woman who had stirred his heart when he was a boy. Neither of them were what they once had been, but they'd both become wiser and stronger, and in time they would surely become closer. They'd been married only a few hours, after all.

Smiling at his absurdity, he decided it was time to retire. He was banking the fire when he heard raw, wrenching sounds coming from Suzanne's room. He stood still, wondering if he was imagining them.

No, the sounds of anguish were unmistakable. He opened the door to her room, wondering if she was having a nightmare. "Suzanne?" he said softly.

She was turned away from him, trying to smother her sobs in her pillow. At the sound of his voice, she curled up more tightly, as if that would make her invisible.

"My darling girl!" He crossed the room and lay beside her on top of the covers. Though he didn't know how much touch she was willing to accept, he could not turn away without trying to offer comfort.

Lying on his side, he wrapped his arm around her waist

and drew her against his chest. She was warm and soft under the covers, and she didn't try to twist away. He drew a deep breath and forced his voice to be steady. "If you are so disturbed by this marriage, we can—end it. Get an annulment since it hasn't been consummated."

He steeled himself for her to say she wanted that, but she shook her head and rolled onto her back so that she was looking up at him. In the dim light coming through the door from the sitting room, her face was blotchy with tears. He felt a rush of tenderness so powerful it hurt.

"No," she said in a husky whisper. "I don't want that. You may be the best thing that ever happened to me. But today made me think of my first wedding."

Some of his pain eased, but he ached for her. "I suppose that was inevitable. You were so joyful that day. So beautiful and so in love with Jean-Louis. To see you was to believe in the power of love. I know that you can't love me as you did him, but—"

"And thank God for that!" she said with bitter fury. "I loved him with the stupidity of the tragically young and naive. I was flattered that such a handsome man of the world had chosen me for his bride. He said that he loved me, and I *believed* him!" She drew a wrenching breath. "I hope to God that I'll never be as stupid again!"

Jarred, Simon asked, "Did he mistreat you?"

She sighed, anger replaced by resignation. "Not by his standards. He needed a wife who was an heiress and attractive enough to be worthy of his wonderful self. He said he loved me because he knew I expected it. He took pride in being an expert lover, so he made sure I enjoyed what he called bed sport." She halted with a shuddering breath.

Sensing that she needed to reveal all her misery so that she could turn away from that past, he said encouragingly, "But?"

She swallowed hard. "At first passion was enough for me, but gradually I realized that any reasonably attractive young female in his bed would be equally acceptable. He never really saw me as an individual. He found his mistresses much more interesting."

Simon could only imagine how painful that must have been for a devoted young wife who had believed herself loved. "Then he was a fool! And not a man of honor."

"His honor didn't include fidelity to his marriage vows. He told me that when I confronted him. But he wasn't angry. He was *patronizing*. He patted my hand and said that soon I'd understand the way things were done in our world." Anger and pain were raw in her voice. "After I gave him an heir, or better yet, two, I could do as I pleased."

Simon swore under his breath. "He didn't deserve you!"

"Perhaps not, but he was sure he deserved my dowry, which was quite substantial." When her voice broke, Simon began stroking her back soothingly.

She resumed, voice shaking. "He was thinking of putting me aside when several years of marriage passed without a child. He considered me worthless."

Simon swore again. "What a thrice-damned fool!"

"His first and only concern was for himself and his reputation, or he would have put me aside earlier." She rested an arm over her eyes to conceal tears. "He was still pondering his dilemma when he decided life would be safer and warmer in Naples and he booked passage for us there."

Guessing where this was going, Simon asked, "Did you reach Naples?"

"No," she whispered. "Our ship was attacked by corsairs. Seeing the inevitable, Jean-Louis shouted at some of the French sailors that he'd reward them richly if they took him away in the ship's boat. They were anxious to leave, too, so half a dozen sailors and Jean-Louis piled into the boat and they tried to escape."

"Leaving you to the mercy of the pirates," Simon said, his voice shaking with barely suppressed fury.

"Of course. I was of no great value to him, and this was easier than putting me aside." Her mouth twisted. "I was lucky. The pirates merely took me prisoner. He was less lucky. The corsairs blew the small boat to pieces. There were no survivors."

"My poor, dear girl," he whispered, drawing her so close that her face was tucked in between his neck and shoulder.

Her voice muffled, she said wearily, "If you and I were in such circumstances, you would have died trying to protect me." It was a statement, not a question.

"Yes." He took a deep breath, not wanting her to be intimidated by his anger at a man now dead. "But I'll do my best to see that we never face such danger."

Her arm came around his waist and she began to relax into him. "I've never told anyone about Jean-Louis because it was hurtful. With you, I can bear to speak."

He was awed that she trusted him enough to reveal the anguish of her first marriage. Surely this was a good omen for their future.

She was all warmth and sweetness as she drifted into sleep, her head on his shoulder, her breathing soft and steady against his throat. He'd wanted more closeness and now they had that. He wanted to give her so much happiness and safety that she would never have to weep again.

He wanted . . . he wanted . . .

With a shock that struck to his heart, he recognized

that the warmth curling through him was as much physical as emotional. He wanted her in every way a man could want a woman. Long-vanished desire was blossoming into life and he wanted so much more than the companionship they'd agreed to.

What the devil was he to do now?

Chapter 9

❧

Lying still so as not to disturb Suzanne, Simon tried to come to terms with the fact that his long years of passionless celibacy had ended, a discovery equally exhilarating and alarming. Mostly exhilarating, but it complicated his marriage enormously. Though he had changed, Suzanne hadn't, and he had pledged to do nothing to distress her.

If she felt different about passion someday, he'd celebrate, but for now and the indefinite future, his job was to protect and cherish her. And teach her how to shoot firearms and defend herself.

Eventually he fell asleep and awoke at first light to find that Suzanne still lay sleeping with her head on his shoulder and her arm around his waist. Her face was peaceful and very young. Carefully he flexed his right arm, which had gone to sleep along with Suzanne.

The motion caused her to stir and open her eyes. She was deliciously tousled, her green eyes making him think of mint leaves. "So I didn't dream last night," she said with a sleepy smile. "You make a marvelous pillow. I can't remember when I've slept so well. What about you?"

"It took me some time to fall asleep," he said honestly, "but when I did, I slept dreamlessly and well."

She rolled onto her back and stretched and he tried not to stare at the way her breasts lifted under the soft fabric of her nightgown. "Perhaps we should continue to sleep together?" Her gaze shifted shyly away from him. "I've . . . never slept all night with a man. I liked having you there."

"Never?" he asked, startled. "Jean-Louis was even more of a fool than I realized."

Her mouth twisted. "So I'm not unnatural for wanting to have you beside me all night?"

"Definitely not," he said firmly. "Particularly not in February!"

She smiled a little at that. "Then join me under the covers for a bit. You must have become cold sleeping on top of them."

"The room did cool down overnight. Give me a moment to build up the fire and I'll join you."

He swung from the bed, knowing he was mad to agree to sleeping together, and also knowing that he couldn't possibly say no. Not when he wanted it so much. This would be a major test of willpower. He'd always thought his was good, but that was before he'd married an enchanting lady.

He added more coal to the fire, then returned to the bed and slid under the covers with her. "It's still early, so lazing here is a good way to spend the time before breakfast."

He was definitely warmer under the covers than on top of them, particularly after Suzanne rolled over and snuggled against him, one hand resting on his chest. She had a faint scent of rosemary, tangy and appealing. He brushed a light kiss on her silky dark hair, thinking he'd never been more content in his life.

This was a good time to raise the topic he'd thought of the night before. "I've wondered how you feel about being touched, *ma chérie*. You have reason to be wary of men. I like touching you, but I don't want to upset you. Tell me what you don't like so I can avoid doing it."

Her brow furrowed. "I've not defined this," she said slowly, "but it comes down to whether a man is touching me with carnal intent. Some men feel they have the right to grope any female they wish. The French émigrés who tried to corner me were like that. Horrible! If I'd had a knife and knew how to use it, I'd have unmanned them!"

"Bloodthirsty but understandable!" he said. "But not all men are like that."

"Luckily not. You aren't. Your rogues of the cellar all seem to be the sort to keep their hands to themselves. Having sailed the length of the Mediterranean with Gabriel Hawkins, I know that he treats women with respect." Suzanne smiled. "He's also mad for Rory and has no carnal interest in any other woman. That makes him safe."

"You can sense carnal intent?" Simon asked, curious.

"Usually. The damnable part is that I like touching. In the harem, I loved having children to cuddle." She sighed. "I'd assumed I'd have children someday, but it's never happened and now it never will."

"Dreams lost," he said softly. "Though sometimes dreams can be reborn. You thought yourself unsuitable for marriage, yet here we are."

She chuckled. "So we are. But that's because you understood and felt much the same way as I."

"In other words, I'm safe," he said with a touch of dryness.

"Exactly, and I loved sleeping in your arms."

He wondered if she would sense the change in him, because his thoughts were definitely carnal. And if she did sense that, what would she do about it?

But for the moment, they were well pleased with each other. He ran a slow, appreciative hand down the lovely curves of her back. "Tomorrow I'd like to get an early start to visit White Horse Manor, but today we can sort out some of the details of life."

"Like my riding habit, boots, and I hope some other clothing as well." Her eyes gleamed. "But the riding habit and boots in particular."

"Before we leave town, I need to call on Lucas's great-uncle and aunt. Lord and Lady Foxton had no children of their own, so they were fond of us young hellions. They were Lucas's godparents, and since he and I were always together, they treated us like brothers." Simon suppressed a swift memory of two boys being welcomed with open arms at Foxton House. "I know they'd like to meet you."

"I'd love to meet them since they are like family to you," she said promptly. "But as godparents, why didn't they take in Lucas when he was orphaned?"

"They were in India at the time. By the time they returned to England, Lucas was settled in with my family and they didn't want to disrupt him again. There were many visits, though."

Suzanne's brow furrowed. "Was Lucas in line to inherit the Foxton title?"

"If he's alive, he would be Lord Foxton. His great-uncle was his grandfather's younger brother. But Lucas had been missing for years and eventually he was declared dead, so his great uncle assumed the title. He would be happy to relinquish it if Lucas turns out to be alive."

They were the ones who had written Simon to tell him of Lucas's presumed death. Keeping in touch with them over the years was a way of keeping in touch with the memories of Lucas.

"So you are family for them," Suzanne said quietly. "I imagine they'll be happy to know you've married. Something positive after too many losses. Our marriage may be . . . unconventional, but it seems very real to me."

"You understand well." He was feeling a strong desire to kiss her in a very carnal way, so he swung from the bed. "I'm thinking of more and more things that need to be done today, so it's time for me to start moving. Shall I see you at breakfast, or do you prefer to rest a little longer?"

She sat up in bed and stretched, as supple and graceful as a cat. "I would not deny you your breakfast fantasy," she said with a smile. "I'll see you downstairs."

He returned to his bedroom by way of the sitting room. He needed to wash, shave, dress, and work on his willpower. Not in that order.

The Foxtons' house was modest but welcoming, the furnishings a mix of comfortable English with exotic Indian accents. It had changed little since Simon's last visit several years before.

The Foxtons had also changed little, though they were a little grayer and more wrinkled. William, Lord Foxton, was tall and lean, his face permanently weathered by years of harsh Indian sun. Anna, his wife, was petite and welcoming, with a sweep of striking white hair. She greeted Simon with a hug. "My dear boy! How is my favorite young rogue?"

"No longer so young and now retiring from the rogue business." He shook Lord Foxton's hand. "It's good to see you again, sir." He drew Suzanne forward. "I wanted you both to meet my wife, Suzanne Duval. We were distant cousins by marriage who hadn't seen each other for years. It was a great blessing to meet again here in London."

"This sounds very romantic!" Lady Foxton clasped both Suzanne's hands. "Welcome to our home, my dear. I'm so happy for you both."

"Thank you," Suzanne said, her smile warm. "I am a fortunate woman."

"Come in and sit by the fire," Lady Foxton said. "I'll ring for refreshments while we catch up on the news."

The two couples chatted easily over tea and cakes before the Foxtons exchanged a sober glance. Her ladyship said, "There is one piece of news. Not news, really, more of a rumor." She crumbled a cake into small pieces with nervous fingers. "But an intriguing one."

When she fell silent, her husband picked up the story. "An old friend thought he saw Lucas in Brussels last year after the emperor abdicated. He was dressed as a monk."

"A monk?" Simon said incredulously. "That does not sound like Lucas. Surely it was a chance resemblance."

"That seems likely," Foxton agreed. "But Carter had met Lucas several times and swore the man looked just like him. The resemblance was that strong."

"Did Carter talk to this monk?"

Foxton shook his head. "No, he said that the monk turned away when he saw he was being watched. Carter tried to intercept him, but the streets were crowded and he lost sight of the man."

Simon felt as if he couldn't breathe until Suzanne took his hand in silent comfort. He swallowed hard. "It's the sort of thing one wants so much to believe, but it seems impossible. You've never received a letter from him, have you?"

"No, nor has his bank ever received a request for money. And yet . . ." Lord Foxton shook his head.

"It is impossible not to hope," Suzanne said softly. "But I've heard it said that we all have someone who looks like a twin somewhere. When I first saw Simon here in London, for a moment I thought he was my late husband, who was his second cousin. Sometimes a simple movement by a stranger conjures someone you know well. That can be very disturbing when it happens."

"What a very down to earth young lady you are," Lady Foxton said. "I'm sure you're right, that it was a chance resemblance. But I wish Mr. Carter had caught up with that monk so he could be sure." Her mouth twisted in self-mockery. "I read too many Gothic novels. I've wondered if Lucas received a head injury and has amnesia so he doesn't know how to come home. Or maybe he was dressed as a monk because he's been working as a spy and dares not reveal his true identity."

"That was my job," Simon pointed out with a touch of amusement. "With the wars over, there is less need for spies, but Mr. Carter's story is interesting. Perhaps I should look into it more deeply."

Lord Foxton's expression eased. "Thank you. I felt the incident should be investigated, but I wasn't sure where to begin. You will have a much better idea how to go about such inquiries."

"Yes, but I'll need as many details as possible," Simon replied. "Exactly when and where Mr. Carter saw this person. What color was the monk's robe? What was going on around him in the streets? Anything else that might help narrow down the possibilities. Where can I find Mr. Carter?"

"He's returned to his estate in Durham, but I asked him the same questions you've asked," Lord Foxton said. "I'll give you my notes."

"That will be very helpful. But you know that it was almost certainly a chance resemblance," Simon said soberly.

"We know," Lady Foxton said. "But we'll feel better if the incident is investigated to the extent possible."

"I'll get on this right away." Simon rose. "It's been wonderful to see you again. Now that I'm back in England, I hope to see you more often."

"So do we." Lady Foxton stood and smiled warmly at Suzanne. "And by all means, bring your lovely wife with you when you call!"

Suzanne blushed a little and the two couples parted with goodwill. But Simon was already thinking about where to start his search for a monk who was almost certainly not Lucas.

As she settled into the curricle, Suzanne said, "Is it possible that Lucas might actually have become a monk?"

Simon said slowly, "Anything is possible, but that seems very unlikely. He was never religious. He barely managed to be an Anglican, much less a Catholic. Perhaps he was disguising himself as a monk for some reason, but it still seems unlikely. If he was spying, why didn't he come home after the emperor abdicated?"

"As you say, anything is possible." She gave a sidelong glance. "You're going to talk to Kirkland about this?"

Simon nodded as he set the horses in motion. "Yes, but first I'll study Lord Foxton's notes. Maybe there will be some clue that will give us more to work with."

"Do you have a portrait of Lucas you could lend to Kirkland? That might be helpful."

He gave a sharp nod. "That's an excellent idea. I have a miniature that's a good likeness. I'll take that along."

After riding several blocks in silence, Suzanne asked in a neutral voice, "Would you rather not go to your estate so you can focus on this investigation?"

He had a painfully intense memory of her warm, pliable body in his arms that morning. "I absolutely do not wish to forfeit my honeymoon, *ma chérie,*" he said immediately. "Do you?"

Her smile lit up her eyes. "I'm looking forward to a few days having you to myself. We still have much to learn about each other."

Yes, and he would relish every moment.

Chapter 10

❧

The weather was cloudy but dry for their trip to White Horse Manor. It was late afternoon and the sun was just beginning to emerge when Simon said, "*Chérie,* we'll be on my land once we turn this corner."

Suzanne had been drowsing in the corner of the carriage, but she came alert at his announcement. "Good! It's been some time since our luncheon and I'm ready for tea."

"We'll make a quick stop here." Simon signaled for the driver to pause when they rounded the curve. When the vehicle had rumbled to a halt at the side of the road, Simon opened the door, flipped down the steps, then offered her a hand down. "There's a fine view across the valley."

She stepped from the coach, glad to stretch her legs, then gasped with surprise. She hadn't thought much about the estate's name, but now it made perfect sense. There was indeed a splendid view across the valley with quilted fields, hedges, copses, and a small, tree-lined river running along the valley floor.

And on the opposite side of the valley, a vast white

horse was galloping along the hills. "What is that?" she breathed. "I've never seen anything like it!"

"Meet the white horse for which this valley was named. These hills are part of the Berkshire Downs, which are made of chalk. The figure is cut deeply into the turf and the depression is filled with crushed white chalk."

"It's remarkable." She studied the abstract shape, which said "galloping horse" without any real details. "Why doesn't vegetation grow over it?"

"Plants try, but the figure is scoured regularly to keep the image clear." He gestured at the white horse. "It's visible from all front windows of the house. Rather magical to wake up in the morning and see that ancient image galloping across the vale."

"I look forward to that." Suzanne climbed back into the travel carriage. "Now I'm even more impatient to see the house!"

"Not much longer," Simon promised. "Many of the servants and their families have been there since my grandfather first bought the manor and they take pride in running the estate well. Mr. and Mrs. Stanley are the butler and housekeeper, Mr. Roper is head groom. They've made my life much easier and they'll do the same for you."

The road had been following a stone wall. Just around the next bend the carriage turned between stone pillars into a long drive, which was lined on both sides with rows of trees and led to a handsome manor house.

Suzanne smiled as they approached. Built of golden-tan stone with a slate roof, the structure seemed to have grown out of the hill. It was friendly, unlike the vast, sprawling palaces of her life in France. "I think I am going to like White Horse Manor very well. How long until I can visit the stables?"

Simon chuckled at her impatience. "Almost immediately, though it's too late in the day to go for a proper ride. But you can choose your mount for tomorrow."

Suzanne was almost bubbling with excitement. The more time she spent with Simon, the younger she felt.

Since the servants knew they were coming, when the carriage pulled up before the house, a dozen interested people swiftly emerged to greet them, led by a middle-aged couple with an air of authority. After helping Suzanne from the carriage, Simon said formally, "Mr. and Mrs. Stanley, allow me to present my bride, Madame Suzanne Duval."

"About time you returned, you rascal!" Mrs. Stanley gave Simon a robust hug, then turned to Suzanne and bobbed a curtsy. "Welcome to White Horse Manor, ma'am. A proper home needs a mistress and a nursery full of children."

The hug Mrs. Stanley gave to her master was proof that she was an old family retainer. Wincing inwardly at the comment about children, Suzanne offered a hand "I'm so happy to be here! My husband has spoken very highly of you and the other servants."

The housekeeper gave a nod of approval. "Aye, I've spent my whole life here at White Horse Manor. This is Mr. Stanley, the butler."

Her husband bowed, less effusive than his wife but equally interested in appraising his new mistress. "Welcome to White Horse Manor, madam."

Simon looked along the row of servants that had lined up in front of the house. "More introductions are needed. Some faces look familiar, but others have grown from children to adults since I last saw them."

Introductions were performed and Suzanne did her best to remember names and positions. Luckily the number wasn't huge, but it would still take time to learn them. As Simon had implied, they seemed to be a contented lot.

After the introductions, Simon escorted her up the broad stairs and into the house. "The bedrooms are arranged like the town house. The mistress's room is to the left, the master's to the right, and a sitting room in between. The rooms are larger here, of course."

She glanced sideways at him. "Which bedroom has the largest bed?"

He grinned down at her with a warmth that curled her toes. "Both beds are large enough for two."

She blushed, a bit embarrassed by how much she enjoyed sleeping with Simon after a mere two nights. She loved having his warm, strong body next to her, and she loved falling asleep in his arms.

Since her wedding, she'd acquired a much better understanding of why marriage was so popular. Passion was fleeting and she'd always felt sad and empty when Jean-Louis finished with her and retired to his own rooms. Or to a mistress. She hadn't wanted to know which.

Marriage based on friendship without the unruly problems of passion was turning out to be as wonderful as Simon had said it would be. Despite his resemblance to Jean-Louis, the two men were so different. Simon saw her as an individual and cared about her. She hadn't known how precious such caring was because she'd never known it. Now she didn't want to be without it.

"I'll wash up quickly," she said. "Then the stables?"

"As you desire, milady. Join me in our sitting room when you're ready." He opened the door to her bedroom with a flourish. "I'm sure you'll find the room comfortable if a little worn. Think about what changes you'd like to make."

The bedroom could use some refreshing of draperies and other fabrics, but it was cozy with warm colors and a soft carpet. The four-poster bed was definitely wide enough for two, with room for a cat and a dog as well. She turned and gave Simon a swift hug, saying, "I know we'll be very comfortable here!"

He gave her a long, warm hug in return. "Till tonight, milady." Then he left her to explore her new quarters.

She was well pleased with what she found. There was

a good-sized dressing room, the chairs and sofa were pleasantly padded when she sat in them, and the windows offered a splendid view of the white horse.

After her brief exploration, it only took a few minutes to freshen up. The sturdy half boots and plain cloak she'd worn in the carriage would do for this visit to the stables.

She opened the door to the sitting room and found Simon standing at the wide windows with his hands linked behind his back as he gazed at the white horse on the opposite side of the narrow valley. She paused in the doorway to admire his wide shoulders and compact strength. Very masculine, and very appealing.

He didn't turn when she entered the room. "It's lovely to watch the horse at dawn, Suzanne," he said pensively. "Especially when there is a little mist and the shape emerges gradually as the sun rises. A shadowy horse turning into light."

She went to stand beside him, so close their sides touched. "Magical."

His arm went around her waist. Standing here with Simon, gazing at a green and lovely England, it was easy to imagine this place as her forever home after too many travels. "Time to see some real lovely horses?"

"You have been deprived of riding for far too long," Simon said with a chuckle. They turned from the window to head downstairs and out the back of the house.

Suzanne took Simon's hand as they walked the short distance to the stables. "I think holding your hand would be far too forward if we were English," she murmured, "but if anyone is shocked, we can explain it's because we're French."

"I'm only half French, but we shouldn't have to explain anything when we're on our honeymoon," Simon said, a smile in his voice.

"You're French enough," she purred in that language.

His hand tightened over hers before he said, "I'm not sure what we'll find in the stables. Mostly workhorses, but there should be a couple of good mounts."

The wide double doors of the stable were open, releasing the familiar scent of hay and horses. As they entered, a wiry man stepped forward to meet them. "Roper!" Simon said, pleasure in his voice. "It's good to see you again. My wife is looking forward to a good ride in the morning, and so am I. What do you have for us?"

Voice sober but eyes bright, the groom touched the brim of his hat. "Welcome, Madame Duval. Colonel, I believe I've found a beast that meets your requirements."

The stables were clean, the loose boxes were spacious, and the horses had sleek, well-brushed coats. Suzanne sighed happily. As a child, she'd haunted her family's stables. When she married and became a countess, such boyish behavior was discouraged, and in the harem she was never near a horse. She had much to make up for.

Wordlessly Simon gave her a handful of carrot chunks. She offered one to the massive plow horse that ambled over to investigate her. "Such a handsome fellow," she crooned as she reached up to scratch behind his ears. He whuffled at her in an interested way, so she offered a chunk of carrot. He lipped the carrot from her open palm, then gave her a friendly head butt that almost knocked her from her feet.

She caught her balance as Simon steadied her. "You haven't lost your touch with horses," he observed. "It will be dark soon. Do you want to look at the riding horses before we return to the house?"

"Of course!" She smiled at the head groom. "Your charges are beautifully cared for, Mr. Roper."

It was hard to tell in the dim light, but he looked as if he was blushing. "We do our best, ma'am. The riding horses are down at this end."

She and Simon followed him down the aisle between

the loose boxes. She caught her breath when they reached the end and she saw an exquisite dapple gray mare. "Oh, she's *beautiful*!" Suzanne breathed.

The mare turned her head and regarded the visitors with dark, gentle eyes. On impulse, Suzanne opened the door and stepped into the loose box despite Simon's sharp, "Suzanne!"

"She won't hurt me, will you, my darling girl?" The mare approached and Suzanne offered a chunk of carrot. Daintily the dapple gray accepted a piece of carrot, then another. "What's her name, Mr. Roper?"

"Luna," he said, satisfaction in his voice. "A silver moon mare."

"I assume she's the horse you found when I asked you to look around for a mount suitable for my wife?" Simon said as he crossed his arms and leaned on the half wall to watch the unfolding scene.

"Aye, she's from Hill Brook Farm." Roper took a similar stance next to him. "Part Arabian and beautifully trained. Will cost a pretty penny if you decide to keep her."

Simon chuckled. "I think there's no 'if' about it. Luna seems as sweet natured as she is beautiful."

"Aye, and well trained." Roper gestured with his chin at the adjacent loose box. "The Duke, the chestnut in the next stall, is a good mount that'll suit your weight well."

Simon looked in that direction and nodded. "A very handsome fellow. I'll look forward to deepening my acquaintance with the Duke tomorrow morning." He entered the loose box and joined Suzanne. "Tomorrow morning you'll find out if Luna is as lovely to ride as she is to look at."

"She will be," Suzanne said confidently. "But now I suppose it's time to go inside and prepare for dinner."

"Exactly so." Simon took her arm and they left the loose box.

Suzanne gave Roper a smile that made him blink. "*Thank you*, Mr. Roper! You have wonderful taste in horses."

She took Simon's arm as they left the stables and walked through the dusk to the house. "I'm so glad we married, Simon. I feel young again."

"So do I." He patted her hand where it rested on his arm. "But I don't suppose that eliminates the darkness of more recent years."

His words were like an icy hand on the back of her neck. There had been so much darkness. "No, it doesn't. I wish I could wash the stains from my soul and be normal again!" She was startled by her vehemence.

"I'd like that, too," he said quietly as they entered the house. "Give it time. Time and happiness can work wonders."

She hoped he was right. As he took her cloak, she studied his handsome face, thinking how dear he had become to her. With sudden hope, she wished that they were both normal newlyweds who were learning to rejoice in each other's bodies.

As soon as the thought took form, her body shrank back, repulsed by the idea of being used sexually.

Yet she was capable of accepting his warm embrace at night. In fact, she loved it. Surely that pleasure was a good omen?

She wished she could be sure it was.

Chapter 11

❧

It was difficult for Suzanne to remove herself from the delicious warmth of Simon and her bed, but anticipation of riding persuaded her to slide out from under the covers. The room was chilly so she wrapped her warm robe around herself and shoved her feet into slippers.

Hoping the day would be fine, she moved to the window and gazed out, catching her breath at the sight of the white horse emerging from the dawn mists just as Simon had described the day before. She sighed happily.

Simon moved so silently that she didn't realize he'd joined her until she felt his body's warmth against her back. She leaned against him. "I find that I am enjoying marriage."

He chuckled. "So am I. It looks as though it will be a grand day for riding."

"Can we ride over to the white horse?" she asked. "I'd like to see it close up."

"It's several miles and you might want to take it easy

your first day back on a horse." He rested a warm hand on her shoulder. "Let's see how it goes."

That made sense. She wished she could banish the uneasy feeling that everything was going *too* well.

By the time Simon and Suzanne had dressed and breakfasted, the sun had emerged and the day was cold and hazy bright. She was bubbling like a happy teakettle as they walked out to the stables.

Roper was waiting with their saddled and bridled mounts. "'Tis a good day for a ride," he said jovially.

Despite her impatience, Suzanne took the time to check the saddle girth and tack. Simon approved. "Ready, milady?" He laced his hands to help her up.

She set her neatly booted left foot in his hands and he tossed her up into the saddle. She landed gracefully as thistledown. She grinned down at him as she adjusted her full skirts to fall over her legs. "One of these days I'm going to try riding astride. I was never allowed that before."

"As you wish, milady," he said agreeably. "But for today, will you settle for looking like a princess on your sidesaddle?" It was no less than the truth. Suzanne's new riding habit was the dark green of the army's rifle companies, and it was a perfect foil for her creamy complexion and green eyes.

"Flatterer," she said with a laugh. "Shall we be off?"

He introduced himself to the waiting chestnut, checked the tack, then mounted. The Duke was a bit frisky at first, but it didn't take long for them to reach an accord. "Behind the stables there's a pleasant trail that follows the hillside. It's good for a gallop when you're ready."

"I'm ready now!" She set off in the direction he indicated at a canter. By the time they were on the trail, she and her moon mare were flying. If her riding was rusty, it didn't show. He kept pace behind her, enjoying the speed and the memories of rides they'd taken together in the days before her wedding.

Eventually she slowed her mount from a canter to a trot. Suzanne was laughing and her face was flushed with pleasure. "How marvelous! Luna is the best horse I've ever ridden. Her gaits are smooth as silk."

Simon pulled up beside her, matching her speed. "The Duke is another fine horse. As you said, Roper has a good eye for horseflesh and he's delighted to spend my money."

"He's spending it well," Suzanne said as she ran her fingers through Luna's silvery mane. "I love White Horse Manor. I'd like to stay here forever, but I suppose we must go back to London and infiltrate the émigré community."

"Yes, but I think it will be more pleasure than pain." He turned to head back to the house. "I'm rather looking forward to it. It's been a long time since I've moved in the sort of French society I knew as a boy."

"Returning to that will be interesting," she said as she turned Luna to follow Simon. "Though it's been a wonderful ride, now I must tour the house with Mrs. Stanley."

"We both have our responsibilities. I need to sit down with the steward and go over the books, which he is keen to show me. But tonight, we can once more indulge in the domestic fantasy of sitting together in front of a fire." He grinned at her. "Simple pleasures, and then a good night's sleep."

Her return smile was intimate, as full of anticipation as his. He was a lucky man. All he had to do was control his unruly male desires.

That was all.

* * *

That night when they retired, Suzanne winced as she climbed onto the bed. "The riding was wonderful, but the sore muscles have arrived with a vengeance!"

"If you lie on your stomach, I'll see if I can massage some of the pains away," Simon offered.

"Thank you!" Suzanne responded by rolling over on top of the covers. Her nightgown fell softly over the curves of her back, bottom, and legs. After a moment of masculine appreciation, he drew a deep breath, then knelt beside her and began to gently massage her neck, shoulders, and upper back.

She sighed with pleasure and relaxed under his hands. "I don't know if this will help with the sore muscles, but it feels wonderful," she murmured.

Her soft body felt equally wonderful to him. Though her nightgown was heavy enough for winter, it was still only a single layer of fabric between his hands and her lithe body. He kneaded his way down her back, making sure no muscle was neglected. Her bottom was round and firm, her thighs and calves a tempting sensual delight.

He was ruefully aware that if they were lovers, this would be a splendid form of erotic foreplay. He would eventually raise the hem of her nightgown so his bare fingers would be touching her naked skin. His hands would work their way upward. . . .

He swallowed hard, trying to suppress the sexual burn spreading through him. This massage would not be allowed if she didn't believe that he'd lost sexual interest and was touching her only as a friend, a brother, might. If she looked at him, she might realize the damning truth.

But she was mostly asleep now, a contented smile on her lips. He gave her bottom a last gentle pat, then climbed from the bed and pulled the covers over her. After banking the fire, he lit the dim night candle that stood on a table across the room and joined her under the covers.

She had rolled onto her side with her back to him, her breathing slow and even. Since the pulse of desire still throbbed through him, he didn't tuck his body around hers, only rested one hand on her hip as he lay on his back.

Closing his eyes, he slowed his breath and concentrated on relaxing, reducing his desire, telling himself he must sleep. And if he had carnal dreams of his wife, no matter as long as he didn't act on them.

His lovely wife, whom he was pledged to treat as a friend . . .

Chapter 12

❧

The night was cold and Suzanne instinctively wriggled back against Simon so that they lay spooned together. He was asleep, but even so, his arm came around her waist. He was so wonderfully warm. . . .

Too warm. A bolt of panic shot through her and she came sharply awake when she realized that a hot, hard part of him was poking against her bottom. She gave a choked cry, jerked away, and stumbled from the bed. "Damn you . . . !" she gasped. *"God damn you to hell!"*

Her cry woke Simon and he jolted awake. There was enough light from the night candle to see the swift procession of emotions as he pushed himself up on one elbow: the instinctive reaction of a soldier reacting to possible danger. Confusion at her cry and words. Then horror as he realized what must have happened.

He swore, then said hoarsely, "Suzanne . . . !"

"You lied!" she exclaimed, on the verge of weeping. "You said you weren't interested in sexual intimacy. I never would have married you if I'd known that wasn't true!"

He swallowed hard, his expression miserable. "I didn't lie. At the time, what I told you was true. It had been so long since I'd felt physical desire that I thought that part of me had died."

She dragged on her robe and wrapped it around her shivering body. "Yet after a mere three days, you're . . . you're . . ." She choked, unable to say how molested she'd felt.

"Believe me, I did not expect this to happen! And certainly not so soon." He climbed from the other side of the bed and pulled on his robe, keeping the broad bed between them.

"You said you've felt younger since our marriage. So have I. Like a young man in springtime." He drew a deep breath. "Our first night together I realized that desire was returning. I was shocked and concerned because I knew this wasn't what you wanted, but I thought my willpower was strong enough to control my reaction when I was with you."

"You were wrong!"

He grimaced. "Obviously my body is not so disciplined in sleep."

"I noticed," she said bitterly. "I speak not as a nervous virgin, but as a woman who has been the victim of male desire far too many times."

He closed his eyes for a moment, his expression agonized as he absorbed her words. Opening them, he said in a rough whisper, "As I said once before, we can have the marriage annulled. The legalities won't be pleasant, but it should be possible since the marriage hasn't been consummated."

She stared at him, feeling as if she was being torn in half as she thought about his kindness, his companionship, his understanding and humor—and his lust. "I don't want to end the marriage," she said haltingly. "I want it to remain the marriage of companionship we both agreed to."

"That's no longer possible," he said reluctantly. "I swore I'd never force you to do anything against your will and I'll keep that promise. But it means no longer sharing a bed. I can't sleep with you and not respond."

She shivered again. They'd both enjoyed that physical closeness so much. But no matter how good his willpower was during the day, he obviously couldn't guarantee the same restraint when he was asleep. "You're right," she said painfully. "I hate the idea of separate bedrooms, but . . . it's the only way."

He nodded unhappily. "I'll leave, but now you need to get back to bed. You look like you're freezing. I'll build up the fire."

He was right that she was shaking with cold, though it wasn't only from the winter night. Keeping her robe and slippers on, she climbed back into the bed and rolled onto her side, pulling the covers over her like a cocoon.

The fire flared as Simon added more coal. Then he pulled a heavy quilt from the chest at the foot of her bed. He shook it out and spread it over her for extra warmth.

"Thank you." She stared at him bleakly, knowing they were equally miserable. "I'll miss sleeping with you."

"And vice versa." His smile was crooked. "For a brief time, we had the marriage we planned on. I wish it had lasted longer."

Needing to know, she asked, "Are you sorry that you've recovered desire?"

He hesitated. "Yes, because it has wrecked the marriage we had planned and both enjoyed so much. But also no, because I feel fully alive. A whole man again. I hadn't realized how heavy my spirit had become until you began to lighten it."

"I'm sorry," she whispered. "I wish I was different."

"Don't apologize. We've dealt honestly with each other and you have nothing to apologize for. But . . ." His voice trailed off as he regarded her, his brow furrowing.

"But . . . ?"

"People change. It's inevitable. I changed rapidly and rather disastrously, but you might also change. What seems repellent now might come to feel . . . less so. Can you open your heart and mind to that possibility?"

She bit her lip. She loathed the thought of sweaty, violent, panting male aggression. Of fear and bodily invasion and helplessness.

But this was Simon, who was unlike any man she'd ever known. Simon, who was honest and kind. "Perhaps that might be possible," she said haltingly. "But it's almost beyond my imagination."

"If your feelings ever change enough that you're willing to allow marital relations, perhaps we might have a child," he said softly. "That's worth some risk, isn't it?"

She closed her eyes against the pain. "In all my years of marriage and then life in the harem, I never quickened. I think I'm barren."

"But you can't know that for sure."

"Gürkan sometimes used . . . devices," she said in a choked voice. "They hurt. I think they . . . damaged me inside."

"Dear God!" For a moment Simon's hand clasped hers in wordless shock. Then he swiftly let go. "No wonder you want to avoid men, *ma chérie*. You have been treated abominably."

"I don't blame all men for the crimes of a few," she whispered. "But you see why I told you that I was no longer fit for marriage."

"And I in my selfishness persuaded you against your better judgment."

"Perhaps against my judgment, but not against my will." She opened her eyes and gazed at him. "I wanted to believe our marriage of friendship would work."

He regarded her gravely. "Know this, Suzanne. All the choices belong to you. All the power is in your hands. Whatever you wish, you may have, even if it is an annulment, or a separation. The choice is yours."

He turned and quietly left the room. She managed to hold back her tears until he was gone. Then she disintegrated into wrenching sobs so intense, there was no space inside her for anything but pain.

Gradually she ran out of tears and lay buried under the blankets, filled with bleak despair. She forced herself to think. For a few bright shining days, she'd thought her luck had changed and she'd found happiness with the one man in the world who could be a perfect loving friend, understanding her as no one else could and not asking the impossible of her.

Their brief Eden had shattered, ironically, because he had become happy. Their marriage had benefited him as much as it had her, bringing him to a level of happiness he'd not imagined and restoring vitality and desire. She couldn't wish him unhappy; she suspected he had a chamber of horrors that matched hers.

Her situation was enormously better than it had been a fortnight before. Thanks to Simon's generosity, she now had the money to live in comfort. She could have a home and friends—along with a return to loneliness that would be all the worse for having been briefly lifted. Their marriage had barely begun and already she was so used to lying with him that his absence made her bed feel achingly empty.

When they were discussing a possible marriage, they had talked in abstract terms about what might happen if one of them regained desire. They'd assumed that if that happened it would be in the distant future. They'd also rather smugly decided that they were French; they could work that out. Discreet lovers were mentioned.

Now that possibility loomed, and the thought of Simon lying with another woman made her want to vomit. She realized that her hands had curled into claws.

She could leave tomorrow and Simon would not reproach her. To spare herself humiliation and notoriety, she could reject the idea of annulment and leave him in limbo, unable to ever take another wife.

But those possibilities were superseded by a promise she had made to him: to do her best to make this marriage work. That meant not giving up after three days. She was, after all, French and very adaptable.

They could continue living together but avoid touching each other, but they both loved it so much. Was there a compromise that would enable them to maintain a mostly satisfactory marriage? Perhaps, though it would be more satisfactory for her than for him. It was worth trying.

Needing to act before she lost her courage, she slid from the bed and pulled off the quilt, then carried it in her arms as she padded from her bedroom, across the cold sitting room, and into Simon's room. She'd not been in it before, but dim light from fireplace coals showed that the layout was much the same as her bedroom.

She was trying to move silently, but was unsurprised when Simon asked, "Suzanne?"

Apparently he couldn't sleep either. "Who else?" She tried to make her voice light and calm. "I've found I don't like sleeping alone."

He sat up in bed and regarded her warily. "Neither do I, but sharing a bed seems likely to be disastrous."

"Perhaps we can find a workable compromise." She cocooned herself in the quilt and gave him a gentle push on the chest. "Lie down, milord."

She clambered onto the bed, lying on top of his covers but close enough that she could roll on her side and drape an arm around his neck. "I promised I would do my best to make our marriage work, not just seize your money and run."

Bemused, he said, "You can do that if you wish to, milady."

"But I don't wish to!" She drew a deep, steadying breath when she realized she was shaking. "For honor's sake as well as for our mutual benefit, I must make a good faith effort to create a marriage that will satisfy us both as much as possible. Which means touching because we both like it so much."

She sensed him studying her through the shadows. "I can't promise to share a bed with you and not become aroused," he said bluntly. "You're a lovely and desirable woman and my wife, and I am no longer a virtual eunuch."

She shuddered. "Don't even joke about that! I hated the fact that men were maimed in order to become eunuch harem guards."

"Sorry, that was an ill-chosen word. But much as I want you in my bed, I can't promise not to upset you again."

"If we have enough bedding between us, I think I can manage," she said, hoping her words were true. "Part of the problem tonight was that your arousal was so unexpected and shocking."

"Unexpected, shocking, and frightening," he said softly. "I'm so sorry, Suzanne."

"Don't apologize," she replied. "The problem is mine, and I will do my best to bridge the gap between us."

"If the answer is to have a lot of bedding, that's easy in February." He wrapped an arm around her and drew her cocooned self over so that she was half lying on his chest.

She hadn't realized how tense she was until she started to relax. With a long sigh of relief, she burrowed against him. "We can't touch each other as thoroughly, but this is so much better than sleeping alone!"

"I agree." He brushed his lips across her forehead. "An American once told me of a frontier custom called bundling in which courting couples share a bed because the young man has to travel so far to visit with her. A board is laid down the middle of the bed and they're supposed to stay on their own sides."

That surprised a laugh from her. "Do you think they do?"

"Probably not, at least, not all the time!" He pulled her closer. "Blankets are softer than boards."

"Thank you," she whispered as she began sliding toward sleep. "For accepting my weaknesses, and for your patience and willingness to try."

"You aren't weak, *ma chérie*. I think you're the strongest woman I've ever known," he said softly. "You survived a sad marriage to a man who didn't deserve you. You survived pirate capture and years as a harem slave. You have the strength of endurance and the ability to change and grow. Since you have decided to do your best to make our marriage work in a way that suits us, I feel hopeful. We both want this. With commitment and intelligence, surely we will succeed."

"I hope so," she said intensely. "I think you're the best thing that has ever happened to me, and I'd be a fool to let you go without a fight."

"I'm flattered." He brushed his hand over her head. "Now rest. We both need it."

She exhaled slowly. Disaster had been averted, but now she must find a way to move beyond the horrors that had crippled her for so long. She owed it to Simon; she owed it to herself.

But tonight, exhausted, she slept.

Chapter 13

❧

Simon awoke feeling much as he did after a battle: battered, drained, and grateful to be alive. He opened his eyes to study Suzanne's face, which was sculpted by the dawn light. There were blotches around her eyes, marks of her previous night's despair.

Yet here she was in his arms and both of them had slept. Granted, there were half a dozen layers of quilt, counterpane, blankets, sheets, and nightclothes between them, but this was infinitely preferable to sleeping alone.

The layers were fortunate because he'd awoken with an erection. Back in the days when he'd been normal, that had been a regular phenomenon. Over time, it had become rarer and rarer and eventually he realized that passion was only a distant memory. He'd thought that state of affairs was permanent, and hadn't much cared.

Then he met Suzanne again. Looking back, he recognized that his compelling wish to marry her had been the first indication that he was coming alive again. He was intensely grateful despite the complications desire was causing.

As he looked back on his life, he suspected that he did not have the right temperament to be a soldier, but circumstances had pushed him into that role. He'd done what was needed and been damned good at it, but he was glad now that he'd be leaving the army behind.

Suzanne stirred in his arms and raised a hand to stroke his face. "Good, we're in the same bed. I didn't dream last night." She tilted her head and gave him a smile that lit up the room. "I'm glad you haven't washed your hands of me."

"I never will." After a moment, he added, "As I said, you hold the power between us, but I'm unable to read your mind. If I do anything you dislike, you must tell me."

"Why are you granting me all the power?" she asked seriously.

"How else will you feel safe?"

She bit her lip. "You're perceptive. Yet it's uncomfortable to feel that I am in control of our marriage. Part of me likes the idea, but you are a seasoned soldier. You are used to action and command. Surely you will eventually resent deferring to me."

He hesitated before replying. "I suspect you're right. But I don't want you to ever fear being honest with me, or be afraid of what I might do."

"I don't want that either," she agreed. "I've spent too much of my life between walking on eggshells and being actively terrified. Better for us and our future would be to share the power. I will tell you when you are being annoying, and you will tell me the same when needed."

"You're never annoying," he protested.

She chuckled. "Up to this point, you've been honest with me, but that remark is worrisome. It suggests a lack of reason on your part."

He laughed, surprised at how buoyant he felt. "Very well, I'll modify my words to say that you haven't been annoying yet, but if you are, I'll mention it."

"That's fair." She sat up and the quilt fell from around her shoulders.

He was acutely aware of the shifting movements of her lovely breasts under her nightgown. But it was now daytime and he invoked his self-control. "We should probably sleep in your bed. That way I'll be the one who has to get up and freeze my feet on the way back to my bedroom in the morning."

"As you wish, milord." She slipped from the bed and immediately donned her sheepskin slippers as protection from the cold floor. "What shall we do today?"

"We'll get dressed and have a fine, leisurely breakfast. We'll take a ride." He grinned. "And this afternoon, I'll start teaching you how to be dangerous."

She looked bemused. "We're having an unusual honeymoon, aren't we? The traditional 'moon of honey' is a time of discovery as two people explore each other's bodies. We aren't really doing that."

"We're doing as much of that as is feasible for the two of us. But beyond passion, I think a honeymoon is a time for two people to give each other their full attention," he said thoughtfully. "We're doing that and exploring each other's minds and spirits, which is even more important."

"Giving each other our full attention?" She smiled wryly. "So we are, but this means I received less than my due on my first honeymoon. Jean-Louis was perfectly willing to initiate me into the mysteries of womanhood, as he delicately called it, but outside the bed, he spent little time with me even on our honeymoon. He was always off hunting and drinking and playing cards with his male friends."

Simon shook his head in amazement. "What a fool my cousin was!"

"So I have come to realize." Suzanne hesitated. "Do you mind when I mention him? Should I stop?"

"Not at all! Whenever you talk of him, I feel better about myself and our marriage."

She laughed. "And so you should!"

A long day of riding and learning how to handle firearms left Suzanne tired but content. Despite the near calamity the night before, she and Simon had regained their ease with each other and were growing even closer. She'd never known a man to whom she could say anything.

Nonetheless, she was a little uncertain about how they would arrange their night's sleep. Simon made it easy. When they went upstairs, he said, "I'll join you in your room when I'm ready for bed."

She entered her room and changed into her nightgown and robe quickly, not wanting to be caught half naked. After years in the harem, she had no modesty left, but she didn't want to make things more difficult for Simon. She'd learned that men were easily aroused if they saw too much bare skin.

But Simon took his time before joining her. She should have known he wouldn't permit any awkwardness. She was sitting up in the bed leaning against piled pillows when he arrived. He moved to the fireplace and began preparing the coals to warm them through the night.

His tone conversational, he asked, "Do you need another massage? It usually takes a few days for sore riding muscles to recover."

"I'd like that," she admitted. "As long as it doesn't make you uncomfortable?"

He stood and brushed his hands off. "If you're asking if that will make me want you more, the answer is yes. But any minor discomfort is more than balanced by the pleasure of feeling you under my hands."

She wanted his touch also, so she pushed the covers back and lay face down on the lower sheet. Simon moved to the side of the bed and began gently kneading her neck and shoulders. "That feels so good," she murmured.

"So do you," he said as his strong fingers soothed her muscles and bones.

On impulse, she asked, "What are you thinking when you do this?"

He hesitated before saying, "That any woman who enjoys being touched as much as you might someday become comfortable with more intimate touching."

Suzanne froze. "Relax," Simon said with a gentle pat on her rump. "If that ever happens, it will be because you want it." Then he returned to gently kneading her back into relaxation.

When she was halfway to sleep, he said, "Now we build a bedtime sandwich."

"Oh?"

"Since you've been living in a hot climate for years, you must need more blankets, so you're the lowest layer." He deftly rolled her onto her back and pulled several of the blankets over her. Then he lit the shielded night candle, which gave only a minimum of light, and extinguished the brighter lamp.

Lastly he climbed onto the opposite side of the bed, lying on top of the blankets that covered her before pulling the other blankets over them both. With a contented sigh, he rolled onto his side and put his arm around her. "This is neater than our impromptu arrangement last night."

Suzanne agreed as she burrowed against him. He was so warm and comfortable. Here they were in each other's arms and, if he had an erection, she wouldn't know about it. "Good night, milord," she whispered. "Thank you for marrying me."

He made a soft, friendly sound before his breathing became slow and steady. She was ready to do the same, but as she drifted into sleep, she wondered if he was right that her love of holding him might someday make her more comfortable with full intimacy.

She hoped so. Dear God, she hoped so!

Their honeymoon might have been unconventional, but it fulfilled the requirement of spending all their time and attention on each other. Suzanne's riding skills had come back effortlessly, and she loved exploring the countryside with him.

Simon's honeymoon concept hadn't involved shooting lessons or teaching his lovely bride a range of dirty tricks she could use in self-defense, but she clearly enjoyed that part of it, too. Her determination to never be a victim again made her an apt student. He'd buy her some weapons that would suit her size when they returned to London.

The sandwich system of sharing a bed was not infallible. Several mornings he'd woken up with a hand resting on Suzanne's breast. She might sleepily move it away, but she wasn't upset.

They were invited to dinner by several neighbors, which he hadn't expected. Suzanne pointed out that he was a major landowner in the area and people were curious about Simon and his French wife.

Though France had been the enemy, Suzanne's charm swiftly won them over. Simon remembered many of the neighbors from his childhood, and he was warmed by their welcome. As Suzanne said later, the only thing that would have made him more desirable to the neighbors was if he were single.

He retorted that the thought of dodging eligible daughters was alarming, and he was grateful that he had a wife to protect him. They'd both laughed. He loved the way they could laugh together. White Horse Manor was feeling very much like home.

The days of their idyll drifted together until a fortnight had passed. March had arrived and the day was lovely and sunny, early spring rather than winter, so they rode across the valley to visit the white horse. The shape was impossible to recognize close up, but Suzanne was intrigued by the crushed white chalk that filled and defined the ancient depressions.

They shared a pleasant picnic lunch on the hillside before heading for home. Their light mood faded when they entered the house and Simon found a letter franked by Lord Kirkland. He broke the wafer and read it, his brow furrowing.

"Bad news?" Suzanne asked.

"Not really, but the honeymoon is over. Kirkland says that the Comte de Chaurry, an influential émigré, is holding an entertainment in three days and a card of invitation will be waiting for us in London. So it's time to return to the real world." He glanced up at Suzanne. "Is de Chaurry one of the émigrés you met when you first came to London?"

She made a face. "Yes. He looked through me as if I was a scullery maid but he wasn't actively insulting."

Simon frowned. "Are you ready to face him and his snobbish friends?"

She smiled wryly. "With you beside me, I'm ready to face anyone."

They were a team now. And if anyone insulted her, he'd break them in half.

Chapter 14

Suzanne did her best to suppress her nervousness as their carriage stopped before the de Chaurry mansion. "I'm glad Jenny will be returning from Dorset this week to start looking after me, but even without her, I'm better dressed than when I first arrived in London." She stroked a hand over her emerald-green silk skirts.

"You look particularly beautiful tonight, and beauty is power," Simon said seriously.

"And if beauty isn't enough, I have those defensive moves you taught me." She smiled wryly at him. "The ability to fight back lends confidence."

"Indeed it does, but I hope that the evening won't require you to break anyone's fingers." He helped her down from the carriage. "From now on, we speak French."

"*Oui*, milord," she said demurely as she took his arm and they ascended the steps to the heavily carved double doors.

Suzanne felt odd as she tried to think in French. Though

it was her native language, in Constantinople she'd had almost no opportunity to use it and she'd been speaking
English since she escaped captivity. At her request, she
and Simon spoke English almost all the time because
she'd wanted to become more fluent.

Constant practice had worked; though she wasn't truly
bilingual like Simon, her English had improved dramati-
cally. Now, alas, she must once again play the role of a
French noblewoman. She had become very good at playing roles, first as an obedient young countess, later as a
submissive harem slave who had accepted her fate.

She was feeling a good deal less submissive since marrying Simon. Drawing on her years as an expensive and
highly polished French countess, she raised her chin and
held the arm of her warrior husband as they entered the
house.

As soon as they stepped into the vestibule, they heard
the sounds of music and laughter and voices chattering in
French. She was instantly jarred into her old life, and remembered how trapped she'd felt as Jean-Louis's wife.
She'd been like a canary in a gilded cage, meant to be admired, not listened to.

"How are you managing?" Simon asked under his
breath.

Simon, God bless him, paid attention to her. "Well
enough, though it's an odd feeling to be in a grand French
household again."

"Agreed. I haven't been in French society for many
years." He smiled at her. "Luckily, we are both very
adaptable."

After Simon gave their names to a footman, they were
escorted upstairs to the hosts, who were receiving guests.
"Colonel and Madame Duval," the footman announced.

"Welcome to my home," the Comte de Chaurry said.
He was silver haired and elegant, as was his very fashion-

able wife. "I've heard you are now the Comte de Chambron?"

"It seems presumptuous to claim the title when I'm not entirely sure," Simon said as he took the other man's hand for a brief handshake. "Several cousins stood between me and the title. France is still too unsettled for certainty."

He drew Suzanne forward. "But there is no question that my wife is the Comtesse de Chambron, as she is the widow of the last verified comte."

De Chaurry's eyes narrowed as he registered that fact. His wife looked as if she'd bitten into a sour lemon when she was presented to Suzanne. In her turn, Suzanne looked ironically amused and was impeccably polite to her hostess.

De Chaurry began to introduce them around the room, Suzanne and Simon were studied thoroughly, but greetings were civil. Halfway around the room, a well-dressed woman who was chatting with friends turned and gave a gasp of shock. "Suzanne, my darling girl, can that really be you?"

Suzanne caught her breath as she recognized the attractive, dark-haired woman. "Madeline de Sevigny! It's been so long!" The two women came together in an enthusiastic embrace. After they released each other, Suzanne turned to Simon. "Madeline and I were neighbors for several years, milord."

"I heard that you died in a corsair attack along with your husband," Madeline said as she stepped back to study Suzanne. "But you are blooming! And your husband also." She turned to Simon, then blinked. "You are not Jean-Louis. He had brown eyes."

Simon bowed. "I am a younger cousin of his, madam, which explains the resemblance. Suzanne and I met before her wedding and we became friends. To my great joy, we found each other again in London."

Madeline nodded approvingly. "Well done, sir. Now I

shall take Suzanne off to meet several of my friends. We have so much to talk about!"

As Suzanne was carried off, de Chaurry drawled, "How fortunate that your wife has found friends. Let me introduce you to these new arrivals." He beckoned two men closer. "Moncoutant, Roubaix, come meet Colonel Duval, who may or may not be the Comte de Chambron."

Moncoutant reminded Simon of a sly, sleek fox, alert and unpredictable. He inclined his head politely, and like Suzanne, he asked, "Which army?"

"British. It seemed the best way to oppose Napoleon. I'm selling out now that the wars are over." He smiled without humor. "Assuming they *are* over. One hears rumors. Do you think the Corsican will remain in containment?"

"I think it unlikely," Roubaix said, his brow furrowed. He was dark and had a face that looked jolly, except for his eyes. "He is a man of great ability and great ambition. He will grow restless in Elba, particularly since our Bourbon king is not sending him the agreed upon allowance."

"That's very short sighted," Simon agreed. "A lion who is not being fed properly is more likely to break from his cage. Do you have any thoughts on what might happen?"

De Chaurry pursed his lips. "One would hope that the Royal Navy can keep him in Elba. But the emperor has too many supporters who will do anything for him. I fear that sooner or later the captors will grow careless and the lion will emerge to fight once again."

Simon sighed. "And our poor France will suffer once more."

"Perhaps, perhaps not," Roubaix said. "I don't think he'll return to France. Italy is more likely. It's only a few miles from Elba and there might be less resistance there."

"That's an interesting thought. But if he goes to Italy

and is proclaimed ruler, how long until his ambitions drive him to conquer again?"

"Not long at all," Moncoutant said. "If he returns to France, he will find a great deal of support. He still owns the hearts of the troops who served under him."

"I think much of his success was that he preached democracy and the common man, but ruled like a tyrant," Roubaix observed. "A man of two faces."

"Both of which are dangerous," de Chaurry said acerbically. "I would love to return home to my lands in Lorraine. But the political situation feels uncertain, which is why I remain safely here among the boring Britons."

"A good number of our compatriots share your wariness." Simon gestured to the groups of well-dressed guests.

"Yes, but many who are less cautious than I have returned to France, so my entertainments are thin of company compared to what they were." De Chaurry gave a very Gallic shrug. "Will you reclaim your family's lands, Duval?"

"I haven't really thought much about that," Simon admitted. "I'm only recently out of the army after years spent in Portugal and Spain. For now, it's good to be in England. I'm half English, you know, so my roots are as deep here as in France."

"What of your wife? She is all French."

"We are still newlyweds," Simon said with a suggestive smile. "We have not spent much time talking about the future."

The other men chuckled knowingly. Moncoutant said, "Understandable! She's very lovely. Is it true that she has learned harem skills that can drive a man to the brink of madness?"

Simon restrained the impulse to plant a fist in the other man's lascivious face. "My wife is a lady. I will not discuss her with any man."

De Chaurry looked disappointed. "Your English blood is showing, but no matter. Let me introduce you to my other guests."

As Simon talked and listened, he found that most of the guests had views similar to de Chaurry. They professed to loathe Napoleon, but they weren't impressed with the aging, ineffectual Bourbon king who sat on the throne.

Most would be pleased to return to their prerevolution stations of vast wealth and privilege, but all recognized that years had passed and France had changed. They hoped that when the political situation stabilized, they would still have wealth and privilege, if not as much as they'd had in the past.

And they all felt that Napoleon's prison in Elba was unlikely to keep him caged forever. It was an interesting evening, though Simon hadn't heard anything that was likely to interest Kirkland. Perhaps Suzanne would do better.

Suzanne was surprised at how much she was enjoying the evening. The de Chaurry "entertainment" seemed to mean conversation, pleasant music in the background, with light, delicious, and very French refreshments and all the good wine one could drink. Kirkland had been right; mingling among the émigrés with an aristocratic soldier husband and a really good new gown made her much more acceptable.

Granted, a few men leered at her and some women turned away rather than be introduced, but most of the émigrés were civil. The unexpected miracle was Madeline. She was a few years older than Suzanne and had been like a helpful big sister guiding a young bride in the ways of the world.

As they exchanged news, Madeline offered condolences on the death of Jean-Louis and quiet sympathy for what Suzanne had suffered in captivity. There were no insults or sneers from her or her friends, but they had a lively curiosity about the day-to-day life of a harem. What did concubines eat, what did they wear, how did they spend their time, and were the Turkish baths as magnificent as they'd heard? How often could a concubine expect to be summoned to her master's bed?

Suzanne had known such questions would arise, and she'd worked out her answers in advance. "The baths are indeed magnificent." She sighed with longing. "Perhaps I can persuade my husband to build one for me. But as for a concubine's romantic life, that varied enormously. My master liked women with unusual features, which in my case meant my green eyes, which he'd never seen before. But otherwise. . . ."

She shook her head and began to lie. "I was considered too small and thin to be very attractive. But even if I was as round and luscious as the females my master preferred—well, even the greatest rake in any realm would never have enough time to pay adequate attention to so many women!" Her expression changed to a smile of wicked satisfaction. "Believe me, my friends, a single husband who lives under the same roof and is interested is much more valuable to a woman!"

That had produced boisterous giggles and stories of honeymoons and husbands and lovers that deflected attention from Suzanne. She didn't mention that the most vital skill she'd learned in the harem was to lie superbly. The reality of her life there was not a subject for superficial entertainment.

She was relieved that no one had called her a whore to her face, though there were women in the room like the Comtesse de Chaurry who had done so in the past. Tonight they avoided Suzanne, but they didn't openly insult her.

Occasionally she and Simon exchanged glances so she could silently assure him that she was all right. He seemed to be moving easily among the gentlemen, talking and listening and learning their opinions.

The hour was getting late when someone stepped on Suzanne's hem and pulled a ribbon trim loose. Ready for a break from the conversation, she excused herself and headed upstairs to the ladies' retiring room. A solicitous lady's maid pinned the ribbon back in place and patted lavender water on her temples.

For a few minutes, Suzanne relaxed with her feet on a brocade footstool, glad she didn't have to talk. When she was ready to return to the fray, she stood and smoothed out her gown. The mirror showed that she looked well tonight, as elegant and calm as a countess should be. But being constantly on guard made this visit with her countrymen tiring. She would see if Simon was ready to leave.

The retiring room was a floor above the drawing room and at the back of the house, so she had to walk the length of a corridor and around a corner to reach the stairs. Sconces gave soft light, illuminating occasional pieces of elegant French furniture. She stopped to admire an elaborate table at the turn in the corridor, thinking that the de Chaurrys must have escaped France with a shipload of furnishings.

"So there's the harem whore." The harsh, slurred voice jolted Suzanne and she spun around to see a male guest. She came sharply alert. Morlaix, his name was. When she'd visited the émigrés on her arrival in London, he'd been one of the men who had tried to corner her. She'd escaped when two servant girls came chattering along the corridor.

This time there was no one else around and he seemed broad and hulking and very drunk. Hoping to brazen this out, she raised her chin and said in her coolest countess voice, "There are no whores in harems, monsieur. Only bored women with too much time on their hands."

"No need to be bored now, your ladyship," he leered as he closed in on her. "I've wondered what harem whores do to please men." With a sudden lunge, he grabbed her arms. "I've heard they can drive a man out of his mind." He tried to shove her downward with one hand on her shoulder while the other hand fumbled with the fall of his trousers.

For an instant she was paralyzed by shock and fear. *Submit or he'll hurt you. Maybe even kill you. You're powerless, you must obey. . . .*

NO! Rage shattered her paralysis. She was no longer a submissive female who feared for her life and had no choice but to obey. She was the wife of a warrior, and he'd taught her how to fight back.

While Morlaix was struggling to unbutton his fall, she jerked her knee upward with furious strength. He wasn't expecting resistance, and her knee smashed dead center into his most vulnerable organs. He howled with agony and jackknifed forward, bringing his throat within easy reach. Suzanne chopped down with the side of her hand, hitting so hard that her hand hurt.

Morlaix gave an agonized squawk and collapsed on the expensive carpet. Burning with rage at every man who had ever hurt or bullied her, Suzanne drew her foot back and kicked him in the belly as hard as she could. Her toes hurt and she wished she'd been wearing her riding boots.

Not caring that her toes hurt, she kicked him again and was preparing to do so once more when strong arms came around her, holding her still. "Enough, *ma chérie.*" Simon's deep voice was in her ear, soothing. "You have dealt with him well, but you don't want to kill him. The authorities would be awkward about that."

She turned and clung to him, shaking. "He wanted to . . . to . . ."

"I know." He patted her back. "Can you stand on your own?"

She nodded. Simon released her and turned to Morlaix. Effortlessly he raised the larger man and slammed him hard against the wall. "Do not ever, *ever,* trouble my wife again," he said in a lethal voice as he stood eye to eye with Morlaix. "If she doesn't kill you, I will. Am I clear?"

Morlaix was still gasping for breath and his gaze was murderous, but he mumbled some kind of assent.

"See that you remember." Simon released his hold and Morlaix collapsed to the floor like a pile of groaning laundry.

As Simon put his arm around Suzanne, she realized other guests had joined them, drawn by Morlaix's cries. One was de Chaurry. The comte drew an unsteady breath as he stared at his guest. The open fall of the man's trousers told the story. "I'm sorry this happened under my roof, Colonel, madam."

The onlookers included several women. One of the younger ones came forward and kicked Morlaix in the ribs, hard, as she swore under her breath. Another followed and spat on him, saying, "Thank you, Madame Duval." Both women turned on their heels and marched down the stairs.

"I'm guessing that Morlaix has made a habit of assaulting young women," Simon said coolly. "A very bad habit." He scooped Suzanne up in his arms. "It's time I took my wife home. Thank you for a generally very pleasant evening, Monsieur le Comte."

He carried Suzanne down the staircase as other guests drew back. She could have managed on her own, but Simon's protective arms felt too good to forego. His warmth, his strength, his kindness. She murmured into his shoulder, "I'm glad you gave me the lessons in defending myself."

"And I'm glad you learned them so well!" At the front door Simon set her on her feet while the butler brought their cloaks and summoned their carriage.

Suzanne was glad to get away. But Morlaix's assault had started her mind spinning in new directions.

Chapter 15

❧

Once they were in their carriage and heading for home, Simon pulled Suzanne onto his lap and held her close again. "The women present almost broke into applause for what you did to Morlaix."

"I would like to think his behavior would get him banned from the houses of his acquaintances, but I'm sure it won't." Her mouth tightened. "And to think he considers himself a gentleman! That vile *cochon*!"

"He is an insult to pigs. Should I challenge him to a duel?" Simon offered. "That's a gentlemanly solution, and the world would be a better place without him."

"You might get hurt!" she gasped.

"I promise you I wouldn't. But I suppose a duel would draw too much attention."

She suspected he was half joking about challenging Morlaix to a duel. But only half. Changing the subject, she asked, "How did you reach me so quickly?"

"I noticed you go upstairs earlier. You hadn't come down and then I heard that howl from Morlaix and had a feeling that something bad had happened." He brushed a light kiss on her hair. "You handled it well, but I'm sorry that it was necessary."

"I'm not sorry," she said, surprised by the realization. "I feel surprisingly good. I survived my return to émigré society, found an old friend, and for the first time, I fought back when a man tried to abuse me. I fought and *won*! That makes me feel strong."

"You are strong, *ma chérie* And getting stronger."

She patted his arm. "I was impressed how quickly you went from suave gentleman to ruthless fighter."

"The advantage of military experience." He smoothed her hair back tenderly. "Are you all right? Will you have nightmares?"

She considered before replying. "I don't think so, and if I do, you will be there."

"I'm glad you're still willing to share a bed with me despite new proof of male bestiality," he said wryly.

"Generalizing is easy, but wrong. Not all men are beasts, and not all women are virtuous. It's best to judge people one at a time." She shook her head. "Enough about that *cochon*. Did you learn anything interesting tonight?"

"Not really. Napoleon looms large in everyone's mind, and most of the men I talked to thought it likely that sooner or later the emperor will break out. They are divided on when and where, and how much trouble he'll cause if he does escape. What about the women?"

"To the extent that they have political opinions, they probably think as their husbands do, but they were much more interested in hearing about life in a harem. There are so many absurd rumors about what it's like!" Her mouth twisted. "I didn't tell them that the worst part was the boredom. Some days it felt that the walls were crushing in on me. Knowing that I would likely never, ever leave . . ." She shuddered.

"No wonder when escape was offered, you grabbed it with both hands and didn't look back," he said quietly.

They had reached the house. Covering her yawn with one hand, she said, "Enough of harems and brutish males! I'm ready to go to bed."

"So am I." Simon lifted her from his lap and set her on the seat beside him. "I'm looking forward to our bed, and may tomorrow be a less dramatic day!"

Despite her fatigue, when Suzanne climbed into her sandwich bed, her mind was too active for sleep. When Simon joined her, she rolled over and lay half across his chest, but her thoughts kept returning to the events of the evening. Morlaix had drunkenly said that he'd heard harem women knew how to please a man. That was true. She was an expert at giving men pleasure and her skill had preserved her life.

Those skills were part of an existence she'd abhorred. But she was free now, safe and supported and protected by Simon. He'd given her everything and asked nothing in return except companionship, and giving that was a joy.

It was time to give back to him. She gathered her resolve, then slid her hand between the covers on his layer of the bed. He slept in a loose linen shirt and soft drawers, and his body was warm and muscular under the fabric. She liked petting his broad chest. He felt so strong, so alive.

She stroked her hand lower, feeling the subtle contours of his torso. Touch. They both loved touching so much, and he was wonderfully touchable.

She had just found the hard jut of his pelvis bone when his hand clamped hard over hers. "Suzanne, what are you doing?" he asked, his voice taut to the breaking point.

"That horrid Morlaix made me recognize that I can give you satisfaction without full intimacy," she said honestly. "I want to please you. And it would be my first step toward breaking the chains that have bound me."

There was a long silence, and she felt the pulse in his hand over hers. "This is . . . appealing, but I don't want you doing something you find distasteful."

"I believe it will make me feel strong," she said slowly. "Strong and free. If you will permit?"

"Of course I'll permit," he said, his voice thick.

He released her hand, and she continued her exploration of his lower body. He really was a splendid male specimen. His breath was quickening and she found that he was almost fully aroused when she grasped him. He gave a suffocated cry and his whole body became rigid. She was pleased to discover that she felt no fear or revulsion because this intimacy was her choice and this was Simon, the best man she'd ever known.

As she kneaded his yielding, heated flesh, her fingers remembered the old skills. She quickly found the rhythm of intensifying his arousal, then slowing down to prolong his pleasure. When he began shaking all over in response, she decided it was time to bring him to culmination. She did so with quick, deft fingers.

"Suzanne!" he gasped. "Dear God, *Suzanne* . . . !" He crushed her against him as his body bucked uncontrollably.

She'd brought a handkerchief to bed in the hope she'd have the courage to pleasure him. As he reached the explosion point, she pulled the handkerchief from under her pillow and captured that hot stream of potential life. He groaned her name again and again at his shattering release, holding her as if she was his lifeline.

Slowly his tension eased and he loosened his embrace. "Thank you, *mon ange,* my lovely angel of the night," he panted. "I hope you didn't find that upsetting?"

"Not at all, it was my pleasure." She relaxed against him, feeling satisfied herself. She smiled into the darkness. "You realize what this means?"

"A number of things," he murmured. "What are you thinking?"

"We can dispense with sandwich sleeping!"

His deep chuckle reverberated through his chest. "Very true! Can you join me on my layer? I don't think I have the strength to move."

Feeling vastly pleased with herself, she rolled from the bed and sorted through the blankets to reach him. She crawled under the covers, glad to eliminate the layers that had separated them. He cuddled her close and kissed her temple. "Sleep well, *mon ange*."

She made a purring sound and rested her hand in the center of his chest. Lulled by the rhythm of his heart, she fell into a deep sleep, wondering what the next day would bring.

Simon woke feeling peace so vast that it seemed a dream. Could it have been? No, Suzanne was curled up against him like a contented kitten, her arm across his chest and a faint smile on her lips.

She stirred and stretched, again like a lithe, lovely feline. He murmured, "Our new servants will be here this week. Shall we tell them that they must never, ever enter our bedrooms unannounced?"

"Not even if they are bearing morning hot chocolate?" she said mischievously.

"Not even then," he said firmly. "These moments relaxing with you are too precious."

They lay together in peaceful silence awhile longer. He idly stroked her back. Then, carefully, her side, before slowly moving his hand to the front of her body.

When he spread his palm over the gentle curve of her

belly, she froze. "I am not ready for that," she said in a tight voice.

He instantly removed his hand. "I'm sorry."

"No need to apologize when I don't know myself what will upset me."

She was trying to keep her voice calm, but he could hear the stress. She had already come a long way in a short time; if she never felt comfortable with greater intimacy, he would still be a lucky man.

He kissed her forehead. "Shall we rise for breakfast? I'm told that Madame Mercier has hired an assistant cook who bakes croissants so light they float off the plate."

"We must certainly sample them!" Suzanne said as she swung from the bed. "Croissants with orange marmalade would be a perfect blending of French baking and British sweets."

"Don't forget the coffee," he said. Even better than a croissant was the fact that he could admire her across the breakfast table.

Simon and Suzanne both browsed newspapers as they enjoyed their croissants, marmalade, and coffee. In the garden outside, daffodils were exploding into bloom in the spring sunshine. Simon thought it was one of those ordinary moments that was also perfect. "I wonder how long we can prolong our honeymoon. At some point I need to start attending to my responsibilities, but I'm in no hurry."

"Those companies where you're a part owner?" Suzanne asked as she took a delicate bite from her second croissant.

"Those, plus the estate. They have good managers but I need to pay attention, visit the premises, meet the people who do the work. I owe it to them, and attention is useful for maintaining productivity."

A maid entered with a silver salver that held a letter for Simon. As she withdrew, Simon broke open the letter. "The world might be catching up with us," he said after he scanned the brief note. "This is from Kirkland and he wants us to call this morning if that's convenient. Both of us."

"I imagine he wonders if we heard anything interesting last night."

"Very likely." But Simon's spying intuition was twitching. There might be more than that to Kirkland's request.

Kirkland greeted them amiably and welcomed them into his study, where he rang for tea and coffee. When they'd arrived and been served, Simon said, "I'm sorry to have no great revelations from the émigrés. I talked to most of the men and they all seemed to think that it's just a matter of time till Napoleon escapes from Elba. When that might happen and what would come next"—Simon shrugged—"no one knows. We learned that Morlaix is a swine who shouldn't be allowed near any female, but I didn't see or sense anything suggesting the group contained a dangerous spy."

"Thank you for looking them over. Even if there is a serious spy among the men you met, events are moving so quickly that it might not matter," Kirkland said flatly. "But émigrés are not the primary reason I asked you to call. You had asked if I might be able to find out more about the fate of your cousin, Lucas Mandeville."

Simon found that he suddenly could not breathe. "And?"

"The good news is that he didn't die when the French sank his ship. He was taken prisoner by the French and sent first to Verdun, then quickly moved to a prison depot. After that the trail becomes murky."

"How murky?"

"From what I've been able to piece together, he escaped by breaking his parole," Kirkland said bluntly.

The shock was almost physical. "No! That's not possible!" Simon exclaimed. "Lucas was always the soul of honor."

Suzanne's warm hand clasped his, anchoring him to reality. "As I understand it," she said in a soft voice, "officers are paroled and allowed some freedom of movement in their community by giving their word of honor that they will not escape?"

"Yes." Kirkland's gaze was steady.

"So breaking parole is considered an unpardonable offense against a man's honor."

Kirkland nodded. "Mothers tell their sons that it's better to die than behave dishonorably. For many people, honor is their lifeblood. Giving their word not to escape and then doing so is considered contemptible. A sin beyond forgiveness."

Suzanne's grip tightened on Simon's hand. "I understand honor," she said compassionately. "But I also understand how a man or woman can be pushed to the breaking point, so that they will do *anything* to survive. Killing an innocent or someone who is helpless—to me, that is true dishonor. To feel oneself being driven mad by captivity and being willing to do anything short of that to escape . . ." She shrugged. "I do not find that unforgivable. Would you rather your cousin was dead?"

Her words started Simon's mind again. Suzanne knew captivity in a way he never would, and she had a compassionate heart. "No, of course I don't wish him dead. It's just that this news is a shock. Lucas was always the one with unshakable integrity and honor. I was the one who became the spy, a trade most gentlemen despise as dishonorable."

"Dishonorable but essential," Kirkland said. "I've lived in these same troubled waters because someone must do this work. I've done things I'm not proud of, but I believe they were for the greater good."

"I've done the same." Simon drew a deep breath. "But shame could explain why Lucas never attempted to return to his family or draw on his money."

"He may have died while trying to get home," Kirkland said quietly.

"That's his most likely fate." Simon sighed. "I don't suppose anything could be done with the sighting of the monk in Brussels."

"There isn't enough information. Someone in Brussels with a picture of your cousin might learn something, but at this distance, it's impossible." Kirkland smiled a little. "I was rather tartly informed that the man was unlikely to be a monk. They live cloistered lives of contemplation in sequestered communities. He was more likely a friar. They live and work in the wider world. I don't know if that's much help."

"Lucas always loved the stories about Robin Hood. He was particularly fond of Friar Tuck," Simon said thoughtfully. Seeing Suzanne's furrowed brow, he said, "Robin Hood and his merry men lived in the forest and robbed the rich to help the poor. It's one of England's favorite legends. There might even be a grain of truth in the stories. I'll tell you more about them later." His gaze shifted. "If I go to Brussels, might I be useful to you there?"

"Quite possibly," Kirkland said, looking interested.

"Then I suppose I'll be going to Brussels."

"No, *mon chéri*." Suzanne's green-eyed gaze was direct and implacable. "*We* are going to Brussels."

Chapter 16

❧

Simon's brow furrowed. "I'm reluctant to take you to the Continent when things are so unsettled."

"Brussels is a very long way from Elba," Suzanne said reasonably. "If the Corsican Monster escapes, we'll have plenty of warning. I'd like to visit Brussels. I hear it's become very fashionable since Napoleon abdicated."

Kirkland nodded. "A number of Britons have taken up residence there. Information and rumors swirl through the city."

"And you'd like to hear about such things?" Simon said dryly.

"Of course," Kirkland said, his expression bland.

Suzanne kept her gaze on her husband as she said quietly, "My old home, Château Chambron, is in northern France, not that far from Brussels. I feel a responsibility to visit and see what condition the estate is in. Has it been abandoned? Did a Bonapartist claim it? I should find out. There may be people there who remember me. There might be some who need aid."

Simon gave a nod of understanding. "I'd like to know also. We are both connected to the estate. It's even possible that I'm the new comte. We should visit."

Kirkland said, "I have a house in Brussels that is currently unoccupied except by a handful of my people. They know the city and the country well. You can stay as long as you wish."

Suzanne's brows rose. "Do you have convenient houses staffed with agents in all major cities?"

"Only those that might prove useful to our work," Kirkland said seriously. "Many people on the Continent have risked their lives to bring down the emperor. Sometimes sanctuaries are needed."

Suzanne had a swift mental image of a vast spiderweb of spies and informants across the Continent, all sending information to England. So many threads held in Kirkland's hands. He had quietly worked behind the scenes of great events, as had Simon.

She had merely spent those years as a captive in a luxurious prison. She had a sudden fierce desire to witness great events at firsthand, perhaps even participate in them. She wanted to go beyond personal survival to acting for the greater good.

Yes, they should go to Brussels.

After finalizing arrangements about the Brussels house with Kirkland, Simon and Suzanne returned home. As they drove, Simon said, "I'll have several copies made of the sketch of Lucas when he was in the navy. I can show them to people in Brussels."

Suzanne frowned thoughtfully. "The pictures you have are old. Could you also have a sketch made of what we think he looks like now? Thinner, older, tonsured, wearing a friar's robe?"

"That's a very good idea. I'll have it done."

When they reached their house, they found their new servants had arrived. Simon had met Jenny Dunne briefly at the wedding, and she looked neat and attractive as she bobbed a curtsy. "Madame Duval. Colonel Duval."

"Jenny, it's so lovely to have you back again!" Suzanne said warmly. "I hope your visit home was a happy one."

"It was good to see my family and friends again, ma'am." Jenny's face brightened at Suzanne's welcome. The women were already friendly, and they should work together well. Simon and his proposed new valet were strangers, however, and Edgar Jackson's scarred face looked surly and defensive.

Jenny said with a note of anxiety in her voice, "Colonel Duval, this is my friend Edgar Jackson. As I said, he was a batman to an officer."

Besides savage facial scarring that just missed his eye, Jackson's left arm and hand had been damaged. He looked like a dog who had been kicked too often. This should be interesting. "I'm guessing it was Sergeant Jackson," Simon observed.

"Yes, sir," he said in a voice that gave nothing away.

"I'm sure the ladies have much to talk about. Why don't you come to my study so we can get to know each other," Simon said. "Were you on the Peninsula?"

"Yes, sir. And the Low Countries campaign before that."

Simon led his potential valet to his small office at the back of the house. "Did you pick up any of the languages of the country where you were serving?"

"A bit of Flemish and French, a bit more Spanish."

A clever man, and the languages could prove useful. When they entered the office, Simon gestured to a chair and sat down on another. "Time for a man-to-man talk to see if we'll suit. First of all, what would you prefer to be called? Sergeant? Jackson? Some other name or nickname?"

The other man blinked. "Jackson, sir. What do you prefer?"

Simon considered. "Colonel Duval, I suppose. More important than names is the question of whether you actually want this position with me, or if you're only here to please Miss Dunne. Be honest now. If you don't really want to be a valet, now is the time to say so. If you prefer a different kind of work, perhaps I can help you find a position that will suit you better."

Surprise, wariness, and doubt showed in Jackson's expression. After a long moment, he said, "Permission to speak freely, sir?"

"Of course. Frankness is essential now."

"Your question does not have a simple answer, sir." Jackson frowned, the scar on his face twisting to make him look very dangerous. "Of course I want to please Jenny. She's the best thing in my life. But I'm not sure if I want to be a valet, and I'm pretty sure I can't do all the work." He extended his left hand, which was gnarled with scars. The tips of two fingers were missing. "I haven't the strength to do everything needed, and I haven't the nimbleness in my fingers." He clenched his hand, which couldn't close fully. "Can't shoot, either."

"I would hope shooting will be unnecessary." Simon considered. Jackson was well spoken and had lost the soft West Country accent that his Jenny still had. He was obviously intelligent, which was something Simon preferred in the people around him. He was also angry at the world, which could be a problem.

But he'd served his country and deserved a chance, and the fact that they were both soldiers should help them understand each other. "Most of the duties of a valet should be within your capabilities and another servant could be detailed to help you when necessary. But let's go back to the question of whether you want be a valet. As a batman, did you resent taking orders from men less intelligent than you?"

A succession of expressions flickered over Jackson's face, ending with a hint of amusement. "Yes, I did. But I don't think you'd be one of those."

"Since I worked mostly in military intelligence, I hope that's true," Simon said dryly. "I was never a Hyde Park soldier, nor do I wish to cut a fashionable swath through London society, so I don't need a valet who has secret recipes for boot polish."

"I can polish boots as needed," Jackson said, his amusement fading. "And a man like me needs to work to survive."

Simon studied the other man intently, looking to confirm his intuition about him. Jackson shifted in his chair. "You've got a stare that can flay a man alive." He began clenching his left hand over his right rhythmically.

"I've been told that before. Very useful when commanding troops or when questioning the enemy. Or testing a man's nerves." He glanced at Jackson's hand. "You're practicing with your left hand to help it work better?"

Jackson flushed and dropped his left arm. "Any reason why I shouldn't?"

"No, you're wise. A friend of mine had a similar injury and he worked it the same way you're doing. He wrote recently and said his hand has improved greatly."

"Good to know." Jackson resumed the hand-clenching exercise.

Simon was impressed by the other man's determination since he knew that exercising a damaged limb hurt. "I think that you have a great deal of ability, more than you've had a chance to use. Would you be interested in a position that would be part valet but include other duties? I might eventually hire a private secretary, but I don't need one now. If you're willing, you could try your hand at that kind of work."

Jackson's brows furrowed. "How do you know I can read and write?"

"Am I wrong?"

"No, sir. I learned from another sergeant who was keen to earn an extra bit of money. What would my duties include beyond polishing boots?" Jackson asked, cautiously interested.

"Some correspondence and organizational work. A good batman carries wider responsibilities than caring for clothing and he needs good judgment, so I think you're already well on your way."

"What if I'm not good at the secretarial work? Would you discharge me without a character?"

Simon shook his head. "No, I'd ask if there was something else you'd like to do."

"I thought you just wanted a valet. Why are you giving me a chance to do more?" Jackson sounded as if he needed to understand before he agreed to do something so unexpected. Another sign of his intelligence.

"My grandparents believed in education and set up schools on the family estate," Simon explained. "Good students were given the chance to study further. Their success has benefited them, their families, and the community. One became the physician for the whole area, another opened a shop in the village so people don't have to travel as far to buy what they need. I've found that there are many talented people who could do so much more if given half a chance. So I'm carrying on the family tradition."

"Then I'm glad to agree. I'll do my best for you, sir." Jackson gave a genuine smile. "And I'll make sure your boots are well polished, too!"

Suzanne looked forward to going to bed with Simon, especially since it had been a busy day and they hadn't had much time to talk after returning home from Kirkland's house. When Simon slid in beside her, she rolled over into his arms and gave a sigh of relaxation. "Now the household feels complete. As soon as Jenny told me that she'd been a lady's maid, I knew she'd be perfect. I'm so glad you think Mr. Jackson will suit also. He didn't seem very amiable when we met him."

"He was feeling ill at ease with the world, but he relaxed after we talked. He's clever and disciplined and I think he'll work out well." Simon drew her closer so she could feel his rich warmth the length of her body even through layers of nightclothes. "When I told him we were traveling to Brussels for a time, he hardly blinked."

"Jenny is delighted by the chance to travel to an exotic foreign land as long as Jackson is coming, too." Suzanne sighed. "I wonder how our quests will go. For Lucas, for Chambron."

"At least we can find Chambron since it must be where we left it. Finding Lucas is quite a different matter."

"There can only be so many religious orders in the area. Perhaps your family friend was wrong and it wasn't Lucas he saw. At least we'll have tried."

Simon stroked her neck and back with a warm, lazy hand. "Are you having second thoughts about going to Brussels? You said once there was nothing for you in France, and Belgium is very French even though it's one of the Low Countries."

"Since meeting you, I've become braver about facing the past," she said slowly. "I'm taking small steps to push fear away. Though I don't wish to live in France again, I do want to be able to visit and remember that life without pain. Brussels is a long step toward France. When we're there, I shall become prepared for a visit to Château Chambron."

"Are you willing to take steps toward vanquishing some of your other fears?" Simon cupped her right breast with a gentle hand.

She froze, her pulse spiking. But he did nothing more, and after a few deep breaths, she was able to relax and recognize that his light, warm touch was pleasant. "That's not so bad," she said. "In fact, rather nice."

"May I go a small step further?"

Her instinct was to say no. Instead she drew a deep breath. "A very small step."

He shifted his hand just enough to gently strum her nipple with his thumb. Even through the fabric of her nightgown, a sharp sensation shot to her loins. She gasped and shoved his hand from her breast as she turned rigid.

His hand stilled on her torso. "You hate that kind of touch?"

She rolled onto her back as she struggled to analyze what she felt. "It's . . . complicated. There is some pleasure and that makes me think of Jean-Louis, who was proud of his lovemaking skills even though he had little thought for me as an individual. But there are also memories of agony from Gürkan. The combination of those feelings is—disturbing."

He was quiet for a long moment, not moving. "I don't know what I can do to counter that."

He started to draw away, but she arrested the motion by covering his hand with hers. Her heart fluttered under their joined hands, so she closed her eyes and tried to calm herself. This was Simon, not Jean-Louis, not Gürkan. *Simon.* Whom she'd known half her life and who had never been anything but kind and protective. As she thought of him, she felt her heart slow to normal.

Silently she guided his hand across her torso from one side to the other. Broad palm, strong fingers, gentle as a kitten's breath as his hand smoothed over her nightgown.

She realized that his gliding touch felt good. Sensual. The fact that she controlled where he touched removed the fear.

Guided by her hand, he continued to caress her slowly. Warmth spread through her, moving to her breasts upward and . . . downward toward her loins. She'd almost forgotten how that felt.

Enjoying the sensation, she moved her hand lower so that he was stroking over her waist. She'd recognized when they started to share a bed how much she enjoyed touching, and this was a more intimate form of touching.

She felt like a cat being petted—until she moved his hand lower yet and she realized how close he was to her most private places. She stiffened. "That's far enough. At least for now."

"Agreed," he said in a thickened voice. He moved his hand from under her hands and curved his arm over her, drawing her close.

Realizing how aroused he was, she exclaimed, "I'm so sorry! I wasn't thinking of you, only myself."

"No matter," he said in a warm voice. "It's good that tonight was about you."

"That can change." She separated herself from him enough to allow her hand to move down his torso and under his night wear.

He gasped and hardened fully when she reached her goal. She smiled in the darkness. She loved giving him pleasure and he loved letting her take charge.

It made for a thoroughly satisfactory prelude to a very good night's sleep.

Brussels

Chapter 17

Suzanne woke early in the warm, unfamiliar bed, sliding quietly from the warm, familiar embrace of her husband. They'd arrived in Brussels so late the night before that not much had registered about Kirkland's house other than that it was well kept by the servants and that it was attractive without drawing much attention.

She opened the window and leaned out to breathe deeply of the fresh air. The delicious scent of baking bread came from somewhere nearby. Suzanne inhaled happily.

The morning was mild for mid-March, with hazy sunshine and daffodils blooming in window boxes. Their narrow street was quiet, but a couple of blocks to her left she could see a park that seemed busier.

"Good morning, *ma belle*." Simon joined her at the window, one arm going around her waist to snug her close. "What is it like to be back in Europe in a city that isn't in France, but feels very French?"

Suzanne leaned into him. "It's interesting and not so

overwhelming as London. I look forward to seeing more of Brussels."

"Would you like to spend the day seeing the sights?"

"It's kind of you to suggest that, but I know you want to start the hunt for your cousin," she replied. "We can admire the city while we search."

"You've read my mind," he said with a half smile. "Kirkland gave me the name and address of a monk who can help us sort out the possibilities. I'll send a message to Frère Antoine before we eat breakfast to ask when we might call."

Suzanne assumed that the monk was another of Kirkland's informants. "Sooner rather than later, I hope."

Simon nodded, his eyes showing resignation tinged with hope. As Suzanne rang for Jenny to help her dress, she sent prayers to whatever deity might be listening that Simon would get his miracle.

After a breakfast of feather-light croissants, exquisite raspberry preserves, and rich *café au lait,* Simon and Suzanne set out to find Frère Antoine, who had invited them to call that morning. Kirkland's household included Maurice, a weathered Englishman with a limp who had lived in Brussels for so long that his French had only a trace of English accent. He had no trouble conjuring up a light double-benched carriage and horse from a local livery.

Simon would have driven if he knew the city better, but Maurice knew exactly where Argenté Abbey was, so he sat on the front seat with reins and buggy whip while Simon and Suzanne held hands in the rear seat. Simon suspected Maurice had been a soldier, and that like the other servants in Kirkland's house, he provided information that might be useful to Kirkland.

It was a pleasant day for a drive. Maurice made laconic remarks about buildings of particular interest, while Suzanne enjoyed the busy narrow streets thronging with cheerful merchants and housewives. "Being in a French-speaking city again takes me back to my childhood," she observed.

"Mostly French speaking, though we'll hear Dutch and a fair amount of English, too," Simon said. "There's a British garrison here, and because living costs are lower in Brussels, a good number of Britons have moved here since Napoleon abdicated."

"That makes Brussels a good transition between London and France. I'll soon be ready to visit Château Chambron. It's not far. South of Charleroi, only a few miles beyond the border between France and Belgium."

She said the words lightly, but Simon saw anxiety in her eyes. He asked, "How do you feel about the estate?"

She bit her lip. "It was very grand, but I wasn't particularly happy there. I want to revisit the place so I can put my life at Chambron behind me."

Simon didn't reply, but he took her hand and squeezed it gently. She had come so far already. He hoped that viewing the home of her marriage would allow her to make peace with that part of her past. He wanted her with him in the present.

Argenté Abbey had originally been in the country, but the expanding city had caught up with it. Weathered stone walls enclosed a sizable estate that included gardens and a farm as well as the buildings of the religious community. The gatekeeper looked dubiously at Suzanne but he rang for a porter when Simon assured him that they were both expected.

The porter led them to a small office near the entrance to the main building. The chapel and cloisters would be private to the monks, but even monasteries must have some dealings with the outside world, and that was Abbot Antoine's role at Argenté Abbey. Black robed and with tonsured silver hair, he rose from his desk with a welcoming smile when Simon and Suzanne entered.

"Colonel Duval, Madame Duval, it's a pleasure to meet you. Is my friend Kirkland prospering?"

That explained the warm welcome. "Yes, and he sends his regards," Simon said. "Do you know him well?"

"We've only met once in person, but he has been a good friend to my order." Abbot Antoine gestured to a pair of majestically carved wooden chairs. "Please take a seat. Would you like some of our Benedictine beer? Our house is rather famous for it."

Simon chuckled. "I'd be happy to partake. I've always been fond of Belgian beers. Suzanne?"

She smiled as she sat and adjusted her skirts. "I'd like to sample some also."

Their host opened a cabinet to reveal bottles and drinking vessels. Abbot Antoine poured full-sized mugs for Simon and himself and a smaller one for Suzanne. It was a deliciously tangy drink, and serving it made for a relaxed atmosphere.

"Now, how can I help you?" the abbot asked. "Lord Kirkland said that you are looking for a relative?"

"Yes, my cousin Lucas Mandeville," Simon replied. "He was in the Royal Navy, missing and presumed dead after his ship was sunk some years ago. But recently a friend of the family saw a religious brother here in Brussels who seemed the image of Lucas. I have this picture from his youth, plus a sketch that shows how he might look now. If it was indeed Lucas who was seen."

The abbot studied the pictures. Setting aside the image of the aristocratic younger Lucas, he tapped the other. "This man looks familiar. The brown robe suggests a Franciscan. They are a mendicant order, sworn to poverty. They travel throughout their provinces to do their work, often staying at different religious communities."

"Did this friar ever stay at Argenté Abbey?" Suzanne asked.

"I believe so. I'm trying to remember." The abbot frowned in concentration. "Yes, a brother who looked much like this one stayed here for several nights around the time of the emperor's abdication last year. The city was crowded because of the celebrations and we had many visitors."

"That was the time when our family friend saw him in Brussels," Simon said, his pulse quickening.

"But surely your cousin is English if he served in the Royal Navy? The brother I speak of was French."

"Lucas lived with my family and spent a great deal of time in France, so he speaks French as well as I do," Simon said, trying to control his rising excitement. "Do you remember anything else about him?"

After long thought, the abbot said slowly, "I believe he was called Frère Jude."

Simon's throat tightened. Jude. Judas, the betrayer. If their theory of what had happened to Lucas was true, that might well be the religious name his cousin would choose. "Do you have any idea where Frère Jude might be now?"

The abbot shook his head. "Friars go where they are needed, so he could be anywhere in Belgium or northern France. There were many disruptions of traditional religious communities under the emperor, so I don't know what places are the most likely. I can list some possibilities for you. The closest is a priory outside Namur where some Franciscans stay, I believe. Our Lady of Mercy."

A youthful monk, perhaps a novice, entered the room with a sheaf of papers and an apologetic expression. "Excuse me for interrupting, Father Abbot."

Simon rose. "My apologies for taking so much of your time, Abbot Antoine. You've been most helpful."

The monk smiled warmly as he stood. "It has been my pleasure. Let me know if your search is successful."

"I will," Simon promised as he took Suzanne's arm.

On the short walk back to their carriage, Suzanne said, "Do you think this Frère Jude could be your Lucas?"

"It's certainly promising."

"Namur is in the same direction as Château Chambron," she said. "We can visit the priory there on our way."

He gave her a quick glance. "You're ready for that?"

She drew a deep breath. "As ready as I'll ever be. With luck, we might find Lucas on the way. What will you do if you find him? Try to coax him back to England?"

"I haven't really thought about it," Simon admitted. "I would like that above all things, but if he has a vocation for the religious life, it's not my place to interfere. It will be enough to know that he is alive and well."

And if this Frère Jude wasn't his cousin—well, Simon had dealt with loss often enough in the past. He would survive losing Lucas again.

As they climbed into the carriage, he told Maurice, "Please take us to the Grand Place. I'd like to show it to Madame Duval."

Maurice nodded and set the carriage in motion. Simon said, "The Grand Place is the heart of the old city and it's one of the finest plazas in Europe. The Hôtel de Ville, the city hall, is magnificent."

Suzanne smiled and took his hand. "So we are successfully combining your search with seeing the sights. An excellent start to our stay here."

"Will you be ready to set off to Namur and Chambron tomorrow?" he asked.

She nodded. "I'm as curious as you are."

He smiled at her, thinking how lucky he was that she'd agreed to marry him. They might still face challenges, but together, they were overcoming them one by one.

Suzanne was feeling hopeful on Simon's behalf. She guessed that he was forcing himself not to be optimistic because if the mystery friar wasn't Lucas, the disappointment would be like losing his cousin all over again. So she would be hopeful for both of them.

Simon pointed ahead of them. "We're almost to the Grand Place. See that tall spire ahead of us? That's the town hall, which takes up one whole side of the square. This was a great wealthy trading city for centuries, so guild houses and other buildings on the square are equally splendid."

As their carriage neared the Grand Place, the shouts of a crowd could be heard. Suzanne asked Maurice, "Is the Grand Place always so noisy?"

He frowned. "Only when there's big news, madam."

"Which doesn't necessarily mean good news," Simon added quietly.

When they entered the square, she saw that a raucous crowd was churning in front of the Hôtel de Ville. An official-looking man stood in front of the city hall holding a document and trying to make himself heard over the clamor while members of the crowd were starting to break into smaller groups and talking animatedly.

"Stop here, Maurice," Simon said when he saw the crowd. As soon as the carriage came to a halt, he jumped from the vehicle and walked toward the nearest cluster of gesticulating men. "Sirs, what is the news?"

A young man swung about and called jubilantly, "The emperor is free and he has returned to France to reclaim his throne!"

Chapter 18

❧

Suzanne gasped, feeling as if she'd been struck a physical blow. There had been so much speculation about if and when Napoleon might burst from his captivity, but the announcement was still a paralyzing shock.

More collected, Simon asked, "Are there any details? Has he reached Paris yet?"

"He landed near Cannes on March first. He returned with the violets, as he promised!" the man exclaimed. "He began marching to Paris with a handful of men at his back and he entered the city at the head of an army. All without a single shot being fired. Not one!"

Another man said eagerly, "Regiment after regiment went over to him as soon as they came into his magnificent presence. The great Marshal Ney himself swore to the king that he'd bring Napoleon to Paris in an iron cage, then bowed his head to his master when they met." The man spat at the ground. "The fat king fled the city the night before, the coward. Long live the emperor!"

"Emperor be damned!" a man in a nearby group roared.

"That Corsican bandit has been a plague to all of Europe, bringing death everywhere he set foot. May the devil take his rotten soul!"

One of the Bonapartists shouted back, "Belgium is truly part of France and it is time that we rejoined our brothers!"

"Bedamned to those French scum!" another man bellowed furiously. "We want no part of them! We need to drive out the damned Dutch as well so Belgium can be free and independent, as we deserve!"

The crowd exploded into an angry mob. Shouts and fists and rocks began flying in all directions.

Simon started to retreat but he was engulfed by two different factions. A hurled stone struck his head and he disappeared into the seething mass of struggling men.

Horrified, Suzanne snapped, "Give me the reins, Maurice! Then get my husband out of there!"

Grimly Maurice thrust the reins at her and leaped to the ground. Suzanne climbed awkwardly into the front seat and concentrated on calming the frightened horse.

Despite his limp, Maurice plowed into the crowd. Suzanne caught her breath with relief when he reached the knot of fighting men and hauled her husband to his feet. Simon was unsteady, but with Maurice's support he began moving toward the carriage. Their progress was slow as they dodged around clumps of fighting men.

It had been a long time since Suzanne had driven a carriage, but she hadn't forgotten how. She turned the light vehicle around so they could depart the way they'd come rather than try to cross the rioting plaza.

Her gaze was fixed on Simon and Maurice and she didn't realize that men were approaching on her other side until a powerful male hand grabbed her left ankle. Her head whipped around and she saw that her attacker was a roughly dressed fellow who smelled like he'd been hauled from a vat of beer.

As he dragged her toward him, he grinned with a

mouth full of bad teeth. "What's a pretty lady like you doin' here? Come with me and I'll show you a good time!"

Fight hard and fast! Remembering Simon's words, she slashed at the man with the buggy whip. Startled, he loosened his grip and she was able to jerk her ankle free.

Swearing, he lunged for her again. Furiously she kicked out, her heel catching the side of his throat. He squawked and fell back. When he regained his balance, he came at her again, raging, and this time he was joined by another drunken lout.

Suzanne lashed out with the buggy whip and managed to strike both men. Before she could wield the whip again, Simon tackled her first assailant, knocking him into the second man. Both attackers crashed to the ground. One side of Simon's head was bloody, but that didn't stop him from kicking the first man in the gut and stamping his booted foot on the other man's fingers.

As the men lay gasping on the cobblestones, Simon swung up onto the backseat of the carriage at the same time that Maurice scrambled in front, grabbed the reins and whip from Suzanne, and sent the carriage bolting out of the square. Shaken, Suzanne clung to the front seat's side rail until they were well away from the riot.

When they were out of earshot of the shouting, she said unsteadily, "Maurice, can you stop long enough for me to change seats and see how the colonel is doing?"

"Yes, ma'am." He pulled the carriage to a halt, murmuring encouraging words to the horse for doing such a good job.

As she clambered back to Simon, she asked, "Were you a soldier, Maurice?"

"That I was, ma'am." He looked energized by the altercation.

Before she was even settled in the backseat, Simon

drew her into a protective embrace. "Are you all right, *ma chérie*?"

"I'm fine." She burrowed into his arms, realizing that she was shaking. "I'm not the one who was just whacked on the head with a rock in the middle of a riot!"

He stroked a hand down her back soothingly. "I wasn't seriously hurt. You were targeted by those ruffians just for being female, which is much worse."

Simon understood so well. She closed her eyes and rested her head on his shoulder as she began to relax. "I'm glad you gave me lessons in fighting."

"I just wish you didn't need them so often!" he said ruefully.

"At least it was over quickly." She drew back to study the laceration on the left side of his head. It was several inches long, but shallow and had mostly stopped bleeding. She pulled a handkerchief from her reticule and began blotting the blood from the laceration. "You lost your hat."

"It could have been worse. Let's save our worrying for Napoleon."

She bit her lip at the truth of his words. "Do you think this news will send Brussels up in flames?"

"I don't believe so. This was just the first reaction to shocking news," Simon replied. "Maurice, you've lived here for many years. What do you think?"

The driver shrugged. "Belgium is used to living under different masters. Folks will settle down and wait to see what happens next." He used the buggy whip to indicate people talking earnestly in front of a butcher shop. "The news is spreading, but most people are just talking, not rioting. Those drunken troublemakers in the square just like an excuse to fight."

Suzanne hoped the men were right. "Do you think Napoleon will be able to stay on the throne?"

"For now, at least. It sounds like the whole army has fallen under his spell again," Simon said soberly. "King Louis's support is thin and his government didn't treat the returning soldiers of Napoleon's Grande Armée well. That means at least half the men in France despise the king, and they're experienced soldiers. Life under their emperor again must look like an improvement."

"I wonder if there's any chance that he'll decide it's enough to rule France and stop invading other countries," Suzanne said thoughtfully. "He's older now. Perhaps his ambitions have dimmed."

"Even if Napoleon swears he'll bury his sword and go to war no more, who will believe him?" Simon asked. "I wouldn't. Surely all the Allied leaders are already drawing up declarations of war against France."

Her hand tightened on his as she thought of all the death and devastation the wars had wrought. "Will there ever be an end to it?"

"I surely hope so," he said quietly. "Luckily, the emperor is a long way from Brussels and he's never managed to cross the English Channel, so Britain should be safe. Do you want to return to London now?"

"There will be time for that if Napoleon decides to invade Belgium," Suzanne said, knowing they must complete their search for Lucas and visit Château Chambron before returning to the safety of England. "We have unfinished business. The sooner we leave for Namur and Château Chambron, the better."

He smiled down at her, his expression warm. "Gallant girl. Shall we leave tomorrow as we planned?"

She nodded agreement. "Since this will be a short trip, little packing will be required."

"Maurice, we'll need a travel carriage and a good team of horses," Simon said. "I assume that will not be a problem?"

"Not at all, Colonel."

"Good. Our next stop today will be at the best gun-smith in Brussels," Simon said. "I assume you know who that is?"

Maurice grinned. "Aye, that I do."

"We're arming ourselves?" Suzanne asked.

"I meant to buy you a good, compact lady's pistol in London, but there wasn't time," Simon explained. "The countryside here may be unsettled, so no more delays."

That made sense to Suzanne. She didn't know if she'd be capable of shooting to kill, but carrying a weapon might help banish her fears. She was tired of being afraid.

Maurice's choice of gunsmiths wasn't far. When he pulled up in front of the shop, Simon asked, "Maurice, is it a safe assumption that there is at least one good rifle back at the house? More likely a small but well-chosen armory?"

"Safe indeed, sir," Maurice said with pride.

Leaving him to walk the horse, Suzanne and Simon entered the shop. A guard was posted visibly at the en-trance, and Suzanne understood why when she saw some of the exquisitely crafted firearms on display. The silver inlaid pistols glittered like jewelry. Deadly jewelry.

As soon as the usual pleasantries had been exchanged with the proprietor, Simon said, "We'd like to see your best lady's pocket pistols."

The proprietor glanced at Suzanne. She tried to look cool and dangerous. "Of course, monsieur and madam." He disappeared into the back of the shop for a few minutes and returned with a velvet-lined tray that held several small, sleek pistols. He set it on the counter reverently. "Would madam like to see which best suits her hand?"

Suzanne picked one up rather gingerly. It would cer-tainly be easier to manage than the full-sized pistol Simon had taught her on. She held it in a shooting grip, examined it, then tried another. "They are beautifully made, mon-sieur, but how accurate are they?"

"Quite accurate for weapons of their size, madam. There is a small shooting gallery in the back of this property where you can test your favorites out."

Her brows rose. "How convenient."

After she'd examined and held each, Simon asked, "Which are your favorites?"

She chose two. At his suggestion, she added a third.

Simon told the proprietor, "I'm also interested in a pair of midweight pistols with the emphasis on ease of use rather than decoration."

Larger weapons appeared. After Simon selected two styles, they moved to the shooting range in the back of the house. The walls and ceiling were padded to reduce the amount of noise generated. Suzanne shot first, carefully loading and sighting down the range. They were indeed reasonably accurate for small handguns and she was rather proud of her marksmanship.

She was unsurprised to find that the model Simon had suggested felt best in her hand and seemed the most accurate. It was relatively undecorated, but she liked the simple, businesslike look of it. "This one, Simon."

"A good choice. Monsieur, a pair of these, please." Then it was Simon's turn. As expected, he was much faster at loading and a better shot, even allowing for the fact that the larger pistols were more accurate. Simon ordered a pair. After both sets of weapons were placed in wooden cases and wrapped reverently, they went outside.

Suzanne would be happy never to have a reason to fire her lovely new pistols. But in a very uncertain world, she liked being as prepared as she could be.

The news of Napoleon's return hadn't reached Kirkland's household yet, so Simon gathered all the servants in the drawing room to make the announcement. He watched faces carefully and saw only dismay or stoic jaw tightening at the news. If there were Bonapartists present, they disguised it well. He'd have been surprised to find any in Kirkland's employ.

He dismissed most of the servants to return to their usual business, though he expected they'd be doing a lot of talking among themselves. Jackson he asked to stay.

Looking wary, the valet did so. Simon asked, "How are your left hand and arm coming along?"

Jackson flexed his fingers. "Well, sir. A little stronger and more flexible." A hint of humor showed in his eyes. "Your ordering me to exercise them at least an hour a day has sure helped."

"Good." Simon set the case of new pistols on the table and flipped it open.

Jackson's eyes widened. "Beautiful weapons, sir. Did you just buy them? I haven't seen these in your luggage."

"Brand new." Simon picked one up, liking the balance, and handed it to Jackson. "Would you be able to shoot this? I assume your experience has been with long guns rather than pistols."

"You assume rightly, sir." Jackson accepted the pistol reverently, feeling the balance and examining how it was made. He raised the weapon in his right hand and sighted along it. "It's a beautiful weapon, sir. I could shoot it, but I don't know about loading. I could likely manage, but I'd be slow."

"My wife and I are going to take a journey south for a few days. The news about Bonaparte might make the countryside a little unsettled. Maurice will drive the coach and will have a rifle and pistol holstered by him. Would you be willing to ride in the seat beside him as the guard? I assume that you could shoot an attacker if your weapon is already loaded."

Jackson's eyes lit up. Working with the confidence of a professional soldier, he lifted the pistol, rested the barrel on his clumsy left wrist, then released the safety and pulled the trigger. The hammer struck with a hard click and his grip kept the barrel steady.

Looking pleased, Jackson said, "Yes, I can do that. A rifle'd be more accurate, but this will take down any bandits who get too close."

"Could you pull a loaded shotgun from a carriage holster and fire it?"

"I think so, if the shotgun isn't too heavy. I'd want to practice first." He stroked the pistol that he still held. "But why are you going to so much trouble to use a cripple? Wouldn't it be easier to hire a guard or two?"

"You're an experienced soldier and your training and judgment are valuable. The same is true of Maurice. Also, I trust you." His eyes glinted. "Am I wrong?"

"No, sir!" Jackson's straight gaze was man to man. "You and your lady have given me and Jenny second chances and a better life than we could've dreamed of. I won't let you down."

"I know." Simon smiled. "And since you believe you can use the pistols effectively, they're yours."

Jackson gasped. "Thank you, sir! They are . . . magnificent! I don't know if I can do them justice."

"If you like, I can buy you a membership in a local shooting gallery so you can practice regularly."

Looking a little overwhelmed but grateful, Jackson said, "That would certainly be helpful, sir. 'Tis practice and drill that makes a good soldier."

"Let us hope these pistols never need to be fired in anger," Simon said quietly. "But with the world turning upside down again, it is best to be prepared."

"Aye, Colonel." Jackson's expression was steely. "We will be."

Chapter 19

❧

Napoleon might be gathering his armies to invade the rest of Europe again, but Suzanne felt warm and safe when she flowed into Simon's arms that night. "What a day it has been! Is your head still aching?"

"Only a little." Simon's hand gently kneaded down Suzanne's back. "Madame Maurice gave me some willow bark tea, which helped. I don't think much of the taste, but honey helped."

"Kirkland has assembled quite a competent household here, hasn't he?"

Simon laughed. "I suspect that all of the servants have aided him in the past, and giving them a comfortable house and regular income is a kind of pension to reward them for past service. It also provides Kirkland with a listening post in the Low Countries and a place for friends and guests to stay." Simon's hand caressed lower. "Very efficient."

"Mm . . ." More interested in Simon's closeness than Kirkland's undoubted efficiency, Suzanne rolled onto her back and caught Simon's hand, bringing it to rest over her heart. He gave a small exhalation of contentment. She thought that tonight was a good time to expand their repertoire of touching.

She tentatively moved their joined hands up to rest on her left breast. His hand lay quietly for long moments, but she could feel the quickening of his pulse beating through her flannel nightgown. Very slowly he began massaging her breast. She forced herself to push thoughts of the past away so she could concentrate on this moment and the pleasure of his touch.

He bent his head and kissed her other breast through the soft flannel. She stiffened at the shock of sensation and he stilled. "It's all right," she whispered. "You can . . . continue."

"Thank you," he murmured in return. "Let me know the moment that you've had enough." He returned to kissing her breasts, the warmth of his mouth triggering a spreading warmth downward through her body.

She concentrated on that growing pleasure as it curled sensually into her most secret core. Heat, moisture, the sensations she'd felt as a young bride when her first husband was applying all his considerable amatory skills to showing her how lucky she was to be his wife.

Sensation began crowding out all the memories of the pain and fear she'd suffered in captivity. She sank into present heat and urgency, glorying in rising passion. Refusing to doubt that she was ready, she raised her nightgown to her waist and drew Simon's hand down to rest on the bare flesh of her belly. He sucked in his breath and she felt his fierce reaction throughout his body—and her own.

With exquisite care he slid his hand lower until his palm rested warmly over the soft triangle of dark hair at the juncture of her thighs. Delta of Venus. The poetic name swirled through her mind as her hips began involuntarily pulsing against his hand. He responded by delicately sliding his fingers between her thighs, finding heat and moist welcome.

With a rough breath, she separated her legs to give him better access. He stroked and teased and built rising flames as she throbbed against his hand. When he touched the most exquisitely sensitive spot of all, she began writhing under the sweet pressure.

With a sudden, shocking explosion, she tumbled out of control and her body was consumed with unexpected ecstasy. Her fractured emotions urged that the time had come to complete their marriage.

She tugged at his shoulders, wordlessly shifting him so that he was suspended over her. His breathing ragged, he followed her guidance, positioning himself between her legs, moving forward into her slowly, carefully. . . .

Until his control splintered. With a ragged gasp, he buried himself inside her. His powerful body surrounded her, pinned her against the mattress with his muscular weight as he rocked into her.

Her pleasure vanished under a shocking torrent of panic. Frantically she realized that she wasn't ready for this invasion, that she wanted him *gone!* She wanted to scream and pummel him with her fists, drive him away from her.

But she couldn't. Not Simon, not after all his kindness and patience.

The quickest route to escape was to marshal the erotic and acting skills she'd perfected in the harem. She was a master of false responses, of making a man feel that he was the greatest lover in the history of mankind. She writhed and moaned and used internal muscles to bring Simon to a swift conclusion.

His shuddering groan reverberated through him and she felt the tension flowing from his rigid body. After a long, paralyzed moment, he rolled to his side, freeing her.

She brushed her nightgown down to her knees, desperately relieved.

But when his ragged breathing was back to normal, he rested his hand on her midriff and said quietly, "We've been honest with each other until now, *ma chérie*. Don't change that and lie with your body because you want to please me. Or escape me."

She froze, afraid to speak, afraid of his anger.

Uncannily perceptive, he said, "I'm not angry with you. We went too far, too fast, and you weren't ready for full intercourse. Then you were deeply upset and reacted in the best way you knew to escape from the situation. Am I right?"

She licked her dry lips before replying. "Yes. I'm sorry. Sorry! It was going so well until it *wasn't!*" She wanted to weep but managed to control herself. "You understand more than I do."

He grimaced. "I should have understood sooner and spared you such a bad experience. But I'm interested in the fact that you didn't seem to find intercourse physically painful as you'd feared it would be because of the injuries you suffered. Was there pain that I didn't recognize?"

She caught her breath, startled. There had been none of the agony she'd experienced in her last months in the harem. "You're right! My body must have been quietly healing. I hadn't believed that was possible."

"But it's very good news," Simon said softly.

She shuddered as she remembered the damage inflicted on her by Gürkan. "I'm grateful for the healing, but horribly sorry that I fell off an emotional cliff and took you with me."

"The falling was quite splendid," he said wryly. "It was crashing at the bottom that was the problem. But I would rate tonight as progress even though we must now retreat some distance. Would you agree?"

She remembered the pleasure she'd felt before panic had kicked in. "We most certainly have made progress!" With a catch in her voice, she rolled against him and wrapped her arm tightly around his waist. "Oh, Simon, *mon trésor*! Thank you so much for your patience. Your kindness and your wisdom."

He laughed a little. "I'm not sure I'm anyone's treasure, but I'm pleased if you think so." His voice softened to a whisper. "And I thank you for your courage and honesty, *ma belle*. We are traveling a far more turbulent road than what we expected when we agreed to wed, but isn't it also a rewarding road?"

She realized there was a note of uncertainty in his voice. Dealing with her fears couldn't be easy for him even though he was doing a magnificent job of it. "Our way forward is indeed turbulent and rewarding." She laughed suddenly. "I have hopes that when we reach the end of this road, we will be boringly normal!"

Chapter 20

⟐

The journey from Brussels to the priory outside Namur passed without incident, which Simon suspected was a disappointment to Jackson. Being trusted as a guard had been a boost to his self-confidence.

The priory of Our Lady of Mercy was smaller than Argenté Abbey, but it was pleasantly placed on a hill west of Namur. Well-kept fields surrounded the walled precinct, and robed monks were starting the spring planting.

The gate guard admitted them readily enough, but they had a long wait in a chilly reception room before the prior emerged to greet them and learn their business. After a terse greeting from the obviously busy cleric, Simon introduced himself and Suzanne and explained their mission before showing the sketches of Lucas.

The prior looked at the pictures and frowned. "I'll have the infirmarer summoned. He might be able to help you. Now if you'll excuse me, Madame and Monsieur Duval, my duties call." On the way out of the reception room, he ordered a young servant to bring the infirmarer, then disappeared.

"Apparently Kirkland's helpful influence doesn't extend this far," Suzanne commented.

That surprised a chuckle from Simon. "Even Kirkland has limits." His brief levity faded. "I wonder if sending for the infirmarer means that Lucas has been ill here. Or perhaps . . . died and is buried here."

"Or maybe he's the infirmarer," Suzanne said calmly. "We'll find out soon enough."

He knew she was right, but it was impossible not to worry. The chance that Lucas was alive was too tantalizing a hope to release. And if he was alive, there was reason to worry about him.

The short, plump, elderly infirmarer walked with a cane and he certainly wasn't Lucas, but he greeted them affably when he entered the reception room. "Good day, Monsieur and Madame Duval. I'm Frère Pascal. How may I help you?" His observant gaze moved from Simon to Suzanne. "Are either of you unwell? I'm not a physician, but I have herbal remedies that may be of aid."

"We're well, but we're seeking information about my long lost cousin and your prior thought you might be able to help us." Simon produced his pictures. "A possible Franciscan friar who looks very like him was seen in Brussels last year. Do you recognize this man?"

Pascal settled creakily on a wooden bench under the window and studied the pictures. "Why, I believe this is Frère Jude!" His gaze lingered on the image of the young Lucas. "He was a fashionable lad! Is that a naval uniform?"

"Yes, his ship was lost in battle and Lucas has been presumed dead for years." Frère Pascal's interested gaze led Simon to add wistfully, "If Frère Jude is Lucas, it's a mystery why he would allow his family to believe him dead, so perhaps this isn't my cousin."

"That I cannot say, but Frère Jude is certainly the image of your cousin." The monk studied the pictures again. "Though not so happy looking."

"The years tend to weigh us down more heavily as we grow older," Suzanne observed. "Has Frère Jude been a patient of yours here at the priory?"

"Not a patient at all," Frère Pascal said reassuringly. "The lad is a bonesetter and he visits the priory every few months to offer his skills to anyone in need of them."

"A bonesetter!" Simon exclaimed. "That's . . . unexpected."

"Perhaps, but he's very good." Frère Pascal patted his gnarled oak cane. "I'd be bedridden if not for his skills. I give thanks to God and Frère Jude that I can get around as well as I do."

Simon supposed that anything Lucas set out to do, he'd do well. But his being a bonesetter was still surprising. Most practitioners learned the trade as apprentices to skilled bonesetters. Often the skills were passed down through families for generations. "You say that Frère Jude visits regularly. Do you know where he is now?"

Frère Pascal shook his head. "He travels around the whole of his Franciscan province, going wherever he feels he might be needed. It's fair to say that he'll probably be here within the next three or four months, but as to exactly when, or where he is now . . ." The monk shrugged philosophically. "Only God in his wisdom knows for sure."

"Do you know other places he visits regularly?" Simon asked.

"He has occasionally mentioned places he has worked, but it's not a regular schedule. He doesn't always stay in religious communities. He's equally likely to travel to a remote village and stay with locals until his work is done."

"Frère Jude sounds like a true servant of God," Suzanne said quietly.

"Oh, he is, he surely his. He has gifted, healing hands." Pascal smiled a little bashfully. "I have felt blessed by them when he has treated me."

"Lucas was always kind and compassionate." Which was true, but could the cousin Simon had thought he'd known so well have been a born healer? "I do wish I could find Frère Jude to discover whether they are one and the same man!"

"I can make a list of places he's been known to visit," Pascal offered. "Though I don't know if it would be a great deal of help."

"That would be a start." Simon reached inside his coat and produced a piece of folded blank paper and a short pencil. "Would it be useful if I sketched a simple map of southern Belgium and northern France?"

The monk blinked in surprise. "It might, though I'm not familiar with some of these places. They are only names to me."

"It's worth trying," Suzanne said.

The reception room contained a small table as well as a bench and several plain wooden chairs. Simon sat down and did a swift sketch of the area, filling most of the piece of paper with the outlines of the country before adding in Brussels and the larger towns and a swath of northern France.

Seeing Suzanne's raised brows, he said, "I was an exploring officer, you know. Maps were a large part of my work."

She smiled. "You're a man of parts, *mon chéri*."

After half an hour's discussion with Frère Pascal, Simon had a map of possibilities. He didn't know if they would be useful, but at least he felt that he was doing something.

Before taking their leave of Frère Pascal, Simon asked

about inns between Namur and Charleroi. The monk gave the name of one that wasn't far, and promised to give Frère Jude a message from Simon if the bonesetter friar appeared at the priory.

When they were back in their carriage and heading south, Suzanne said, "Progress is being made."

"I hope so. But I could spend a great deal of time chasing around this part of the world without success." Simon sighed. "It occurs to me that if Frère Jude really is Lucas and he hears that I'm looking for him, he might choose to avoid me for the same reasons that he has never communicated with his family."

"You might be right. There is no way to be sure," Suzanne said. "But you have a plan of action now, and the area Frère Jude travels through is not enormous. It's worth investing several months in the search." She smiled a little. "At the least, we'll see a selection of peaceful farms and fields and eat many fine country meals."

He laughed and took her hand. "You're right, milady. Now we'll find that inn and dine on good country cooking, and we can start speculating about what we'll find at Château Chambron."

"It will be my turn to be nervous," Suzanne said wryly. "But my quest is simpler than yours, I think."

"What do you expect to find at the château?" he asked.

"I don't really know." She frowned. "I assume people are living there. Perhaps a powerful Bonapartist official has appropriated it. The property is beautiful and valuable."

"What would you like to find?"

Her answer was slow in coming. "I would hope the occupants are people who will love the place and be happy there. Happier than I was."

"Would you have a claim on the property since you're the widow of who might have been the last legitimate owner?"

"Jean-Louis was not a man to explain legal issues to a mere female," she said dryly. "But my guess is that the property would go to the nearest surviving male relative, along with the title. Quite possibly you."

"I sincerely hope not! I have enough responsibilities in England." He squeezed her hand. "But at least curiosity will be satisfied by tomorrow night."

She smiled back at him. "Yes, and I'll be able to relegate the château to the distant and unlamented past."

Simon hoped that was the case. But the past could be a Pandora's box, with unexpected complications like this hunt for his cousin, who may or may not be alive.

Never mind. Tonight, a good dinner and a good night's sleep with his warm and winsome wife awaited him.

Suzanne was pleased with both the country inn dinner and a quiet night sleeping in Simon's arms. She hoped that in a few days she would recover from the panic she'd felt the night before. Soon, she hoped, she'd be ready to try again.

The next day's journey was about thirty miles, the same length as the day before. She held tightly to Simon's hand as Maurice drove them along an unkempt road leading into Château Chambron. "We're barely in France, I see. I never realized how close the estate is to the border with Belgium. Jean-Louis was very focused on Paris and on being French. He considered French-speaking Belgians to be second-class Frenchmen. I'm not sure if he ever visited Brussels."

"Did he own any other properties besides the château?"

"There was a rather grand house in Paris, but I believe that was rented. Long gone now, I'm sure."

She gazed out at the drive that led up to the château. It was lined with tall elms that met above the track like a forest tunnel. "This drive was better kept when I lived here. I suspect that the estate has seen better days."

A herd of small deer bolted across the road and disappeared into the woods on the other side. She remembered those deer. From the size of the herd, they had prospered.

The carriage emerged from the tree-lined entrance road and for the first time she saw the château. She gasped with shock. "Dear God!"

The once magnificent palace was a burned-out wreck, the roof collapsed and the stone blackened with rain-washed soot. "I wonder what happened here?" Simon asked calmly, his clasp comforting on her icy fingers. "And when it happened. Not too recently, I think."

The splendid formal gardens in front of the château were wildly overgrown. She'd loved the château's many gardens; they'd been her favorite part of the estate. Her mouth dry, she said, "The left wing wasn't too badly damaged. Someone could live there."

"Perhaps." Maurice pulled the carriage to a halt in the semicircular drive in front of the ruined front entrance. Simon climbed out, flipping down the step and helping Suzanne down. She took his arm and they walked along the overgrown path that led toward the left wing.

The heavy door that opened into the wing suddenly swung open and a young man stepped out, a rifle in his hands. His clothing was ragged and his furious eyes were wild. "Leave immediately if you value your lives!"

They stopped and Simon moved his hand to Suzanne's waist so he could shove her out of the way if this madman decided to shoot. "We have no desire to hurt you," he said mildly. "May I ask who you are?"

"I'm Philippe Duval, the Comte de Chambron," the young man snarled. "This place is mine, and trespassers will be *shot*!"

Chapter 21

❧

Suzanne caught her breath, stunned, as the hard metallic snap of firearms being cocked sounded behind her. Jackson and Maurice were training their guns on the young man, and Maurice barked, "Stand down!"

For a terrifying moment, violence thickened the air, ready to erupt into blood. Then a thin young woman darted out the door. Her pale blond hair fell over her shoulders and her gaze was frantic. "No, Philippe!"

She lunged at the rifle and dragged the barrel down, sunlight glinting on her wedding band. His weapon fired and the sting of black powder filled the air, but the bullet lodged harmlessly in the ground.

"I'm sorry, my love, I can do no more," Philippe said in a raw whisper as he sagged against his wife, on the verge of collapse.

Ordering her heart to slow down, Suzanne studied the young man's face. He appeared ill and half crazed, but his dark hair and chiseled features proclaimed that he might well be blood kin to Simon and Jean-Louis.

Deciding that the women should take over, Suzanne said in her most soothing voice, "There is no reason for violence, Monsieur le Comte. We are mere visitors and likely relatives of yours."

The young man's hand jerked on the rifle, though he didn't seem to have the strength to lift it. "You won't have Château Chambron!"

"We don't want it." Suzanne made a calming hand gesture toward Simon and the men on the carriage and walked toward Philippe and the young woman. "I am Suzanne, and it's a pleasure to meet you."

Philippe looked baffled but automatically clasped her proffered hand. His own hand was burning hot, and this close Suzanne could see the signs of a dangerous fever. Speaking to the young woman, she said, "You are Madame le Comtesse de Chambron?"

"I don't know." She brushed her hair back wearily. Her face was lovely but gaunt, and her clothing was just short of rags. "Perhaps. I am Marie Duval." Her French had a touch of German inflection.

"Your husband is unwell. Surely he should be lying down? I swear that neither of you are in any danger from us."

"I protect what is mine!" Philippe said in a barely audible rasp, weaving in his tracks.

"Marie and I will help you inside where you can get some rest," Suzanne said firmly. "You must preserve your strength in case a real enemy approaches." Quietly she removed the rifle from his slack grip and handed it to Simon.

"Yes," he said dazedly. "Yes, I must be strong."

With Suzanne on one side and Marie on the other, Philippe allowed himself to be guided back into the damaged remnants of the palace.

Suzanne remembered this west wing reception room as gracious and well furnished, but she wouldn't have recognized this wrecked entryway as the same place. The grand furniture, paintings, and carpets were long gone, and the only furnishings were a couple of battered chairs and a table that might have been salvaged from the servants' quarters.

A wide, crude pallet had been laid out by the fireplace, which contained only ashes from a fire that must have kept the young couple from freezing during the chilly spring nights. With the fire burned out, the room was cold and darkly clammy.

Marie was awkward as she helped Suzanne lay her husband on the pallet. Suzanne winced when the stretch of the other woman's worn gown revealed that she was well into pregnancy. These poor children! Marie couldn't be much more than eighteen or nineteen, and her husband was only a couple of years older.

Suzanne felt Philippe's forehead. It was scorching. Guessing that chills would follow soon, she pulled the ragged covers over him. "How long has he had this fever?"

"Two or three days. I think it comes from worry and exhaustion, or I'd have it, too." Marie's voice was a whisper. "I can do nothing to help but sponge him off with cool water when the fever burns worst."

Bemused, Simon had quietly followed them inside, willing to let Suzanne take the lead. He leaned the discharged rifle against the wall, then offered Marie his arm in a courtly gesture. "Madam?" After leading her to the nearest chair, he asked, "Are you only recently arrived here? It doesn't appear that you've had time to settle in."

"You are most tactful," Marie said with a weary wisdom beyond her years. "We've been here only about a fortnight after walking halfway across Europe. Philippe was sure that when we arrived, we'd find the home he has been yearning for. Instead, *this*." Her gesture included the abandoned, devastated château.

Simon leaned against the table, his arms crossed unthreateningly, while Suzanne took the other chair. "I'm familiar with the Duval family," Suzanne said with massive understatement. "Where does Philippe fall on the family tree?"

"He's the son of the last comte to live here before the wars drove him out. Jean-Louis Duval."

What? Concealing her shock, Suzanne said, "I knew Jean-Louis well. He had a wife, but no children."

"Philippe never met his father's very grand second wife. His father said that the woman was a shrew and he didn't want his only son to be persecuted by her."

"How . . . protective of Jean-Louis," Suzanne said in a somewhat choked voice. "Who was Philippe's mother?"

"She was the daughter of a farmer, so beautiful that the young comte fell instantly in love with her." Marie smiled fondly at her husband. "You see how very beautiful Philippe is. But his mother died in childbed, and the comte was so heartbroken that he couldn't bear to have his son in his house because he looked so much like his mother."

"How was he raised?"

"His father took him to his mother's family. They loved him and cared for him well, so the comte only visited his son occasionally. He gave Philippe his gold ring engraved with the Chambron arms and encouraged him to learn farming so that someday he would be able to manage the full estate of Château Chambron."

"Then the wars began and everyone's plans shattered," Suzanne said. "Jean-Louis left with the second wife and died before he could return."

"Years later Philippe learned that his father and the wife had died on shipboard during a corsair attack." Marie sighed. "Philippe wanted to return here to claim his inheritance, but he was an officer in the Grande Armée and he wasn't free to come back until after the emperor abdicated."

Suzanne's startled glance flicked to Simon, whose expression reflected her own shock. So the self-proclaimed new comte was a Bonapartist. Wonderful.

Suzanne felt a sudden desire to giggle. How Jean-Louis would have hated the very idea! Simon didn't look enthralled either, but he was unlikely to hold Napoleon against a young couple in such distress. At least, she hoped he wouldn't.

"Outside, you said you might be relatives," Marie said. "How are you connected to Philippe?"

"I'm a Duval by marriage, like you. My husband is a second cousin to the late Comte de Chambron, so he's also a cousin to Philippe." A second cousin once removed? Suzanne would work that out later. "Do you have any means of support? Can the family who raised Philippe take you in?"

"We did go there, but strangers are living in the house and they drove us off. We came here because there was nowhere else to go." Marie smiled wryly. "I found some root vegetables in the old gardens and Philippe was able to snare some rabbits before he fell ill. I don't know how . . ." She stopped speaking, her expression bleak as she pressed her hand to the curve of her belly.

Deciding it was time to reveal who she was, Suzanne said, "I am doubly a Duval by marriage because I was Jean-Louis's wife. The grand one, though I didn't feel very grand."

When Marie shrank back as if Suzanne were a poisonous viper, Simon said reassuringly, "Her shrewishness was much exaggerated. I find her remarkably good tempered."

Not looking convinced, Marie asked, "Is this château your home?"

"Not anymore. I was very young when I married Jean-Louis and I knew nothing of his legal affairs. I have no idea who the heir is. That's for the lawyers to decide." She leaned forward and took Marie's hand in both of hers. "What I do know is that we are kin and you need proper food and a proper house and Philippe needs medical care. Our home is in England, but we have been recently visiting in Brussels. You must come and stay with us until your husband is well and the situation is sorted out."

A small sound came from Simon. Suzanne turned and gave him a look that dared him to disagree with her. He gave a short nod of acceptance.

Suzanne rose. "It's too late in the day to make the whole trip to Brussels, but we can stay at an inn tonight and get some proper food into you."

Marie bit her lip as she looked at her husband. "Travel will be hard on him."

"Staying here will be even harder." Suzanne glanced at Simon. "We can manage in the coach, can't we?"

"I'll ride outside," he said. "We can lay a shutter across the inside seats to create a platform long enough for Philippe to lie on. You and Marie can sit on the other ends of the seats and make sure that he isn't jostled off on a rough road."

"That should work," Suzanne agreed. "Marie, what possessions do you want to take with you?"

Marie was too exhausted to protest being carried off by near strangers. "We have very little." She stood and pulled a canvas bag from a pile of neatly folded garments. It took only moments to add their pathetically few belongings. As she tucked a stained, folded shirt on top, she said, "The most valuable thing we own is Philippe's rifle."

"I'll take charge of that," Simon said. "I think you'll understand that I prefer to keep it out of his reach until he's in his right mind again."

Marie nodded and looked around to see if there was anything else to take with her. Despite the couple's acute poverty, Marie was well spoken and seemed gently bred. Suzanne asked, "Are you French? You have a slight accent I'm not familiar with."

"I'm from Lorraine, where there is much influence from Germany, but we are still French." She cocked her head curiously. "And you? You seem entirely French, but you said that you and your husband live in England?"

"I am French and he is half French and half English. He is equally at home in both countries." Better not to mention that he was an officer in the British army until some later date.

Simon stepped outside and called Jackson in. Together they wrenched a battered shutter about the right size from a window and laid it across the left side of the coach. They padded the top by folding the young couple's pallet in half and laying it over the shutter.

Then they wrapped Philippe in the remaining blankets and carried him to the carriage. He was unconscious of being moved and his breathing was labored. Marie sat on the forward seat and held his hand—the hand that bore the Chambron signet ring.

Suzanne sat opposite on the rear seat, ready to help hold Philippe on his makeshift bed if the carriage lurched badly. She silently prayed that they'd get this young couple to civilization in time.

They set off with Simon sharing the outside driver's seat with Maurice and Jackson. It was a tight fit but manageable. Maurice set the horses at a slow pace to minimize jostling of the sick passenger.

Marie was almost as exhausted as her husband. By the

time they reached the main road, she was folded over, dozing with her head on her husband's shoulder, still holding his hand.

Suzanne wondered how all this would work out, but one thing was certain. They couldn't leave these young people to die alone in a ruined palace.

Chapter 22

⫻

They found a clean country inn only a few miles up the Brussels road. Madame Moreau, the grandmotherly landlady, clucked over the condition of Philippe and Marie and called for her grown children to get the young couple settled in a ground-floor room.

Experienced with nursing sick people, Madame Moreau managed to get willow bark tea down Philippe, then warm beef broth and a sleeping draft so he could rest. For Marie, she provided a hip bath, hot water, and a worn but clean shift to sleep in. Marie almost whimpered with happiness. After eating two bowls of hot, nourishing soup, Marie was sleeping as soundly as her husband on the cot that had been brought in. Suzanne was grateful to let Madame Moreau take over the nursing care.

Because the inn was small and everyone ate in the common room, she and Simon weren't alone together until they withdrew to their small bedchamber. She watched him a little warily, uncertain how he felt about the day's events. As Simon unfastened the laces at the back of her gown, he said with dry amusement, "I didn't expect that you'd clutch a pair of Bonapartist asps to your bosom."

She smiled ruefully as he helped peel the gown off, his hands warm on her shoulders. "I didn't expect it, either. But they're kin and they're in dire straits."

He folded her gown over the foot of the bed and went to work unlacing her stays. "True enough about the dire straits," he admitted, before pressing a kiss on the side of her neck that sent tingles to Suzanne's toes. There were advantages to not having her lady's maid with her.

As he finished with her stays, he asked, "Do you believe he is Jean-Louis's son?"

Suzanne inhaled deeply, glad to be down to her loose shift. Turning to Simon, she replied, "He certainly looks like a Duval. Jean-Louis was in his thirties when we married. He could have sired any number of children by then."

Simon removed his coat and cravat, revealing his broad shoulders so that he looked pleasingly informal. "You're right about the Duval resemblance. The bigger question is whether Philippe is legitimate."

"That's much less likely. The story Philippe told Marie about Jean-Louis having been smitten by love for a beautiful farm girl . . . ?" Suzanne began braiding her hair. "Perhaps, but smitten by lust is much more likely. I'm sure Jean-Louis would never have stooped to marrying a girl so far beneath him. I never heard a hint of rumor that he might have had a first wife."

Simon stripped down to his loose shirt and drawers, then pulled the covers down so they could retire. The bed was not large, so they would have to sleep close. He was fine with that. "Might he have arranged a false marriage ceremony to get a beautiful girl to lie with him?"

Suzanne frowned as she slid into the bed. "I wish I could say that he wouldn't, but I can't. Marie's story sounds like the kind of lies aristocrats use to seduce pretty girls, and then cover up the existence of illegitimate children. But I'm sure Marie believes the tale, and I suspect that Philippe does, too. He has a gold Chambron signet ring that she said came from his father."

"Jean-Louis might have had a drawer full of rings to give out," Simon said cynically.

"Quite possibly." Suzanne gave a sigh of relaxation as Simon drew her over to him. "Even if Philippe is legitimate, it might be difficult to prove. There has been too much chaos in France, and the château is a charred ruin along with any records that might have been stored there."

"Do we want to allow him to succeed in his claim to be the latest Comte de Chambron? The house may be a ruin, but the lands are extensive and valuable. You have a claim on a widow's jointure at the least."

Suzanne said firmly, "I imagine you're right, but proving my claim sounds time consuming and difficult. It's much easier if I just let you support me in comfort."

He laughed. "I'm happy to do so. You haven't been very expensive so far. Don't you have any desire to claim what you're entitled to?"

"Depending on what Napoleon does, there might not be anything to claim," she pointed out. "What about you, milord? There's a good chance that you're the nearest legitimate heir. Don't you want to claim *your* rights?"

"Not really. I thought about it this afternoon as we were driving here. I have enough responsibilities in England, and sufficient income as well. I would be inclined to allow Philippe to have the title and estate. Since he was raised on a farm and schooled in agriculture, he's probably better prepared to manage the lands than I would be."

"The title and the property may be separate issues," she said thoughtfully. "If the estate isn't entailed to the next comte, Jean-Louis could have chosen to leave it to his illegitimate son. Perhaps Philippe will have the estate while you become the next Comte de Chambron?"

"Perhaps, though it doesn't seem very important just now," Simon observed. "Did Jean-Louis have a lawyer who might have his will and other legal documents?"

"Yes," Suzanne said. "I met Monsieur Morel once and signed papers when he told me to. He lived near Paris and had an office with a number of hardworking clerks. He might still be there. He seemed like the sort of man who could survive all the political changes of the last years."

"Maybe we can look him up later, when and if the world calms down again." Simon stroked his hand down her side, sending curls of warmth through her. "But for now, are you interested in testing more boundaries?" His hand slid around her waist and down, coming to rest quietly with his palm on the juncture of her thighs. She felt the warmth through the soft linen of her shift.

She sucked in her breath, tense from what had happened before, when pleasure had turned to panic. But the pleasure had been real, and she dearly wanted to overcome the panic.

After a quiet moment of steeling herself to go forward, she moved her hand down his torso and discovered that he was certainly interested in what might happen. When she clasped him, it was his turn to catch his breath. She smiled into the darkness, pleased at how he reacted to her. "Perhaps we should start here to render you . . . less interested? Then we could explore those boundaries again. More carefully this time."

He laughed and bent for a kiss, his mouth warm and provocative. "You are a brave woman to keep trying. And I am a very grateful man!"

She laughed with him, then focused on driving him a little mad. With her harem skills she could have finished him quickly, but she chose to tease and caress slowly, and she found that the intensity of his pleasure created a surprising echo in her. As his breathing quickened, so did hers. As his heat and pulse rate increased, so did hers, and lingering fears dissolved into the richness of *now.*

"Suzanne . . . ," he gasped when he culminated, crushing her to his convulsing body. *"Mon ange . . ."*

She clung to him, shaking and aroused. When he raised her shift and touched her with exquisite skill, it was swiftly her turn to convulse. She bit his shoulder to keep from crying out, for this time she felt only pleasure. *Simon, Simon . . .*

"Mon trésor," she murmured when she could speak again. Safe in his arms, she drifted into sleep, thinking that someday soon, panic would be no more than a sad, distant memory and they could lie together with boring normality.

No. Sharing a bed with Simon would never be boring.

The next morning dawned sunny and pleasant. Wordlessly they indulged themselves by lingering in bed for extra minutes, just holding each other as golden bands of sunlight slowly moved across the bed.

Eventually Suzanne sighed and rolled out of Simon's arms with a fleeting caress for his whiskery jaw. "I do so like waking up with you."

He propped himself on one elbow and smiled at her, thinking how lovely she was with tousled morning hair and fewer shadows in her green eyes. "The feeling is mutual, *ma chérie.*" He stretched and swung from the bed. "Now we begin what might be a complicated day."

He did a quick shave as she brushed out her shining dark hair. Thick and luxuriant and with hints of auburn, her hair was always a mesmerizing sight. He was lucky he didn't cut himself with his razor.

After they dressed and descended to the ground floor, they made their way to the bedroom at the back of the house shared by the younger Duvals. Simon tapped on the door. A couple of minutes passed before Madame Moreau emerged carrying a tray with empty mugs.

"How is Philippe?" Suzanne asked.

"The crisis has passed but he is still very ill, very weak," the landlady replied. "He will not be able to travel for several days."

"Would a physician help?"

"A physician couldn't do more than I've done." She sniffed. "And there is none nearby I'd trust with my dog, much less a person!"

Simon smiled, liking her plain speaking. "What about Madame Duval?"

"With warmth and food and a good night's sleep, she is better, but fragile. Very worried for her husband, of course, plus there is her condition."

"So they need several days of rest before traveling to Brussels," Suzanne said.

"That is what I recommend," the landlady said. "Now I must go and see how my kitchen is managing."

"Thank you for all you're doing," Simon said. But he was not enthralled by her recommendation.

The kitchen seemed to be managing well even without the mistress. Simon and Suzanne settled at a small table by a window and were served well-flavored sausage, sweet pastries, and strong hot coffee. After a bite of the sausage, Suzanne remarked, "You look like you're tempted to abandon our cousins here to their own devices."

Simon smiled ruefully. "Am I that obvious? Of course we can't leave our newfound relatives ill and alone. Even when they're recovered, they're going to need help to establish themselves."

"Help and money," Suzanne said.

He shrugged. "I can provide both."

"You're very generous."

"As you said, they are kin, and in dire need." Simon smiled dryly. "Isn't that what families are for?"

Suzanne bit into a flaky pastry. "Yes, but you hate sitting around here doing nothing when you might be searching for Lucas, yes?"

She was learning to understand him very well. "We've already established that we can't just walk away," he responded.

"Not permanently, but perhaps we can ride away for a few days," she said. "We should be able to hire a couple of decent horses here in the village and travel to some of the other places on the list Frère Pascal gave us. Maurice and Jackson can return to Brussels and come back with a vehicle better suited to carrying Philippe to Brussels, and visit with their ladies as well."

Simon's mood brightened. "That's an excellent idea. Waiting around here for several days would drive me mad." He swallowed the last of his coffee and stood. "I'll speak with Maurice and Jackson."

Suzanne washed down the last bite of her pastry with the rest of her coffee. "And I'll talk to Madame Moreau and Marie. I'm sure that madam will know who might have horses to hire. With luck, we'll be on our way by midday!"

Suzanne found the landlady in the kitchen eating her own breakfast. Suzanne explained what they'd like to do, adding that they'd leave enough money to cover costs for the young Duvals for a week's worth of bed, board, and nursing treatment.

Madame Moreau nodded. "It will be better if you go off rather than having that military-looking husband of yours prowling about restlessly and alarming my other guests. Horses are easy— my husband and I own a farm and he has riding horses that should do." She frowned at Suzanne. "Or at least they'll do if you're a good rider. They aren't mounts trained for fashionable ladies."

Suzanne smiled. "I am not a fashionable lady rider, so I should be able to manage. If I can't buy or borrow a riding habit, I'll ride astride."

Madame Moreau clucked disapprovingly. "That wouldn't be proper for a lady, which you are even if you don't admit it. We have a sidesaddle and my oldest daughter has a habit that would fit you, though she made it herself and it's very plain."

"Plain is preferred in these unsettled times. If she's willing to let me borrow the habit, I'll be very grateful."

She and the landlady exchanged a rueful glance about the unsettled times before Madame Moreau finished her coffee and got to her feet. "I'll find a boy to guide you and your husband to the farm. It's not far."

"And I'll talk to Marie to tell her what we have in mind. I hope she won't feel abandoned if we go off." Suzanne resignedly recognized that if Marie was very upset, Suzanne would have to stay at the inn when she'd much rather ride with Simon.

Hoping for the best, Suzanne quietly entered the sickroom to find Marie. Philippe slept sitting up against a pile of pillows to help his breathing, though it was still labored. But his color had improved from the day before.

Marie sat on a chair by the bed, her worried gaze trained on her husband. Suzanne beckoned her out to the corridor so their talk wouldn't wake Philippe. "You look better today," she said approvingly.

"Warmth and good food make a great difference," Marie said with a smile. "I don't know how to thank you."

Suzanne squeezed her hand. "No need for thanks. You are family. Are you comfortable here at the inn?"

"Oh, yes! Madame Moreau reminds me of my grandmother," Marie replied. "She is so kind and did much for Philippe. She is as good as any physician."

"Would you be comfortable staying here while my husband and I leave for two or three days to continue the journey that brought us to Château Chambron? He is seeking a man who is very dear to him," Suzanne explained. "Our servants will go to Brussels and return with a carriage that can carry Philippe in more comfort. But truly, we will return. We are not abandoning you!"

Looking worried, Marie said, "Have we become too great a burden for you?"

"Not at all." Suzanne paused a moment, struck by a new thought. "Heavens, Philippe is my stepson! That makes you my daughter-in-law." She eyed Marie's expanding middle. "And this is my first grandchild on the way. I must think of myself in a new way. Perhaps I should begin to wear a cap like the elder ladies do."

Marie laughed, as Suzanne had hoped she would. "You, a grandmother! I cannot imagine that." Her voice softened. "But you have been as a mother to us."

"Then I shall give you a bit of motherly advice. Ask Madame Moreau if she needs any mending done. Having busy hands will give you less time to worry."

"I'll do that," Marie said meekly. "I want to be useful, not a burden. But I don't know how we'll ever be able to repay you and your husband."

"No need to worry about that now. You are family, after all." She was happy to be related to Marie, and no doubt she'd become fond of Philippe when he wasn't waving a rifle around. "Now I'll find my husband and we'll look into hiring horses, but I'll come to say good-bye before we leave. We won't be gone long."

Marie gave Suzanne a swift hug. "I hope you and monsieur find the man you are seeking."

So did Suzanne.

Chapter 23

~∞~

The boy assigned to guide Simon and Suzanne turned out to be a Moreau grandson about ten years old. He chattered cheerfully as he led the way down a lane to the family farm. Apparently most of the meat and vegetables and dairy served at the inn were grown there, and his mother was the best cook in the world.

As the grandson skipped ahead of them, Simon took Suzanne's hand and they strolled along the lane enjoying the birdsongs and vigorous spring greenery. Suzanne remarked, "There seem to be more and more people in our lives, so riding across country with only you sounds very appealing." She glanced up at him through her dark lashes. "Positively romantic."

He loved that she felt that way, but he was having second thoughts. "With France so unsettled and disturbing all her neighbors, it might be dangerous for the two of us traveling alone."

"But you were an army exploring officer, yes? You

must have spent much time in Spain riding alone through hostile territory, and here you are, alive and well," she pointed out.

"I relied on my uniform and a fast horse to keep me out of trouble, but I'm wondering if it's wise to take you."

"You'd rather sleep alone with your horse?" she teased. "Travel always brings some risks, but this country is quiet and we will have good horses and weapons. Shouldn't that be enough?"

"Probably," he admitted. "But being a husband makes me feel very protective."

"Protectiveness is a fine trait in a husband." Her smile was angelic. "I have complete faith in your ability to keep me safe."

He laughed. "How can I argue with that?"

"You can't. We'll be fine." She shivered. "If Napoleon's armies start to march, that will be quite another matter."

"They will march," Simon said grimly. "But not just yet. It will take him time to organize his forces again." But damnably, it probably wouldn't be much time.

The lane ended in the Moreau farmyard. Monsieur Moreau came out to greet them, having heard already about the inn's unusual guests. He was a vigorous man in late middle age, and his shrewd gaze seemed to assess them for honesty and horsemanship.

"My grandson says that you're interested in hiring a pair of saddle horses for a few days," he said. "All my horses are over there in the paddock. Take a look, and I'll join you in a few minutes, after I give this scamp a sweet cake as a reward for his efforts." He ruffled his grandson's hair affectionately.

The grandson happily followed his grandfather into the farmhouse for his treat while Simon and Suzanne crossed to the paddock. It contained the full range of horses from great, strong draft beasts all the way down to a grandchild-sized pony. Suzanne sighed happily. "So beautiful. All horses are beautiful."

"Some are more beautiful than others," Simon said. "There appear to be several mounts that will meet our needs for a few days."

After a brief study, Suzanne said, "I like the looks of that golden chestnut gelding with the blaze down his nose."

She moved to the gate and opened it far enough to slip inside the paddock. After closing the gate behind her, she drifted toward the horses. Simon's nerves twitched at the sight of her entering a paddock full of unknown beasts, but he controlled the impulse to call her back.

Monsieur Moreau joined him and frowned to see Suzanne inside the paddock. "What the devil?"

He made for the gate, but Simon gestured him to stay where he was. "My wife is very good with horses."

Suzanne reached out a hand to the chestnut and murmured soft words that Simon couldn't make out. But equine ears pricked up in interest and three full-grown horses and the pony ambled over to greet her. Laughing, she stroked velvety noses and murmured more words, probably telling them what very fine horses they were.

"You spoke true, Duval," the farmer said with some amazement. "All of 'em would love to have her throw a saddle over their backs."

"She was always a horse charmer, even when she was a slip of a girl." Simon glanced at Monsieur Moreau. "Are you willing to let us hire two horses for three days? If so, we need to discuss the fees."

It took only a few minutes to work out the details. By the time Suzanne came over leading the chestnut, the transaction was settled.

A larger dark bay followed her hopefully. He looked a likely mount, so Simon entered the paddock and made the beast's acquaintance. After checking him out, Simon said, "You have fine horses, Monsieur Moreau. May we hire these two?"

"I think I'll have to let you have 'em," the farmer said with a grin. "They obviously don't want to leave your lady."

Simon chuckled. He knew exactly how the horses felt.

Amazingly, Simon and Suzanne managed to ride out not long after noon. Maurice and Jackson had already left for Brussels with the carriage. Suzanne's borrowed riding habit was plain dark blue and a little large, but she wore it with dash. Simon decided that she would look good in a potato sack. She waved at Marie and the servants who'd come out to bid them farewell.

As they rode through the village on the road east, Suzanne said, "It may be a little late to ask if you know where we're going."

He chuckled. "I was an exploring and intelligence officer. I always do my research before setting out. Our first destination is the Church of St. Agnes in a village about three hours' ride from here. Frère Pascal said that church is one of the places where Frère Jude stays sometimes."

It was a fine day for a ride. The road they traveled carried little traffic, but farmers were cultivating the fields, and cattle that had grown thin during the winter were grazing contentedly on the lush spring grass.

After a couple of hours, they stopped to enjoy Moreau cheese and bread and a good red wine. "This is very romantic," Suzanne said as she shook crumbs out of the linen napkins the inn had provided. "Though probably I shouldn't mention that my backside is a little sore."

"I think that rubbing your lovely backside to make it feel better would be very romantic," Simon said earnestly.

She laughed, and he felt the pleasure in their being able to have such a teasing conversation. When they rose to resume their trip, he patted her very lovely backside as he prepared to help her up into the saddle.

She grinned and did the same to him.

Their leisurely enjoyment of the journey ended when they reached the Church of St. Agnes. After they tethered their horses, they entered the small church. It wasn't grand, but sunshine poured through the stained glass windows and the old stone walls radiated peace.

A cassocked priest knelt before the altar deep in prayer. By mutual consent, Simon and Suzanne sat in the last pew. When he saw her close her eyes, he realized this was a fine time to attempt prayer, though he'd never been very good at it.

He closed his eyes and concentrated on the peace that was an essential part of this small church. When his mind was as still as it was likely to get, he thought about what he should pray for.

Peace for the nations of Europe so that no more men would die on the battlefields? He sent a fervent prayer heavenward, though peace seemed far too vast and unattainable for a sinner like him to pray for, not with Napoleon igniting flames in Paris.

But he could certainly send up a prayer of gratitude for Suzanne, who had brought joy undreamed of with her warmth and trust and honesty. So gratitude for her, and also a prayer that she would fully heal from the terrible scars of the spirit she had endured. She deserved peace and happiness.

Was it too arrogant to ask God to bring Lucas back to him? The best of his friends, the brother of his heart. But for all he knew, Lucas had been dead for years and Simon was chasing a phantom of hope. Better to pray for peace for Lucas's soul, whether he was living or dead.

Peace . . . He realized he was holding Suzanne's hand.

He released it when he heard movements from the kneeling priest, but not before squeezing her fingers. She opened her eyes and smiled at him. Peacefully.

The elderly priest used the railing to help himself rise, but he turned with a welcoming smile. "Good day. I'm Père Martin. May I help you?"

"I hope so," Simon said as he pulled out the sketches of Lucas. "I'm looking for a long-lost cousin of mine who may now be a Franciscan friar and bonesetter. I was told he sometimes stays here when he does his work in this area. Do you know him?"

Père Martin gave a pleased smile as his gaze settled on the picture of Lucas as a friar. "Frère Jude! Of course, he is always most welcome here. He has been here for several days and left no more than two hours ago."

The shock was like touching a red-hot poker. Simon swallowed hard. "Did he say where he was going next?"

The priest thought a moment. "He said he'd be heading east on the Liege road, I believe."

"How was he traveling?" Suzanne asked. "Is he on foot?"

"No, he rides a mule." Père Martin smiled tolerantly. "He worries that he is not honoring his vow of poverty by owning a mule, but I always assure him that riding allows him to travel farther and do more of God's work."

Could this friar be Lucas, who'd loved horses as much as Simon did? He'd know soon enough. "Thank you, Père. We'll take that road and hope to catch up with him."

Simon spun and headed for the door at a swift pace, almost unbearably excited. He was almost at the door when Suzanne caught his arm and whispered, "Put something in the collection box!"

"Oh. Right. Of course." He always donated to a church's poor box, and today he'd almost forgotten when he had the most reason to be grateful. He dropped in a large handful of coins before going outside.

He did remember to stride to Suzanne's horse first so he could help her mount. While she settled on the chestnut's back and adjusted the fall of her skirts, he said in a constricted voice, "I don't actually believe this will be him. I've been letting myself hope too much."

"At least you will have certainty," she said softly as her gloved left hand gently brushed his cheek. "If Frère Jude isn't Lucas, there will be no other places to search."

Her words gave him a measure of calm. Certainty would be welcome. He swung onto his horse. "Thank you for your sanity."

"You've often been sane for me. Come, let us finish our journey." She set her horse off at a swift trot, which was saner than the gallop he wanted to use. But they covered ground swiftly. The road was almost empty except for a couple of farm wagons and one annoying flock of geese that reduced them to a slow walk to avoid damage to the squawking birds.

After a brisk hour of riding, he saw the figure of a man on a mule in the distance. Abandoning sanity, he kicked his mount into a gallop. As he closed in on the healthy, well-groomed white mule, he identified the brown Franciscan robe. The friar had fair, tonsured hair, tanned skin, familiar shoulders, but he seemed to have little curiosity, because he didn't turn to see who was thundering up behind him.

"Frère Jude!" Simon called as he slowed his gallop. "Frère Jude?"

He guided his horse to the mule's right side and leaned over to grab the other beast's bridle. As he forced both mounts to a stop, he asked urgently, "Lucas?"

The friar turned his head, and Simon found himself looking into the startled blue eyes of his cousin Lucas.

Chapter 24

❧

Shocked, Lucas whispered, "Simon?" He instinctively reached out and for an instant his hand clasped Simon's with fierce recognition.

An instant later his expression shuttered and he yanked his hand back. Clutching his reins with knotted fingers, he said, "You shouldn't be here."

Still barely believing, Simon retorted, "Why not? I only wish I'd found you sooner, Lucas!"

His cousin was shaking his head. He was too thin, and in his brown friar's robes and sandals, he looked like a stranger. And yet at the same time, he was achingly familiar—Simon's companion of countless races and wrestling matches and late-night conversations. "Lucas Mandeville is dead. I am Frère Jude now."

Suzanne galloped up and pulled her horse to a halt. A little breathlessly, she said, "Good day. I'm Suzanne Duval, and pleased to meet the cousin my husband loves so much."

Lucas stared, appearing jolted by her arrival and on the verge of flight.

Voice soothing, Suzanne said, "A family reunion after so many years calls for food, drink, and discussion. The logs under that flowering apple tree will be a good place." She rode to the logs, which looked as if they were destined for future fires, but in the meantime could act as an informal picnic area.

Dismounting, she dug into her saddlebags. "And you thought I'd brought too much food, Simon!"

Simon was amused and grateful for her intercession, since he found that he didn't quite know what to say to his long-lost cousin. He also dismounted and tethered both horses before he collected the jug of wine and a pair of pewter drinking vessels from his saddlebags. "That's a fine-looking mule, Lucas."

Jarred from his bemusement, Lucas said, "Yes, the Magdalene has carried me for many miles."

The Magdalene? An interesting name for a mule. When Lucas still looked wary, Simon said, "Do sit down so we can break bread together, Lucas. There are many years to catch up on. I'm not going to abduct you and take you back to England against your will, you know."

Still looking uncertain, Lucas dismounted, tethered the Magdalene, and seated himself on a stump opposite Suzanne's log. Gracious as a duchess in her own drawing room, she sliced several pieces of cheese and a couple of rounds of bread from a baguette, then wrapped the food in one of the two cloth napkins Madame Moreau had packed.

She handed Lucas the bundle, then poured wine into one of the pewter drinking vessels. That also was given to Lucas. "Breaking bread together is a primal form of connecting with others, isn't it? Plus, it tastes good."

Lucas actually smiled. "Very true, Madame Duval."

"Please, call me Suzanne. We are family, after all."

Lucas politely waited for her to lay out bread and

cheese for two on the other linen napkin. After she poured wine into the other vessel, he bit hungrily into his food.

Simon had taken a seat a couple of feet down the log from her, leaving space for her to set the napkin of food between them. After sipping the wine, she offered it to Simon. The sharing was quietly intimate.

He was glad they had enough food and wine for Lucas. Simon was wondering how to start a conversation about why his cousin had vanished when Lucas said, "Belated congratulations on your marriage, Simon. How long have you two been wed?"

Simon and Suzanne looked at each other. "It's only been a few weeks," he said, mildly surprised. "It feels much longer." She had been a part of him since they'd first met, he realized.

Suzanne grinned at him. "I hope you mean that in a good way, *mon chéri*."

"That very way," he said with a smile. Turning to Lucas, he explained, "We first met many years ago. You had gone into the Royal Navy by then, but I'm sure I wrote you about attending the wedding of my cousin, the Comte de Chambron, and how I'd become friends with his young bride."

Interest engaged, Lucas said, "You're that Suzanne? Simon went on about your beauty and charm at great length."

"Really?" Suzanne gave Simon a sideways smile. "I thought you were mostly impressed with my riding. Other than that, all my focus was on my wedding."

Looking as if he was enjoying himself, Lucas said, "As I recall, Simon, you said you hoped you'd meet a girl like her when you were ready to settle down."

Simon drew in a steadying breath as he thought of the intervening years. "That's what I did. *Exactly* like her. But it was a long and complicated journey from then to now." His sober gaze held Suzanne's before he turned back to Lucas. "A long, complicated journey for all of us, I think. What happened to you, Luke? We were informed that the French had sunk your ship and you were missing and presumed dead. And then . . . nothing."

Lucas started crumbling his bread into small pieces. "I don't want to talk about it. I'm not fit to be speaking to either of you after what I did."

"A year ago, at the time of the emperor's abdication, a friend of the family, Mr. Carter, thought he saw you in Brussels dressed as a monk, and he told your great-aunt and uncle about it."

Lucas looked up swiftly. "My aunt and uncle. They are well?"

"Yes, but they miss you deeply. They still grieve." As Simon did. "Even though it was the faintest of hopes, they asked if I could investigate. Since I spent the last years as an army intelligence officer, they hoped I might be able to come up with more information, even though I was mostly on the Peninsula."

Lucas swallowed hard, his throat working. "I wish you had just accepted that I was dead."

"Well, I didn't. I asked a friend who is also in the intelligence business if he could learn something from his connections in France. He inquired and found that you'd survived the sinking of your ship and that you'd been captured and interned in France."

Lucas had finished his bread and cheese and now his fingers were knotting together in his lap. "Don't say more," he whispered. "Please!"

Simon continued inexorably, "He said that you'd broken your parole and escaped, and had likely died trying to get out of France. And that was all that was known until Mr. Carter saw you in Brussels."

"Yes, I broke my parole!" Lucas snapped. "Being interned at Verdun was bad enough, but then I was sent to the depot at Bitche, which is one of the circles of hell. The commander was known for his viciousness and he took a special hatred for me. He said I'd never be exchanged because he intended to see me in hell first."

His voice dropped to a raw whisper. "So when I could bear no more, I broke my parole and escaped and I've been in hell ever since."

"I'm sorry, Lucas," Simon said softly. "I can only guess at your pain. But I can't be sorry you're alive."

There was a long silence. Then Suzanne said briskly, "I know that honor is a gentleman's lifeblood, as vital as the air he breathes. But honor is not always rigid and immutable. It can take new shapes in new circumstances."

She stood and refilled their wine before sitting again in a flurry of skirts. "Simon spent years as an intelligence officer. A spy. There are those who consider such work dishonorable, but it is vital. Wellington himself said that he could not have succeeded in Spain without the work of his intelligence officers, and Simon is one of the chief among those. He's also the most honorable man I know."

Lucas raised his head. "What Simon did was different. He served his country. I broke my word and disgraced myself forever."

"Oh? I'm a mere female, but as I understand it, the system of parole requires honor on both sides. The captive gives his word that he won't escape, and the captor promises to treat him as a gentleman and exchange him for an officer of equal rank. It seems to me that the commander at the Bitche depot was not upholding his side of the bargain and you were justified in escaping before he could drive you to your death."

Lucas frowned as if he'd never thought of the matter like that. "Yes, he behaved dishonorably, but I still broke my word."

Exasperated, Suzanne stood and stared down at Lucas. "The world is a complicated place, and following the narrowest social rules is sometimes folly. Simon was a spy, and he served his country and saved lives. You were a naval officer who served your country, was captured, and escaped. You damaged no one by doing that."

She caught his gaze, steel in her eyes. "And I was captured by corsairs and enslaved and became a whore to one of the cruelest men in the Ottoman Empire. There are women who have recoiled upon hearing my story. They considered me filthy, disgraced, dishonored beyond redemption."

She drew a deep breath. "If I accepted their judgment, I would have no choice but to take my own life. But I do not choose to accept that! I choose to *live*. That is a choice you can also make, if you dare."

Simon was stunned by what she had just revealed to a virtual stranger. He stood and wrapped an arm around her shoulders, drawing her tight against his side. "I have never been prouder of you, *ma chérie*," he said quietly.

Lucas was staring at her, shocked to his core. If he chose to condemn Suzanne, Simon might have to break his neck. But he said quietly, "You're a very brave woman, Madame Suzanne. I don't have your kind of courage."

"Think about it and maybe you'll find out otherwise," Suzanne said tartly as she let Simon draw her down to the log, his arm still around her. "But don't *wallow.*"

Lucas blinked. "Wallow?"

She gave him a humorless smile. "After catastrophe wrecks one's life, one is entitled to wallow in misery. To howl and pound the earth and cry out to the heavens. But at some point, enough! You have chosen to redeem your sins in service to those in need, and that is admirable. But continuing to berate yourself for your shortcomings after all these years is self-indulgence. Wallowing."

He swallowed hard. "Wallowing."

"Unless you enjoy hating yourself, of course," she said cordially. "That's quite a different matter."

Amazingly, Lucas began to laugh. "Simon, you've found yourself a spitfire."

Simon laughed, too, deeply relieved to see the old Lucas. "My lady has many facets, and one of them is fire." He raised their joined hands and kissed her fingers. "She's right, you know. I've done my full share of wallowing, too."

"Perhaps it becomes a habit," Lucas said in a low voice.

"Habits can be changed," Suzanne said, her voice compassionate. "Though it takes time."

Thinking it was time to change the subject, Simon said, "I've been perishing of curiosity about how you have become a friar and bonesetter. How did that happen?"

"You talk about life being complicated, which it is, but this was simple. I was injured when escaping from the depot at Bitche. By the time I stumbled into Belgium, I was half dead. A farm family found me in their barn, and because I had obvious broken bones, they called the local bonesetter, Frère Emmanuel." Lucas smiled a little. "Emmanuel means 'God is with us,' and if ever God was with a man, it was Frère Emmanuel."

"You learned the skills from him?" Suzanne asked.

"Yes. Frère Emmanuel came from a family that had been bonesetters for generations. He was getting old and frail and had no son, so I became a kind of apprentice. I traveled with him and cared for him and learned his skills. I found the work interesting and it was deeply rewarding to help those in need. So I stayed with him. It was impossible to imagine going back to my old life in England, where every man would scorn me for behaving dishonorably." He glanced at Suzanne. "Perhaps I was wallowing."

She smiled at him. "I didn't say a word."

"Have you never wished to return to England if only for a visit?" Simon asked. "The Foxtons would be overjoyed to see you. Not to mention that there's a title and inheritance waiting for you. Your uncle will gladly return both of those to you."

Lucas hesitated. "That is the life I didn't think I could return to."

"That was then, this is now," Simon said. "Years have passed. Have your feelings changed?"

When Lucas didn't reply, Suzanne said, "Of course you've taken vows, but even with a true vocation, perhaps you could visit your aunt and uncle?"

"Actually, I haven't taken vows." Lucas frowned. "Since I traveled with Frère Emmanuel and lived the life of a Franciscan friar, people assumed that is what I am. But I have never felt that I had a true vocation. Frère Emmanuel always said that if I did have a vocation, I would be sure of it, as he was."

"Perhaps your vocation is for healing," Simon said. "You have the bonesetter skills and Frère Pascal in Namur said you had healing hands. Those skills can be exercised anywhere without following the Rule of Benedict."

Lucas smiled humorlessly. "Can you imagine an English lord who practices as a bonesetter?"

"Actually, yes," Simon replied. "The English aristocracy has more than its share of eccentrics. Why not a lord whose eccentricities are actually useful?"

Lucas's eyes lit with laughter. "You make a compelling case, Simon, but my life is here."

"It doesn't have to be," Suzanne murmured.

Lucas gazed at her, something in his eyes that looked like longing. Simon remembered how his cousin had always enjoyed the company of females for friendship as well as flirting. A life of celibacy had never seemed possible for him, much less likely.

Lucas rose from his tree stump, tall and too thin but undeniably Lucas. "You have given me much to think of, but my work is here. Simon, it has been a blessing to see you again. Thank you for caring enough to hunt me down."

Simon hid his disappointment. "Is it all right to tell your aunt and uncle that you are alive and have been living the religious life here in Belgium?"

"Yes, but I'd prefer you not tell them of my disgrace." He offered his hand. "Bless you, Simon. And Suzanne." He turned and gave a bow that was more courtier than cleric. "I am so glad that you and Simon have found each other."

Suzanne gave him a swift kiss on the cheek. "So are we. You know that our door will always be open to you."

He smiled down at her. "You are gracious."

Simon said, "We're staying in Brussels for now, perhaps for a month or two, perhaps longer. Here is the address." He pulled out a pencil and a small piece of paper and jotted down where to find them. "And if you choose to travel to England, you know where to find us there."

"Perhaps someday I shall." But the words seemed mere courtesy. Lucas turned, swung onto the Magdalene, and set off on his road again.

There was no more to be said. Simon helped Suzanne onto her chestnut, he mounted the bay, and they turned back to the road west.

Their search had been successful beyond Simon's hopes. But he wished he had his brother back again.

Chapter 25

Simon was silent as they rode west after meeting Lucas. His expression was remote and Suzanne thought it best to leave him to his silence. After an hour of travel, she saw a small inn ahead. "The horses are tired and so are we," she said. "Shall we stop for the night here? It looks pleasant."

He agreed, saying only the bare minimum as they booked a room and dinner for the night. They groomed their horses together since the landlord was busy. Suzanne had always liked tending to her own horse. It was soothing and the horses seemed to like it.

As Simon brushed out his horse's mane, he said, "Lucas's mule was very well kept. He always loved horses."

"A trait that must run in your family," Suzanne observed. "The Magdalene is his most constant companion and surely his friend as well."

Simon gave a muffled grunt that sounded like agreement. They dined on thick bean soup flavored by a ham hock and bolstered by good bread and a decent white table wine. Then it was dark and time for bed.

Simon stripped off his outer clothes and lay on the bed with a sigh. Suzanne slid over to him and rolled onto her side, resting her open hand in the center of his chest, where she could feel the strong beat of his heart against her palm.

He laid his hand over hers. "Thank you for your patience with my grouchiness."

"You're not grouchy. You just have much to think about," she said. "Are you disappointed about today?"

"That's the right word," he said slowly. "Disappointed. It was an unexpected miracle to find Lucas alive and well. But I suppose on some level I thought that if I did find him, we'd immediately regain the kind of friendship we had as boys. As close as brothers. Now I realize that was foolish."

"The caring is still there between you. The longer you talked together, the more I saw signs of the young man you grew up with. But you've been living very different lives for many years, and he has deliberately turned away from his youth. He never expected to see you again and I don't think he knew what to do. He was glad to see you, though. I'm sure of that."

In a voice of bleak acceptance, Simon said, "I believe he was, but I don't fit in to his life anymore."

"Not his life as it is now. But meeting you has surely stirred Lucas's thinking. What the results might be, I can't even guess." She shook her head in the darkness. "I did sense that he envies what you have. What *we* have."

"What do you mean?"

"We have warmth and companionship together," she explained. "His life is very solitary. He moves from place to place rather than living in a community as the monks do, and he doesn't have a true religious vocation to balance what he's missing. Unless he always preferred solitude?"

"No, Lucas was more outgoing than I. He liked people of all sorts. Men, women, children, young and old, rich and poor. People who know Frère Jude like him, but it's still a lonely life."

"Perhaps cutting himself off from normal human interactions is part of his self-punishment," she suggested.

"You may be right, but nonetheless, he seems content with his life. One can do much worse." Simon sighed. "I hope he'll visit England before it's too late to see his great-aunt and uncle. It would mean so much to them."

"Perhaps he will. As you said, he knows where to find you." She exhaled warm breath against Simon's shirt-sleeved arm. She ached for his sadness at losing his cousin in a new way, but at least he was not alone.

Simon shifted to his side so she rolled onto her back. When he bent into a kiss, she gave a purr of pleasure because it was so warm and lovely and unexpected. She guessed he might be wordlessly expressing his gratitude that he was not alone.

His hand slid down her torso, rounding over her hip and down her thigh. She tensed for an instant when he pulled the hem of her shift up to her shoulders, exposing her bare skin to his caresses. Tension swiftly melted into pleasure at the intimacy of his bare skin on hers.

She wanted to protest when he ended the kiss, until he moved his lips to her breast. Arousal shot through her, pooling deep inside. She began moving her hips restlessly, wanting him to touch her there, between her legs.

He took his time. After honoring both breasts, his mouth trailed down her torso, tongue licking and breath warm against her skin. Lower, lower . . .

She gave a choked cry when he reached her most secret, yearning places. His lips and tongue, knowing and teasing, raised her desire to fever pitch until she could bear no more. She cried out, her fingers locking into his hair as her body convulsed.

As she melted bonelessly into the mattress, he gave a sign of satisfaction and rested his head on her soft abdomen. The whiskers on his cheek prickled pleasantly against her. Her clutching fingers relaxed into petting as she whispered, "Oh, *my* . . ."

He gave a low laugh. "Have you not done that before?"

She didn't want to take anything away from this special moment, but honesty compelled her to say, "Yes, when I was very young. But he was more interested in impressing me with his skill than in pleasing me." After a moment, she added, "I was pleased then, but nothing like as much as now because you *do* want to please me."

"Always, *mon ange*," he whispered. "Always."

The ride back the next morning was relaxed, with the normal amount of casual conversation exchanged between Suzanne and Simon. They had almost reached the Moreau farm when he remarked, "Whenever you look at me, you blush."

She looked at him, and blushed. "Yes, but in a good way."

Mercifully, he changed the subject. "I don't know how long we'll be in Belgium, but I'm thinking about asking Monsieur Moreau if he'll sell us these horses. They're sound and well trained and would probably cost us less than buying similar mounts in Brussels. What do you think?"

"I like the idea," she said. "I love riding, and these are both fine beasts. I like Hercule here almost as much as my sweet Luna back in England. Your Achille is also a fine fellow."

"He has first rate stamina and I think he'll be a very

good horse for long distance riding if I turn exploring officer again." Simon patted the sleek dark neck of the bay.

"Are you in danger of running out of money?" Suzanne asked. "This has been an expensive journey."

"I brought more cash than I thought I'd need and I've spent almost all of it, so it's good we'll be back in Brussels soon, where I can call on my banker," he admitted. "I should have enough to buy these horses and saddles and get us back to the city, though."

"I am fortunate to have been almost penniless during my early days in London," she said thoughtfully. "It makes me really appreciate being married to a rich man."

He chuckled. "I'm not rich beyond the dreams of avarice, but I'm grateful that I can afford to buy what I need without having to think hard about it. Except for a castle. I could not afford a castle."

"Who needs a castle when we have White Horse Manor?"

"My thoughts exactly. But I suspect we will need these horses."

Since Monsieur Moreau had raised and trained the horses for sale, it didn't take long to agree on a price that included the saddles so that Suzanne and Simon could ride on their return to Brussels if they wished.

They arrived at the inn to find that Maurice and Jackson had returned with a wagon that was covered and had good springs. With a well-padded pallet on the floor, Philippe should be able to travel in reasonable comfort. Marie assured them that he was recovering well and sleeping most of the time, which should help him heal.

They left the next morning after exchanging affectionate hugs with the Moreau family, who waved them off with invitations to return soon. Maurice drove the wagon with Jackson at his side, Simon and Suzanne rode, and Marie traveled with her husband inside the wagon.

The journey was unremarkable until they neared Brussels, where the traffic became increasingly heavy, and included soldiers as well as elegant carriages and farm wagons. They entered the city behind a company of marching Dutch-Belgian troops.

Simon's expression became grim. Edging his mount toward Suzanne's as they made their way along the crowded streets, he said, "There must be news of possible war."

Suzanne said, "More likely to be probable war?"

Simon nodded. Even so, it was a surprise when they reached their house. As the wagon and the two dusty riders halted in front of the building, Jenny ran out to greet them, her face tense. "The Duke of Wellington has just arrived in Brussels, and he's taken a house only a block away!"

Simon swore under his breath. *Probable* war had become inevitable war. And he suspected that Brussels would be the headquarters for the British and Dutch-Belgian troops.

Chapter 26

❧

The conversation that Simon knew was coming took place the morning after they arrived back in Brussels. At breakfast, Marie said shyly, "Sir, Philippe would like to speak to you at your convenience."

"After breakfast then," Simon said. "Would you like more coffee, Marie?"

"Please." She spread marmalade on a warm croissant. "I'm so hungry now!"

"I think that's natural," Suzanne said. "I assume that Philippe wants a man-to-man talk with my husband and female presence is undesired?"

Marie nodded. "Yes, but I shall make him tell me everything afterward."

"I'll do the same with Simon," Suzanne said, and the two women laughed. Simon was glad to see that they were becoming good friends. Suzanne needed the chance to make more female friends.

Simon finished off his coffee and stood. "I'll go up to see Philippe now. If you hear shouting, ignore it."

He was only half joking. Philippe was in a situation that would madden any man. At least he wasn't armed this morning.

Simon entered the spacious bedroom that the young Duvals shared to find that Philippe was now wearing a robe and sitting up in a chair by the window with a blanket tucked over his lap. Simon offered his hand. "Good morning to you. You look much improved."

Philippe shook hands with conscious strength. "Thank you. I feel weak as a kitten but that's much better than I felt several days ago." He grimaced. "I imagine you know why I asked to speak with you."

Simon took a chair. "You're grateful for our help, furious that you've had to accept it, and you're too well mannered to blame us for the fact that help is needed."

That surprised a laugh from Philippe. "That's a good summary. I loathe that I cannot even support my wife, and . . . and I don't know when I will be able to." He began nervously plucking the blanket on his lap. "And I have even less idea when I will be able to repay you."

"When times are difficult, it's usual to turn to family to help, and we are family," Simon said matter-of-factly. "But your situation is difficult. Even if no one disputes your claim to the estate, it's expensive to buy seed and livestock and equipment and to hire labor."

Philippe grimaced. "I know. I thought that when we returned to Château Chambron, it would be the well-run estate I remembered. Instead . . ." He drew a shaky breath. "I don't even know where to start to make the estate productive again."

"Do you know who handled your father's legal affairs? I presume he used a *notaire* for contracts, wills, deeds, things of that nature. Your father's *notaire* would be able to help you determine your legal position. Perhaps there are funds available to invest in the property."

"I'd like to think so, but that seems too good to be

true," Philippe said pessimistically. "The *notaire* is a Monsieur Morel in Saint-Denis, just north of Paris, but I've never met him. My father intended to draw up a will leaving me the estate, but I don't know if he did. I was told that he had to flee without warning." He shrugged. "I hope that with the emperor back on his throne, the courts will support me in my quest."

"He is on the throne now, but I don't know how long he'll be able to hold it with the Allies raising armies to invade France and depose Napoleon once and for all."

"The emperor has defied the odds again and again!" Philippe said angrily. "He will this time, too!"

"Perhaps, but the odds against him are very steep." Deciding it was time to reveal that they were on opposite sides of the long wars, Simon said, "As I've said, you and Marie are welcome to stay here as you recover and sort out your future. But you should know that I was a colonel in the British army and I've only recently sold out. Suzanne and I do not want this house turned into a political battlefield, but I understand if you're uncomfortable staying under this roof."

Philippe recoiled in his chair, sucking his breath in with a sound like a hissing snake. "Why did you take in an enemy? To humiliate or destroy us?"

"I don't see you as my enemy. I will concede that some of Bonaparte's reforms have been excellent and well overdue, such as his reform of the legal system. But his desire to conquer the world and in the process cause the deaths of whole armies of men, not to mention France itself—" He bit his tongue to keep from saying more in that vein. "That I cannot forgive."

"I wish Marie and I could leave this house!" Philippe said with sudden violence. "But we are trapped. I cannot subject her to life in that hovel in her condition, and I—I am too weak even to storm out raging."

"Don't think of us as the enemy," Simon said again, his voice conciliatory. "Think of us as family. Suzanne was bemused to realize that she is your stepmother and she is about to become a grandmother, but she and Marie are becoming fast friends. They are wise not to let politics interfere with the ties of family and friendship."

"I wish I could do the same," Philippe said, his eyes bleak.

"I am not asking you to forswear your allegiance to your emperor or to forget your valiant service. As I've said, you are welcome to stay here while our world re-arranges itself. I ask only that you do not work for Bona-parte while you live under this roof." Simon smiled a little. "I promise not to talk politics if you also refrain."

"I promise," Philippe said reluctantly. "But I wish you were less generous. It would be easier if I could despise you."

"Life can be damnably awkward that way," Simon said with dry amusement. "One of the best men I've ever known was a French major who captured me. I managed to escape and don't know his fate, but I hope he is alive and well somewhere."

That won a reluctant smile from Philippe. "I'll try to remember that the enemy is a political entity, not individ-ual men." He gave an exhausted sigh. "Thank you for coming. I need to sleep now. I wonder if I'll ever feel strong again?"

"You will. In Spain I had a vicious fever like the one you've endured. It was a long time before I fully recov-ered, but I did. And here I am, fit and able to annoy you."

Philippe laughed. "You had best go before I run the risk of liking you." With an exhausted sigh, he slouched back in his chair and closed his eyes. "Suzanne, a grand-mother?"

"Difficult to believe, but I'm sure she'll be a good one."

Simon considered asking if his reluctant guest would like help in getting to the bed, but decided against it. Philippe was already accepting more help than he wanted to.

Quietly Simon left the room and headed down the stairs. Suzanne and Marie were waiting for his return in the breakfast room. "No daggers were drawn," Simon said succinctly. "Philippe was appalled to learn that I was a British army officer, but will reluctantly accept our hospitality on the basis of being family. We have mutually agreed not to discuss politics."

Marie gave a sigh of relief. "My place is at my husband's side, but I do not want to leave." Her protective hand lowered to rest on the expanding curve of her stomach.

"And we do not want you to leave," Suzanne said warmly. "I like having family around me. And I am so looking forward to being a grandmother!"

They all laughed since it was impossible to imagine a woman who looked as lovely and young as Suzanne being a grandmother, but as Simon had said to Philippe, she'd be a very good one. Aloud, he said, "Suzanne, Philippe said that Jean-Louis's *notaire* was Monsieur Morel in Saint-Denis. That's the man you mentioned, isn't it?"

She nodded. "I only met him once, when Jean-Louis took me there to sign some documents. Then I was stashed in a room with tea and cakes while the men went off to discuss important things that were too complex for frail female minds to comprehend. Very tedious it was, too."

Simon smiled at her acid tone. "I need to visit my local banker this morning, so I'll ask if anyone there recognizes Morel's name and knows if the fellow is still practicing in Saint-Denis. If he is, I can write to learn if he has any of Jean-Louis's papers."

"It would be useful to know where Philippe and I stand," Marie said thoughtfully. "If anywhere."

It sounded like Marie had a practical streak, which would serve her and her husband well in their uncertain situation. Simon suspected what the young couple needed was a good forger to produce a will in Philippe's favor. That wasn't something one could ask the local banker about, though.

The day had started with rain, but when the sun came out in early afternoon, Suzanne sought out Simon in the small room he'd turned into an office. "Would you like to go for a walk? The Parc de Bruxelles is said to be very fine and so far we've seen almost nothing of Brussels."

"That's an excellent suggestion." He set his pen into its holder and stood with a long stretch. "Mail sent on from London arrived while we were away and I'm required to pay some attention. Life was easier when I was in Spain and out of reach of stewards and business managers."

"Much simpler," she agreed. "Merely a matter of dodging bullets and finding enough food to eat."

He chuckled. "Most of the time it wasn't that bad, but a stroll in the sun with my lovely wife is infinitely preferable to either bullets or business documents."

When they stepped outside, she drew a deep breath and tightened her shawl against the cool April air. The park was only a few minutes' walk away and it was very large, surrounded by grand public buildings and private palaces. Within the park boundaries were broad tree-lined walkways, fountains, beds of colorful spring flowers, and equally colorful men and women enjoying the weather and the chance to meet friends.

"There are certainly a great many soldiers here," Suzanne remarked as she strolled along with her arm in Simon's.

"Brussels already had a British garrison," Simon said. "Now that Wellington has made the city his headquarters, more soldiers are flooding in every day."

"Spies too, I'm sure. No doubt Kirkland will be very interested in what you have to report."

"Sadly, no one knows what is going on, so spies must resort to guesswork and looking over each other's shoulders," Simon said. "Only Bonaparte knows his plans, and even he probably doesn't know what he'll do next."

Another couple was approaching and the man said with pleasure, "Colonel Duval, it's good to see you here! Are you looking to secure a new command?"

"Major Beckett! A pleasure to see you as well. I'm out of the army now. But I have secured a lovely new wife." Simon performed the introductions and pleasantries were exchanged before they all moved on. As they continued through the park, Simon said, "I need to get cards printed for us since it looks like there will be considerable socializing during our stay."

"And social gatherings are useful for gathering information."

"Exactly. Also good for getting free food and drink," Simon said promptly.

"I'm going to need some new gowns as well as calling cards," Suzanne said. "This could get expensive."

"Why do you think I went to the bank this morning?"

She chuckled, and then smiled sweetly when another military man hailed Simon. There were several more such encounters.

As they turned their steps toward leaving the park, Suzanne pointed at four cavalrymen trotting along the road that bounded the park. They were dressed in all black uniforms and rode shining black horses. "Who are those dramatic fellows?"

"Black Brunswickers, a corps of German volunteers

raised by the Duke of Brunswick after the French took over his duchy. They're fine fighters."

"Decorative too." Suzanne's eyes narrowed. "Do they have silver skull badges on their hats?"

"You have sharp eyes. Soldiers often try to outdo each other with extravagant uniforms." Amusement sounded in Simon's voice. "Wellington allows officers to wear whatever they wish, but he does forbid carrying umbrellas into battle because it doesn't look soldierly."

"He's right," Suzanne said, smiling at the mental image of umbrella-carrying officers. "I should think one needs both hands for reins and weapons!"

They walked past the fountain when they turned to leave, feeling a playful spatter of droplets driven by the breeze. On the other side of the fountain, a cluster of people surrounded a lean, upright man in a blue frock coat. Though nothing like the gaudily dressed soldiers scattered through the park, he had an unmistakable aura of authority that compelled attention.

Her voice hushed, she asked, "Is that Wellington?"

Simon glanced in the direction she indicated. "Yes, the Iron Duke in person. *The Conqueror of the Conqueror of the world.* The man whom everyone expects to be the savior of Europe."

"That's quite a burden to carry," Suzanne remarked.

"He's up to the fighting, but I don't envy him the politics. Half the men around him are probably angling for high army positions or to be on his staff. I imagine he wants to call in the men he worked with and trusts from the Peninsula, while the army headquarters back in London are pressuring him to take on young men from powerful families who have no military experience."

"Being a hero is not enough so that he can choose his own staff?" she asked incredulously.

"He'll get some of the men he wants, but he'll probably have to accept some useless fools as well."

218 *Mary Jo Putney*

"Dodging bullets is beginning to sound easier than navigating the political currents," she said frankly.

"Bullets are only now and then. Politics are forever."

Suzanne chuckled. "That was true even in the harem. The politics were endless and sometimes lethal."

Simon was about to reply when his voice changed. "The duke has seen me and he's heading this way."

Suzanne glanced over and saw that Wellington had broken away from his entourage and was striding purposefully toward them. "Colonel Duval! Good to see you. I didn't know you were in Brussels."

"We came to Brussels on some personal business, sir," Simon said as the men shook hands. "Allow me to introduce my wife, Suzanne Duval."

The duke turned his appreciative gaze on Suzanne. She managed a greeting, but felt absurdly shy. He'd been a distant, godlike figure in her mind, and here he was in person. Not godlike, but certainly a man who radiated power and authority, and one who was on easy terms with her husband.

Simon said, "I heard that you traveled from Vienna to Brussels in a mere week?"

"Not a week I care to repeat," Wellington said tersely. "I heard you sold out?"

"After the emperor's abdication, it seemed time to tend to my own affairs." He smiled fondly at Suzanne. "Which have gone very well, as you can see."

Other people were beginning to come after Wellington. "I've business to attend to as well," the duke said. "Call on me first thing tomorrow. There's something I'd like to discuss."

"Of course, sir." They settled on a time before Wellington's attention was claimed by a flirtatious and very expensively dressed lady.

As Simon took Suzanne's arm and they resumed their

journey from the park, she said, "I wonder what he wants of you."

"Perhaps he'd like me to become an unofficial staff member," Simon said thoughtfully. "I know the work, and since I'm not a serving officer anymore, I could be brought on quietly, with fewer political complications."

Suzanne bit her lip, not saying anything. With war coming, this couldn't be good.

Chapter 27

Wellington greeted Simon promptly when he showed up for their meeting the next morning. "Sorry to invite you over so early, but it was the only time available for the next several days."

"I can only imagine the demands on your time."

"Not only military and political, but social," the duke said wryly as he gestured Simon to a chair. "The population needs to be reassured that Bonaparte isn't going to march into the city next week."

Simon seated himself. "That's not likely, but with Napoleon, who knows?"

"Exactly, which is why I wanted to talk to you." Wellington sat opposite his guest, his expression serious. "The emperor has always been an impatient devil. It was a mistake for him to break out of Elba while the Congress of Vienna was still in session. With leaders from all the Allied nations there, we immediately declared him outlaw for breaking the Treaty of Paris." The duke gave a dangerous smile. "And we were able to agree on a strategy to defeat him once and for all."

."His error is our good fortune," Simon said. "I gather that the plan is for the Allies to field half a dozen armies in a great arc across half of Europe, then to all march on France and crush Paris. Britain and the Dutch-Belgians are here at the western end of the arc, the Prussians are immediately to the east, and the Austrians and Russians on the eastern end."

Wellington nodded. "But it will take time for the Allies to organize those armies. Napoleon can move much more quickly. He may not have the support of all the citizens, but the army is solidly behind him, and they're some of the best, most experienced soldiers in Europe." He scowled. "While my best troops were sent to North America to teach the Americans a sharp lesson. They've been recalled, but moving my Peninsular army back here will take time, and I don't think we have enough of that."

"Napoleon has always preferred attack to defense," Simon agreed. "If I had to guess, I'd say he'll try to defeat the different armies one at a time rather than waiting for them to surround him. Belgium is closest to Paris and he thinks of it as part of France and rightfully *his*. He'll probably try to split the British and Prussian troops so he can hammer the armies separately."

Wellington gave an approving nod. "I see your wits haven't dulled since you sold out. You are officially out of the army now, aren't you?"

"Yes, it's official. I'm a civilian again."

"Good." Wellington frowned. "There's a damnable shortage of military intelligence available. Because we're in a limbo of not quite war, I'm forbidden to send cavalry scouts into northern France to see what's going on."

"Have you been able to bring Colonel Colquhoun

Grant in? He's extraordinary at intelligence work." Simon knew that, having worked closely with Grant.

"He'll be in charge of the official intelligence operation, but he's regular army. You no longer are." The duke fixed Simon with a gimlet stare. "You're as good at intelligence work as Grant, and you're no longer an officer. Plus, with your French heritage, you can travel through France as a Frenchman."

Simon had sensed this was coming. "So you'd like me to go into France as a civilian to see what I might observe."

The duke nodded. "I need to know which way Bonaparte is going to jump and you might be able to figure that out. But it could be dangerous since you wouldn't be in uniform. If you're caught and charged as a spy, you'll likely be shot."

Which had almost happened to Simon in Portugal. He thought about it. His ability with languages had led to his doing other intelligence work out of uniform, and he'd damned near died because of that.

In the past he'd accepted the risks as part of his job, but then he didn't have Suzanne. Life was more appealing now than it had been in his army years.

But the simple fact was that he could not say no. Not to Wellington, and not to his own sense of himself and his duty. "I have personal business that gives me good reason to travel to Paris. If I should happen to see something interesting, naturally I would want to share that information."

"Good man," the duke said as he rose to his feet. "Sorry to be so abrupt, but now I must meet with some of my staff to look at maps."

"And tonight you'll probably have to go to a dinner party and look calm, all knowing, and completely certain that victory will be ours."

The duke gave a bark of laughter. "Exactly. On your way out, give my secretary your address so that you and your lovely lady will be put on the various invitation lists. It's going to be a spring filled with frivolity, and that's another kind of war."

They shook hands and Simon left, leaving his address with the secretary as requested. He'd thought his spying days were over, but apparently not.

Interesting times.

Suzanne was waiting for Simon when he returned from his visit to Wellington. Seeing his expression, she took his arm and guided him into his small office. After closing the door, she said, her lovely face sober, "I'm not going to like this, am I? Will you be joining his staff on a volunteer basis?"

He turned and enfolded her in an embrace, absorbing her warmth and inhaling her familiar scent of woman and tangy lemon. "Something you'll like even less, I'm afraid."

She stiffened and moved away, looking up into his eyes. "What?"

"Wellington isn't allowed to send cavalry scouts into France, so he wants me to become a civilian spy because I can be an authentic Frenchman," Simon said succinctly.

Her face became so pale that he feared she would faint. She folded into a chair and said, "Tell me how you intend to proceed."

He took the other chair, hoping to God that this didn't destroy the sweet, hopeful relationship they'd been building with such care. "I thought I'd pay a visit in person to Monsieur Morel in Saint-Denis. I have legitimate business with him and it will give me a good excuse to travel through northern France and Paris."

She considered his words, then gave a short, decisive

nod. "It's a good reason since it's true. We need a well-used carriage for the journey. We don't want to look too prosperous."

"We?" he said, startled. "I'm going alone, Suzanne."

"No, you are not," she said calmly. "We shall be quite unexceptional if we travel as a couple of modest means going to Saint-Denis to inquire about a possible inheritance. It's a story that even a suspicious policeman will believe because it's true."

"I don't want you to risk yourself, Suzanne," he said vehemently. "I couldn't bear it if you were hurt."

"What a coincidence." She gave him a cherubic smile. "I feel exactly the same about you."

He glared at her. The intelligence officer in him realized that she was right: an unremarkable couple traveling together was less likely to attract attention than a man traveling alone. "You are too beautiful to travel unnoticed."

"It isn't difficult for a woman to make herself look drab and careworn," she retorted. "You will also have to change your appearance to look less like an officer because you move with too much confidence and authority. You must already know how to do that since you've done this work before."

"I have, and I'll do it best alone! I don't want you to come with me."

"Is it that you don't want me with you, or that you don't want me to risk myself? Those are two different things."

He gave a sigh of exasperation. "You know I always want you with me under ordinary circumstances, but not when going into possible danger. In a difficult situation, I'd be distracted by worry about you."

"And vice versa." Her gaze was serious. "I'm not completely useless, you know. You have taught me how

to fight when that's required and how to defend myself."
She frowned. "Before we leave, I'd like a few practice
sessions in that shooting gallery you and Jackson have
been visiting."

He stared at her, his heart hurting. Hellacious to imagine anything happening to her at any time, but if he was
responsible? The thought was unbearable.

"A quiet carriage ride to Paris is not such a dangerous
matter, is it?" she said in a soft, coaxing voice. "French citizens do it all the time. We would be taking well-traveled
roads and we'll both be armed. We traveled to Château
Chambron and back with no trouble. This would likely be
the same."

He shook his head. "France is worried and soldiers are
gathering and eager to fight. Nor can we know what orders
might be issued that would affect travelers. Napoleon
might close the northern borders."

"France is a large, vigorous nation. Napoleon and his
ambitions may be center stage in the eyes of the world,
but below that most of the population is going about their
usual business, which includes *notaires* and wills and
legal proceedings."

"We might have a safe, easy journey," he admitted.
"But we can't know if that's what will happen. France
might explode with us in the middle of it."

"Life is always uncertain and potentially dangerous.
We could step into our street and be flattened by a runaway carriage," she pointed out. "Why not allow me to
join you on this first journey? We can be there and back
in less than a fortnight. If it is clearly a detriment to your
work to have me with you, I'll accept your judgment and
be an obedient wife." She frowned. "Well, perhaps I will.
I can't promise."

He had to smile. "As always, your honesty is admirable and rather terrifying."

She smiled back, knowing she had won. "I do think I might be useful. Women can learn things that men can't, just as the reverse is true."

"But don't look so beautiful that women hate you and men always remember you." His brow furrowed. "We need to get official French citizenship papers and I don't know if I can arrange that from Belgium."

"Why don't we travel as Belgians? We can pass as Belgian as easily as French. The accent is only slightly different." In the middle of her words, she slid into the accent of Brussels, and did it very well. "There has always been much coming and going between France and Belgium and it shouldn't be difficult to arrange the papers since we are living here at the moment."

"That makes sense," he agreed. "Should we leave in about a week? We'll need new clothing and the chance to develop the characters we intend to play." He concentrated for a moment, donning the persona of a quiet man of middle means who was content with his lot in life.

She started to reply, then blinked. "You've changed how you look! You don't seem like a soldier anymore. Your posture is less upright. But it's more than that. You're easier to overlook now."

"I've done this sort of thing before," he pointed out. "But are you sure you can look suitably drab for a journey to Paris?"

She laughed, then closed her eyes for a long moment. Her face became still and she somehow became less lovely. Less memorable. It was as if she was turning down a lamp and had gone from illuminating a room to being a faint hallway night light.

"You really can make yourself look almost average!" he said. "I wouldn't have thought it was possible, *ma belle.*"

"I have had to be an actress often in my life," she said

ruefully. "I'm glad I don't have to act with you, but I still have the skills."

She stood and leaned into him for a hug. He enfolded her in his arms, wanting to stay in this safe, warm moment forever. Yet danger lay ahead. How much, he couldn't know. But he couldn't escape the feeling that the world was about to come crashing down all around them.

Chapter 28

❧

After leaving Suzanne, Simon went in search of Maurice. He found the older man sitting in the sun in front of the small stable behind the house, smoking a pipe, and looking content with his life. "Given your long acquaintanceship with Kirkland," Simon said, "I'm guessing that if I want to get papers that prove my wife and I are native Belgians, you would know how to go about it?"

Maurice's eyes glinted with amusement. "I expect I could. What names would you want on them?"

"Our own. We're not pretending to be different people, we just want to travel into France to visit a *notaire*. Given the uncertainty of the times, it might be easiest if we're Belgian, not French or English. Duval is a common name."

"Very sensible." Maurice gave a puff on his pipe. "Anything else you need?"

"A small, somewhat worn but respectable carriage. French currency. Maps of France and Paris to guide us on our way. We're just two average people making inquiries about a possible inheritance. We don't want to attract attention."

"Hard to do with a woman like madam."

"She has promised to look drab and unmemorable," Simon explained.

"I'll believe that when I see it," Maurice snorted, unconvinced. "Do you want me to drive you?"

"We would seem too prosperous. We're respectable, but far from wealthy."

"A good choice when traveling in uncertain times," Maurice agreed. "Finding a coach is easy, but it'll take a few days to get your Belgian identification papers."

Simon nodded. "While you're at it, could you have a set of papers made up showing us to be French citizens? I'll give you the names and places that make sense for that. We want to leave in about a week."

"That will be enough time." Maurice rose in a leisurely fashion. "I'll get to work on the papers right away."

Simon returned to the house, mentally listing what else needed to be done. He'd arrange for Suzanne's target practice. He'd also find a small, easily concealable knife for her to carry. He still felt uneasy about taking her into a potential war zone, but since she was determined, she'd be as prepared as he could make her.

That meant both prayers and weapons.

The next days were busy as Suzanne prepared for her trip to Paris. Working together, she and Simon drew up a Duval family tree to the extent they knew it. There were too many limbs cut off by violence. Too many question marks. She had the impression that Monsieur Morel had served the Duval family for many years, so perhaps he would be able to fill in some of the blank spaces.

She was glad to have several practice sessions at the shooting range. Not only did her marksmanship improve, but she became more at ease with handling her new pistols. If she ever needed to use them, she must be quick and confident.

Simon also gave her advanced lessons in self-defense, including a hold that cut off blood to the brain and could render a person unconscious in seconds. She accidentally knocked him out when practicing it. He'd woken blinking a horrifying couple of minutes later and emphasized that the hold shouldn't be held for long or she'd risk injuring the brain of her victim.

Just as important but less dramatic was augmenting her wardrobe. The city's most fashionable modistes were too busy to produce new garments quickly, so Suzanne ordered only some grand gowns to be worn after they returned from France. She was able to buy a plain bonnet and a ready-made cloak, and she and Jenny made several garments that suited her role as a modest wife of modest circumstances.

But when shopping for fabric, Suzanne found a length of beautiful, blazing red silk that gave her an idea. She bought enough material to make a gown that could easily be made flamboyant, working on it privately so no explanations would be required. She'd almost finished the gown and was hemming the full skirt when Jenny came looking for her with a question.

Jenny's gaze immediately fastened on the scarlet gown. "Goodness! It's . . . very bright. But the fabric is beautiful and that color looks well with your dark hair."

"It's not a very respectable color, though, is it?" Suzanne held up the garment to her face, which showed the color but not how very low cut the bodice was. "I don't know that I could bring myself to wear it in public, but . . ." She gave a delicate pause. "I think the colonel would like to see it in private. Don't mention this, though. It's to be a surprise on the right occasion."

Jenny smiled conspiratorially. "I won't mention it even to Edgar!"

Happy to change the subject, Suzanne said, "He seems much happier these days."

"Oh, yes! He's almost his old self again now that he has a job and he's useful. The exercises the colonel suggested have been helping, too. His left hand will never be what it was, but it's much better. He can do almost anything with it."

"Good for patting his sweetheart?" Suzanne said teasingly.

Jenny blushed and excused herself. Smiling, Suzanne finished hemming the scarlet gown, then carefully wrapped it in plain linen and put it at the bottom of her travel case. She might not need this gown, or the pistols, but she liked to be prepared.

Two days before their planned departure, she was doing her final packing when Simon entered the bedroom with a bouquet of fragrant spring flowers, which he presented with a flourish. "For the loveliest of ladies, *ma belle*!"

"How nice of you!" She buried her nose in the blossoms, enjoying the scents—and realized that something different was buried inside. Curiously she separated the flowers and found a neat little dagger in a leather sheath. She blinked and pulled it out. "You are so romantic, *mon chéri*!" She clasped the weapon over her heart and gave a soulful sigh. "Flowers fade but a dagger endures."

He grinned. "I thought that if I was going to bring more potential mayhem, I should include flowers. The sheath can be strapped to your ankle or thigh, or perhaps concealed under your stays. Try it different ways to learn where it is both comfortable and accessible."

"Will you give me a demonstration of how to carry and use it?" she asked. "I'm sure there are useful techniques."

"I like to hold a knife with the blade pointing up for an underhand stroke." He demonstrated with the knife in the sheath so there would be no accidental injuries. "It's easier to block an overhand stroke than one coming up from below."

She took the sheathed weapon and tried striking both ways. "I see what you mean." She slid the dagger from its sheath and examined it more closely. "It's a lovely little knife that fits my hand well."

"As with the pistols, it's good to have weapons that are comfortable and easy to use. When danger strikes, the faster you can respond, the better. If you have to think about what to do, it may be too late."

They did a little mock scuffling with the sheathed knife so that she had a better sense of how to use it. "You're quick," he said approvingly as he dodged back from a strike that could have sliced into his abdomen and done serious damage if the knife wasn't in its sheath.

"I'll practice more strikes to get a better feel for it," she promised. Then she sat on the edge of the bed and drew her skirts up provocatively. "Shall we try to decide the best location for wearing the dagger?"

His eyes darkened as he caught one ankle, then bent to kiss her inner thigh. "This will take time to determine," he said huskily.

"We have time," she murmured as she pulled him onto the bed with her. They ended up laughing together as hands slipped below clothing with mischievous intent.

They had learned well what pleased each other and it wasn't long until laughter became moans and muffled cries. Suzanne convulsed under his touch before yielding to boneless relaxation and deep internal throbbing.

As she struggled for breath, she wondered when she

would be able to open herself to him entirely. The mere thought made her tense until she forced herself to relax. They had come so far already. Surely someday she would be capable of full marital intimacy.

But for now, all her attention should be on driving her husband to madness. And she knew exactly how to do it. . . .

The day before their departure, Simon found Suzanne attaching a ribbon to an otherwise very plain bonnet and asked, "Will you join me for a serious discussion with Philippe? He's less suspicious of you than of me."

She set the bonnet aside and rose. "He's much less so than he was."

He offered his arm. "True, but the topic of the discussion will raise his hackles."

Together they climbed up to his bedroom. Simon tapped on the door and Marie called, "Come in."

She and her husband were side by side on the small sofa, sharing morning coffee. He was well enough to walk a few steps, though still weak. Simon thought how much better he looked than when they'd found him at the ruined château.

Philippe's brows arched as he regarded his visitors. "Have you come to throw us out of the house now that we're better?"

"Nonsense!" Suzanne said briskly. "We're here to discuss a matter of business."

Marie rose. "I'll leave so you'll have your privacy."

"No need," Simon said. "Stay, this affects you also."

Philippe frowned. "Now I am getting worried." Marie took his hand nervously.

"It's nothing dire. I've found the name and address of your father's *notaire*, Monsieur Morel. He's still practicing in Saint-Denis, so Suzanne and I decided to visit him in person to discover the state of the Chambron legal affairs. My guess is that even if he has a copy of the will, there won't be any money, but it won't hurt to ask."

"I also want to find out if there is anything left of my dowry," Suzanne added. "I'm not optimistic, but I'd like to know."

"Would you be willing to give me a power of attorney so I can act on your behalf?" Simon asked. "You could specify how you would like any monies to be handled, if there are any."

Philippe frowned, but Marie said mildly, "Don't be so suspicious, *mon chéri*. If we hadn't trusted Simon and Suzanne, we'd be dead by now. I for one will be glad to know where we stand."

At her words, Philippe said reluctantly, "Very well, I'll give you a power of attorney, but do you think it's safe to travel into France with conditions so uncertain?"

Suzanne smiled. "Simon and I have had this discussion. There is no reason to worry overmuch. If an army starts marching toward us, we'll simply move out of the way. Quickly!"

They all laughed together, and Philippe called for pen, paper, and a lap desk so hc could write the power of attorney. When he was finished, he handed it to Simon but said to Suzanne, "I would like a word with you in private, Suzanne. Marie, would you mind leaving with Simon?"

His wife looked surprised, but she obediently led the way out of the room with Simon behind her. After the door closed, Philippe turned an intense gaze on Suzanne. "Will you tell me how my father died?"

She took the chair opposite him, sensing his craving to know more of his father. "I think that you know we were sailing to Naples. Jean-Louis knew a number of the people at the Court of Naples, and hc also thought it wise to be out of France."

Suzanne hadn't been sure she'd like Naples, but she'd obediently gone along with her husband's plans. She was always obedient in those days.

"A storm pushed us farther south than usual, and I'm told the corsair ship was farther north than such vessels usually venture. The corsairs attacked at dawn and caught our crew unaware. All was chaos and confusion." She drew a deep breath as she remembered the shots and screams and flames. The bodies . . . "The pirates swarmed over the main deck, cutting down all who opposed them."

"Battle is always chaos," Philippe said grimly. "What happened to my father?"

She considered how much to say. There was no reason to tell him that the father he idolized was a craven coward. "Jean-Louis was not the man to grovel before pirates." She looked down, not wanting Philippe to read anything in her eyes. "It was . . . very quick. I don't think he knew what hit him. He and the others who would not submit were buried at sea. Everyone else, including me, was taken prisoner and enslaved."

"I'm glad to know he went down fighting, as a Duval should." Philippe swallowed hard, then bluntly asked an even more difficult question. "Do you think I am a bastard? I was always told that my parents fell passionately in love and married very soon after, but now that I am grown, I wonder if my father really would have wed a woman of much lower station, no matter how beautiful or how much he loved her."

"I'm sorry, Philippe," she said gently. "I simply do not know. I was in the nursery when your parents met." She hesitated, picking her words carefully. "The man in his thirties whom I married was unlikely to have wed a girl of modest birth, but as an enraptured youth, he might have done so."

"If I was legitimate, wouldn't he have taken me to be

raised in his own home?" Philippe's words were a plaintive cry.

"Not necessarily. Since your mother was of modest birth, he might not have wanted you exposed to the sneers of the aristocratic circles he preferred. Or perhaps you are illegitimate, but you were his only son and he cared for you. We may learn something from the *notaire* that will be illuminating. Simon and I will always be honest with you, you know." Honest, and kind when possible.

"I almost wish you weren't," he said, looking very tired again. "But thank you for answering my questions. Have a safe journey." He closed his eyes, exhausted once more.

She rose and left the room quietly. It would be a great disappointment if Monsieur Morel was able to tell them nothing useful.

The next morning, Simon and Suzanne set off for Paris, the passionate and perilous heart of France.

Chapter 29

~⟡~

The trip through northern France to Saint-Denis was blessedly free of incident. They took the main Brussels-to-Paris road, which was busy with more soldiers than one would see in peaceful times. Suzanne was glad that no one paid any particular attention to them.

Apart from the journey to Château Chambron, Suzanne had done no traveling in Europe since she was captured and enslaved. She wasn't surprised to learn that Simon was a practiced traveler who knew how to manage everything from deeply rutted roads to changing horses to ferry crossings.

She recognized that even though he was driving their small carriage, he was also keenly observant of everything around them, including the military units. Wellington had chosen his spy well.

Saint-Denis was about a hundred fifty miles from Brussels, and traveling at a relaxed pace, they reached their destination in the middle of the fourth day. As they entered the compact town on the northern edge of Paris,

Mary Jo Putney

Simon said, "This road we're traveling on is actually where Morel's office is. Shall we stop by and set up an appointment with Monsieur Morel?"

"We might as well. If we're lucky, he might even be available to talk to us," she replied. "I must admit that I'm impatient to hear what, if anything, he has to say."

"I'm curious, too." Simon smiled at her. "It's time to turn on your aristocratic charm and beauty again."

"And you must return yourself to being a wellborn senior officer." To her amusement, he did just that, becoming more formidable under her gaze.

She must have successfully done the same, because when they left the carriage and horses at a livery across the street, Simon said, "Come, *ma belle*. You will have every man in the office, including the *notaire* himself, rushing out to gaze at you."

She laughed. "I don't think he's the susceptible sort. I'll settle for his being polite and available."

The *notaire* was housed in a substantial building with marble steps leading up to the entrance. The heavy brass knocker also spoke of discreet success.

When a clerk admitted them, Simon said in a voice that assumed he would be obeyed, "We are Monsieur and Madame Duval and we wish to see Monsieur Morel on matters pertaining to Jean-Louis Duval, the Comte de Chambron."

The clerk's eyes widened. "Come in, monsieur and madam. I'll see if the *notaire* is available."

He led them to a comfortable reception room, then disappeared down the corridor beyond. He returned in only a few minutes. "He is pleased to meet with you. If you will come this way?"

They were escorted deeper into the house to a handsomely furnished office dominated by a massive desk of shining mahogany. The man behind the desk was in late middle age, and as handsome and well-furnished as his office. He rose as they entered. "Good day, Monsieur and Madame Duval. I have not heard the name of Jean-Louis Duval for a long time."

His gaze moved to Suzanne, and he sucked in his breath with audible shock. "Madame la Comtesse, is that really you? I thought you were dead!" His eyes narrowed as he studied Simon. "You are not Jean-Louis."

"No, I am not." Simon took a seat alongside Suzanne as the *notaire* gestured for them to sit.

Morel signaled to his clerk, who was hovering by the door. "Refreshments, please. My guests have been traveling and must be hungry. Close the door behind you."

He settled behind his desk again, clasping his hands before him on the embossed leather surface. "Madame la Comtesse, I do not doubt your identity, but I must verify that. Do you recall when we first met?"

She nodded. "Jean-Louis brought me from the house in Paris, saying there were certain legalities that must be performed. He didn't bother to explain, of course. You were courteous to me but dismissive. I had the feeling you barely noticed my existence."

"I actually noticed you with great pleasure, but I've learned it isn't wise to pay too much attention to the beautiful young wife of an older husband, no matter how innocent one's admiration is," he explained wryly. "Then what happened?"

"I signed the documents like a proper and obedient young wife," she said, trying to recall what it had been like to be so young. "Then you and Jean-Louis had important men's business to discuss, so I was sent off to the library. The books were all legal tomes so there was nothing very interesting to read."

She stopped, struck by a more pleasant memory. "But as you did today, you ordered refreshments for me. There was a lovely tea that smelled of . . . of jasmine, I think. And exquisite pastries. There was one of *choux* pastry with raspberry preserves and cream flavored with a liqueur. One of the loveliest things I've ever eaten. Do you have the same chef?"

The *notaire* chuckled. "Indeed I do. Thank you, madam. I do not doubt your identity." He turned to Simon. "The Duvals breed true and you certainly have the look of the family. Where do you fit in?"

"I was a second cousin of Jean-Louis." Simon reached inside his coat and drew out a folded paper. "Suzanne and I drew up a family tree that shows what we know. We thought you might have additional information."

The *notaire* unfolded the large sheet of paper, scanning it quickly and nodding. "Ah, there you are, Monsieur Duval. Your father, also Simon Duval, married the English lady and moved to England just before the Peace of Amiens ended. I know nothing more of your branch of the family, and I cannot verify your identity because you never visited my office and ate pastries."

"I can verify it," Suzanne said. "Simon and I first met when he and his parents attended my wedding to Jean-Louis. There was a grand fortnight-long house party for family members. Simon was one of the few guests who was close to my age and we became friends. After the wedding, we went in very different directions, then met again in London several months ago. There is no question but that he is the Simon Duval I knew." She raised her left hand, where her gold wedding ring caught the light. "Finding each other led to the result you see."

The *notaire* accepted that. "Since you have remarried, I presume you know for a fact that Jean-Louis is dead?"

Her mouth twisted. "He died before my eyes. There is no doubt about it." In terse words, she described what had happened.

The *notaire* listened quietly, then said, "Thank you. I'm sorry to have put you through that, but now I have confirmation for my records."

There was a quiet knock at the door; then two servants arrived with trays of food and drink. Monsieur Morel had obviously decided his visitors were important because the trays contained savory bites like small sandwiches and hot cheese puffs as well as sweets including—oh, joy!—the *choux* pastry with cream, raspberries, and orange flavored liqueur. Plus coffee, jasmine-scented tea, and wines.

As Suzanne and Simon took advantage of the refreshments, Morel returned to his study of the family tree, jotting notes in several places. He reached the bottom of the page and became very still. "You have included Philippe Duval. You know of him?"

"He and his wife are currently living in our house in Brussels," Suzanne said. "Obviously you've also heard of him. Do you have a copy of Jean-Louis's will? If so, does he mention Philippe in it?"

The *notaire* took off his spectacles and polished them carefully. "This is a delicate matter, Madame le Comtesse. How long have you known of Philippe's existence?"

"Less than a fortnight," she replied. "Simon and I visited Château Chambron to see what condition the estate was in. We found that the château had been burned down and Philippe and his wife were living in the ruins and in dire straits."

"It doesn't upset you that your husband had a natural son whose existence he concealed from you?" Morel asked curiously.

Suzanne shrugged. "Not really. Jean-Louis never spoke to me of important matters. He allowed Philippe to believe that he is legitimate. Philippe wants to believe, but he's doubtful."

"And justly so. Jean-Louis never suggested to me that his son was the product of a legal marriage." The *notaire* hummed thoughtfully. "Your late husband left his affairs in a confused state, I fear."

"An understatement," Simon said dryly as he removed Philippe's power of attorney from his inside pocket. He handed it to the *notaire*. "We are all interested in whatever clarity you can offer about Jean-Louis's estate."

Morel studied the power of attorney carefully, including the witness signatures. "This appears to be in order." He sat back in his chair and steepled his fingers. "You are both among those with a right to know about the will and its dispositions. It is an unusual document. I can produce it for you to study here in the office, but if you like, I'll summarize the points that affect you."

"The summary, please," Suzanne said firmly.

The *notaire* looked at Simon. "You are the heir to the title of Comte de Chambron. I can say with reasonable certainty that the heirs between Jean-Louis and you are all deceased. Congratulations, Monsieur le Comte."

Simon was still for a long moment. "I regret that so many of my kin have died."

"Inheritance usually comes from a bittersweet hand," the *notaire* said. "If it makes you feel any better, no property or monies are attached. Properly speaking, you would also inherit some ceremonial regalia that goes with the title, but I have no knowledge of where it might be."

"Probably at the bottom of the sea," Suzanne said dryly. "Jean-Louis would have brought such trappings with him to Naples so that the locals would know his rank."

Simon shrugged. "So the title is an empty shell. I never aspired to it and I certainly never expected to inherit any money or property from my cousin."

"Titles can be useful socially," Suzanne said with amusement. "Much grander to be announced as the Comte and Comtesse de Chambron when we attend a ball."

Simon chuckled. "You are already the Comtesse de Chambron, milady. But apparently now you will no longer endure the humiliation of having a commoner husband.

Will you mind if I renounce the title? It seems wrong to claim it when my future lies in Britain."

"The title holds no joy for me," Suzanne said slowly. "I do not wish to be the Comtesse de Chambron again. I am much happier as Mrs. Simon Duval."

He caught her hand for a moment and their gazes met with mutual agreement. He kissed the back of her hand before relinquishing his clasp.

Monsieur Morel gave a discreet cough. "There are more provisions that will interest you," he said. When he had his guests' attention, he continued, "Jean-Louis did leave a not inconsiderable amount of property. Since Château Chambron was not entailed, he left it to his 'beloved son, Philippe Duval.'"

"So the estate really is his!" Simon said. "He'll be very happy to know that. Perhaps he can sell some of the land to raise money to restore the rest of the property."

"That shouldn't be necessary," the *notaire* said. "Because of the uncertain state of the French economy, I persuaded Jean-Louis to transfer the bulk of his fortune to England. London is banker to the world, and the investments I made on his behalf have prospered. Most of that sum was bequeathed to Philippe. He won't have wealth unlimited, but the income will allow him to make the estate profitable again if he uses it carefully."

"I think he will," Suzanne said. "Philippe seems truly dedicated to the land and now he will be able to restore it to productivity. This will be a great comfort to him and Marie. They are expecting a child, so their lack of resources was upsetting."

"You are both very generous," Morel said, tilting his head to one side curiously. "You want nothing for yourselves?"

"As you know, my mother was English and her fortune remained there," Simon explained. "My inheritance provides all that we'll need."

"There is another important provision of the will," the *notaire* said. "Madame de Chambron, you were so young that you probably weren't aware of this, but your father was an expert negotiator, and the marriage contract drawn up with Jean-Louis protected your dowry to a remarkable degree. That money is also in England, and it's quite a substantial amount."

Suzanne's jaw dropped. "So when I was doing piecework to keep from starving, I had a fortune sitting in a bank a few miles away?"

Simon gave a slow whistle. "How ironic."

After a long moment of silence, he said, "You could have kept all this money for yourself, Monsieur Morel. You have been a remarkable protector and manager of the Duval family assets."

Hearing the unspoken question, the *notaire* said dryly, "I serve the law, Monsieur le Comte. Honor is not the sole preserve of the aristocracy."

"So I have found myself," Simon agreed. "I trust you have been well compensated for your efforts?"

"My fees are quite adequate." The *notaire* cleared his throat in a meaningful way. "The Morels have handled the affairs of the Duvals for generations. I gather your financial life will be based in England, but naturally I will be pleased to handle any matters that involve France."

Simon glanced at Suzanne, who gave a small nod. "We will welcome your assistance here," he said.

Looking pleased, Morel continued, "I would like to meet Philippe Duval when he has the opportunity to come to Saint-Denis."

"I'll tell him that," Simon said. "I'm sure he'd like to meet you also."

With the prospect of Philippe becoming an important client, Morel asked, "How was he raised? What has he been doing all these years?"

"His mother's family raised him on a farm in the general area of Château Chambron," Suzanne replied. "He was well educated for a farmer's son. He went to war several years ago."

"As one does," Simon said dryly. "He was an officer in an infantry regiment."

"What of his wife? What is her background?"

In other words, would Marie be an appropriate wife? "Marie is from Lorraine," Suzanne said. "Her father was also a man of the law, but an *avocat*, not a *notaire*. She is intelligent, practical, and she and her husband are devoted to each other."

"Good, all good," Morel murmured. His voice became brisk. "What I've given you today is an overview of your situation, but I must prepare official documents for your signatures and get the most up-to-date figures for the bank accounts. Can you return in two days so all that might be finalized?"

"Of course. Can you draw up two copies of everything? I'd like to have them in separate places if we should chance to be stopped at road barriers on our way back to Brussels."

The *notaire* grimaced. "That's a wise precaution, but I'll need another day."

Suzanne said innocently, "That will give us time to see a little of Paris. It's been so long since either of us has been here." She would enjoy seeing the sights, and Simon could observe troop movement and perhaps gather other information. "Monsieur Morel, can you suggest a hotel in Paris that might be a good place to stay? Convenient and not too grand."

The *notaire* considered. "The city is full to the brim with all the, mmm . . . political excitement, but one of these hotels should be able to accommodate you." He wrote down several names and addresses and handed them to Simon. Rising, he said, "Then I shall see you in three days, and let me say it has been a pleasure to meet with you both."

He shook Simon's hand, then bowed to Suzanne. "Now if you'll excuse me . . ." He rang for the clerk, who escorted them out.

As they stepped outside, Simon asked quietly, "If you'd known you had a fortune, would you have accepted my proposal of marriage?"

Suzanne was silent as they waited for a wagon to pass before they crossed the street. "No," she said at last. "I felt too damaged to marry again. I would have refused you." She turned her head to gaze up into his gray eyes, cool to mask his feelings. "And that would have been the greatest mistake of my life."

Chapter 30

⁕

Suzanne felt as if they were on a second honeymoon, one very different from the blissful peace they'd enjoyed at White Horse Manor. They found a room at one of Monsieur Morel's suggested hostelries, a small inn on a side street not far from the Tuileries, the great sprawling imperial palace where Bonaparte was rebuilding his empire. Paris buzzed with energy, marching troops, and an undercurrent of danger.

Like any couple on a honeymoon, they admired the sights of a great city in springtime, and as Suzanne had predicted, no one took much notice of them. She'd actually spent a good deal of time in Paris because Jean-Louis had preferred it to the country, but she'd seen only the narrow aristocratic society inhabited by her husband. Though she'd made friends among the women and had lived well, she'd never walked the teeming streets with an interesting, protective man at her side.

They crossed the bridges over the Seine to the Left Bank and back again, then visited the glittering jewel box of Sainte-Chapelle, which was surely the most beautiful chapel in France and quite possibly the world. They ate food from street vendors and looked into some of the most fashionable shops in Europe. They even walked by the grand mansion where Suzanne had lived with Jean-Louis, but she felt no connection or nostalgia for it. The girl she'd been and that life she'd lived felt infinitely far away.

Suzanne's favorite place was the glorious Cathedral of Notre-Dame, where they admired the stained glass windows and lit candles for the people they'd loved and lost. She even lit one for Jean-Louis, her thoughts bittersweet. He hadn't been a particularly good husband, but she would never forget how entranced she'd been by the handsome, charming man she'd wed when she was only a child. A different lifetime.

Simon knew the city at street level and he enjoyed showing her around, but even he couldn't identify all the different kinds of troops they saw marching in the streets. Most were infantry, but there were also cavalry units in flamboyant uniforms and once a procession of horse artillery, the wheels of the gun carriages making a deafening clatter on the cobblestone streets.

On the second day, they'd been strolling in the Tuileries Gardens when they saw a group of colorfully garbed soldiers leaving the palace. In the center of the group was a handsome, impatient man with dark red hair. Soldiers began bringing out horses. The redhead mounted his and waited for his aides to do the same.

Simon drew Suzanne back to the edge of the gardens as they watched the soldiers. "That is Marshal Ney," he said softly. "He was called the Bravest of the Brave by Napoleon himself. A cavalry leader and one of the best soldiers in Europe, though perhaps a little too impetuous, which is not always a good thing in a subordinate."

Fascinated, she said, "Isn't he the one who became a commander for King Louis XVIII and vowed he'd bring

Napoleon back to Paris in an iron cage when the emperor escaped Elba and returned to France?"

"The very one," Simon agreed. "When he and his troops encountered Napoleon, his men began shouting, *'Vive le emperor,'* and the whole force put itself under the emperor's command. Led by Ney."

She frowned. "How could he betray his vows to the king so easily?"

"He changed his mind," Simon said dryly. "I'm not sure it was done easily, but it's hard to look at the face of a man with whom you've ridden into battle and order your soldiers to shoot him down."

She shivered as she tried to imagine doing such a thing. "Do you think the emperor ever considers what his actions cost everyone around him?"

"If he did, he would never be able to do the things he's done."

Ney and his aides had ridden off, so she took Simon's arm and they headed back to their inn. They would be leaving in the morning, first to go to Monsieur Morel's office, then on to Brussels after they'd signed the necessary papers.

When they reached the inn, the garrulous innkeeper, Monsieur Gagnon, greeted them after they rang to be let in. "Eh, my children, have you enjoyed your time in Paris?"

Suzanne generally let Simon do the talking, and she did so now. "It's a grand city, Monsieur Gagnon. It makes our Brussels look like scarcely more than a market town," Simon said. "Though my business here didn't prosper, I'm happy to visit again after too many years away." He glanced fondly at Suzanne. "And to show Paris to my bride."

Suzanne smiled and batted her lashes, trying to look not very bright since she didn't want Gagnon to think much about her.

"Ah, you are newly married?" the innkeeper said jovially. "Come into my quarters and have a glass of wine with me."

Simon agreed readily since he was always interested in hearing what people had to say. Gagnon shared a cozy ground-floor apartment with his aging mother, who poured wine for her son and his guests, then retreated into a rocking chair in the corner and lit up a foul-smelling pipe. After they were seated on worn but comfortable chairs, Gagnon asked curiously, "You mentioned that your business hadn't prospered?"

"We came from Brussels to look into a possible legacy from my wife's uncle. Luckily we expected little, because that is what we found." Simon sipped at his wine, a robust red. "There was about enough to pay the costs for this trip."

Suzanne said innocently, "But we've seen Paris, and in such exciting times!"

Gagnon snorted. "Too exciting! The madness of kings and emperors." He shook his head. "Most Frenchmen want a liberal government with a Parliament that speaks for the people. Rather like what the British have, but better because it would be French. But what do we get? Tyrants who make promises to obey the will of the people, but then go ahead and do whatever they want. They listen to no one. Bah!"

His mother pulled her pipe from her mouth long enough to spit out, "Hang the bloody emperor!"

Gagnon said uneasily, "That's not a wise thing to say, *ma mère*."

"I spit on the emperor's grave!" She jammed the pipe stem back in her mouth and began rocking furiously.

Gagnon lowered his voice, looking nervous. "Pay no mind to my mother. My father and both of my brothers died fighting for France. It is a hard thing for a mother to accept."

"No mother could forget such losses," Suzanne said

warmly, thinking that Gagnon probably didn't like Napoleon, either, but was too discreet to say so to strangers. "We women pray for peace. Do you think there will be a new war?"

Looking troubled, he poured himself more wine. "No one knows. But it is easier to rally a nation to fight the enemy than it is to agree on bitter political issues."

Simon sighed. "I fear you're right, Monsieur Gagnon." He swallowed the last of his wine. "Come, *ma petite*. We have a long journey ahead of us and it's time we retired. Thank you for the wine and your thoughts, monsieur. We'll return to Brussels and pray for peace."

Suzanne also rose and took her leave of the innkeeper and his mother. She and Simon didn't speak until they were in their bedroom. As she set her cloak and bonnet aside, she said, "Do you think he's right about what the people of France want?"

"Yes, most people want peace and prosperity with a good job, enough to eat, and time to enjoy friends and family." He peeled off his coat. "But leaders like Napoleon find no glory in peace."

They left Paris early the next morning when the streets were largely empty except for farmers driving in carts of produce from the country, and the ominous stamp of marching feet as new military units entered the city.

Their stop at the *notaire* was only long enough to sign the required papers to the accompaniment of coffee and pastries. Then Monsieur Morel sent them off with best wishes for a safe journey. Simon felt there was unusual intensity in that farewell, and suspected that their return to Brussels would not be as smooth as the journey to Paris.

His feeling was confirmed not far north of Saint-Denis when he saw a manned barricade across the road ahead.

He said under his breath, "Look dull, *ma petite*. I believe we are about to have our papers checked."

She drew in her breath. "Napoleon doesn't want information about Paris moving north toward the Allied headquarters?"

"That's my guess." He pulled up his horses at the barrier and greeted the guards politely. The guards studied the identity papers and asked questions about why they had come to Paris all the way from Brussels. Simon answered the questions patiently, avoiding any unnecessary comments. Suzanne sat beside him looking nervous and mousy. Eventually they were waved on.

Suzanne breathed with relief as they continued on their way. Simon warned, "I doubt this will be the last time we're stopped and searched."

"I think we should conceal the documents from Monsieur Morel. They aren't obviously valuable like jewels, but they represent a considerable amount of money. If the guards can read the bank statements and see how much is involved, they might think we're aristocrats fleeing Napoleon's return."

"That's a good idea. What kind of concealment are you thinking about?"

"I'm a seamstress. When we stop for the night, I'll stitch one set of documents into my cloak and the other into the lining of your travel case."

Simon nodded. "With luck, they won't be disturbed. But if hidden documents are found, we'll look very suspicious."

"I thought of that. It will make me feel better to be doing something that might help us to get out of France safely," she explained. "I have a couple of other ideas that might be useful. Even if they aren't, staying busy is better than fretting."

That was a sentiment he understood. At least he had driving the carriage to help occupy his mind.

They passed through two more road barricades that day, and the farther north they traveled, the surlier the guards became. Their Belgian credentials weren't challenged specifically, but the level of suspicion was rising.

As darkness fell, they reached a posting inn where they'd stayed on their way south. "Let's stop here for the night," Simon suggested. "It's reasonably comfortable, and after dinner, I'll talk to the landlord about different routes north, and what he's heard from other travelers. A slower, less traveled road might have fewer guard posts."

"You can work on that while I hide the documents." Suzanne made a face. "I'll be glad to get back into Belgium!"

After an adequate dinner, Simon sought out the landlord while Suzanne ascended to their room and pulled out her travel sewing kit. Besides concealing the legal documents, she had a couple of ideas that were so foolish she wouldn't even tell Simon. But in an uncertain situation, they might be useful.

When Simon joined her later, he said, "I hope you've been more successful than I. There is a turnpike that will go part of the way, but we'll have to get back on this road eventually. The landlord thinks that civilians like us are getting through to Belgium, but he isn't sure."

"Then we must continue to look dull and harmless. The sewing project has gone well, though." Suzanne displayed what she had done. Her cloak was a double layer of felted material and she'd been able to tuck one set of the documents between the layers of the upper back. The fabric was heavy enough that the addition of the documents was barely noticeable.

"Very nice," Simon said as he inspected the cloak. "What will you do with my travel case?"

"I've already done it," Suzanne replied. "The case had a hand-stitched oilcloth lining already. I was able to unpick one seam, insert the documents, and sew it up again."

Simon looked more closely. "It's impossible to see where you resewed it! You really are a first-rate seamstress."

"It's more challenging than being a countess," she said with amusement. "Being a seamstress requires intelligence and skill. All a countess needs is an expensive wardrobe and a feeling of superiority."

"Now you are a double countess," Simon said as he began to undress for bed. "Isn't that more work? Twice the wardrobe, twice the sense of superiority?"

"Not really. All I have to do is ignore my rank twice as hard!" Suzanne yawned. "Shall we see if the bed is any more comfortable than it was on the journey south?"

"Even if it isn't, I have you and you're soft," he said with mock smugness.

She laughed and threw a pillow at him. When they settled into the bed, she was indeed wonderfully soft and warm, yet even with Suzanne in his arms, Simon had trouble falling to sleep. Danger was gathering, was in the very air.

And he didn't know if they would be able to avoid it.

Chapter 31

❦

The next day they took the toll road that paralleled the main Brussels road for a distance. Since it was a toll road, it was in better condition, but less traveled because it cost money. It had barricades at several of the tollgates, though. The bored guards were very thorough and suspicious. They growled over Simon and Suzanne's identity papers and searched their carriage, finding nothing of interest.

After that happened twice, Simon said, "I'm leaving the turnpike at the next tollgate. The main road is at least busier so the guards have less time to harass us."

Suzanne said, "I wonder how many French troops are doing this sort of work?"

"If there are this many on all roads out of Paris in every direction, it could be quite a few men," Simon observed. "If they are concentrated on the roads leading north to Belgium, that says something interesting about what Bonaparte's intentions might be."

"But we don't know if there are barricades in all directions."

"Such are the joys of intelligence work," Simon said wryly. "One's ignorance is so much greater than one's knowledge." They rounded a bend and saw the next toll-house. It had been turned into a guardhouse and the swinging gate was now manned by three French soldiers.

Simon's senses snapped with an instant warning of danger. The soldiers looked like the kind of swaggering bullies who enjoyed throwing their authority around, and Simon caught the smell of sour wine. They'd been drinking heavily by the look of it, and their gazes all went to Suzanne.

The sergeant in charge, a great hulking brute, barked, "Show me your papers!"

Simon produced their identification from an inside coat pocket. Maurice had artistically aged the papers before handing them over, and the wear had become more authentic in the last several days of use.

The sergeant frowned at Simon's identification. "This looks fake to me."

"It's genuine!" Simon protested. "My papers have been accepted at every other guard post on our journey."

"Maybe the soldiers manning those posts aren't as smart as we are." The sergeant elbowed the man next to him and they both laughed as if there had been a joke. "You look like a bloody English spy to me!"

"I'm as much a Frenchman as you are!" Simon replied indignantly. "Now I live in Brussels, as true a French city as Paris. Twenty years Belgium has been part of France, and it's waiting for the emperor to make it French again."

"Sounds just like what a spy would say," the sergeant said, elbowing the man beside him again. Clearly they were itching for a fight, and being bullies, they wanted to pick on an easy target. Worse, their glances kept flicking to Suzanne, who was doing her best to be unobtrusive but was still quietly attractive and undeniably female.

Would a bribe help? Some officials would accept money

and wave them through, while others would see it as proof of criminality and they'd be in much worse trouble. Usually he made such decisions in an instant, but he realized that fear for Suzanne was clouding his judgment.

Before Simon could decide on the best course of action, the sergeant snarled, "Get out of the carriage so we can search you." He smiled viciously. "And ask you more questions. This time, I want honest answers, you traitor!"

If Simon was alone, he'd fight back with a ferocity that would have astonished the sergeant, but if he did that now, what would happen to Suzanne? The soldiers were armed, ready, and eager to shoot someone, and his wife was right in the line of fire. The knowledge was paralyzing.

Impatiently the sergeant grabbed Simon's arm and yanked him from the carriage, than hurled him to the ground with bruising force. "Take this spy and his wife into the building and we'll see what they know!" He grinned wolfishly, ready for torture.

As one of the soldiers hauled Simon to his feet, Suzanne said in a throaty purr, "Oh, I'm not his *wife*! I scarcely know the man. Except in one way!" She tittered musically. "He has a boring wife in Brussels, but he was in Paris and wanted a little fun so I said I'd accompany him on his way back to Belgium."

All three men stared at her. While the sergeant had been bullying Simon, Suzanne had slipped off her cloak so it lay on the bench seat of the carriage.

Under the cloak, she wore a dark red morning gown with a white cotton fichu tucked modestly around her neckline, but as she spoke she tugged off the fichu. She'd altered the gown with a shockingly low neckline that revealed a riveting expanse of creamy curves, turning her from a prim wife into a sensual temptress.

A quick tug at her hairpins and waves of shining dark hair tumbled over her shoulders and throat as she swung gracefully down from her side of the carriage. "I'm an honest working girl so I made sure the fellow had his fun."

Her sultry gaze moved over the French soldiers, coming to rest on the sergeant. She circled the carriage toward him, every part of her body signaling wantonness. "But sometimes I like giving it away for free to a *real* man!"

Simon and the soldiers were equally stunned. Suzanne took the sergeant's arm, saying throatily, "Sergeant, let's go inside and I'll show you a *very* good time."

She cast a coy glance at the other two soldiers. "Don't worry, my lads, there's enough to go around!"

Staring at Suzanne, one of the soldiers said in a hoarse voice, "Should we just shoot 'im, Sergeant Fabron?"

Simon saw a pulse jump in Suzanne's jaw. "Now don't you go and do something hasty, *mon chéri*!" she said coaxingly as she reached out to caress the soldier's wrist. "He owes me half my fee and I won't get it until we reach Belgium. A girl deserves to be paid, doesn't she?"

The guards were entranced enough to go along with her wishes. Fabron said, "Lamont, before someone else comes along, take this sod and the carriage around to the back of the tollbooth. Gag 'im, tie 'im to a wheel, and search 'im down to 'is bare bollocks to find the money he's supposed to give the wench. If it isn't on him, search the carriage. Berger, you stay out here and man the barricade."

"Thank you, Sergeant Fabron," Suzanne cooed. "Now let's you and I go inside for a little fun." Trailing the delicate white silk fichu in the air like smoke, she sauntered seductively into the tollbooth turned guardhouse, which was the size of a small cottage. Every movement she made was an exercise in provocation.

Eyes glazed with lust, the sergeant followed her inside, slamming the door behind him. Lamont, the soldier who had been ordered to move Simon, abruptly jammed the butt of his rifle into Simon's solar plexus with a force that produced temporary paralysis. Then he shoved his prisoner into the carriage and led the horses and vehicle around to the back of the guardhouse. As he struggled to recover, Simon heard muffled sounds coming from inside the guardhouse. Was that a female cry? The sound of a blow? *What the bloody hell was going on in there?*

Behind the guardhouse was a shed and a small paddock containing a sturdy dapple gray gelding. Lamont tethered the carriage horses, then turned to Simon with an expression of anticipation. "Maybe I should start by shooting your bollocks off? That would make it easy to find out whether you've hidden money down there."

Simon hadn't fully recovered from the blow, but if he didn't act now, he was dead. As the soldier dragged him from the carriage, Simon kicked out ferociously, feeling bone shatter as his boot smashed into the soldier's jaw.

Lamont gave a choked cry as blood sprayed from his mouth. Simon ripped the rifle from the man's hands and bashed him on the side of his head with the wooden stock. Lamont collapsed and Simon swiftly tied him up and gagged him with his own cross belts and dirty handkerchief.

He checked that the rifle was loaded and half cocked, then raced around the guardhouse, staying low. He paused before rounding the corner and saw Berger, the other soldier, staring avidly at the door of the guardhouse. Suzanne emerged looking deliciously rumpled. "Now it's your turn," she purred as she beckoned to the soldier.

She moved normally and her words were convincing, but Simon was sickened to realize that the dark red of her gown bore almost invisible darker stains of blood. She was trembling even though she managed to sound seductive.

Berger stammered, "I . . . I shouldn't leave the barricade."

"Sergeant Fabron will be out in a moment when he's

recovered from"—her voice choked off for a moment—
"from so much more than he expected! But this is a quiet
road, so let's get a bit of a start for what comes next." She
went up to him and raised her face for a kiss. He eagerly
complied—and as Simon watched, Suzanne clamped on
the blood vessels of his neck to block the flow to Berger's
brain.

She was shorter than the soldier so the angle was difficult, but the hold worked well enough that Berger sagged
away from her, looking confused. Simon closed in on the
pair and swung the stock of the rifle into the back of
Berger's skull with vicious force.

As the soldier dropped like a puppet whose strings had
been cut, Simon spun around to his wife. "Dear God,
Suzanne, are you all right?"

"Did you think I didn't know how to be a whore?" Her
face white, she folded to her knees and vomited into the
grass. Simon knelt beside her and wrapped one arm
around her cold, shaking body as she breathed in short,
frantic gasps.

After long moments, she raised her head and whispered, "Not . . . really hurt. But I had to let him *handle*
me. He said he liked it rough. Then he lay down on the
cot and explained in vile detail what he wanted me to do.
He . . . he didn't expect me to fight." She drew a harsh
breath. "Until I knifed him. Then . . . and then . . ." She
retched again.

She stumbled as she tried to rise. Simon helped her up,
aching for her shock and horror. A bruise was forming on
her left cheekbone and she began to sob as she turned into
his arms. He held tightly to her as long as he dared and
wondered what the devil had happened in the guardhouse.

Worried about passing time, he said in his calmest
voice, "We're going to have to get out of here as fast as

we can on horseback. That will be quicker than the carriage. There's a riding hack in the paddock in back. Go and exercise your horse magic on him so he can be saddled. I'll move the soldiers into the guardhouse and make sure they aren't going to escape anytime soon."

"Fabron . . . won't be going anywhere." She wiped her mouth again as she turned to go around the guardhouse.

Ruthlessly suppressing his concern for her, he set the rifle down and hauled one end of the barricade out of the roadway so travelers could pass if they came by. Most people would be so glad to avoid paying the toll that they wouldn't look around for toll keepers or soldiers.

Next he dragged Berger into the guardhouse and dropped him to one side before he turned to the cot to examine the sergeant's body. Simon's gut clenched and he understood why Suzanne had been so sick. The man's breeches were unfastened, revealing a mass of bloody tissue. There were a dozen other stab wounds in the massive body, one a slash across his throat. So much blood . . .

He drew a long, shaken breath, forcing himself not to look away. He guessed that Suzanne had gone temporarily berserk after Fabron had "handled" her. That had driven her to this frenzied retaliation for all she had endured at the hands of men.

He ached at the knowledge that his wife had been forced to such violence.

Face grim, he retrieved the two French rifles from outside and set them behind the guardhouse before dragging the still unconscious Lamont inside to join his fellows. As he'd hoped, Suzanne was in the paddock talking to the dapple gray, which required her to calm down and speak softly so as not to alarm the beast.

A quick, efficient search of the French soldiers indicated that Lamont and Berger would survive, though their injuries would keep them off the battlefield for a while. He collected all their weapons, along with a canvas bag containing bread, cheese, sausages, and a jug of wine.

He also took all the blankets except the blood-saturated one under Fabron and carried them outside with the weapons and food. Suzanne had coaxed the gelding close enough to get hold of its bridle. Hearing Simon, she turned, her green eyes huge and stark as she waited for her husband to recoil with loathing or rage.

Simon said only, "He deserved it." Then he entered the shed. Inside he found the gray's saddle and a set of sizable saddlebags. Military equipment. As he emerged with both, he said, "You can ride this fellow and I'll ride the piebald carriage horse. It will be awkward since he's not trained for riding, but he's a docile beast and I can manage him. We can lead the other horse. I don't want to leave any horses here in case one of the soldiers wakes up soon and wants to pursue us."

"We can use the other carriage horse as a pack animal," she said, leaning her forehead into the gray's neck. She looked numb and achingly fragile.

"Good idea. While I pack everything we need, you should sit down and rest," he said gently. "We have some hard riding ahead of us."

She nodded and settled on a crude bench set against the back wall of the guardhouse. She barely had time to lean back before they heard the sound of a heavy wagon approaching along the road. They both stiffened.

A hoarse voice said cheerfully, "A bit o' luck here! No one on duty at this tollbooth. Let's get on by before the keeper returns."

Simon and Suzanne held still, barely breathing, until the crunch of wagon wheels had faded from hearing. Suzanne drew a deep breath and got to her feet. "I assume we'll travel cross country until we're back in Belgium. Do you know the way?"

"I've been studying maps since I arrived in Brussels and I have a compass if necessary, but all we need to do is head north and avoid French troops and barricades," he replied as he started saddling the gray. "Belgium isn't far. We'll probably have to spend tonight in a French barn, but tomorrow we'll be back in Brussels."

She nodded mutely and began hauling their bags from the small carriage.

Working together, they were soon ready to leave. They hadn't taken much luggage to Paris, but enough that it was convenient to have a pack animal. Simon folded one of the blankets to make a riding pad for the bay. The other blankets he wrapped around the rifles to disguise what they were.

When everything was packed, he helped Suzanne into the gray's saddle. Since she was riding astride, her blood-stained scarlet skirts fell untidily over her knees and revealed her ankles. She seemed barely aware of that. She could change into clean clothing later, but now it was more important to leave this place of blood and violence.

They set off north, leaving the carnage behind them. But Simon knew that neither of them would ever forget.

Chapter 32

❧

Suzanne rode north through lanes and fields, following Simon blindly and barely aware of her surroundings. Her thoughts were a whirlwind of terror and blood.

Efficient as always, Simon found them an isolated barn with enough hay for the horses and a rain-filled live-stock watering trough where she could wash up. As she did, images of Lady Macbeth trying to wash the blood off her hands filled her mind.

Simon helped her as if she was a child unable to manage, including giving her a shirt and his spare pair of trousers to wear because she'd be riding astride again the next day. The clothing was enormous on her, but it was comforting to wear his things. She was also glad that she didn't look at all like a woman.

After she had washed and changed, she found that he'd groomed the horses, then made a comfortable nest for them with a blanket spread over a deep pile of straw. "Sit down and have something to eat before sleeping. Do you want to start with some wine?"

He offered her a jug but she shook her head. Fabron had smelled of sour wine . . .

Not questioning her reaction, he passed her a piece of slightly stale bread with a slab of good cheese on top. She realized that she hadn't eaten since breakfast at the inn, and the food helped steady her.

Dead men's food . . .

Suppressing the thought, she followed the bread and cheese with a swallow of the wine. A merciful white, not blood red. She wondered if she'd ever be able to drink red wine again.

They ate and drank without speaking and watched the sun slide below the horizon. The sunset was beautiful. And blood red . . .

She decided she'd had enough to eat.

When they were done, Simon packed the food and drink back in the canvas bag. "Time to rest," he said soothingly. "We've had a rather tiring day."

She smiled humorlessly at his understatement. Very English.

"Can you stand to be touched, or would you prefer to take a blanket and roll into a ball well away from me?" he asked, his voice calm. "I understand that you might not want to be close to a man."

The question jarred her from her daze. "How can you even bear the thought of touching me?" Her voice cracked. "After what I did!"

"Come here, *ma petite*," he said softly as he extended a hand toward her. "Let us face the night together."

Desperate for the comfort he offered, she took Simon's hand and stretched out beside him. The golden straw under the blanket rustled in a friendly welcome. Simon drew the other blanket over them and pulled her close.

She was cold, so cold, but his warm body and embrace began thawing the ice in her heart. "I didn't mean to do it," she whispered. "But he was like Gürkan. A similar size and build and a cruel, evil soul."

Simon gently touched the bruise on her cheek where the sergeant had struck her for no particular reason other than to demonstrate that he was powerful and she was helpless. "He was a brute, *ma petite*. Did he injure you in any other way?"

Guessing what he didn't want to ask, she said, "He didn't rape me. There wasn't time for that. He wanted . . . other things first."

Simon winced. She sighed and said half to herself, "Though I'd rather regretted that I didn't have the opportunity to kill Gürkan myself, I never truly imagined myself capable of being so vicious. But I was."

"His behavior put you into a killing rage, like an ancient berserker warrior in a battle fury," Simon said matter-of-factly. "The rage boiled over and you lost all control."

That was what her anger had felt like, she realized. It had been an uncontrollable force that boiled up in her body like molten lava and made her want to annihilate her enemy. As she did.

Simon's explanation didn't take away her horror at her behavior, but it was an explanation that helped her make sense of what she had done. She began weeping silently into his shoulder while his warm hand stroked down her back.

When she'd spent all her tears and had no more, she asked, "How do you understand this so well?"

After a long silence, he said heavily, "I experienced something very like what you did. The experience was . . . shattering. I wasn't sorry for the result, but I loathed myself for how I had done it. How vicious and uncontrolled I'd been."

"What happened?" she whispered, wanting to know, not sure she had the right to ask when she could feel his pain.

He drew a rough breath. "It was on the Peninsula. I came upon a deserter who had just raped and murdered two young children. A brother and sister."

"Oh, no!" Suzanne gasped with horror, her nails biting into her palm as she imagined how he must have felt to discover such evil.

"Their bodies were still warm, but it was too late. They were already gone. I had a bayonet and a rage that knew no bounds." Simon drew a ragged breath. "I cannot regret ridding the world of a monster, but I did regret becoming a monster myself."

"I'm sorry, so sorry," she whispered, able to envision a scene that must have been similar to the one she had created earlier this day. Then, because she needed to know, she asked, "Have you ever done anything like that again?"

"No." His arm had tightened around her shoulders, and she sensed the effort he made to relax. "I am a soldier. I've killed sometimes when it was needful, but never again with that annihilating rage. Once was enough."

"Oh, yes!" she said so fervently that Simon laughed a little.

"I doubt you'll ever do such a thing again, *ma chérie*. A lifetime of rage was burning through you. Some men need killing and Fabron was one of them," Simon said. "He is now part of your past, as is Gürkan. Don't let them live on in your mind and torment you."

"That's good advice, though it will take time for me to drive them from my thoughts." She cuddled under Simon's warm arm and rested her head on his shoulder as she began to relax. She had survived the horror of slavery and Gürkan, and she would survive this. She had behaved savagely, but she vowed not to let that one act poison her life. *No wallowing.*

"I thought I was done with war, yet here it is on our doorstep again," Simon said. "I will continue to do unofficial exploration work for Wellington because it must be done, but I'll do it alone in the future."

She cringed inwardly. "I caused too much trouble."

"No, but today I realized that when you're with me, I'm too concerned for your safety," he explained. "That clouded my judgment and slowed my reactions. Dangerous."

"If you'd been alone, would you have been able to fight your way free of three hostile French soldiers?"

"Nothing is sure in such a situation," he replied, "but I've escaped similar situations unscathed."

"I'm sorry I was a liability," she said in a small voice. "I thought I was helping."

"Your presence was necessary on this trip to the *notaire*. There was no way to predict that we'd run into drunken soldiers hungry for violence. What you did to distract Sergeant Fabron was brilliant even though it played out in unexpected ways," Simon said thoughtfully. "At the end of the day, what matters is that we both escaped relatively undamaged." His arm tightened around her. "But on purely military scouting trips, I'm better off alone."

A few days earlier she might have argued with him, but no longer. His military experience and understanding were far beyond anything she would ever master. "Very well, I won't pester you to travel on journeys where I would be a nuisance."

He breathed a sigh of relief. "Good."

"You thought I'd be stubborn, didn't you?"

He chuckled, then brushed a kiss on her forehead. "Yes, but one of the many things I like about you is your intelligence."

"That's sometimes more true than other times," she said ruefully.

"Such is the nature of being human." He yawned, covering his mouth with one hand. "I'm going to sleep like a hibernating bear. It's been a tiring day."

That it had been. "Will any sound that suggests danger wake the bear up in an instant?"

"Yes, it's one of those skills one learns in the army. Luckily this seems a peaceful place. I hope you can sleep also, milady." He tucked her close and relaxed.

He fell into sleep almost immediately, his slow, steady breaths soothing. She wasn't surprised when she thought of how much he'd done this day, taking down one of the soldiers, then managing their escape and quietly caring for her when she fell to pieces. He deserved his rest.

Though she was also exhausted, her mind was too jangled for sleep. She forced her body to relax, muscle by muscle. Then she made herself remember the whole horrible encounter with Fabron, refusing to avoid a single moment.

Then she hurled the experience into a mental bonfire and let the flames consume every vile touch, every bit of rage, every wash of shame, every searing emotion. The mental exercise left her shaking, but distanced from what had happened. She had devised this technique as a way to endure the worst of her experiences in the harem.

Because above all else, she was a survivor. She would not allow monsters to destroy the goodness of her new life.

Thinking of goodness, she patted her sleeping husband. How had she been so lucky as to find a man of such kindness and understanding? Well, actually he had found her. She hoped he didn't regret how complicated their bargain had become.

That was a thought for another day. For now, finally, she could sleep.

* * *

Suzanne was dozing peacefully when rustling in the straw jerked her awake. Not an enemy. The sound was too small for a soldier, and far too close. A rat?

Warily she sat up and looked around. Simon slept on, presumably recognizing that sounds from her were unthreatening.

More rustling. The dim light in the barn caught the movement of a small creature, but it didn't move like a rat. A cat—that was it. A small, scrawny cat was nosing at the food bag. It skittered backward when she moved, staring at her anxiously. Poor hungry little fellow. It seemed to be having a worse day even than she was.

Moving slowly, she reached out for the bag and pulled it close, then felt inside. Ah, the cheese. She broke off a chunk and pulled it out, then broke off a smaller piece and tossed it toward the little cat. It jumped nervously, then crept forward warily on its belly till it reached the tidbit and bolted it down. Suzanne tossed another piece and this time the cat didn't back off as far before moving in to devour.

She continued tossing small pieces until the original chunk was gone. When the cat saw that no more food was coming, it sat back on its haunches and daintily washed its small face. Then it vanished into the shadows.

Smiling, Suzanne relaxed back on the blanket and rolled an arm over Simon. Feeding the hungry was rewarding.

Suzanne woke the next morning when something small, cool, and moist touched her cheek. Surprised, she opened her eyes and saw a hopeful little tabby cat almost nose to nose with her. She decided it was a half-grown kitten, not yet a full-fledged cat. A skinny gray tabby with golden eyes. The little puss had been there a while, she guessed, since her shoulder was warm as if a tiny little fur blanket had been resting there.

She moved her hand slowly to the cat and scratched its head. She was rewarded with a treble purr. The cat arched its back and turned under her hand, the long tail a happy banner. Suzanne got a close view of the little fellow's backside. A "he," not an "it."

He head-butted her cheek. She laughed and Simon stirred to wakefulness beside her. "It appears you have company," he murmured.

"This little fellow was trying to get into the food bag last night, so I gave him some cheese. He must have liked it."

"Food is a fine basis for a relationship." Also moving slowly, Simon sat up. "I think he's trying to convey that it's breakfast time."

"Can we spare more cheese?"

"Go ahead, we have enough to get us back to Brussels and then some." Simon extended his hand and the little cat sniffed it, then licked his fingertips. "His coat is rough and he's half starving, but he's not feral."

"I think he's a barn cat who wants a position as a house cat." Suzanne pulled out more cheese, setting down a small piece for the cat, then handing a larger piece to Simon, along with the last piece of bread. Since there was still a good supply of cheese, she gave more to the cat.

The three of them ate in companionable silence. Then it was time to pack up, saddle the horses, and resume their journey.

Suzanne thought the cat had gone about his feline business, but after Simon helped her into the gray's saddle, the tabby appeared from nowhere and leaped onto her stirruped left foot. Then he began earnestly hauling himself up her trousered leg, his nails tiny little needles that stabbed through fabric and into skin. He made it up to her knee and jumped on the saddle between her legs, looking vastly pleased with himself.

"I think our scouting party has acquired a new recruit,"

she said, unable to resist scratching his scrawny little neck. "Can I keep him?"

"As long as you're both willing, I don't see why not. He wouldn't have shown up here if he had a real home." Simon had just fastened the supply saddlebags on their packhorse, so he unlatched one side and pulled out a folded shirt. "You might want to put this under him so he doesn't curl his claws into any sensitive bits of your anatomy."

"Good idea. Those claws are *sharp*." She tucked the folded shirt under the little tabby. He settled into the soft fabric and looked ready to ride all day. He smiled at her and she smiled back. Pets were very cheering. "I should give him a name."

"Once you do, he's yours," Simon said with a grin as he swung onto the saddle pad he'd improvised on the bay's back.

"Leo, I think. That's a proper feline name."

"Very well, Leo and milady. Northward, ho!"

Tonight they should sleep in Brussels after what she fervently hoped would be a boringly uneventful day.

Chapter 33

❧

The ride north was more than uneventful; it was delightful. The day was pleasant and sunny, full of late spring beauty before the summer heat. In the middle of a patch of woods, they forded a shallow river. As their horses scrambled up the opposite bank, Simon said, "We have just passed from France into Belgium."

"I'm glad!" she said. "Shall we stop and stretch our legs and have a bite to eat?"

"A good thought. The horses can drink from the river and there's plenty of grass for grazing." He dismounted and helped Suzanne from her horse. "How is little Leo doing? He hasn't tried to bolt?"

"No, he seems quite happy to travel along. He's very attached to me. Literally!" She lifted the little tabby, who promptly dug his needle claws into the shirt that had become his traveling bed. "He's not doing your shirt any good, though."

"It's an old shirt, and even if it wasn't, it's worth sacrificing for such a charming addition to our party."

Suzanne passed Leo to Simon. He was a nice furry little handful who purred, and also yawned to reveal a mouthful of sharp teeth. Lucky he wasn't a biter.

After a pause to scratch Leo's head, Simon set him on the ground. The cat bounced under a shrub to relieve himself. Then he returned and made it politely known to Suzanne that he was ready for another meal.

She dismounted and pulled the food pack from a saddlebag, then tossed a bit of cheese to Leo, who consumed it eagerly and looked hopefully for more. As she gave him another bit, she said, "The cheese may run out before we reach Brussels at this rate."

Simon chuckled. "His enthusiasm is charming, but save some for us, *ma chérie.*"

They settled next to each other on the grass and enjoyed their picnic. Suzanne loved this relaxed time with Simon. No distractions, no danger for the moment.

She discreetly admired her husband's handsome face, which no longer made her think of Jean-Louis, who had glittered with wit and charm over deep layers of self-absorption. Simon had similar bones and build and coloring, but when she looked in his face, she saw calm authority and subtle humor and deep kindness.

She liked that his dark hair was getting pleasantly shaggy and that he let her doze for a few minutes with her head on his lap before they continued. With him, she felt safe and cared for and understood.

What made this day so intensely, painfully wonderful was the knowledge that when they reached Brussels, the hammer of impending war would come down on them. Simon would almost certainly be sent away to do his hazardous exploring work, and the city would fill with would-be warriors and worried women. Of which she would be one, so she wanted to capture every moment of this simple happiness to hold in her heart.

All too soon, Simon woke her from her doze with a

kiss on her temple. "Time to resume our journey, milady. And at the end, we shall find good food and a hot bath and a large, comfortable bed."

"I'm not sure which of those sounds best!" She raised her head from his lap and leaned in for a proper kiss. Simon's arms circled her and he drew her into a leisurely continuation of that kiss. He had a wonderful mouth, so sensual and welcoming. By the time they broke apart, they were both panting.

Simon drew a deep breath and stood, offering her his hand. "Later?"

She rose and gazed into his gray eyes, which were not cool at all. "Later!"

Not releasing her hand, Simon said, "You seem to have recovered from yesterday better than I could have imagined."

"It helps that I have had a great deal of practice at overcoming dreadful experiences at the hands of men." She hesitated, looking for the words to explain. "This time, I had you, who understood my berserker rage. Because of that, I better understood myself, which was a very long step toward accepting my own darkness and beginning to heal."

"I'm glad I was able to help," he said quietly.

"More than you can ever know," she replied in a similar tone. Her voice turned brisk. "But now we must resume our journey because we must reach Brussels before we run out of cheese!"

Simon laughed and helped her onto her horse with little Leo on her lap. Not long after their lunch stop, they intersected the Charleroi-to-Brussels road and their pace increased. It was a long day's ride, but for Suzanne, they reached Brussels too soon, and her perfect day with Simon was over.

At least they had made it to Brussels before the cheese ran out.

Barely.

When Simon, Suzanne, and Leo entered the house, weary and travel stained, the inhabitants immediately started gathering. Maurice and Jackson arrived first. "We'll take care of the horses, but first, what news, sir?" Maurice asked.

"Bonaparte is certainly mobilizing, but it's not clear when or where he'll aim his armies," Simon said succinctly. "It may well be Belgium, though."

Philippe and Marie emerged from the drawing room at the front of the house. He was using a cane for balance, but looked much stronger and was walking well. Marie was beside him, and her gaze went to Suzanne. "Suzanne, did you know you have a cat on your shoulder?"

"So I do," Suzanne said amiably. She reached up to scratch his head. "His name is Leo. He's a country cat who has decided to move to the city."

Simon said, "Philippe, I need to talk to you and Marie. Not bad news at all. Give us time to bathe and change and we can discuss what we learned over a late supper."

Jenny appeared, looking rather appalled. "Madam, your clothing!" she exclaimed, staring at Suzanne's oversized and travel-stained men's garments.

"We had to travel quickly." Suzanne made a face. "Suffice it to say that it was easier to get into France than it was to leave. But as you see, we're fine. I hope you like cats, Jenny!"

"Indeed I do. Young and skinny as this fellow is, I imagine he'll want to go to the kitchen for a meal." Jenny scratched Leo's head, then expertly removed him from Suzanne's shoulder without his claws inflicting further damage.

"I must arrange a bath and help you to change," Jenny continued. "Madame Maurice, do you like cats?" On receiving a positive response, Jenny handed Leo over to the older woman.

Madame Maurice cuddled Leo to her ample bosom and cooed feline noises at him. "I'll fix you that supper after I feed this young rascal."

As the cook headed off to the kitchen, Simon predicted that Leo was going to live very well in this house. Then he followed his wife up the stairs to wash up and change into proper clothing. The day was far from over.

Madame Maurice's dinner was tasty and invigorating, a fine stew of beef and vegetables braised in beer, with bread and more of the same beer to wash it down. Simon told himself he must remember to thank Kirkland again for this amazing house filled with comfort, good food, and experienced spies.

Philippe was twitching with nerves, so Simon put him out of his misery as soon as he'd eaten enough to mitigate his ravenous appetite. "The news is mostly good, starting with the fact that Château Chambron is yours, and your father very specifically left it to his 'beloved son.'"

Philippe swallowed hard, and Simon guessed that that acknowledgment meant almost as much as inheriting the property, at least for tonight. Later it would be the estate that mattered.

"The estate, but not the title," Philippe said in a low voice. "My birth was not legitimate, was it?"

"No," Suzanne said gently. "The title must go to Simon. But you were Jean-Louis's only child. He loved you and provided very handsomely for your future."

Privately Simon thought Jean-Louis could have done a much better and fairer job of raising Philippe, but for a man who was selfish by nature, this was a good effort. Monsieur Morel's generous guiding hand was surely visible here.

Simon passed Philippe his copy of the will. "In more good news, there is also a substantial monetary inheritance. It's rather inconveniently located in London now, but when the political situation stabilizes, you can move the funds here if you like. I strongly suggest that you continue using Monsieur Morel for estate and financial matters. He and his family have served the Duvals for generations, and it was his intelligence and honesty that preserved your inheritance."

He handed over a bank statement. Philippe looked at the column of numbers and gave a breathless whistle. Marie looked over his shoulder and gasped. "It's a fortune!"

"It's not enough to live as grandly as Jean-Louis did," Suzanne said. "And really, there is no need to live that grandly. But used well it should be enough to get the estate back on its feet."

"I strongly suggest that you abandon the château," Simon said. "Repairing it could easily cost your whole inheritance."

"The Château Chambron has been the home of the Comtes de Chambron for centuries," Philippe said unhappily.

Marie laid her hand on his. "It's just a house, *mon chéri*. And it was very uncomfortable living in the ruins! A more modest home for us and money for planting are much more important." She smiled at her husband. "All I need is a house that contains you and is clean, comfortable, and well provisioned. That will be infinitely better than a burned-out palace."

"You're right. I know you're right." With visible regret, Philippe mentally abandoned the family home he'd once yearned for. He raised his gaze to Simon. "Can I transfer the money I'll need for a spring planting before it's too late?"

Simon shook his head. "That will take time and planting won't wait. Since I have already established a banking relationship here in Brussels, I can advance you enough to get started immediately. You can repay me once you have access to your own funds."

Philippe clasped Marie's hand hard, his expression baffled. "Why are you so generous to us? When we first met, I threatened you with my rifle!"

"You were defending what you loved most. I would have done the same. We are family, as I've said before. Family helps family." Simon guessed that Jean-Louis's erratic attention had given Philippe little faith in family support. But he was learning.

"The decisions are yours, of course, but in your position, I'd head down to the estate with a wagon full of seed and farming equipment," Suzanne said thoughtfully. "When you were camping out in the ruins, you were too ill to meet any of the local people, but there must be men and women who worked for the estate in better days and would be pleased to have jobs again."

Marie asked Suzanne, "Most sizable estates also have cottages and tenant buildings scattered about. Is that true of Château Chambron? One such house would suit us for the foreseeable future."

"Yes, there were a number of smaller residences in different locations around the estate," Suzanne replied. "I'd suggest looking for one that isn't currently occupied and being flexible and generous with any of the former tenants and laborers who have been planting crops and keeping livestock on the property since Jean-Louis abandoned it. Deal with them tactfully, and they will reward you with their loyalty, I think. Jean-Louis tended to be . . . rather too aristocratic."

"Luckily, I wasn't raised as a true aristo." Philippe smiled at his wife. "But even so, Marie is in charge of tact and charm."

Marie smiled back at him. "When shall we leave, *mon chéri*?"

"You're not coming with me!" Philippe exclaimed. He

turned to Simon and Suzanne. "Can Marie stay here until the estate and the future are more settled?"

"Of course," Suzanne said warmly. "I would miss her sorely if she were to leave now."

Marie scowled. "The fact that I am with child doesn't make me useless!"

"No, but if the armies of France invade Belgium, one of the routes might be right across your estate," Simon said bluntly.

"He's right." Philippe touched his wife's shining blond hair. "You and our child are too precious to risk in a war zone. If there is danger, it will be easier for me to deal with it if I'm alone."

Marie looked as if she wanted to argue, but her good sense won out. "Very well," she sighed. "But if armies do start marching over the estate, for heaven's sake, get out of the way!"

Philippe smiled with rare humor. "One reason I survived years as a soldier is that I know what armies are like. I have a keen sense of when to retreat and when to go to ground and hide. I'll be safe, and so will you."

Marie caught her husband's hand and held it to her heart. "I know you are right," she said intensely. "But it will be hard to say farewell."

Simon glanced at Suzanne and their somber gazes met. Yes, the farewells would be agonizing for all of them—and in a world on the brink of war, there was no way to avoid them.

Chapter 34

❧

Outside the dining room where the financial discussions had taken place, Jenny and Jackson were waiting, holding hands. She was blushing and looking very pretty, while he looked confident and determined. They exchanged a glance, and then Jenny blurted out, "Madam. Sir. We want to get married!"

"As soon as possible," Jackson added. "Maurice knows a Church of England vicar here in Brussels, and he says we can arrange a marriage quickly."

"How wonderful!" Suzanne exclaimed. "I've been expecting such a happy announcement, and here it is." She guessed they had decided to marry as soon as possible because of the impending war. In a world falling into fragments, they needed to weld themselves together into one loving unit.

Understanding that need, Simon said warmly, "This calls for a celebration!"

Maurice and his wife and several other servants had crowded in behind the happy couple, so Simon continued, "Maurice, I'm sure that this house's cellar must contain champagne. Time to break out a couple of bottles to toast the happy occasion."

Maurice grinned. "Champagne coming right up, sir!"

As everyone chatted and waited for the champagne, Suzanne studied Jackson, amazed at how much he'd changed since Simon had hired him. Then, Jackson had been like a wary dog who had been kicked too often and no longer trusted anyone, except Jenny, who had never lost faith in him.

Now he was confident and protective of his lady love. Simon had said Jackson had become a competent valet and a very good secretary and his daily exercises had improved his hand beyond what anyone had thought possible. Some of the damage would never heal, but no matter. Jackson was ready for what the future might bring, and he and Jenny would face it hand in hand and heart to heart.

Pray God that everyone under this roof did have a future.

After a toast to the young couple's happiness had been drunk, Suzanne and Simon retired, pleading fatigue after their long ride. When they reached their bedroom, Simon quietly closed the door behind him. "First thing in the morning I'll send a note to Wellington's house to inform him that I've returned. I expect he'll want to talk to me tomorrow."

Suzanne sighed and began pulling the pins from her hair. "Then he'll send you off within the next day or so. I hope you can be here for Jenny and Jackson's wedding." Her smile was unsteady. "I've accepted that you're safer traveling fast and alone. Just . . . be sure you survive to come back."

Simon crossed the room and embraced her as if storing up as many memories of touch and closeness as he could.

"I don't want to leave, but it's needful. Knowing which way the enemy will march is the difference between victory and massacre."

"I understand." She bit her lip until the urge to cry passed. "Duty is a harsh mistress. I could scream and weep and beg you not to leave and you'd still go, and we'd both be even more miserable because of my attempts."

Simon chuckled, his expression wry. "You are so wise, milady. Remember that I spent years roaming around Portugal and Spain as an exploring officer and never suffered a major injury. This should be less dangerous."

She leaned back in his arms and gave him a crooked smile. "I don't think I want to know what you consider a *minor* injury! It would probably just make me worry more. My job, I presume, is to stay here and keep the household safe and sane."

"Exactly." He frowned. "I think it very unlikely, but if the French should invade, the city will run mad. Stock supplies of food and ammunition before then, and if trouble comes banging on the door—well, use your best judgment for keeping everyone safe. If rumors of French invasion send half the city fleeing to Antwerp or Ghent, it will be wisest to sit tight here and not risk getting caught in a mob of panicky people."

She shivered. "I agree. Staying here should be safe enough. I'm French and so are half the other people in the household. Brussels is at heart a French city and I wouldn't think Napoleon and his generals will want to burn it."

"I pray you're right, but in war, anything is possible." He took her shoulders, gazing into her eyes as if sheer force of will could keep her safe. "If the worst happens and you must flee Belgium, go home to England and wait for me. I'll find you there."

She couldn't bear the thought of leaving Brussels without him. Home was where Simon was. "We've been talking too much. Time is running out. Let's not waste another moment. Unlace me, please." She turned so he could undo her gown and stays.

"With the greatest of pleasure, *ma belle*." His deft fingers unfastened her gown and stays with amazing swiftness even with pauses for provocative touching.

She turned back to him, yanking off her outer layers. "You're wearing far too many garments, milord. Tonight I want to show you all that I am, and I want to take all that you have."

He caught his breath, understanding her meaning. They'd married in winter and began sharing a bed under layers of blankets. Advancing spring had meant fewer covers and increasingly thorough explorations of each other's bodies, but they had never seen each other unclothed. Suzanne simply hadn't been ready to feel that vulnerable even with Simon.

One night in bed as they held each other, he'd murmured that someday he wanted to see her as God had made her, but being Simon, he'd said nothing more. He'd left the choice to her. Tonight she chose to take the final steps that would bring their marriage to a state of intimacy that she had been unable to accept until now.

After all that had been between them and the separation that was to come, it was time to be the woman Simon deserved.

"As milady desires." He'd removed his coat earlier, and now shirt and trousers and undergarments went flying, along with several buttons. His gaze remained locked on her as she sat on a chair to strip off her stockings and toss them aside.

She was equally riveted by the sight of him. The magnificent shoulders and broad chest that she'd discovered with touch. Narrow waist, powerful thighs. The exact right amount and pattern of dark, masculine hair. He was beautiful in the way only men could be, sleek with power and potent masculinity, equally warrior and protector.

Her throat tight, she stood and slowly drew her chemise over her head, revealing herself fully. He whispered, "You are even lovelier than I dreamed, *ma belle.*"

He stepped toward her and she held up a hand to stop him. "There is one more thing you must see." Steeling herself, she turned so he could see her back. She felt his stillness when he saw the scarlet tattoo that marked the curve of her derriere. "The mark of Gürkan," she said flatly. "So all would know who owned me."

She could *feel* his silent rage flashing like lightning behind her. Then Simon stepped forward and gently kissed the tattoo. "And now the mark of the bravest, freest woman I've known."

With his words and his gesture, the last of her shame vanished. She turned and kissed him with fierce urgency. Body to body, skin to skin, heat to heat.

There had been increasing passion between them, but she'd never initiated it and never like this. He met her with the fullness of desire that he'd been banking until she was ready. Now she was ready, *mon Dieu,* she was ready!

The bed was only a few steps away. She'd pulled the covers all the way down earlier, and now they tumbled onto the sheets together, hands and mouths eager, inventive, devouring. She had a dizzy moment of wondering why it had taken so long to get to this place, and then she stopped bothering to wonder.

Later this night, they would take their time, but not now, not for this coruscating explosion of need. They were lying on their sides, hands demanding, mouths engaged, legs tangled together. Then his fingers slid between her thighs and she cried out with the intensity of the sensations.

When her hips thrust against him, he breathed, "Now?"

"Now!" For the first time, she pushed him onto his back and mounted him, feeling his full strength and heated nakedness. Slowly at first, to make sure that they were properly aligned. Slowly still because she was tight and wanted to savor the rich sense of joining. And slowly because she saw that she was driving him mad, his chest heaving and his eyes wild as his hands cupped her bottom, holding her against him.

Control vanished into mutual madness, incinerating and devastatingly right. They had been building toward this since their marriage and the first delight in touching.

No, they had begun this long journey to intimacy when she was fifteen and he was seventeen and they had felt the power of innocent mutual attraction that could not be acted on because it wasn't their time.

Now was their time and she couldn't bear to waste another moment before this ultimate consummation. She shattered, locking her body to his with arms and legs and biting his shoulder as he poured himself into her.

Utterly spent, she lay gasping as she melted against him, wanting her skin as close to his as humanly possible. He pulled the covers over them and said with a hint of laughter, "I think you now most certainly have had all of me."

She had to laugh, too, and then she wept with completion and joy. And Simon, being Simon, understood without words.

Chapter 35

❦

Simon woke at dawn and knew that he'd never been happier in his life. Suzanne was draped across him, head on his shoulder, a smile on her face, one arm around his waist, and a glorious cascade of darkly shining hair spilling over her upper body.

Beyond her, on the corner of the bed, he saw that little Leo had the cat genius for passing through doors because he was curled up on the foot of the bed. He blinked at Simon, then closed his eyes again, looking as happy as Simon felt. Of course they were both happy—they were sharing a bed with Suzanne Duval, the double Comtesse of Chambron, who was quite possibly the loveliest woman in Europe.

Lovely. Gallant. Kind. Understanding.

Beautiful in all ways.

He transferred his attention from feline to female, stroking Suzanne's hair gently so as not to disturb her, but her eyes opened and she smiled up at him. "Good morning, milord," she murmured, looking very like her cat.

"And a good morning to you, milady." He gave her what was surely a besotted smile. "I was just thinking of what magnificent hair you have, and how long it will take you to brush the tangles out since it didn't get plaited last night."

"It will take a long time, but I don't mind because it made you happy." She smiled mischievously. "Mind you, I wouldn't want to make a habit of it! Loosened hair is for special occasions only."

"Which last night most certainly was," he said with a laugh, his stroking hand sliding from her hair to her waist and points south.

She purred and pressed against him as if trying to see if it was humanly possible for them to get any closer. Her hand started to wander also, with electrifying results.

He caught his breath. "It's rather—ironic is the best word, I suppose. Last night you said you could scream and weep and beg me not to go and make us both miserable, and I'd still have to leave. But this is far worse, *ma belle*." His whole body clenched at the knowledge of what must come. "Now it's even harder to leave, and I'll be even more miserable because I've never been so happy in my life."

She made a sound that was part sigh and part rueful laughter. "The same is true for me. Yet still you must go or you would not be the man you are."

"Let's not waste what time we have." He licked her throat, which was conveniently close. Her fair skin was silky smooth and deliciously edible. "You did most of the work last night. Shall I do most of it today?"

He saw a flicker of tension in her eyes as she considered how she would feel if he was looming above her, a male with alarmingly greater weight and strength than hers. He said softly, "You can always change your mind in the middle, *ma belle*, in which case I'll simply roll over and you can ravish me at your leisure."

Another instant, and she gave him a wicked seductress smile. "Very well, milord. Let us discover how it works that way."

It worked *very* well.

As he walked to Wellington's house for a two o'clock meeting, Simon told himself sternly that he shouldn't call on the commander of the Allied armies to discuss matters of life and death wearing a ridiculous cat-in-the-cream-pot smile on his face. He thought he had his expression under control by the time he reached his destination. The trick was not to think of Suzanne.

It was really, *really* difficult not to think of Suzanne.

When he reached Wellington's house, he was greeted by a young aide whose job was to sort the general's visitors into useful sheep and useless goats. Simon obviously qualified as a sheep since the aide said, "Colonel Duval, welcome! I'll take you up to the duke's office."

"I'm not actually a colonel anymore," Simon said mildly as he followed the aide.

The young man flashed a quick smile. "Around here, sir, it's once a colonel, always a colonel."

Which was true; military rank tended to stay attached to a man for the rest of his life. Simon didn't really mind. He'd earned the rank, unlike being the Comte de Chambron, a title that he still couldn't quite accept.

The aide announced him at the office door, then vanished. Simon stepped inside to find not only the duke but also Lieutenant-Colonel Colquhoun Grant, Wellington's chief exploring officer on the Peninsula. He and Simon had often worked together, and Simon had taken over many of Grant's duties when the Scot spent two years as a French captive.

Wellington glanced up from a map. "Ah, good. I'll be

interested in hearing what you saw in France, Duval. You know Grant, of course."

"Indeed I do, sir." Simon offered his hand to the rangy Scot. "Good to see you again, Grant. I hear you're now in charge of the duke's intelligence operation."

Grant returned a rare smile as they shook hands. "Yes, and I hear that you've abandoned the army."

"I tried, but I'm not sure how successful I've been," Simon said dryly.

"Damned useful that you're officially a civilian now," Wellington said. "What did you see on your trip to Paris?"

"A great deal of military activity." Simon pulled a folded paper from inside his coat. "Here's a list of the military units I saw in and around Paris."

The duke and Grant studied the list together, frowning. Wellington said, "Boney is certainly planning something. What's your best guess, Duval?"

Simon had thought about this. "The emperor isn't going to sit tamely in Paris and wait for the Allied armies to close in from all sides. He'll strike boldly and try to take out the opposing armies one by one, and my guess is that his first march will be north to Belgium."

"Think he'll go after Blücher and his Prussians first?" Wellington asked.

"Maybe, though I think it more likely he'll come straight at us because our army is weaker," Simon said bluntly. "About a third of our soldiers are experienced British troops, but most of your Dutch-Belgian troops are not battle tested."

"They'll run like rabbits unless stiffened by the British." The duke nodded, looking grim as he studied the list of military units Simon had seen. "Not to mention that we're almost certainly outnumbered. If there is a pitched battle, we'll need the Prussians to carry the day."

Grant said, "If Bonaparte can drive a wedge between

us and the Prussians, he'll do it, and then swing around to crush our Anglo-Dutch army."

"Bonaparte may not make the decision purely on military considerations," Simon said a little hesitantly. "This is merely my opinion, but I think he's angered by the description of you as 'the Conqueror of the Conqueror of the World.' His critics point out that he's never fought you face to face. I suspect he wants to prove that he can defeat you. That *he* is the Conqueror of Conquerors."

"Schoolroom games," Wellington grunted. "A damned foolish way to run a war!"

"True," Grant said with a humorless smile. "But I can see Bonaparte doing that."

"What matters is where and when he marches," Wellington said. "Gentlemen, it's time to look at some maps."

A large map of northern France and Belgium was pinned to the wall, and the three of them gathered in front of it to discuss possible French lines of march, roads, terrain, likely weather, and whatever other factors might play into the emperor's decisions.

Among the three of them, they had a great deal of information about the territory. The discussion was useful but inconclusive. Wellington frowned at the map. "The devil of it is that a wrong guess on the direction of the enemy's march could be fatal. Mons? Charleroi? A different route into Belgium? Moving an army is like herding elephants. March in the wrong direction and it's almighty difficult to turn your force back the right way."

His gaze moved from Simon to Grant and back again. "Which is why I need you fellows to figure out where the emperor is going in time to prevent disastrous errors. Duval, I'd like you to pay attention to this area." He swept his hand over the map to the south and southwest of Brussels, an area that included Charleroi, Mons, and France all the way to Paris. "Grant, look to the east and the area south of the Prussians. You both know the kind of information I need. Duval, how soon can you leave?"

Steeling himself, Simon said, "Tomorrow, sir."

Wellington gave a nod of satisfaction. "Good." Then he turned his attention to Grant, and Simon quietly withdrew.

On his walk back to the house on the rue de Louvain, he bought a bouquet of lilacs and lilies from a flower seller as he thought through all that had to be done before he could leave. It was a surprisingly short list. He'd be traveling light and camping most nights. From experience he knew exactly what was needed.

Suzanne must have been waiting for his return because she emerged from the drawing room as soon as he entered the house. When she saw his face, she drew a deep breath and asked, "When?"

"Tomorrow. I'm sorry, *ma chérie*," he said quietly.

She accepted the flowers and bowed her head to inhale the scents, or perhaps to hide her expression. "You'll miss the wedding."

"I know."

She raised her head, expression under control. "On the positive side, Philippe has his wagon packed with seed and farm tools, and he's ready to head off for Château Chambron first thing in the morning."

"He's worked fast! Excellent. This way, I can travel with him and help him get on his feet, and it's right on the way for me."

"Is there anything I can do to help you prepare?"

He shook his head. "I only have to shove a few things into my saddlebags."

She nodded, her gaze still on him. They seemed to have run out of words. He lightly brushed his knuckles under her chin. "I'll see you later, *ma chérie*."

At least they had one more night together.

* * *

This last night was luminescent with pleasure and pain. By the time Simon and Suzanne had exhausted themselves, it was almost dawn. Simon had his arm around his wife, holding her as close as humanly possible. She was trembling and he knew she was struggling not to cry.

"I won't be gone long," he said softly. "I think this war will be over in weeks, not months. Certainly it won't be years."

She turned to look up at him, her eyes stark. "Think of me at midnight, and I will think of you at the same time. Since you'll be traveling, you might not always be able to manage the exact time, but know that when midnight strikes, I will be thinking of you. We may not be together in our bed, but our minds can hold thoughts of each other."

He felt like weeping. Instead, he clasped her hand and held it against the center of his chest. "Minds and hearts, *mon ange*. Always you will be in my heart."

He leaned down to kiss her, and they found that they had the strength to make love one last time.

Chapter 36

❧

Brussels

Mon chéri Simon, I thought of you at midnight last night and the night before, and warm thoughts they were! Tonight I decided to write my thoughts down. I don't think these words will ever be read, but no matter. Holding the pen and form-ing the words focuses all my attention on you.

Brussels bustles, though it is sadly flat for Marie and me now that our husbands are far from our sides. But today was a perfect spring day, so we walked in the park along with what appeared to be every other Briton in Brussels, and a good few others.

Should I be thinking of myself as British now that I have an Anglo-French husband who seems to be more British than French? I shall have to think on that. We usually speak French in bed—have you noticed?

You might be in Château Chambron by now. I hope all is going well for Philippe.

You are always in my heart, mon chéri.

Suzanne

On the road to Château Chambron

My darling Suzanne,

I am thinking of you at midnight, mon ange. After a night on the road, I realized that thinking isn't quite enough so I have dedicated one of my small notebooks to writing you. I write my midnight thoughts to you in my cramped, private version of shorthand that I use for observations when I'm working. This uses very little paper and no one else would be able to read these words, but that's all right. This little journal is merely a way of recording my thoughts of you.

We're making reasonably good time considering that we're traveling in a heavy wagon. My horse Achille is rather bored at being tethered behind us, but as you know, I gave Philippe the two carriage horses that we took out of France. The one that I rode when we escaped seems pleased to return to his accustomed work.

I feel some guilt that we essentially stole them, but I don't know any practical way to compensate the owner. Or even a way to locate the owner, given that they were hired horses. But Philippe will treat them well.

The horses have informed me that they wish you were here because your magical horse talent makes them happy to do as you say. You may have noticed that it works equally well on me!

Always in my heart, ma belle . . .

Simon

Brussels

*Simon, do you remember how I met my old
friend and neighbor, Madeline de Sevigny, at the
émigré gathering in London? She's here in Brussels! I met her today when Marie and I were walking in the park. I was so happy to see her again,
and she immediately embraced Marie as a friend.*

*Madeline says that half the London émigré com-
munity has come to Brussels to see what will happen, as if this was a great carnival. No doubt the
warier ones have already made arrangements to
flee north to Antwerp if Napoleon's army invades
Belgium. Fools. If they're that afraid of the heat,
they should move farther from the fire, back to
London, for example!*

*Madeline says that she and some of her friends
keep busy organizing ladies' teas and excursions
and charitable works since so many men are off
doing military things. Like you, mon coeur! It will
be pleasant to have some mild diversions with
other ladies.*

*I hope all your diversions are of the mild sort. . . .
Suzanne*

Château Chambron

*Greetings, mon ange. Philippe is invigorated
now that he is healthy and secure in his ownership
of the estate. He hasn't threatened me with his rifle
even once! The château looks even worse than
when we saw it, which has made Philippe accept
that he must let it go. Instead he bends his efforts
to finding the estate's long-time tenants.*

Many here remember him and he has been wel-

comed back with enthusiasm. On the drive down, we discussed your advice about treating his people as friends and partners rather than being lordly and annoying. From what I am seeing, the people of France are tired of lords and dictators and want to be treated with dignity and respect. Or else!

But the best moment of the day came as Philippe was talking to the once and future steward of the estate. Madame and Monsieur Cordier, the maternal grandparents who raised Philippe, heard that he had returned, so they rushed to find out if it was true. They all fell weeping into each other's arms. It was a most affecting sight. Less complicated than when I found Lucas.

The Cordiers had been forced from the house where he was raised (I'm not sure why), but they are now living in another sturdy farmhouse, and it has room for Philippe to stay for the time being. They are desperate to meet Marie and welcome their great-grandchild into the world, but they agree it is best for her to stay safely in Brussels for the time being.

Tomorrow I set out for Paris, to find what I can see along the way. I'm sure it will be safe—I've seen no threats yet.

You are always in my heart, ma chérie, and I wish you were in my bed. Better yet, in our bed in Brussels—it's more comfortable. My regards to your current bedmate, the little Leo.

Simon

Brussels

Mon chéri Simon, the city grows busier and more excited, waiting, waiting, waiting! Here we

*are at the end of the first week of June. The days
since I've seen you seem so long, though it hasn't
really been that many. Yet it seems like forever!*

*You will find this amusing: I have become in-
volved in charitable work helping out camp followers. The other ladies are impressed at how
unshockable I am. Of course they know nothing of
my past, and I prefer to keep it that way.*

*But the work is needful, as you like to say. Many
of these women have been following their men for
years. They act as nurses and laundresses as well
as sharing beds. Some women have lost several
husbands to death over the years, but because few
women follow the army, those who do are always
in demand and can have a new man as soon as
they are ready. One woman said she accepted an
offer from a corporal as she was burying one husband, but if she'd waited to get back to the camp,
she could have had a sergeant!*

*Too often, these women and their children need
food, clothing, medical care. Madeline and Marie
and other ladies like us do our best to help. Marie
tires very easily now and I'm somewhat worried
about her, but I imagine being tired is natural this
close to her time.*

*I so wish you were here, my Simon! You are in
my mind, heart, and soul, but selfish creature that I
am, I want you in my arms. Take care, beloved. You
must come back to me. No other outcome is
acceptable.*

Always, your Suzanne

Somewhere in France

*For the last two nights, milady, I've not been
able to think of you as much as I wished because I*

*have been on the run, being pursued by a French
patrol. They have become suspicious of me. Me, a
loyal, innocent, and harmless son of France! I'd be
quite outraged if I wasn't in truth a spy.*

*I'm glad this isn't a proper letter so you will
never know the full truth of what has happened.
You'd find it upsetting. To be honest, I have found
it upsetting.*

Simon paused over his notebook, thinking of what had
happened and wondering how much to tell Suzanne.
Even in his midnight thoughts, he didn't want to tell her
the whole story because she would be horrified.

After the long pursuit, he and Achille had both been
close to collapse as he tried to get back to Belgium. Because they weren't far from Château Chambron, as a desperate last resort he directed his mount to the old château
in the hope that he could find a place to hide in the ruins.

When he pulled up in front of the wing that was still
standing, his dismount from Achille was perilously close
to a fall. He was stiff and aching all over from too many
hours in the saddle, and he clung to the stirrup to keep his
balance while he waited for his body to start working
again.

"Simon!" The shout echoed over the ruined gardens in
front of the château.

Simon grabbed for his pistol and swung around before
he even wondered who would know his name. It was
Philippe emerging from the door of the wing that was still
standing. Uncertainly Simon lowered the pistol. "What
are you doing here? Aren't you supposed to be plowing
and planting or whatever a farmer does at this season?"

"I took a few hours off to do some searching in the
ruins." Philippe surveyed him. "What are *you* doing here,
looking like a corpse walking?"

"I'm being pursued by a French patrol. If you listen,

you can hear the hooves of their horses." Simon paused and could hear just that. The soldiers were very near. "I came here hoping to find a place to hide." He regarded his cousin, who had served in the emperor's army, and wondered if Philippe would turn him in.

Philippe frowned for a long moment, as if considering whether to help or hand him over to the soldiers. Then he snapped, "Quickly now, come inside. You have little time."

He grabbed Simon's arm with one hand and Achille's reins with the other and half dragged them both inside. The horse's hooves rang on the old marble floor. "Go up the stairs and turn right. I'll show you where to hide after I take your horse to one of the rooms in back."

"Must have . . . my saddlebags," Simon panted.

Swiftly Philippe unfastened the saddlebags and yanked them off the horse, dropping them on the floor. "I'll bring them upstairs after I hide your horse."

Simon lurched to the stairs and hauled himself up along the railing, which was unsteady but didn't fall apart under his weight. Achille clopped dutifully into a passageway that ran to the rear of the house. Simon hoped to God that the animal's weight wouldn't cause a floor collapse.

As instructed, he turned right. Philippe caught up with him quickly, the saddlebags slung over one arm. "The room over the entrance has a hidden closet with a listening hole to the receiving room below. Our ancestors were suspicious, cousin. You can hear what is said by the French soldiers when they get here. I'll try to convince them that no one has come by. If they decide to search the place and find you, I'll have to pretend I didn't know you were here."

"Of course. Don't want to endanger you."

Philippe helped him into the hidden closet. The floor was cluttered with rubble but Simon didn't care. He folded himself down against the wall by the corner that had the listening hole. "If they drag me out and shoot me in front of the house, thank you for trying to help, Philippe."

"A wise man once told me family is family. Now I need to find my old cane so I look convincingly crippled." With a last swift smile, Philippe shut the closet door.

Simon closed his eyes and prayed that he would survive to see Suzanne again. The hoofbeats neared, then stopped, all too close.

A moment later, the heavy old door knocker was bashed into the door half a dozen times. Then the distinctive tap of the cane as Philippe hobbled to the door and opened it.

A soldierly voice said, "We've been chasing a damned English spy. Did you see a man on a horse gallop by?"

"No, I've neither seen nor heard anyone."

Another, older voice said with surprise, "Captain Duval! I haven't seen you since our forces were disbanded and we were sent home. Is this ruined palace your home?"

Philippe chuckled. "How good to see you alive and well, Captain Weiss! I live nearby in an honest, comfortable farmhouse. This château was once owned by an aristo." He spat. "Now long gone, God be thanked! I am trying to recover from old wounds, so I decided to practice my walking by coming over here. A very grand place it was once, though peasants like me were never welcome inside. I was curious to see if anything interesting remained in the ruins, but if so, someone else got here first."

"May all aristos burn in hell!" one of the soldiers said harshly. "Like the one who lived here is probably doing!"

Amid laughter, Captain Weiss said, "We must be off now after that damned spy. There was a lane that split off the road to the château. He must have gone that way. He can't last much longer." After a moment's pause, he asked, "Will you be fit enough to rejoin the army, Duval? We need experienced officers like you if we're going to take down Wellington."

Philippe sighed wearily. "It depends on how soon the next battle is. I fear I may always need this devil's crutch." He thumped the floor a couple of times with his cane. "But good luck, *mes amis*! Fight well and know when to duck."

Laughter and farewells were heard and the soldiers' horses rode off. Simon gave an exhausted sigh. It looked as if he would live to run another day.

Chapter 37

❧

Simon had managed to struggle to his feet by the time Philippe returned. "I wish I knew more words beyond 'thank you'! May I stay in the ruins tonight? I'll be off early in the morning."

"Nonsense, you're coming back to the Cordiers'," Philippe said briskly. "You need a proper meal and a bed and a good night's sleep."

"And maybe a bath?" Simon asked hopefully. "A basin of warm water and a towel would be wonderful. A basin of *cold* water!"

Philippe laughed and lifted the saddlebags. "We can do better than that. Come along now and hold tight to that railing. I don't want you to waste my lies by breaking your neck. I'll collect your horse."

"He deserves pampering far more than I do," Simon said as he started carefully down the stairs. "I've never met a horse with a more gallant heart. I don't think I can ask him to go on again tomorrow, though. He needs rest."

"So do you, but I'm sure you're more careful of your horse than yourself," Philippe said dryly. He left the saddlebags at the bottom of the staircase and disappeared into the back of the house, returning with Achille about the same time Simon reached the bottom of the steps. "If you want to leave him here to rest, I can lend you a decent hack that will be fresh and ready to go."

Simon patted Achille's neck. The horse managed a friendly whuffle, but he looked close to breaking down, which would be a terrible thing to do to such a good mount. "Thank you. I'll take you up on that."

Philippe tossed the saddlebags over the horse and fastened them, then led the way outdoors. Achille picked his way down the steps very carefully. "It's about a mile to the Cordiers' house along a path through the woods. Do you want to ride or walk?"

Neither, actually, but the lure of food and a bed were too powerful to resist. "I'll walk," Simon said. "That will spare Achille and give me a chance to stretch my legs out."

Philippe nodded and led the way around the ruined château to the path through the woods. Simon said, "Aren't you going to ask if the soldiers pursuing me were justified in their belief that I am a spy?"

Philippe glanced over Achille's back. "I think it's better I don't know. That way I can't tell any lies if they come back."

Wise man. As they made their way through the growing darkness, Simon said quietly, "I love France and mean it no harm. It is my father's country. But I hate war and want to see an end to it."

"I was so proud and excited when I joined the army," Philippe reminisced. "Willing, even eager, to lay down my life for France. I was very young, only seventeen. Seven years ago. Long enough for me to have now seen too much of war." After a dozen more steps, he said, "Now I want to live for Marie, for my family. My true family, the Cordiers, not the father I worshipped but who barely remembered my existence."

Glad that Philippe had become more clear-sighted about Jean-Louis, Simon said carefully, "He could have done better by you. But he chose wisely when he gave you to the Cordiers to raise and in the end, he left you all he owned."

"He did, but . . . he was an aristo," Philippe said in a matter-of-fact voice. "The Cordiers gave me things beyond price. I can't wait to bring Marie to them. They will love her and she will love them."

"Who could not?" Simon said. His tight muscles were beginning to loosen, which made him even more aware of his exhaustion.

After another few minutes of walking in silence, Philippe said, "In these last weeks, I have come to realize I would lay down my life for France if necessary. But I will not do it for the emperor."

"He is a great and terrible man," Simon said. "He has done some fine things for France, but he seems unable to exist without war. Even if he manages to pull off a victory over Wellington and the Prussians, in the long run he cannot defeat all his enemies. Trying to do so will just cause the deaths of too many men. Too many of them our French brothers."

Philippe sighed. "I want an *end* to this. I hope whatever information you are carrying will bring that end closer."

"So do I!" Simon said fervently. "Is that why you were willing to help me?"

"Not really." Philippe laughed. "I did it because family is family!"

The Cordier Home

*I owe Philippe eternal gratitude for helping me
elude my pursuers, and even more for bringing me
to the home of his grandparents, the Cordiers.
They have clucked over me, fed me, given me a hot
bath, and now a bed, sadly empty without you. I
slept for hours and so missed my midnight
moments with you, mon ange, but I have a candle
so I'll finish my account by thinking of you. I shall
tell you the whole story when I am home again.*

*Imagine kisses and much, much more. MUCH,
much more . . . !*

Simon

Philippe's horse was good, though not as good as
Achille. Fortified by food and a good night's rest, Simon
continued north, hoping to God he would be able to deliver his information in time. As Wellington had said, if
an army heads the wrong way, reversing direction is difficult and potentially catastrophic.

Simon had spent days in France studying military movements, troop concentrations, and everything else that might
help determine Napoleon's plan of attack. Now he knew
where the invasion would come, but his knowledge would
be useless if he couldn't get it into Wellington's hands,
and time was running out.

Crossing the border was difficult because the French
were doing their best to block all traffic and information
from getting through. Luckily Simon was an expert at
avoiding pickets and sliding through enemy lines.

He had almost reached Mons, a town west of Charleroi, when he saw an Anglo-Dutch cavalry encampment.
Giving thanks, he rode into the camp and waved down
the first officer he saw, a captain. "I'm Colonel Duval,

one of Wellington's exploring officers. Please take me to your commanding officer."

The captain looked doubtful. "You don't look like no colonel. General Dornberg won't want to waste his time talking to just anyone."

"He'll listen to me." Simon sharpened his voice to command. "Take me to him *now!*"

Not entirely convinced but intimidated, the captain led Simon through the camp to the largest tent. After a short discussion with the soldier guarding the entrance, the captain waved Simon inside with a "you asked for it" expression on his face.

Simon entered and saw General Dornberg in full, dazzling cavalry uniform, sitting at his breakfast table with several junior officers. Even though he wasn't in uniform, Simon snapped his best salute. "Sir, I'm Colonel Duval of Wellington's intelligence staff. I have vital dispatches that must be sent to his headquarters in Brussels immediately."

Dornberg frowned. "Where's your uniform?"

"Under special orders from the Duke of Wellington, I've been gathering intelligence in civilian clothing, thereby risking summary execution if I was caught by the French," Simon said flatly. "Luckily I wasn't, quite." He held up his dispatch case. "Send this to Wellington *now*. He's waiting for this report."

"I'll be the judge of that." Dornberg held his hand out for the dispatch case.

Simon was reluctant to hand it over, but Dornberg was a senior officer and his troops would be affected by the information, so he gave the case to the general.

Dornberg opened the case and scanned Simon's concise, carefully written report. "Napoleon is going to come through Charleroi? Absurd! All indications are that he will come through Mons, and my men are ready for him."

"The emperor has done his best to confuse us, and he has been successful. But I have the latest information and it is vital that it be sent to Wellington immediately."

"I won't waste his time on this," Dornberg growled. "Now get out of my sight, whoever you are!"

Simon wanted to do murder, but killing a general surrounded by armed officers was not a good idea. Teeth clenched, he spun on his heel and marched from the tent, leaving the dispatch case behind.

Outside, he swung onto his tired horse and thought about where he could get a fresh mount for the ride to Brussels.

It was late evening when Simon reached Wellington's headquarters, and by then he never wanted to see a horse again. Here, at least, he was recognized and let through immediately.

The duke was conferring with several aides when Simon entered his office, but he got to his feet, his expression intent. "You have information?"

"I do. The French army is going to be coming up through Charleroi, not Mons." Simon followed that statement with a brief summary of what he'd observed to reach his conclusion.

Wellington swore. "By God, Napoleon's humbugged me!" He waved at a chair. "Sit, Duval, before you fall over."

Simon gratefully obeyed as the duke snapped orders at his aides to reroute the army south toward Quatre Bras, which meant "crossroad." This particular crossroads was where the Brussels-Charleroi road intersected the Nivelles-Namur road, and all four routes were paved, swift thoroughfares.

After the aides had bolted off to carry out the duke's orders, he said to Simon, "I have still to attend the

Duchess of Richmond's ball to allay fears and rumors, but you should go home and get some rest, Colonel. I may well have need of you again."

Simon levered himself out of the chair. "Does your calling me colonel mean that I'm drafted back into the army?"

"Yes, but for now, go home."

This was one order Simon was more than willing to follow. Home and Suzanne.

Chapter 38

⚜

Suzanne woke that morning with Leo curled up on the pillow next to her face. It was mid-June and it seemed as if Simon had been gone forever. At least she had Leo, but it was not at all the same.

As she ate breakfast, she mentally listed what she needed to do this day. Not much, really; the household ran very smoothly and would even if she wasn't here. But it felt like a secure base for watching what might come.

The day was pleasant, so Suzanne had decided to walk through the park, then call on Madeline to see if her friend or one of the women's group knew a good midwife who was still in the city. She'd donned her hat and was about to step outside when the door knocker sounded. Since she was right there, she swung open the door and blinked at the tall, shabby man on her doorstep.

"Madame Duval?" was the hesitant question. "Suzanne?"

The rich voice was familiar. Suzanne looked more closely and gave a sudden gasp of shock. "Frère Jude!"

She stepped back from the doorway. "Please come in! I'm sorry I didn't recognize you at first."

He entered with an apologetic smile. "That's because I'm not Frère Jude anymore. I never really was, I think, so I must be Lucas Mandeville again."

He took off his hat and she saw that the top of his head didn't shine anymore because the tonsure was filling in with his tawny hair. "What should I call you? Monsieur Mandeville? Lord Foxton?" She smiled tentatively. "Foxy?"

He laughed at that. "Lucas will do. Is Simon home?"

"He's . . . been away for several weeks," Suzanne said. "But I'm sure he'd be over the moon to know you're here. Will you stay? Please? Until he comes home?" Assuming Simon *did* come home, which was the kind of horrid thought it was impossible to suppress.

"I'd like to stay here for a while, at least. Is there stabling nearby for the Magdalene?"

"Of course there is." Suzanne laughed as she peered out the window and saw the white mule tethered patiently to the iron fence in front of the house. "There's a stable behind the house and Maurice is probably there. He'll be happy to settle the Magdalene. I'll have a room prepared and order tea and sandwiches for you."

"I'd like that." He gave her a gentle, beneficent smile that made her wonder how much of a friar he still was. She guessed that even he didn't know.

She gave orders for the room to be made up and for food to be brought to the drawing room. Lucas joined her soon and attacked the sandwiches as ferociously as a well-mannered man could.

When he'd cleared two platefuls of food, she topped off his tea for the third time. "Perhaps it's presumptuous of me to ask when you barely know me, but Simon talks of you and thinks of you as a brother, which means you're my brother-in-law."

He smiled at her. "You are desperate to ask questions. Feel free to do so."

"You say you are no longer Frère Jude, but he was your life for many years. Was it meeting Simon that made you decide to become Lucas Mandeville again?"

He nodded. "It was . . . shockingly wonderful to see Simon again. The shock was first, but it got me to remembering all that was good in my early life. I realized that if I felt a true vocation for the religious life, I would have taken vows by now. I craved solitude and needed to serve others, but I can have those things outside the religious life."

"Did you convert to Catholicism?"

He smiled. "I consider myself a fellow traveler. A mule-riding fellow traveler." He paused to consume a small tea cake in one bite and swallowed it with obvious pleasure. "Your lecture on not wallowing was very potent. I have wallowed long enough. Since I exiled myself from the life I was born to, only I could free myself from that exile.

"I also realized how much I want to see my great-aunt and uncle again. Apart from Simon, they are my closest family. How selfish it was of me to think only of myself and not of them!"

"Pain does that," she said quietly.

"Pain, and shame. I felt too dishonored to associate with honorable people," he said quietly.

"Honor matters, but rigid definitions of it are not to be worshipped as gods!" she said with exasperation. "Being a mere female, I think one's obligations to friends and family matter more than self-crucifixion over abstract definitions of honor."

Lucas gave her a slow smile. "How very wise Simon was to marry you. Having decided not to wallow, I fulfilled my obligations to the communities I visited by sending another friar whom I'd trained. He is a truly good man, a good bonesetter, and will get better. I travel a different road now."

"Is that why you came to Brussels? To see Simon as a first step to returning home?"

"That is a large part of it. But . . ." He smiled a little bashfully. "You'll think this is absurd. But I often have a sense of where I am needed. I have a strong feeling that I'm going to be needed here. I'm no surgeon, but I'm good at splints and resetting bones into joints and such things."

"War is coming, so your instincts are correct," Suzanne said. "I fear there will be much to occupy you very soon!"

She thought a moment, then asked, "Incidentally, have you learned anything about midwifery? You may soon be the only person around with any medical skills."

Lucas looked startled. "I've delivered several babies in dire straits, but I'm no expert. Why do you ask?"

"Our cousin Marie is very near her time and the midwife we'd engaged has fled the city," Suzanne explained. "I'm going to try to find another, but if I'm unsuccessful, it will be good if someone in the house knows how to deliver a baby!"

"Bonesetters are at the very bottom of the medical hierarchy, so I shall pray that you find a proper midwife," he said gravely. "But if you don't, well, I shall do what I can."

"What is the medical hierarchy?" she asked.

"Physicians are at the top. They study in universities and are gentlemen. Surgeons are lower. They work with their hands and are really just tradesmen whose tools are blades and saws. Midwives are necessary but ignored as much as possible. Bonesetters are peasants," he explained with a glint of amusement in his eyes.

"Given that you're a peer of the realm, you might change that. Your nickname will be Lord Foxton, the Bonesetter Baron!"

"I sincerely hope not!"

She laughed. "We'll see. Let me show you to your room. You must want some rest. Or perhaps a hot bath?"

"Bliss unbounded." He smiled and rose to his feet. "Thank you, Suzanne."

"You are always welcome with Simon and me," she said sincerely. "I'm off to find a midwife, but I shall see you later."

She guided him up to his room, then left the house on her midwife hunt. As she walked through the busy streets, she wondered what Lucas would do with his future. In some ways he was like a newly hatched chick. But he was intelligent and he'd find his way. And with luck, he'd move back to England and live close enough to Simon for them to be great friends again.

Suzanne had had no success in locating an available midwife, so after she returned home that evening, she visited Marie's room and urged her not to have her baby for at least a week. Marie laughed, but said she could make no promises.

Tired by the long day, Suzanne retired to her room and settled at her desk to begin writing her nightly message to Simon. It was her favorite time of the day because the house was silent and she could focus on Simon.

Mad, Mad Brussels, 15 June 1815

I am addressing you early tonight because I want to feel you close, my Simon. The days are dragging like years and rumors are sweeping through Brussels like wildfire. "The French are

*coming, the French are coming, flee for your
lives!!!" I'm told the roads and canal to Antwerp
are as full as they can hold. Your advice to sit tight
here in our safe, comfortable house is very wise.*

*The French might be coming—indeed, I'm sure
they will, eventually—but I've not heard any reliable information that says they've entered
Belgium. The Duke of Wellington is very visible
and very social, making quips and attending balls
and throwing dinner parties to calm people's fears.*

*He intended to go this evening to what should
be a dazzling ball given by the Duchess of Richmond. He is probably there now, being calm and
charming. If you were here to take me, I'd like to
attend, but you aren't, alas. I'm sorry I never saw
you in your uniform. I have no doubt that you were
a magnificent sight.*

*Sometimes at midnight I feel that our minds do
briefly touch and I can sense your warmth and wit
and kindness. No doubt that is merely fancy on my
part, but I enjoy the illusion.*

*Marie has given up our daily walks because she
is too tired. Not surprising considering all the
extra weight she's carrying. She's also rather restless and Madame Maurice confided to me that the
baby could come at any time. I find this a terrifying thought! Particularly since I've just learned
that the midwife who has attended her has left the
city. I must find another one. Soon!*

Should she tell him about Lucas's arrival? No, she was
tired and that was too important a story to rush.

*That is enough for this evening's musings, mon
coeur. Take care, and now I will sleep and imagine*

*you beside me. Leo tries to comfort me but he is so
very small!*
    Your Suzanne

Though Suzanne was tired, she felt too restless to go to
bed. Something was about to happen but she didn't know
what.

Her intuition was confirmed when the metallic blare of
bugles shattered the night. The call to war.

She jumped to her feet, heart pounding, then opened
the window and listened as menacing sounds filled the
night sky. Drums, harsh and insistent. The piercing wail
of bagpipes with their wild, primitive summons to battle.
The sounds of marching feet, then the rattle of wagons
and gun carriages. A cacophony of war. The front door
opened and she heard the voices of Maurice and Jenny
and Jackson as they left to learn what was happening, and
observe the mustering of the troops.

She couldn't bear to join them, but she listened for a
long time until she heard the front door open again. She
frowned, wondering who had returned. A little warily, she
went down the stairs—and there was Simon, turning from
locking the door. He was crumpled and filthy and weaving with exhaustion, and the most beautiful sight she'd
ever seen.

"Simon," she whispered. *"Simon!"* And she raced down
the last of the steps and straight into his arms.

Simon wasn't expecting to be tackled by an armful of
warm, wonderful, clean woman, but he didn't mind even
though the momentum of her embrace slammed him back
against the front door. "Suzanne," he breathed as he buried
his face in her hair. "Suzanne, *mon ange.* I'm filthy, you
know."

"I know, but I do not care." She pulled her head back

enough so that their mouths could meet in a long, heart-felt, all-consuming kiss.

Stress fell away, dissolved in her wonderful, warm Suzanne-ness. Finally he broke the kiss. "Much as I'm inclined to stay like this for the rest of the night, I think I should wash off the travel grime and eat a meal before I ravish you. Or is it your turn to ravish me? I forget."

She laughed and stepped back. "My turn, I think."

"That's good. I'm not sure I have the strength to be the ravisher."

"Come down to the kitchen. There should be hot water there and you can wash up while I find you food." She wrapped a supportive arm around his waist and steered him toward the steps that ran down to the kitchen and servants' quarters. "You can tell me what is going on out in the world."

"The French are invading through Charleroi," he said succinctly. "There will be a battle soon, maybe several. Wellington has been waiting to see which way the emperor will jump. As of tonight he's moving out and preparing to engage. I could tell you far more if you wish, but let's save that for later."

"We have better things to talk about," she agreed.

They'd reached the long kitchen. At one end there was a decent-sized hip bath and a screen that could be placed in front of it for privacy. A heavy bucket of water was always warmed by the kitchen fire. Simon had just about enough energy left to dump the hot water in the hip bath, along with some cooler water so he wouldn't poach.

He moved behind the screen and started stripping off his travel-stained garments. "Is the screen necessary? I'm quite sure you've seen everything."

She laughed and handed a glass of red wine over the screen. "I don't want another woman to come in and see how lucky I am!"

"I'm a fairly sorry specimen just now." He subsided into the water and closed his eyes as he sipped the wine, feeling delightfully pampered. "Speaking of which, where is everyone? I'd have thought that the drums and bugles would have woken up the household."

"I think most of the household has gone out to see what is happening. Except Marie, of course, and Madame Maurice, who is sitting with her."

From what he could hear, Suzanne was slicing food, meat or bread or cheese. At the moment, he wasn't particular. She continued, "Where will the troops assemble before they march out?"

"The Place Royale in the lower town." He sipped more wine. "It will be a madhouse there."

"Many good-byes," she said softly. "I'm lucky that I'm saying hello tonight."

He thought about not saying more, but better she was warned. "Wellington might want me for something else, but he did tell me to come home and get some rest tonight."

"Oh." Suzanne's voice was distinctly unenthusiastic. "While you're splashing, I'll go upstairs to get your robe. I don't suppose you want to put those clothes on again."

"Definitely not." He applied himself to scrubbing thoroughly, from the top of his head to his toes. He was reluctant to emerge from the warm water, but falling asleep in the hip bath wasn't appealing. He'd climbed from the tub and had toweled himself reasonably dry by the time Suzanne returned with his robe and a pair of heavy socks.

Since he was properly decent and clean, he gave her a long, warm embrace after he emerged from behind the screen. Lord, he'd missed her!

The feeling was mutual. She moved away reluctantly. "The sooner you're fed, the sooner to bed."

He smiled. "Don't expect much when we get there."

"We'll see." She gestured toward the table. Ham, cheese,

bread, a slice of meat pie, and more wine. It was the best meal he'd seen since he'd left the Cordiers' house.

As he dug into the food, she poured wine for herself before saying, "I have really good news—Lucas has shown up on our doorstep and he's sleeping upstairs. He was almost as tired as you are."

Simon looked up from his food, delighted. "Lucas is here? Or rather, Frère Jude?"

"He is now Lucas again, having decided it was time to leave Frère Jude and his self-imposed exile behind." Suzanne sipped her wine. "He said he felt he would be needed here."

"He always had an uncanny ability to do that," Simon said as he applied himself to the meat pie again. "I once was tossed by my pony and broke my arm. Lucas felt something was wrong and came and found me." He swallowed a bit of pie. "Similar things happened more than once."

"That's a useful ability! I suppose he's now being drawn by the knowledge of the upcoming battle and its victims."

"Very likely. He was always a better man than I." Simon took a thoughtful swallow of wine. "His ability to find me was a result of how close we were, I think. I might have a touch of the same thing, because I could never quite believe he was dead. It seemed that somewhere out there, he must be alive. And he was."

"I'm so glad for both of you." Suzanne set her half-empty wineglass down and asked the question whose answer she didn't want to hear. "How long do you think it will be before you find out what Wellington wants of you?"

"I don't know." Simon pushed his plate away, no longer hungry, his gaze on Suzanne. "Perhaps twenty-four hours."

She stood and extended her hand. "Then let's not waste any of that time, *mon chéri*."

Chapter 39

❧

Suzanne fell asleep with a smile, safe in Simon's arms. And was wakened by a woman's wrenching cry of agony.

Beside her Simon also blazed into wakefulness. "What?"

"Marie!" Suzanne was already out of the bed. She grabbed her robe and barely had it on before she threw the door open and raced down the corridor.

Behind her, footsteps and male voices sounded. Simon called, "Lucas!"

"I'm glad to see you home, Simon!" Lucas said. "We'll talk later."

Both men moved fast, but it was Lucas who was first in the door after Suzanne. Marie was writhing on a bed covered with drenched sheets. Madame Maurice was holding her hand and trying to soothe her. The older woman looked up in relief when Suzanne and the men entered. She looked as if she'd just realized that having children was not the same as delivering them.

"Suzanne!" Marie cried out as she thrashed across the bed. "Suzanne, *mon amie!*"

Suzanne immediately caught the younger woman's sweaty hand. Speaking in French, she said, "It's all right, Marie, it's all right! Remember, only yesterday Madame Maurice said that having babies is perfectly normal—it just hurts a lot. This will be over soon, though it will feel much too long. And won't you and Philippe be so pleased with yourselves when you can hold that child in your arms!"

"Philippe, *mon coeur*," Marie said raggedly. "I so wish you were here!"

"He would be if he could, but he can't. He's creating a home for you at the château. But there is someone who can help. Simon's cousin Lucas, the medical man, is right here, and between him and Madame Maurice, you'll be well taken care of." She brushed a towel over Marie's sweating face with her free hand. "We'll all take care of you."

"Don't leave me, Suzanne," Marie begged, her face contorted as another contraction wracked her. "Please don't leave me!"

"I won't. I'll be right here until I can hold my new grandchild." Suzanne used her most soothing tone. "It's going to be a boy, I'm sure. Remember Madame Maurice said that because you're carrying low? She says she's always right about such things. Philippe will be so proud! Men seem to be extra pleased with themselves when they have a son, as if that's even more of a miracle than a daughter. So foolish!"

Marie began to relax as the contraction passed, but she held tight to Suzanne's hand. Suzanne glanced up and saw that Lucas and Madame Maurice were talking in low voices. The older woman looked very worried and Lucas was nodding gravely.

Then Lucas moved to the side of the bed and spoke to Marie, his voice deep and wonderfully calming. "This is your first, isn't it? Of course it's alarming, but don't worry, when you have your second it will all be easier. Now I'm going to examine you because that's what we medical men do." He shot an ironic glance at Suzanne. Continuing, he said, "Simon, help Madame Maurice collect supplies. She knows what is needed."

"Of course." Simon had managed to hastily drag on a shirt and a pair of trousers. Lucas wore a similar but shabbier outfit that Suzanne recognized from when he'd appeared at her door. She made a mental note to find him more suitable clothing than a Franciscan habit or the regrettable garments he was wearing.

But though he looked like a rag picker, his wonderful deep voice was calm and his intelligent presence spread confidence throughout the room. "The baby is turned opposite the usual way, Marie," he said. "It's called a breech birth. That means he's an independent little fellow! I'll see if I can turn him around so he can arrive more quickly."

As Lucas worked to manipulate the baby to a better position, Simon and Madame Maurice arrived with hot water and towels and fresh bedding. Jenny also entered to gently sponge Marie's perspiring face and help with the bedding.

But Lucas's expression was grim as he tried and failed to reposition the baby. His voice was always soft and his hands gentle, but damnably, nothing he did helped. Suzanne guessed that Marie's small-boned body was making this delivery more difficult and dangerous than normal.

Throughout an endless day, Suzanne continued to hold the girl's hand. Once she had to get up to stretch her legs and relieve herself. Jenny moved in to take Suzanne's place, but Marie was fretful and asked Suzanne to come back as soon as she could. "I will, *ma petite*," Suzanne promised.

Lucas stood and followed Suzanne from the bedroom. To her pleasure, Simon was heading toward her. When he arrived, she leaned into his embrace, drawing his warm strength into her as she worked the fingers of her right hand to drive the numbness away. "My poor exhausted darling!" he murmured. "Her condition is grave?"

"Very," Lucas said wearily. "I've been unable to turn the baby and they're both growing weaker."

Simon made a pained sound and his arms tightened around Suzanne. "You haven't found an experienced midwife?"

Lucas shook his head. "Not with Brussels in chaos. I wish I could hand this over to someone with more experience! There is so much I don't know about birthing."

"I don't know if a midwife could do more than you have, Lucas," Suzanne said. "If I was having a baby, I'd trust you. But after this, I'm rather glad I don't seem inclined to having babies!"

Suzanne had spoken as she had to lighten the mood a bit, but in a small, selfish part of her mind she resented losing these hours with Simon when he might soon be gone, never to return. But how could she abandon Marie? Impossible.

"Do you think Marie and the baby will survive?" Simon asked.

"I hope so, but I don't know," Lucas said in a barely audible voice.

"I'll get some proper clothing on and come back to Marie in a few minutes," she said, looking down at her rumpled dressing gown.

"I'll have tea and sandwiches sent up," Simon said. "I don't suppose that my presence in the sickroom is desirable."

Suzanne would like having him close, but this crisis wasn't about her. "It's not a terribly large room."

Simon lifted her chin with one finger and kissed her. Not a deeply passionate night kiss, but a pledge of unity and mutual support. "I'm going out to find what news there is. From the sound of guns, there is a battle in progress south of Brussels. Close enough for us to hear, but not so close that we need to expect French soldiers in our streets."

At least Simon was here, not in the middle of that battle. She would like to stay in his arms forever, but that wasn't possible. She patted his backside so he'd know that she wasn't completely exhausted and he reciprocated with a chuckle.

Marie's labor stretched from before dawn into the day as she grew steadily weaker, hardly moving except when wracked by contractions. Suzanne had heard that labor could sometimes take two days and couldn't imagine how anyone endured it.

A raging thunderstorm struck, darkening the sky. As lightning flashed garishly outside, Lucas took Marie's hand and said, "Marie, look at me. I've heard of a method that might aid you in giving birth, though I've never done it or seen it done. Suzanne and I would support you in a kneeling position and let gravity help the process along. Are you willing to try that?"

Despite her pain and exhaustion, Marie's reply was a clearly whispered, "Yes, if you think that best."

"Good girl." Lucas gestured to Suzanne and between them they managed to raise Marie and move her onto her knees with her legs spread. Lucas took most of her weight while Suzanne kept her balanced.

Once she was stable, Suzanne held one hand and massaged Marie's back until another contraction began. Lucas said firmly, "It's time now, Marie. You're tired and he's ready. Now push, *push!*"

Marie whimpered, head drooping and sweat-drenched blond hair falling tangled over her face. Her whole body strained for an agony of time. Until she cried out and her son was born in a rush of blood and fluids, feet first. He was a frightening bluish color.

"Well done, Marie! Now you can relax," Lucas said,

but his expression was grave. He and Suzanne helped Marie lie back on her mangled pillows. Then he held the tiny baby in his large hands, his eyes closed and his lips moving as he—prayed, perhaps?

Suzanne couldn't breathe, couldn't bear the thought that after all this pain and struggle, the child wouldn't survive. She didn't know if Marie could endure such a loss.

But as she stared at Lucas, she sensed a kind of heat radiating from his hands, invisible but powerful. The power flowed through his palms and into the infant.

Abruptly the baby started thrashing and howling indignantly and his skin began turning pink. It was the most beautiful sound Suzanne had ever heard.

Marie had looked unconscious but now her eyes opened and she reached for her child. *"Please!"*

Lucas tenderly gave the infant into his mother's keeping. "Here he is, Marie, and a fine strong boy, just as Madame Maurice predicted."

Suzanne could have sworn that she saw that mysterious power move through Lucas and the baby into Marie like a wave of healing love. Marie's eyes closed and she wept as she whispered prayers of gratitude and cuddled her son skin to skin.

Looking ready to collapse, Lucas went to work cleaning Marie and preparing to cut the cord. "Suzanne, thanks so much for your help. You did a splendid job."

Suzanne whispered, "Lucas, what just happened? What did I see?"

He smiled at her, exhausted but at peace. "Sometimes God smiles."

Dripping from the rain, Simon returned after full darkness fell, his expression grim. As he entered the house, he saw his cousin in the drawing room, his lean body stretched out in a chair. He held a brandy glass in one hand and looked as if he never wanted to move again.

Hearing Simon, he glanced up and smiled. "Marie and her son are resting and well. She's going to name him Simon Lucas."

Simon's throat tightened. "I am honored."

"As am I." Lucas raised his brandy glass in a toast. "May he have a long and happy life with fewer wars than our times have known."

"Amen to that." Simon desperately needed to see Suzanne, but he also needed to talk to Lucas. To *be* with Lucas. He sank into the chair opposite. "I was very worried. It looked like a difficult birth."

"It was, very. But when Suzanne's time comes, she won't have the same problems."

"Why do you say that?" Simon asked quizzically.

Lucas grinned, looking like the brother Simon had missed so much. "If I tell you, you'll hit me."

"Why?"

"She has the most magnificent hips."

Simon grinned back. "She does, and if you're noticing, it's fortunate that you've given up the celibate life." His face sobered. "Suzanne fears that she is barren."

"The past doesn't always predict the future. Wait and see." Lucas finished the brandy in his glass with one long swallow. "Sometimes God sends miracles. This brandy comes close to one, by the way. You have a most excellent cellar."

"Credit goes to the gentleman who owns the house and to his people who care for it and for us while we are guests here." Simon stood. "Where is Suzanne?"

"Your beautiful and intrepid lady is sleeping the sleep of the just and exhausted in your bedroom."

Simon nodded and reached to grasp his cousin's hand in both of his. "I am so very glad to have you back, Lucas!"

"And I'm glad to be back." Lucas added his other hand to the fervent four-hand clasp. "Thank you for accepting me in all my sins, Simon."

"Of course." Simon gave a ghost of a smile. "Family is family." His smile vanished. "I'm going off to join Wellington. If I don't come back, know that our friendship has been one of the best things in my life."

Lucas muttered a very unspiritual word under his breath, then rose to his feet and gave Simon a powerful hug. "Go with God, my almost brother."

Simon hugged Lucas back, telling himself he mustn't break down. Then he pivoted and headed up the stairs to find his wife.

As Lucas had said, Suzanne lay collapsed on their bed, fully clothed but resting peacefully with Leo on the far side of her pillow, his little whiskers twitching. Simon stripped off his coat and lay behind her, drawing her against him. His brave and gracious lady, too precious for words.

Eyes not opening, Suzanne whispered, "How soon until you must leave?"

"Within the hour," he said quietly. "I have just enough time to find my old uniform and say farewell to you."

Wordlessly she rolled over and wept silently as they clung to each other. But she didn't ask him not to go.

Chapter 40

A single kiss led to swift lovemaking, neither of them speaking since words would hurt too much. After, as they lay together in a tangle of limbs and clothing, Suzanne asked quietly, "What is the military situation, and what part will you play in it?"

"Napoleon simultaneously attacked the Prussians at Ligny and the Allied forces at Quatre Bras," Simon said succinctly as he rose from their bed and began to change his clothing. "The Prussians were defeated and Marshal Blücher is withdrawing to the north in good order. The Quatre Bras battle was more of a draw, but it prevented the French from taking control of the crossroads there."

"And those roads are critical to moving armies." Suzanne frowned. "With the Prussians retreating north, will Wellington have to do the same to maintain contact between the two armies?"

"You're getting very clever at military tactics!" Simon said approvingly as he dug into his clothespress to find his folded uniform. "Exactly. It's likely that there will be another larger, more decisive battle in the next day or two and it will be fairly close to Brussels." He found his scarlet uniform coat and shook it out. Like him, it was showing signs of wear. "I thought I'd not wear this again."

Suzanne swung from the bed and began to change into her nightclothes. "Why did you bring it here? Intuition?"

"I suppose that's why." He began to put on the uniform. "The emperor's exile to Elba seemed inconclusive. Not like peace had really arrived. And I thought if the wars returned . . ." With a sigh, he shrugged into his coat. "Soldiers are needed."

"Once a soldier, always a soldier," she said, her voice not quite steady.

"And once a spy, always a spy." He sighed as he buttoned his coat. "I'm sorry, milady. I wanted to give you a peaceful, pampered life. Not this." His gesture encompassed the military chaos of the city.

"We may get there yet." She unpinned her hair and let it fall in a hypnotic cascade. Her gaze on him, Suzanne began brushing out the shining length so that it could be braided for the night. "What does Wellington need you for?"

"To command a Dutch-Belgian regiment. Their Sixth Infantry fought at Quatre Bras and the commander and many of the officers were killed or wounded. Since I speak good French and adequate Dutch, the duke thought I was the best available replacement."

She frowned. "Have you much battlefield experience? I thought you spent most of your time as an exploring officer."

"Most of the time. Not always." He gave her a reassuring smile as he dusted off his tall shako hat. It had two bullet holes in it, a fact he would not point out to Suzanne. "I've had enough battlefield experience to manage this command. All I have to do is order the regiment to form a square, then amble around inside the square looking confident and saying 'Hold, lads!' in two languages."

She managed a twisted smile. "Don't forget the part about ducking!"

"I won't, *ma chérie.*" He embraced Suzanne one last time, never wanting to let her go. How many soldiers and their loved ones were embracing this same way, weeping inside at the circumstances that were tearing them apart? Too many.

Throat tight, he gave her one last kiss, full of tenderness, not fire. She was trembling in his arms. When he pulled away, she kissed her fingertips and touched them to his lips as she regarded him with her great, grave, green eyes. So lovely. So very, very dear . . .

On the verge of breaking, he turned and left the room. *Always in my heart . . .*

He buried thoughts of Suzanne when he stepped out into the corridor and found Jackson waiting in his infantry uniform. Patches of brighter fabric on the left arm marked the crippling wounds he'd suffered. "What the devil are you doing?"

"Going with you, Colonel." Jackson saluted, his gaze steady.

"Good God, man, you've been married even less time than I have!"

A glint of humor showed in Jackson's eyes. "A fact Jenny and I are both aware of, sir. But some things must be done."

Simon thought back to the tired, broken man Jackson had been when they'd met. With time, the confidence of doing a job well, and the love of a good woman, he was now a man ready to face whatever might come. To deny him the chance to meet this challenge would be to deny his manhood.

"I'll be grateful to have you with me," Simon said honestly. "But as my wife said to me, be sure to duck when you have to!"

Jackson grinned. "I'll do my best, sir."

Side by side, they descended the stairs and set out to war.

Worn out by the long day and night, Suzanne came awake groggily the next morning, her arms around the pillow that Leo slept on. A steady, saturating rain still fell. She'd been roused by Jenny's knock before her maid quietly entered the room with a cup of hot chocolate and a fresh crescent roll. "Miss Suzanne?"

Trying not to think of the parting with Simon, Suzanne sat up so Jenny could set the tray on her lap. "How are Marie and the baby?"

Jenny smiled. "Happy and healthy. She is very pleased with herself and can't wait to show her husband their son. Do you have any idea when that might be?"

Suzanne glanced out the window at the rain, knowing that the roads would have turned to mud by now, and sighed. "Not really. Soon, I hope. What other news is there?"

Jenny's gaze dropped as she smoothed the covers around Suzanne. "Edgar has gone off with the colonel."

"What?" Suzanne exclaimed. "He shouldn't have done that!"

"Yes, and no," Jenny said with a sigh. "He thought it was his duty."

"How admirable and maddening." Suzanne bit into her flaky crescent roll rather savagely. "But I'll admit that I'm glad he'll be there with Simon."

Jenny nodded. "The injured from yesterday's battle

are coming into the city. The more badly wounded are in wagons, but the ones who can walk are staggering along the streets, needing water and food and care. Mr. Mandeville asked that you come down and help when you're ready."

Suzanne swore in a most unladylike fashion, swallowed most of her hot chocolate in one scalding gulp, and set the tray aside. "And I thought yesterday was tiring! Find me a gown that bloodstains will wash out of. And join me? It sounds like many hands will be needed."

"Yes, ma'am." Jenny smiled wryly. "Keeping busy will be good for us!"

And so it was. When Suzanne was dressed in sturdy, practical clothing with a wide hat to ward off the rain, she found that Lucas had set up a street infirmary. An overhead canvas awning protected the work area from the rain and it looked like most of the members of the household were already helping the wounded. There were several wooden chairs and two long tables of different heights, buckets of water with ladles, and boxes of bandages and ointments and other supplies.

Suzanne said, "Lucas, what do you want me to do?"

He helped a wounded Belgian soldier onto the table. "A lot of this is common sense. Take off the old bandages, clean the wounds, removing any bits of grit or material that shouldn't be there. If you find a musket ball deeply lodged, best to call me.

"Then pour gin over the wound to reduce the chances of inflammation"—he grinned—"don't let the patients drink it. We don't have unlimited supplies. Bandage the wound as lightly as is feasible, and send them on their way. Many were billeted here in the city and if they can make it back to their billet, they should be taken care of."

Suzanne drew a deep breath and pitched in. Jenny was at her side, Maurice helped lift men who couldn't move easily, and Madame Maurice was almost as good at cleaning and bandaging wounds as Lucas.

It was approaching midday when Suzanne heard a voice call, "Madame Duval!" She looked up and saw Janet Allen, one of the camp followers she'd met at the informal shelter that had been set up to aid the women and children who followed the army. Janet was young and vigorous and had pitched in to help the volunteer ladies.

Suzanne liked her and they'd become friendly. Usually Janet was imperturbable, but today she looked frantic, her saturated red hair falling in dripping corkscrews around her face. Suzanne exclaimed, "Janet, what's wrong?"

"I've learned that my Jack was wounded in the battle yesterday! He and several of his mates who'd also been injured were heading back to the city, but his leg was badly torn and finally he couldn't walk anymore. He may die out there in the rain, or a French soldier might come along and kill him because he's an easy target! Please, ma'am, can you do anything to help him?" Her voice was desperate and tears mingled with falling rain on her face.

Wondering if it was possible to help, Suzanne asked, "How far away is he, and can you find the exact place?"

"It's several miles south on the road toward Quatre Bras. One of his mates drew me a map. I've walked that road and I know I can find him, but I'll need help getting him home."

"Is the territory where he was left under French control now?"

"It might be," Janet admitted, "but soldiers don't usually bother camp followers. We're no danger to them."

The reverse wasn't always true, but Suzanne felt a powerful impulse to help. To do something *active*. Maurice was a few steps away and temporarily unoccupied, so Suzanne said, "Mrs. Allen needs help to bring her wounded husband back to Brussels. Can you find us a cart with wheels wide enough to manage the mud, plus canvas to cover the cart to protect Corporal Allen?"

Maurice snapped a couple of questions at Janet, then nodded. "Aye, I can find a cart and a pair of strong mules to pull it. I'll come with you to help push the cart out of the mud."

"*Thank* you!" Suzanne said gratefully, knowing his strength and knowledge of the area would greatly increase their chances of success. She crossed the infirmary to where Lucas was treating the wounded arm of a member of the King's German Legion.

Briefly she explained what she was going to do. She half expected him to object, but he nodded understandingly. "Risking yourself as a sacrifice toward Simon's safe return home?"

She winced. "You are altogether too perceptive, Lucas. My mind knows that ritual magic isn't going to help him, but this is worth doing for its own sake."

He laid a quiet hand on her shoulder. "Just be careful, Suzanne. Simon needs you."

"And I need him." She gave Lucas a crooked smile. "Pray for us, almost brother. I'm sure you're better at it than either Simon or I."

He smiled, then turned away to help a man being carried between two friends. She hoped Lucas could pray and bandage at the same time.

The journey down to Jack's location was wet, muddy, and utterly miserable, though they made decent time under the circumstances. The corporal was just where his friends had described, in a copse of dense trees a little way off the main road. They seemed to be in a kind of no man's land and hadn't seen any soldiers from either side in the last half hour.

Suzanne looked around uneasily, feeling that danger could come from any direction, but Janet leaped from the cart. "Jack. *Jack!*"

Her young husband had been half unconscious, saturated by rain and looking frighteningly pale, but he jerked awake and made an instinctive reach for a weapon before he recognized his wife. "Janet, is that really you? You're mad, my girl!" But he crushed her into his arms when she knelt beside him.

Maurice allowed them a minute for their reunion before saying, "Time we got a move on. There are safer places for hugging."

That was undeniable, so working together, they managed to get Jack into the back of the cart, under the canvas and wrapped in a blanket. They were about to head back to the road when a deep voice shouted in French, "Who is back there!" The shout was followed by several shots.

The rescue party froze in panic. After an instant of frantic thought, Suzanne said, "I'll go out and talk to them. I'm the only one here who is French and I should be able to convince them that I'm just a camp follower looking for my husband."

Maurice frowned. "That's not safe."

"We're in the middle of a bloody war zone!" she swore. "Nothing here is safe! But I have the best chance of keeping us all in one piece. If they want to take me off for questioning or something, head for Brussels as soon as we're out of sight. One way or another, I'll get away from them and manage to make my way home."

More shots were fired. Not waiting to argue further, Suzanne called out in French in a frightened feminine voice, "Please, sirs, I'm a camp follower looking for my husband! I'm unarmed. I'll come out but, please, don't shoot me!"

"Show yourself!" the deep voice barked.

Suzanne emerged from the woods, hands held high and stumbling in the mud. It was easy to look harmless and terrified. Though she had her knife and one of her pistols, she doubted they'd be any good against the half dozen mounted men of the patrol.

The leader with the deep voice was a lieutenant. He said sharply, "Your name!"

"Suzanne Duval, sir," she said, her voice quavering. The name was common enough to be harmless.

"What outfit was your husband in?"

What had Simon said? "The Dutch-Belgian Sixth Infantry."

"They fought well," the lieutenant said with grudging respect. "The great Wellington made a mistake, and if not for the Dutch-Belgians, we'd be in Brussels now!"

"And a lot drier!" one of his men muttered to general laughter.

"She might know something useful. Gerard, take her up with you and we'll bring her along to headquarters."

"But I want to find my husband!" she wailed, backing away.

Gerard, a burly sergeant, said not unkindly, "The battle was fought yesterday. He's either recovering or dead. Now behave yourself and you won't get hurt."

He extended his hand. She took it reluctantly, put one foot on his foot in the stirrup, and with his tug, managed to scramble up behind him. Her seat wasn't very comfortable, but at least the sergeant was warm to hold on to.

The men rode for a couple of miles, chatting idly as they studied their surroundings. They all seemed to be experienced soldiers, loyal to the emperor and ready to fight. They also complained about the weather and the food and the usual things soldiers complained about. They weren't monsters like the guards she and Simon had met on their way out of Paris.

The group halted in front of a handsome stone tavern with a sign proclaiming it as La Belle Alliance. French soldiers milled around, and there were several artillery pieces in front. Gerard told Suzanne, "Off with you. You're about to become a very lucky woman."

She scowled at him, unable to think of any good interpretation of his comment other than getting out of the rain. He just grinned at her.

The lieutenant dismounted and escorted her inside. The tavern was warm and blessedly dry, and good food smells scented the air. Her captor explained to a captain sitting at a desk how they had found her and thought she might be worth interrogating.

The captain nodded and got to his feet. "I'll see if he wants to do it himself. If not, I'll question her."

While she waited, Suzanne took off her cloak, which had given up any attempt at water resistance, and wrung it out, creating a small stream of water. One of the officers in the room snapped for her to stop making a mess. She bowed her head meekly and donned her wet cloak again.

The captain returned. "He wants to talk to you himself."

Suzanne wondered who "he" was. An intelligence officer? Perhaps a general?

She was led into a dining room. Sitting at the table was Napoleon Bonaparte, the emperor of France.

Chapter 41

❦

Suzanne gasped and sank to one knee. "Sire! Your Majesty!" A simple country girl wouldn't know the proper way to address an emperor, but as long as she looked overcome with awe, she should be safe. That wasn't difficult to do, either.

Though the vigorous young general who had led France to victory after victory was gone and he'd become a fat, pasty-faced man who didn't look very healthy, Napoleon was still a compelling figure. He radiated power and confidence. No wonder people followed him, even when he led them to their deaths.

Not displeased by her reaction, the emperor waved a hand. "Get up now," he said good-naturedly. "Look at me, girl."

Suzanne stood, trying to look modest and dazzled. Again, it wasn't difficult. "She has a look of my Josephine about her, doesn't she?" the emperor mused.

Though he'd set his empress aside because Josephine gave him no heirs, it was said that the emperor had never stopped loving her. As several aides murmured agreement about her appearance, Suzanne said, "If so, I am honored, Your Majesty."

The emperor asked her the same questions the lieutenant had. Her name. Her reason for being on the road. Her husband's name and outfit. Then he asked, "You are French?"

"Yes, sire, I was born not far from here. My husband also is French."

"Then why is he in the Dutch-Belgian army?" Bonaparte asked with a frown.

"He wasn't given a choice, sire." She thought of Simon and tears began welling up in her eyes. "All he wants to do is survive and come home to me, and it may already be too late. I fear he was taken captive by the enemy. I may never see him again!" Thinking of Simon made it too easy to cry.

"Someone give her a handkerchief," the emperor ordered, as uncomfortable with a woman's tears as most men were. "You were following the Anglo-Dutch army, hoping to find your husband, *oui*?"

"Yes, sire."

"What are they doing now?" he asked, his gaze suddenly sharp.

What to say? With sudden ferocity, she thought, *Confusion to the enemy!* "After the defeat of the Prussians at Ligny and the sad showing of the Allies at Quatre Bras, the Anglo-Dutch are retreating north. Fleeing, really. It's a mad scramble. Many of the camp followers weren't able to keep up. It's said that the Prussians are fleeing to the east, perhaps to the River Meuse. I do not speak of my own knowledge," she added conscientiously. "But I heard it said by reliable men."

"Good, good," the emperor praised, looking vastly pleased. "Now we divide the British and Prussians and destroy them both!"

Suzanne kept her face blank, as if ignorant of military strategy. Well, she was fairly ignorant, but the false information she'd given the emperor should benefit the Allies.

The emperor barked, "Bring me maps!"

The captain who had escorted Suzanne into the imperial presence asked, "What should I do with the girl?"

Bonaparte waved an impatient hand. "Take her to the kitchen to be fed, then lock her up until this is all over."

He'd already forgotten her before she even left the room. The captain took a firm grip on her arm and marched her to the kitchen, where half a dozen cooks were toiling to feed all the important people who had taken over the tavern. "Feed her some soup or something," the captain ordered. "Then call a guard and have her locked up in the cellar."

A frazzled female scullion said, "Over there in that corner out of the way, girl. Don't drip any mud near the food! I'll bring you some soup."

Suzanne obeyed, scanning the room as she did. There was a back door. A male kitchen servant stepped through the entry and returned a couple of minutes later carrying a large sack of potatoes. So it wasn't locked.

She perched on the stool in the corner. The soup arrived in a large mug along with a chunk of bread. Leek and potato soup, very tasty and warming. Suzanne sipped from the mug, her cloak gently steaming in the warmth of the kitchen.

The head cook bellowed a command that sent a flurry of movement among his assistants. And while all attention was on the chef, Suzanne quietly stood, edged along the back wall, and slipped out the back door. She finished the soup and set the mug on the ground by the wall, since stealing it seemed more a crime than lying to an emperor.

Now what? The steady rain hadn't abated, and on this side of the tavern, no one was in sight. But surely that building across the yard was the stables. Acting as if she was a servant at the inn, Suzanne crossed the open space and entered the stables. There were a dozen stalls, all of them occupied.

Time for that horse magic Simon said she had. She walked along the row, sizing up the potential mounts, and stopped dead at the sight of a lovely gray mare. Good God, this was surely the emperor's famous mare Desiree! Despite the horse's friendly whuffle, Suzanne swiftly moved on.

At the far left end of the aisle was a young red roan who pricked his ears forward in interest as she approached.

Since she still had some of the bread she'd been given, she offered it to the gelding. He ate it with interest, then nuzzled her affectionately. She smiled with delight. "We're going on an adventure, my handsome red friend!"

The tack room was on the other side of his stall, so she collected what she needed and entered the stall, speaking soothing words. She was about to saddle the roan when two men entered the stables, talking heatedly about military tactics.

Suzanne dropped to her knees in the straw, her heart hammering, but they didn't come down to her end of the stables. She heard them saddle two mounts and ride out, still arguing. Thank heaven she hadn't chosen one of those two horses!

She waited until she was sure she was alone again, then stood and saddled the roan and led him from his stall. He was lively but willing to accept her. She used a mounting block to scramble onto his back. Since she wasn't wearing a riding habit, her lower legs were uncovered. She tried to arrange her wet cloak, to cover them a little better, with limited success.

No matter. She rode out with confidence, as if there was nothing odd about her appearance. There were surely stranger sights in a war zone.

She passed by the men and artillery pieces in front of the inn without attracting much notice. But once she reached the road and turned north, a man said loudly, "Eh, that's a woman!"

Another man barked, "Stop her! That's an officer's horse!"

"Come on, Red," Suzanne said as she kicked the horse into a gallop that sent mud splattering behind them. "We are going to *fly* back to Brussels!"

If there was a pursuit, it wasn't a serious one. She guessed that she wasn't important enough to bother with when a battle was being planned.

When she felt they were safe, she slowed to a fast trot and considered who, if anyone, she should tell about her encounter with the emperor. From what she'd observed on the trip south in the cart, the Allied troops were digging in just south of a village called Waterloo. She might be able to find someone there who would be interested in what she'd seen.

It was full dark by the time she reached the hive of activity that was the Anglo-Dutch army. A few inquiries brought her to an inn called the King of Spain, which was said to be Wellington's headquarters.

She attracted great interest as she drew her filthy horse to a halt in front of the inn and swung her equally filthy self to the ground. "I have dispatches for the duke!" she announced in her most commanding tone. "Someone look after my horse."

A bemused soldier stepped forward to take the reins as Suzanne marched into the inn, dripping mud and water. "I have just seen the emperor, and I have information for the duke," she announced. "Tell him that the wife of Colonel Simon Duval is here."

More confusion, and one kind man handed her a towel to mop the rain off her face. Lord Fitzroy Somerset, Wellington's military secretary, entered the common room. She'd met him several times.

He stared at her. "Mrs. Duval, is that really you?"

"Yes, though rather the worse for wear." She smiled at him. "I've just seen the emperor and have some information that might be interesting."

Somerset gave a soft whistle and ushered her from the common room. When they were in private, she gave him a brief summary of what had happened to her. "The duke will want to hear this," he agreed.

After a few minutes waiting, she was escorted into Wellington's presence. His brows arched. "Mrs. Duval? You look like you've had a difficult day."

She smiled tiredly. "Hasn't everyone? But I didn't expect to meet Napoleon Bonaparte along the way."

The duke indicated a chair. "Tell me."

"Thinking I was a camp follower, a patrol took me in for questioning," she said as she started the tale of how she'd come to be personally interviewed by the emperor.

She ended by saying, "When asked what I had observed of the Allies, I said the British-Dutch forces were fleeing north toward Brussels and the Prussians were heading east toward the Meuse rather than retreating north in good order. I hope I added to the confusion among the French."

"Excellent work!" Wellington exclaimed. "Did the emperor believe you?"

"He seemed to," she said slowly. "I think he wants the Allies to be in disarray so he can move in and make a decisive strike."

"That sounds likely," the duke said soberly. "Knowing what the enemy is doing is vital and unbelievably difficult, even when the armies are only a few miles apart. If what you told the emperor contributes to his making errors of judgment, you've served your country well today."

"I hope so," she said with a sigh. "I want this to be *over*. With your permission, I'll head back to Brussels now. My household will be very worried at my absence."

"God willing, this matter will be over in a few days,

but it will be a near run thing," the duke said. "A very near run thing. Thank you for what you've done, Mrs. Duval."

She inclined her head and withdrew. She went outside, still dripping, and found that her horse had been properly fed and watered and was ready to travel the ten miles or so back to Brussels. Telling herself that she was equally ready, Suzanne asked one of the soldiers in front of the inn to help her onto her mount. Once her aching body was secure in the saddle, she started on the last leg home.

It was well past midnight when she finally reached the house on the rue de Louvain, but lights were still visible inside. She tethered the weary roan and knocked on the door. Maurice threw it wide open when he saw who was on the doorstep. "Thank heavens you're home safely, ma'am!"

"I couldn't agree more," she said with a tired smile. "Could you have someone look after my horse, please? He deserves oats and a really good grooming."

Maurice peered over her head at the muddy roan. "I don't recognize your mount."

She peeled off her saturated cloak and let it collapse in a muddy heap on the tile floor. "I have taken up a career as a horse thief. How did the rescue mission turn out?"

Maurice smiled. "We brought Corporal Allen here along with three other wounded soldiers that we found on the way home. All have been treated and are doing well. Janet Allen is staying with her husband and keeping an eye on all the patients."

Suzanne closed her eyes and uttered a fervent prayer of thanks. "I need food, a hot drink, and a hot bath, not necessarily in that order."

"And you shall have them!" Jenny came flying into the reception hall and gave Suzanne an enthusiastic hug despite her soggy state. "Now tell us of your adventures!"

Moving at a more moderate pace, Lucas appeared and handed her a glass of brandy. "I also want to hear what has happened. Sit and tell us all."

Madame Maurice appeared and wrapped a warm blanket around her. "This way, ma'am," she said as she guided Suzanne into the drawing room.

Suzanne subsided into a chair as Lucas knelt to start a fire to ward off the cool, wet night. She felt a deep sense of peace to be here with these people who all meant so much to her. All she lacked was Simon.

Dear Lord, look after him, she prayed silently. *Let this all be over, and bring him home to me!*

Chapter 42

❧

The rain had stopped. That was the first thing Suzanne noticed when her eyes reluctantly opened. What time was it? Midmorning, it appeared. After her exhausting day and late night return, her household was letting her sleep late.

And Leo was sleeping on her head, his little body a warm band across her skull. She smiled as she reached up to pet him. "Could you see your way clear to pulling the bell cord? No, I suppose not." She rolled across the mattress and pulled at the cord while Leo rolled down her pillow with an indignant squeak. Luckily, he was of a forgiving nature.

Suzanne had barely had time to pile pillows against the headboard and prop herself up when Jenny arrived with a tray. "How are you feeling today, ma'am?"

"As if a herd of horses galloped over me," Suzanne reported. "But it would have been worse if you hadn't drawn that hot bath for me last night. And woken me up when I fell asleep there!"

Jenny smiled and arranged the bed tray over Suzanne's lap. "You deserved every bit of pampering we could give you! When Maurice and Janet and the others came back and reported how you'd given yourself up to the French soldiers to save them . . ." She shuddered.

"I knew I had the best chance of coming through unscathed." Suzanne swallowed a delicious mouthful of hot chocolate. "Luckily I didn't have time to think about it or I would have been too afraid. Now tell me what has happened in the world while I was away."

"It was reported that Wellington was retreating and French troops were about to enter the city. Many people panicked and they were fighting to get away to Antwerp." Jenny smiled. "You're lucky to have missed that."

"Cowards and good riddance," Suzanne said callously. "But what about the armies? Is there any word from them? I hate not knowing!"

"We all do! Which is why early this morning Maurice rode down to that village, Waterloo, to find out. The two armies are lined up across a wide valley, about a mile apart. He says Wellington has a good defensive position. All was quiet when Maurice left. He thinks the emperor is waiting for the ground to dry enough to maneuver his artillery pieces."

Suzanne swallowed hard and set down her half-eaten crescent roll. "I wonder how long until the ground dries."

"Maurice thought maybe around noon."

Suzanne looked at the clock on the mantel. It was after 11:00. Suddenly grim, she finished her chocolate and set the tray aside so she could get out of bed. "Time to find myself something to do so I don't go mad with waiting."

"Mr. Mandeville has set up his street infirmary again. I'm going down there when you don't need me."

"I'll go with you." Suzanne swung from the bed, wincing at muscles aching from all the riding the day before.

"I've never done much nursing, but I do like helping and the soldiers are so grateful."

She and Jenny shared a glance, and Suzanne felt they were thinking the same thing: that if they helped strangers, perhaps strangers would help their men if necessary. It was only superstition, but still it felt good to help others.

She began to dress and tried not to think of the huge battle involving tens of thousands of men that would soon begin just a few miles away. *Be safe,* mon chéri, *be safe!*

As Simon had told Suzanne, commanding this Dutch-Belgian regiment would mostly be a matter of strolling around looking confident and telling the men to hold their ground. So far, his words had been prophetic. The Sixth Infantry was a militia regiment that had done nothing but weekly drills and beer drinking before Napoleon had returned from exile, but they had stood their ground at Quatre Bras.

The regiment also suffered a number of casualties during that fight, particularly among the officers. Captain De Jong, the senior surviving officer of the Sixth, had been grateful when Simon had shown up to take command the day before.

He was even more impressed by the fact that Simon and Jackson both had a working knowledge of Dutch as well as French. Simon and his batman had spent much of the previous day ambling around the regiment, creating bonds with soldiers and noncoms. The regiment was now settled into position, but waiting for the battle to begin was hard, damnably hard.

De Jong had also been talking to his men, and he met Simon in the center of the infantry square by the company colors. The colors were a pair of banners that carried the flags of the Kingdom of the Netherlands and the Sixth regiment, and they were the visible signs of the regiment's pride and honor. A regiment that lost its colors never recovered from the shame of it, so the banners were well guarded.

Simon glanced along the Allied line of battle, saying to De Jong, "It's an impressive sight, isn't it? Flags and uniforms from half a dozen nations, not just the United Kingdom contingents from England, Scotland, Ireland, and Wales, but Dutch and Belgian units from the Netherlands. Hanover, Nassau, Brunswick. And we can hope that ten or twelve miles away, the Prussian army is marching to join us."

De Jong, an open-faced young blond man, followed Simon's gaze and nodded thoughtfully. "I hadn't really thought about it that way, but we're part of a great enterprise, aren't we?"

"Shakespeare's play *Henry V* has a line where the king is addressing his outnumbered troops just before the Battle of Agincourt," Simon said softly. "He says something like 'Gentlemen in England now abed/Shall think themselves accursed they were not here.' On a day like today, it's not just England, but all the Allied lands."

"It's a noble sentiment," De Jong said, his brow furrowed. "The words move me. But more of my mind is saying that I'd rather be at home abed with my wife!"

Simon laughed. "So would I. But this is where I need to be."

"And I'm very glad of it, Colonel," De Jong said more seriously. "After Quatre Bras, I can no longer say my men are raw troops, but one battle does not a seasoned soldier make."

"It's a good start, though." Simon nodded at the four rows of dark blue uniformed men that formed the sides of the square. "The Sixth and the other Dutch-Belgian troops fought bravely at Quatre Bras and saved the Allied army from disaster. Good men. You have a right to be proud of them."

"I am." De Jong made a face. "But we're militia. Most of the time I captain a fishing boat."

Simon smiled. "The world needs fishermen more than soldiers."

"I look forward to returning to fish herding rather than commanding men!" De Jong said fervently.

KA-KA-KA-BOOOOOM!!!!!

Their idle conversation shattered as the French cannon began blasting with thunderous power that shook the ground and numbed the ears. The soldiers of the Sixth flinched and some turned pale, but most looked glad that the battle was finally joined.

A French cannonball landed menacingly a dozen yards in front of the square, bounced, then continued rolling toward the regiment. As one of Simon's men moved curiously toward it, Simon ran forward, bellowing. "Out of the way! That cannonball can kill! Out of the way!"

Startled, the troops in the path of the rolling ball scattered to the sides. His voice pitched to carry as far as possible despite the cannonade, Simon barked, "French gunners like to 'graze' cannonballs like this, firing low so they skip along the ground. They roll farther and do more damage than if they were launched higher. Pass the word on! *Stay clear of any rolling cannonballs!*"

Impressed and unnerved, his soldiers did pass the warning on and they became adept at dodging the occasional cannonball. Despite their care, though, a couple of cannonballs struck the square, wounding and killing a dozen men. Simon had arranged with the regimental surgeon to set up a treatment area and in each platoon there were men designated to carry the wounded there for treatment. As the day continued, the treatment area grew larger and the square became smaller as men were wounded and pulled from formation.

The attacks became progressively more lethal. A series of cavalry charges roared up the slope at the Allied lines.

Heavy horses carrying cavalrymen were a terrifying sight to an infantryman on the ground, and once again Simon's experience helped.

"Don't fall back!" he shouted. "Horses won't charge into an infantry square. Hold your fire until the order comes, then aim for the horses!"

Terrified but determined, the soldiers of the Sixth held their fire until the order came. *Ready! Level! Fire!*

Muskets blasted, the air filled with the burning stench of black powder, horses screamed and crashed to the ground. The cavalry charge broke and the horses swerved around the square. The soldiers of the Sixth gave a whoop of triumph.

That was the first charge. There were many more to come.

As the most experienced soldiers, Simon and Jackson headed wherever the fighting was fiercest, wherever the men of the Sixth needed help or encouragement. Jackson's weak hand was of no importance here. What mattered was his calm, his advice, the dark humor that made beleaguered soldiers laugh.

Simon was grateful that Jackson had insisted on coming because on a day like this, the regiment needed all the strength and experience it could get. He'd been in enough battles to recognize how perilous the situation was. Outnumbered and outgunned, the Allied armies were close to the breaking point.

But that didn't mean they'd break. His teeth bared in what wasn't a smile, Simon gave the order to fire and another cavalry charge broke on their infantry square.

Nightfall was coming, unless eternal night came first.

Suzanne was growing adept at basic nursing, and she'd taken to carrying a notebook and pencil so she could record messages and addresses from wounded soldiers who feared they would never make it home.

Most messages boiled down to "I love you." Tears stung her eyes as she wrote the words down and swore the messages would be delivered.

Lucas was amazing, ever-calm as he practiced his bonesetter art along with treating open wounds. Bones that were broken were set, and twice Maurice was sent to find more laths for splints and more lengths of bandage to hold the splints in place. Soldiers Lucas treated wouldn't have to worry about bones healing crookedly. If they lived, they would heal straight and true.

And the wounded kept coming. Their street infirmary was receiving men wounded earlier in the day, and they brought news of the fighting at the same time. As Suzanne patched a battered sergeant in a dark green Riflemen uniform, she asked, "How is it going, Sergeant?"

"Bloody awful." He flinched as she treated his wounded arm with gin. "Sorry, missus, but there ain't any nice words strong enough. 'Tis a nightmare, with more French than Allied troops. And they're more experienced, and they've got more and better guns."

Trying not to show her fear, Suzanne started work on a bayonet slice across the sergeant's cheek. "Are our troops retreating?"

"Nay, we're holding. Bloodied, battered, but holding." The Rifleman sucked his breath in at the vicious sting of gin on his lacerated cheek. "If you're sending up prayers for your man, pray that the bloody Prussians reach the field in time to help. Otherwise . . ."

Suzanne drew in a slow, shaky breath. Pray for Simon, pray for the Prussians to arrive. She could do that.

She *would* do that.

* * *

"The Prussians have arrived, the Prussians have arrived, the Prussians have arrived!" Word moved across the Allied lines, reinvigorating the battered troops. The balance of the battle changed as Prussian troops poured in from the east.

The emperor played his last card by sending his Imperial Guards, the finest troops in Europe, who had never been defeated. Until this evening, when the tidal wave of the empire broke on the steel of the British Guards regiments.

The summer days were long, but even so, nightfall was only a couple of hours away when Wellington ordered a general advance, sweeping his dark cockade hat forward in a fierce command. Shouting with battle fever, the Allied armies advanced down the slope to meet the French head on. The battered Sixth rushed forward, raging to defeat the enemy once and for all.

Simon and De Jong led the way, but the regiment scattered into smaller groups as it rushed forward. Some of the men became involved in hand-to-hand combat with clusters of stubbornly resisting French fighters. Other members of the regiment swooped deeper into the valley of death. Simon was in a high, wild state dictated by warrior's instinct.

That instinct drove him when a French heavy cavalryman thundered forward to ride De Jong down. The blond fisherman was doomed, until Simon lunged forward and drove his sword into the cavalryman. The rider fell off, mortally wounded, but Simon couldn't avoid the steel-clad hooves of the great horse.

He crashed to the ground, his vision dimming. Pain, numbness, falling. His last thought before tumbling into darkness was of Suzanne. *Always in my heart . . .*

Chapter 43

❧

It was well into the evening when Suzanne wearily approached Lucas with a hunk of good local cheese. She broke it in half and offered him the larger chunk. "Eat, almost brother," she said, her voice raw from so much talking. "We aren't running out of patients and we need to keep up our strength."

He bit into the cheese as if it were an apple. She did the same, then swallowed hard as something vital twanged deep in her heart.

She couldn't breathe, couldn't think. *Simon!* She stared at Lucas. "Simon. I'm sure something has happened to him. Dear God, *Simon!*"

Lucas also froze for a long, agonized moment before he said, "I don't think he's dead. But he may be seriously wounded."

An injured soldier was limping toward Suzanne, but she waved him off. "Go to that woman over there—she'll help you." Suzanne wiped sweaty, bloodstained hands down her skirts. "I must find my husband!"

This time the rescue party was Suzanne, Maurice, and Lucas, though they used the same cart as the day before. It was now stocked with medical supplies, blankets, and a basket of food and drink. Lucas drove the cart. Because they were armed, Maurice and Suzanne kept watch on all sides for any roving French soldiers or looters.

The road was jammed and chaotic as wagonloads of the wounded lurched toward Brussels and desperate family members forced their way south. Lucas was an expert driver and the small cart could be maneuvered better than most through the teeming mass of vehicles.

They had almost reached Waterloo when Suzanne spotted a familiar figure on horseback heading toward them. "Jackson!" she shouted as she waved frantically. "Edgar Jackson!"

Seeing them, he kicked his horse faster and met the cart as Lucas pulled over on the verge. She called, "Jackson, where is Simon?"

Looking ill, he said, "He was alive when I left him in surgery, but he was hurt bad, ma'am. I was coming to get you."

Maurice called, "The battle. Is it over?"

"Aye, and we won! Blücher's Prussians arrived after a brutal cross-country march. That turned the tide. The French army broke and is fleeing south as fast as they can go."

Victory was a relief, but a distant one compared to the urgency of reaching her husband. "Take us to Simon!" Suzanne demanded. "How was he wounded? How badly?"

"He got trampled by a French heavy cavalry horse after he saved one of the officers of the Sixth. He's got some sword slices and broken bones, but it's the skull injuries that are the worst."

After that, there was no talk. A grim-faced Lucas pushed the cart and horses as fast as possible in such a crush of traffic. In a few days it would be the longest day of the year, but it was still near dark when they reached the village of Waterloo.

Jackson led the way to one of the homes that had been commandeered by the surgeons. Suzanne tumbled from the cart and headed for the front door, shuddering at the sight of a pile of amputated limbs that had been tossed out an open window.

Inside, she grabbed the arm of a blood-splattered orderly. "My husband, Colonel Duval! Where is he?"

The orderly thought a moment, then gestured toward the back of the house. "He's not a candidate for the cutting ward so he was taken into the dining room. Should be there if he's still alive."

Heart pounding, she thanked the orderly as she pushed past him, praying Simon still breathed. She was dimly aware that Lucas and Jackson were behind her and guessed that Maurice was guarding the precious cart and riding horse.

The dining room was lit by a single lantern and the air was thick with the scents of blood and injury. There, on the dining room table. Simon was stretched out on it, probably in deference to his rank. He looked like a carved image of a warrior saint, so still, so still. . . .

Suzanne picked her way through half a dozen other injured men to reach Simon. His uniform was torn and stained with blood and mud. Dear God, a huge hoof print was clearly visible on his lower left leg!

"Simon?" she whispered. Then louder, "Simon?"

He didn't react. She caught his right hand and checked for a pulse while holding it. There was a thready beat, but she had the sense that Simon was far, far off, and could easily slip away entirely.

Lucas joined her and began a quick examination with experienced hands. "He has a broken leg, a broken arm, probably some broken ribs. But the most dangerous injury is to the head." Lucas delicately touched the blood-saturated hair. "Head injuries are the devil to diagnose and treat."

Suzanne knew that it was possible for a man to survive severe head injuries, but no longer be himself. That would surely be a fate worse than death. "Can we take him back to Brussels?"

"I don't know if he could survive the journey," Lucas said painfully.

"I saw what you did with Marie," Suzanne said in a low, intense voice. "You're a healer. Can't you heal Simon?"

"It doesn't work like that!" Lucas said, his expression agonized. "Such miracles are rare and I can't predict when one might happen. I can't bear the thought of failing with Simon."

"And I can't bear the thought of your giving up without trying!" Suzanne retorted. "Do your best, almost brother. If you fail, well, Simon and I won't blame you. But I will never forgive you if you don't try!"

Lucas collected himself, becoming wrapped in stillness as he drew inward. Then he placed a light hand on each side of Simon's head. Lucas's eyes closed and his lips began to move in a silent prayer.

Suzanne felt as if heat was building inside Lucas. On impulse, she covered his nearer hand with hers. Heat, healing, a power that flowed from Lucas. Was some of it being drawn from her? She felt dizzy and had to concentrate on staying upright and connected to Lucas.

Silently Jackson covered Lucas's other hand. The heat increased, creating an invisible light that filled Simon and spilled over them all.

Simon drew a deep breath, coughed, and his eyes opened. Dazed, he breathed, "Suzanne?"

She wanted to weep. "I'm here with Lucas and Jackson. You've been injured and we're going to take you back to Brussels."

"The battle?"

"Won, sir," Jackson said. "When Blücher arrived with his Prussians, the battle turned our way. The French are fleeing in disarray."

"Good . . ." Simon's eyes closed, but his breathing was strong.

Relieved beyond words, Suzanne said, "Jackson, can you get a couple of orderlies with a litter to carry Colonel Duval out to the cart?"

Jackson nodded and went in search of orderlies. Suzanne wondered if Lucas would also need to be carried out since he seemed so weak. She didn't feel much stronger.

But they both managed to make it outside to the cart, though Lucas moved like a sleepwalker. Suzanne swiftly spread two blankets on the floor of the cart, and the orderlies briskly laid Simon there. Suzanne ordered, "Lucas, you're all done in. Lie down beside Simon."

Silently Lucas obeyed and Suzanne spread her last blanket over them both. Then Maurice turned the cart and they headed back to Brussels. Lucas's hand rested on Simon's the whole way, lending his strength to his almost brother.

The miracle held, and Simon was still breathing when they reached the rue de Louvain in Brussels.

Heaven was a soft bed with a kitten purring in one ear and a sweetly scented female form on the other side. Simon hurt everywhere, but maybe his eyelids wouldn't be so bad?

Cautiously he opened his eyes. Yes, he was in his bedroom in Brussels with Leo to his left and Suzanne to his right. His left arm was bandaged. Splinted, even. His left leg was, too. But his right side worked, so he stretched out his right hand to pat Suzanne's arm.

She woke with a sleepy smile and reached up to touch

his cheek. "*Mon chéri,*" she murmured. "Are you returning to the land of the living?"

He blinked at her. "If I don't, you'll be a very wealthy
widow."

Her smile turned mischievous. "Indeed, but I find you
most useful in warming my bed. Leo tries, but he is only
little."

"What day is this?"

"June twentieth, two days after the battle. Which we
won. You've been sleeping since we brought you back to
Brussels. The Prussians and other Allied troops have
chased the French army most of the way to Paris by now,
I believe, and you can retire once more from active military duty."

"I like that idea." He was beginning to feel stronger,
more engaged with the idea of being alive. "One of my
officers, Captain De Jong. Do you know if he survived?"

"He did, and yesterday he called here to see how you
were faring. He says you saved his life, and he will ship
his finest preserved fish from the Netherlands to wherever your home is."

"White Horse Manor," he whispered. "It seems forever since we honeymooned there."

"Three months, but three very eventful months." She
kissed Simon's right hand in the middle of his palm. Her
voice unsteady, she said, "You were near death, but Lucas
saved you. I believe he has a divine ability to heal, though
he says it doesn't happen often. I'm just thanking heaven
that it worked for you!"

"So am I, *mon coeur.*" He gazed into her green eyes,
caught in an intimate bond beyond words. Even so, he
would try to speak. "We have come on such a long journey together. Remember when I found you in your London boardinghouse and you thought I was mad when I
proposed marriage?"

"I still think you were mad," she said with a twinkle as her hand clasped his. "But mercifully you were persuasive as well."

"We've shared so many words," he said hesitantly, "yet when I was sliding into death on the battlefield, I realized I had never said that I love you. You know I do, don't you?"

"I do." Her hand tightened on his. "But I like hearing the words. Would you like to hear that I love you?"

"Yes," he said firmly. "You may repeat that several times."

She laughed. "I love you, I love you, I love you, my handsome and lovable lord. I'm not quite sure when it happened, but I went from loving your touch to simply loving you."

"Speaking of touch, do you have any idea of how long I'm to be trussed up like a Christmas goose?"

"Lucas says that the bones are healing remarkably quickly. I suspect that is part of his miracle." Her smile turned even more mischievous. "But I am very inventive. Shall we experiment to learn what parts of you are working?"

Ignoring the pain on his left side, he rolled toward her to touch his lips to her warm, welcoming mouth. His beloved, his heart. "By all means let us experiment, my love. And we shall learn whether saying words of love has made lovemaking even better than before."

"I think that would be impossible," she murmured. "But I yearn to find out!"

Epilogue

❧

White Horse Manor
Berkshire, England
July 1815

Simon would never tire of admiring the play of light and cloud shadows over the galloping white horse carved on the opposite side of the valley, and the sofa in their private sitting room gave him a splendid view. The view became even better when Suzanne breezed in, looking delectable in a shimmering green silk gown that turned her eyes a mesmerizing shade of emerald.

"Good afternoon, *mon chéri!*" She bent and brushed a kiss on his head. "It has been far too long since I've seen you!"

"Almost three hours. Since we lunched together. Definitely too long." He caught her hand and tugged her down beside him on the sofa so close their bodies touched. As enthusiastic about her arrival as Simon, Leo promptly deserted his position on the sofa back to claim his lady's lap.

"What did the surgeon say when he examined your leg?"

"It's healing well and I should be able to abandon this cane in a fortnight and ride perhaps a week or two after that."

Her brows arched. "And your interpretation of his advice?"

Simon grinned at her. "I believe what he meant to say was that I'll be riding with you by next week."

"I am somehow not surprised." Suzanne clasped his right hand with her left and used her free hand to scratch Leo's head, which sent the little cat into ecstasies. "I asked Stanley to send up tea so we can admire the white horse together."

"It's a very peaceful occupation."

They chatted idly for a few minutes until Stanley arrived with a tea tray that held tea, sandwiches, and cakes, and a smaller tray piled with letters. "The post has arrived," he announced.

"Are there any letters from Belgium?" Simon asked.

"I believe so, sir." Stanley set the tea tray on the low table in front of the sofa and handed over the smaller tray, which held a letter opener as well as the letters. Leo instantly jumped on the table, acutely interested in the sandwiches. Suzanne gently removed the cat while Simon sorted through the pile.

"Most of these are business, but . . . ah! Here's one from Philippe."

"Good!" Suzanne offered Leo a shred of ham from one of the sandwiches. It was accepted with great enthusiasm. "I've been worried since the whole French army marched right by his estate."

"And ran back in the other direction after the battle." Simon broke the wax seal and scanned the letter. "He sends fond greetings and assures us that there was not much damage to the estate apart from the soldiers trampling two of his fields of rye. He rather casually mentions that the surviving wing of the château was burned down, which is a blessing since it will no longer attract wandering vagrants. I think that's aimed at me."

"Undoubtedly," Suzanne agreed. "What does he say about Marie?"

"She's written her own note on the lower half of the page. She loves the estate and adores the Cordiers and says she never expected to have a family like them. Young Simon is possibly the most beautiful and intelligent infant in France and motherhood is wonderful." Simon handed her the letter so she could read it herself and opened another.

"This one is from Maurice. He says that a box of excellent salted herring was delivered to the house with compliments from Captain Pieter De Jong, and do I wish it to be sent here?"

"Let the household in Brussels enjoy it, but I like that Captain De Jong honored his fish promise after you saved his life." Suzanne looked down at Leo. "His ears perked up when herring was mentioned."

"Better give him more of the ham," Simon advised. "Here's a note from Kirkland. He thanks me for my efforts in Belgium, but suggests that in future I not try so hard to get killed because he knows you would disapprove."

"He's quite right about that! Are there any others from Belgium?"

Simon riffled through the pile. "A letter from Lucas!" He broke the wafer and scanned the precise handwriting. "He's returning to England! He asks if he can stay here for a while, and is there room in the stables for the Magdalene?"

Suzanne laughed. "Of course there is! Both of them

are welcome to stay here as long as they wish. White Horse Manor is a good place to relax and adjust gradually to being an English gentleman again. It will also be useful to have a medical man around the place, especially one who can occasionally perform miracles. He's up to three, but more miracles are always welcome."

Simon glanced up. "He saved Marie's baby and he saved me. Which is the third?"

Suzanne gave him a Mona Lisa smile. "You said you'd mentioned to Lucas that I didn't think I could have children, and he told you not to judge the future by the past."

Simon stared at her, dumbfounded. "Suzanne," he breathed. "Are you saying what I think you're saying?"

She laughed with delight. "Apparently all I needed was a better man, and there are no men better than you!"

"Mon ange!" He leaned over and swooped her onto his lap in a flurry of green silk skirts. Leo leaped away with an indignant squeak, but managed to land neatly in the middle of the tray of sandwiches.

Simon gazed into her enchanting green eyes. "There are certainly no better women anywhere than you, my brave beloved." So he kissed her.

Always in my heart . . .

Author's Note

Waterloo is a feast for military history buffs, not to mention that it's wonderful material for a novelist. Two of Europe's greatest generals faced off against each other and Wellington's forces won, ending Napoleon Bonaparte's imperial ambitions after far too many years of war.

I wrote about Waterloo before in my novel *Shattered Rainbows*, including the Duchess of Richmond's famous ball and a more detailed battlefield experience, but this time I was writing about spies and intelligence workers, which took me to events around the edges of Waterloo. The research was an education in how vital intelligence gathering was, and how difficult transmitting information was in an era when everything had to travel by horse and hand.

Simon's character was inspired by the real Colonel Colquhoun Grant, Wellington's most valued intelligence officer. On the Peninsula, Grant was captured and held for two years by the French, and even then managed to send information back to Wellington.

After the emperor escaped from Elba and Wellington made Brussels the headquarters for his Anglo-Dutch army, Grant was made chief of intelligence and did his usual thorough job of observation and analysis. He was the first to realize that Napoleon wasn't going to attack through the Belgian city of Mons, but through Charleroi.

Grant's report was sneered at by General Dornberg in Mons, who didn't pass on the vital dispatch that Wellington had been waiting for. Despite this enormous frustration that left Wellington at a disadvantage, Colquhoun Grant made it back to the army in time to take the field at Waterloo, an experience I gave to Simon.

Another interesting incident I discovered was the English camp follower who was captured by the French and questioned to find out what she knew of the movements of the Allies. I doubt that she, unlike Suzanne, was interrogated by Napoleon himself, but the incident does show how desperate armies were for information.

The most interesting thing I learned in this round of research was how Waterloo was truly won by Allied nations. Many histories are very Anglocentric, but it wasn't England alone that defeated Napoleon. The British army was made up of soldiers from all over the British Isles, which meant a lot of them were Scottish, Irish, and Welsh.

Nor did the British army take the field alone at Waterloo. A significant number of Wellington's troops were Dutch-Belgian, along with military units from various German states such as Brunswick, Nassau, and Hanover. (The state of Hanover owed fealty to the British Crown since the royal family was descended from George I, the elector of Hanover.)

Nor could the battle have been won if the Prussian troops under Prince Blücher hadn't reached the battlefield in late afternoon after a ferociously difficult march over difficult terrain. Some of Blücher's staff were reluctant, not entirely trusting the British, but Blücher had promised Wellington to lend support, and he was not the man to break a promise. His troops made the critical difference. Though Blücher was in his early seventies, he led the way.

As Wellington famously said, the battle was a near-run thing, and without the Prussian troops, it would almost certainly have gone the other way. There is a famous picture of Wellington and Blücher shaking hands about 9:30 that evening near La Belle Alliance, the tavern that Napoleon had used as his headquarters.

The irony is that the name means "the Beautiful Alliance," a phrase that could be used to describe the coalition that brought the emperor down. Cooperation was as beautiful a thing then as it is now.

Please read on for an excerpt from

SEDUCTION ON A SNOWY NIGHT,

available now!

NEW YORK TIMES **BESTSELLING AUTHORS**

MADELINE HUNTER
SABRINA JEFFRIES
MARY JO PUTNEY

*This winter, steal away with the reigning queens
of Regency Romance*

. . . plus one or two dukes, one heiress, and one
headstrong beauty—to a surprise snow storm, the comfort of a blazing fire, and the heat of a lover's kisses . . .

"Hunter's effortlessly elegant writing exudes a wicked
sense of wit."
—*Booklist*

"Anyone who loves romance must read Sabrina
Jeffries!"
—**Lisa Kleypas,** *New York Times* **bestselling author**

"Putney's books are the literary equivalent of catnip to
historical romance fans."
—*Booklist*

Bombay, India
Summer 1816

Dawn was the best time of day here. Night had cooled the air and the savage heat of high noon was still hours away. The air was fragrant with scents unknown in England, and in the trees bright birds were busy about their early morning business.

Lady Diana Lawrence, the blackest sheep of her generation of the noble Lawrence family, curled up on the teak bench of her bedroom's balcony and admired the morning mists floating over the field that lay beyond the house. Dim shapes resolved into an elephant. An oxcart. A graceful woman in a sari carrying a bundle of sticks. The timeless rhythms of India.

She felt a sudden sharp longing for the mists of home drifting over the still surface of the Broads. Water birds and reeds and fishermen in low boats gliding across the silvery waters.

She'd left England over seven years before. The general reason was her craving to see the world; the specific one had been the shattering pain of a doomed love affair. In the years since, she'd traveled widely and seen many strange and wondrous sights.

After several years of traveling ever eastward, she'd come to rest in India, but she'd never felt that she would stay here forever. Perhaps it was time to go home, because England was home and always would be.

She took a sip of her cardamom-flavored tea. That tea would be something she would take home with her. She asked her companion, "Do you think you'd like England? It's not as warm, but I guarantee you'll continue to eat regularly."

He yawned, showing sharp feline teeth, then tucked his white nose under his long black tail. The Panda was a pragmatist. As long as there was food, he would be content.

Now the sky had lightened enough to read the letter that had arrived the evening before from her favorite niece, Lady Aurora Lawrence Vance. She was known as "Roaring Rory" in some circles, just as Diana had been proclaimed "the Dashing Diana." Or even "the Devilish Diana." More proof of how alarmingly alike she and Rory were.

But Rory's life had taken a surprising turn toward love, marriage, and stability. Though not, Diana was sure, tedium.

Having savored the anticipation long enough, she opened the oilcloth packet that had protected the letter on its journey halfway around the world.

> *My darling Aunt Diana!*
> *So much news to share! (Oh, I must be careful or I will run out of exclamation points before the end of this missive!)*
> *For someone who always found the prospect of marriage deeply alarming, I'm finding the reality quite deeply wonderful.*

Diana laughed, feeling Rory's bubbling personality as strongly as if she were in the room. She returned to the letter.

Once more I give thanks to my wonderful visit with you in India because that led to being captured by corsairs on the way home, which was not wonderful but did lead me to meeting Gabriel, which never would have happened if I'd been more sensible and less captured.

When I wrote my last letter, I believe that I said we were leasing a rather absurdly large house in London because it was the best available. I also mentioned that we were looking for a modest estate near London.

However, instead of buying an estate of our own, we decided to make Gabriel's grandfather's estate, Langbridge, our country home. It's very sensible because Gabriel will eventually inherit the property and he wants to become acquainted with the land and people. Having spent so many years at sea, he says, it will take time to learn farming and estate management.

Of course he's learning quickly and enjoying the challenge. Most of all, he loves having a stable full of horses and being able to ride whenever he wishes, which wasn't possible in his sea captain life. Now we ride together, which is a high point of our days. Or was—I'm not riding as often now for reasons I'll get to soon.

But the real issue is not learning the land, but the fact that his grandparents are getting old and they need us. His grandmother is a darling and we plotted together to persuade the men that the move was a good idea.

The negotiations made the Congress of Vienna

*look straightforward! The years of estrangement
after Admiral Vance disowned Gabriel made matters awkward, but Gabriel wants to make up for
those years, and his grandfather, once England's
most rigid retired admiral, now yearns for
Gabriel's company and decided he was willing to
accept my unruly self as part of the package.*

*I miss Cousin Constance dreadfully, but we ex-
change letters often, the United States being much
closer than India, though not precisely close.
We're collaborating on new stories.*

*She sends her love to you, along with the happy
news that she and Jason now have a baby boy!
Named Richard Gabriel Landers in honor of
Jason's father and my Gabriel. She assures me that
he is the best and most beautiful baby in North
America.*

Diana thought nostalgically of the fun the three of
them had had when Rory and Constance had come for a
long visit, the only members of the Lawrence family to
make it all the way to India. Those months were the most
enjoyable Diana had experienced here. Constance was illegitimate, the daughter of Diana's least reliable brother, but
she had grown up sweet and kind and wise. She was
Diana's second-favorite niece, though really she shouldn't
make comparisons. Rory and Constance were both wonderful.

*Constance and I also have another book baby!
(Oh, dear, the exclamation points are breaking out
again!) The Shining Blade, our corsair book, has
now been published and is quite the rage! Have I
thanked you lately for sending our first books to
your publisher friend in London? He has done well
by us, under the stern eye of my father, who han-*

*dles all our contracts and makes sure we aren't
swindled.*

    *Have you ever thought of publishing your own
work? Not novels, I'm the one with the lurid
Gothic imagination, but your travel journals.
They're quite wonderful—you have such a keen
eye and a sense of humor about the travails of
travel, and warmth for the people you meet and the
differences and the similarities. among us.*

Diana's brows arched as she considered. She'd never
really thought about that. Her journals were her private
thoughts and sketches and reflections, but travel memoirs
were popular and few were written by independent, not to
mention scandalous, ladies. This was definitely worth
considering. She returned to reading.

    *I probably shouldn't ask this, my favorite aunt,
but have you considered returning to England?
You are missed here by everyone, most of all by
me. You could stay with us in London—the house is
so large you'd never have to see us if you didn't
want to!*

    *Plus—I'm also increasing, slightly behind Con-
stance, who is ever more efficient than I am. It
won't be long now! (Clearly I haven't written in far
too long! Blast, more exclamation points have escaped!)*

    *Gabriel is delighted but also rather anxious de-
spite my assurances that Lawrence women are famously fertile and never, ever die in childbirth. As
you know, I put the "rude" in "rude good health."*

    *I'd like you to be godmother to this new little
person, as you were for me. You were the best god-
mother! The globe of the world you gave me was
the most marvelous present I ever received and in-*

*spired my own adventures. It has a place of honor
in our library.*

*   And—if you don't mind and I have a girl, I want
to name her Diana.*

Diana swallowed hard when she read that, sharply aware
of how much she missed her family. Most of them were
quite enjoyable people, and now that she was thirty and officially a spinster, they wouldn't be trying to marry her off
to some boring, bossy gentleman. They wouldn't *dare!*

Books by Bestselling Author
Fern Michaels

___**The Jury**   0-8217-7878-1 $6.99US/$9.99CAN

___**Sweet Revenge**   0-8217-7879-X $6.99US/$9.99CAN

___**Lethal Justice**   0-8217-7880-3 $6.99US/$9.99CAN

___**Free Fall**   0-8217-7881-1 $6.99US/$9.99CAN

___**Fool Me Once**   0-8217-8071-9 $7.99US/$10.99CAN

___**Vegas Rich**   0-8217-8112-X $7.99US/$10.99CAN

___**Hide and Seek**   1-4201-0184-6 $6.99US/$9.99CAN

___**Hokus Pokus**   1-4201-0185-4 $6.99US/$9.99CAN

___**Fast Track**   1-4201-0186-2 $6.99US/$9.99CAN

___**Collateral Damage**   1-4201-0187-0 $6.99US/$9.99CAN

___**Final Justice**   1-4201-0188-9 $6.99US/$9.99CAN

___**Up Close and Personal** 0-8217-7956-7 $7.99US/$9.99CAN

___**Under the Radar**   1-4201-0683-X $6.99US/$9.99CAN

___**Razor Sharp**   1-4201-0684-8 $7.99US/$10.99CAN

___**Yesterday**   1-4201-1494-8 $5.99US/$6.99CAN

___**Vanishing Act**   1-4201-0685-6 $7.99US/$10.99CAN

___**Sara's Song**   1-4201-1493-X $5.99US/$6.99CAN

___**Deadly Deals**   1-4201-0686-4 $7.99US/$10.99CAN

___**Game Over**   1-4201-0687-2 $7.99US/$10.99CAN

___**Sins of Omission**   1-4201-1153-1 $7.99US/$10.99CAN

___**Sins of the Flesh**   1-4201-1154-X $7.99US/$10.99CAN

___**Cross Roads**   1-4201-1192-2 $7.99US/$10.99CAN

Available Wherever Books Are Sold!
Check out our website at **www.kensingtonbooks.com**